IT

Pieces In The Dark

Nick Sambrook

Book 1 of 3

CHAPTER 1 - PIECES IN THE DARK

It was a sea you wouldn't want to swim in, laced with froth and rendered opaque grey-green by the heavy clouded sky above, mixed with assorted floating kelp and driftwood, churned in the waves against the dark, rocky shoreline below.

The strong, warm, onshore wind was humid and stinging with sea spray; a follow-on from the previous day's storm.

The West Coast sand was harsh, dark grey flecked with coarse black volcanic rock, making it rough to sit on and baking hot to walk over. It was a stark contrast to the bright East Coast beaches, with their blue, calm, clear waters, soft white gently sloping sand, and picturesque shores.

Alone on the top of the dunes he closed his eyes and rested his arms and head on his knees. He sat with his bare feet in the hot sand, and rubbed a flat pebble between his fingers.

It had been three days now, and Sam's head was still throbbing and numb. The warm salt wind and the sound from the sea just seemed to exist in perpetuity. He felt detached from it, and yet somehow he was more awake than he had ever been before in his life, and probably more than anyone else ever had, or at least it seemed that way.

He had hoped the sea air would bring him round a bit more, and help him recover, but it just made him feel more remote, like watching life go by from the inside of a café window on the street.

It seemed not to matter to the world if he were there or not, just another blade of grass on the edge of the beach, incidental. Like the pebble, he was just part of the environment; picked up, randomly moved, washed over, buried, and then just left.

He may have been on this earth, but he seemed disjointed from it; not involved, detached, as if no longer an integral part.

He saw things differently now too, everything seemed to have so much more perspective, depth, context, and meaning than from before. What he now knew was utterly vast and profound.

Unsurprisingly, given the weather, he was totally alone on the beach that morning, which was unusual here for late March.

Not even the usual small selection of overweight New Zealand seagulls had bothered to turn up. Kapiti Island lay several miles offshore, and in the sea mist it looked grey and bland in the distance like a gravestone in the half light.

On the days when the sun had been out, and the air was clear, it had been alive with the bright greens of various trees that echoed with exotic birds and coloured vegetation that contrasted with the rich blue skies and the calm blue- green sea.

At night the island, with its ragged steep hills, would be silhouetted by vast burning sunsets from the West, fire that would ripple over the sky like chequered flames on the underside of a burning log.

The scale of what he had experienced and the knowledge he now possessed was impossible to come to terms with. He wasn't just trying to recover from the impact it had made on his mind and body, he was also trying to come to terms with the vastness of what he had been exposed to, the change to his mind, what it all meant, and how it fitted together, if at all.

His perception of everything was just so different now. He saw things in a completely different way. Things that in the past were now contextualised, he processed information in an odd way, collated and analysed in a broader fashion, correlated. He could see things, and his mind would be exploring every aspect of what he was looking at, questioning it, and determining its relationship to everything else.

Life before seemed so much simpler and less complicated, but now it was a totally new existence, like a baby being born into a room of noise and pain and strange concepts, trying to cling to the cosy memories from a world that was safe and warm only moments before.

He just sat there. Just sat, there. Looking, at nothing. Thinking, of nothing. Trying to empty his mind. But still he had thoughts that he couldn't stop floating in. The everyday things he couldn't block out, the feeling of the wind on his face, the sound of the waves, and the sand around his feet.

You just couldn't get away from everything. Your senses wouldn't allow it. It had been three days now. Three, very long days. Today was the first time Sam had really been out of bed and moved around.

Wanting him to get some air, his girlfriend had dropped him off at the beach here in the car, while she drove to town to get some urgent supplies. She had been worried about leaving him alone for any length of time, but being in a holiday home they hadn't got much food in. She had tried the local pizza delivery service last night as a last resort, which was so bad that it only left the other remaining option - which was starvation.

She thought that getting some air would do him good, and get him out of and away from the house. Sitting him by the pool in the grounds seemed a bit pointless, as the storm the day before had filled it with assorted leaves, branches and muddy water.

He had laid in bed the night before, and all the previous day, listening to the roaring wind outside the patio window. He hadn't slept much as the noise outside was too loud and his head was still throbbing. At times it seemed to be trying to get at him, as if it had something personal against him. It had certainly unsettled him somewhat, and by the morning he felt uneasy and defensive, especially as he hadn't shaved or washed for some time.

So now he felt a bit nervous about sitting too close to the shoreline, especially after having remembered the scenes from watching the newsreels of the Indian Ocean Tsunami nearly three months earlier.

There had also been a couple of earth tremors locally, which apparently happened quite regularly around here. One had hit just after they arrived at the house, and that had unsettled him too. The feeling and sensation and emotion weren't something you could describe to people who hadn't experienced it.

Having the earth literally move backwards and forwards underneath you was a very disturbing thing when you had spent all your life assuming it wouldn't ever move. An unsettling, disjointed failure of trust; almost an injustice. Something that you had become used to being solid and unmoving and reliable, changing into an unstable shifting, rumbling platform was an unnerving affront. It's the one thing you depend on to be there, unmoving, and when it isn't, it disturbs your soul, your confidence, and makes you question in your mind everything you have come to believe and rely on.

Ironically this was exactly what was now going on in his head. A new perspective, confused questions, and doubt about everything he had ever known or relied on in the world. He didn't have any friends around to talk to either about it, and he didn't want to discuss it with Brina yet. He didn't want to frighten her or spoil her holiday. He didn't know where to begin. His head was just a mess of logic, knowledge, and information firing here and there, as if his brain was almost humming.

He felt pretty much under attack too, sort of repressed. So to try and make himself feel better he had at least forced himself to get up, managed a shower and a shave before being brought out. This all made him feel a little more comfortable in himself - it was just everything else that seemed to be the problem.

There never seems to be enough oxygen here, he thought. He had noticed it a few hours after stepping off the plane. At first he just thought it was because the air was purer or cleaner than the air in London, which of course wouldn't be difficult, but after a few days he had just continued to feel lightheaded.

Maybe it was just that there were fewer rainforests in the southern hemisphere, or maybe Australia burns off all the oxygen in the air before it reaches the North Island. Or perhaps it just converts it into plant form, and floats it over.

He looked again at the mass of seaweed and grey-green vegetation swilling around the rocks. Whole floating armadas of collective ecosystems blown inexorably eastwards, only to end up liquidised on the volcanic rocks, and mashed up into piles or rotting organic stuff on the dark grey sand.

Thinking again, thinking, now thinking laterally, and casting his mind now to distant Australian shores. The estuaries, with branches falling into them, flooding, water lifting and carrying leafy branches, plants, and insects into mats of floating vegetation. Sweeping out to sea, and mixing with kelp, algae, and flotsam. All piloted by the odd small furry animal.

All this ending up months later across the ocean here into mounds of rotting tossed salad and the remaining living survivors on the beach. All having a total lack of appreciation for the journey, and the exciting views.

Three days earlier he had been relaxing quietly on the bed in the warm late afternoon sun in the holiday home, set in its own grounds up in the hills overlooking the coast. There was very little sound; just birds singing quietly and the slight easterly wind blowing the light drapes gently into the bedroom. Brina was dozing on the bed next to him, her long blonde hair still tied in a folded up pony tail from when they had been swimming.

She had a white cotton sheet wrapped around her naked body for comfort, security, and to keep the warm breeze off her as she laid on her side facing away from him with her head on two white pillows.

A little while earlier he had been doing quite a lot of swimming, and then followed it up by showing off to her with some old weights he had found in the pool house. The heat had worn him out quickly and left him giddy and looking like an idiot, so they had decided to go and rest inside, out of the afternoon sun.

Situated a few miles from the coast and up on the hillside overlooking the coastline below, the house itself was very large single storey building in levels going up the hill, with several bedrooms. It had about an acre or two of land and was situated on its own, and was much too large for just the two of them really. It had come up as a last minute cancellation deal, but it was fine, and somewhere with a lot of space to relax.

The bedroom was very large, expensively furnished with quality fabrics and dark Rimu wood furniture. It had a dark stone tiled floor, a walk-in-wardrobe, and a massive en-suite bathroom. Open patio doors led onto a colonial styled terracotta floored veranda, which gave a lot of cover from the midday sun.

With it being mid-afternoon the sun was lower in the West, and now shone through the half-open long windows and through the thin cream billowing curtains. It filled the room with light and warmth, together with a hot fragranced breeze.

He listened sleepily to the warbling songs of the exotic blue and black Tui birds feeding off the flax and kowhai trees. This was combined with the gentle constant noise of the cicadas outside, who sang to each other in the dense trees of the bush around the hillside grounds.

He was so relaxed and happy, just resting on the cool mattress and cotton sheets on his back, with his head on soft pillows. The heat of his body was soothed by the gentle air flow over his skin.

He had changed out of his swimming shorts at Brina's request, and so he had just quickly thrown a pair of boxer shorts on. She had changed out of her bikini and into a soft white cotton sarong, which was now on the floor by the bed. With her arms and shoulders now bare she had wrapped the sheet around herself for protection, and now peacefully laid asleep, breathing slowly, with her back to him, as a white, slightly bent cocoon. It was just bliss. He had not relaxed this much in a long time.

It was wonderful here. They had spent several days at the house and had explored the area around them. This had given them a relaxing break from all the tours and flights they had done, which had taken them all around the North and South Islands over the last three weeks; packing in as much as possible, seeing everything, doing everything, and working through the list of tourist 'Must See's'.

Sam's idea of a holiday was to cram as much in as possible and leave all the relaxing and resting to when you got back. Brina's idea of an holiday was somewhat different from his, but she had gone along with everything, and had enjoyed herself, just happy to be with him.

It was clear she was making the most of the time in the holiday home now, a break from hotel rooms, their own space, resting and sunbathing by the pool as much as she could - not to mention being able to finally wear the bikinis that she had so carefully selected before they left. Now she had her own space and peace and they could spend some time sleeping and easing out the aches and pains from the walking, diving, climbing and jet boating.

She definitely wasn't one of these precious types, but every girl had her limits. It was easy to wind down now, that feeling of a 'job well done' after all they had achieved in such a short space of time. They had a week or so now to recover, switch off and rest, with a well-earned sense of achievement and time to allow it all to sink in.

In this idyllic, post-coital sleepy state, he had been lying motionless for several minutes now, in a sort of half awake, half sleeping state, yet not able to quite drift off to sleep like Brina, but not willing to risk waking her up either by trying to move. The last half an hour or so had been somewhat physical, and he was both energised and drained.

He had always had trouble getting to sleep, or more to the point, 'switching his brain off'. His mind seemed to use that time when he went to bed to run through everything over and over, almost as if it had been too busy during the day to think straight and needed that time to catch up.

A bit like a mother running around all day after her children and only having time to herself once they were safely tucked up in bed. It was a strange time, all the thoughts seemed much clearer and logical and straightforward, and it was much easier to solve problems without the distraction of the day.

He had gotten into the habit long ago of keeping a writing pad and pen by his side of the bed, next to his compulsory glass of water, to jot down notes to help him remember his ideas and solutions and what he needed to do the following day. He got so much done at that time of night, and would often leave complex work until late at night or the early hours, at which point in time things often didn't seem to be much of an issue after all.

Switching off to go to sleep though was still a problem. He had tried lots of techniques and self-help methods but none had worked very well. It was as if there was something else there all the time, working his mind, not letting him rest.

He hated that state between awake and sleep where irrational and out of proportion thoughts went over and over in his head. Pathetically silly, trivial things, which during the day would be dismissed in a moment. Like trying to work out if you had said something that had upset someone earlier that day, unable to do anything about it and then your brain goes over and over it in all ways possible trying to get an answer, but unable to move forward stuck in that limbo state. When in the cold light of day it was simple, obvious, and in any case, irrelevant.

He didn't often sleep very deeply, and dreaming was only remembered occasionally, so waking in the morning was always a struggle, as was actually getting up. He relied heavily on his own autopilot and routine together with lots of help. So to say he wasn't a 'morning person' was an understatement.

The autopilot facility was a great help, just relying on his body to get up washed, dressed, and fed in routine. Although it was a little disconcerting sometimes to realise suddenly that you are at the wheel of a car and had been driving for half an hour with no memory of how you got there. However as soon as he arrived at work he was firing on all cylinders until late, almost unable to stop. It was the starting again that was the problem.

Dreams, when they came, were very varied and erratic, his brain trying to resolve its emotional issues in an unrestricted state, with the normal over-riding logical controls switched off. He didn't have many bad dreams, or frustrating ones, or the generic ones like falling or being chased. But when he did they were very varied in content, and darted from one scene to another, invariably using references to people and places in his past.

He did occasionally talk in his sleep. In fact only the month before he woke himself up shouting out a warning to someone in a dream, and continuing to experience the scene and call out in panic for a minute after waking up. Just as well Brina hadn't been with him.

Just recently though he had started to experience one-off sounds that would bring him from deep sleep state to wide awake, sounds like a barking dog; clear and precise and sounding absolutely real, and just a few yards away, which would leave him sitting upright looking around in the darkness in silence.

The worst had been a woman screaming in absolute terror, feral and animalistic. His eyes wide open in the dark, he seemed to carry on hearing it even though he was awake, even though it had never been there. However he still sat in silence straining his ears to try and hear anything more, but nothing, with sweat on his neck and body, clinging to the bedclothes.

After a long, deep breath the created sound was gone, and his mind was left trying desperately to fathom out what was going on. His mind was hunting his senses for any useful information, while at the same time trying to wake up and at the same time manage the panic.

When his brain finally stopped trying to make sense of things, he would get up and walk around for a while before going back to bed. Just as well, he thought, that we didn't live our lives in a dream, what a complete mess everything would end up being.

Sam sighed deeply, folded his arms, tucked his fingers under his armpits, rested his thumbs on his chest, and stared up into the top corner of the wall opposite.

He remembered when he was a young boy in bed in the half light of his bedroom. He recalled how he was able to stare long and hard at a point on a far wall, and could gradually phase his eyes in to make the wall seem to zoom closer to him. So it appeared, literally, that he had brought the wall only a few inches away from his face, or as if he was standing right up next to the wall with no peripheral vision but that his whole view was just taken up with a small portion of the wall.

It was a strange effect and one he had to concentrate on to achieve and hold. He wasn't able to do it at will, he had to be relaxed and half asleep to make it occur, but it was always controllable, like a built-in macro vision feature.

Sometimes he would wake up from a dream with his eyes open, and already be in the same zoom mode, which could be quite alarming. His whole field of vision would be taken up with just a small area on the wall up close, just like a telephoto lens, and he would no longer be able to see anything else in the room unless his concentration broke, and then the rest of the room snapped back in.

It was just like moving his head instantaneously from the pillow to a few feet from the wall. If only he could turn his head around it would be just like an out of body experience, but he couldn't. It was likely just caused by a weakness he had in one eye, and his brain simply trying to make sense of the difference.

Of course, when you are young and don't understand things, it can be quite alarming to have these strange visions and perception. When you grow up though you learn, understand, read, and find out what it is caused by. You then also read of other people that have experienced it. He had even read an article on it in a magazine some years ago, but couldn't remember the name for it. There was also a micro version of it, where some people would see things 'small', and seemingly from far away. Ordinary people would become 'little people' and seem to do strange things, nothing paranormal, just a different way of seeing things. It was surprisingly common, one in a few hundred or so, but just something in the past people had been a little reluctant to 'fess up' to in case they were thought to be mad or delusional.

As the years went on he had grown out of it, and forgotten about it, until he started using computer terminals a lot and had noticed similar effects. He had ended up only using very high frequency screens because anything less than a 120hz refresh rate looked as if they were flickering, and he just got headaches and a pain behind one eye.

He had even forgotten he could do it, and it had been a very long time since he had thought about it or even tried to do it, but as he couldn't sleep, and didn't want to wake Brina up by getting out of bed, he had a go at doing it again. It had been several years since he was this relaxed and happy, if only he had remembered to cover himself in a sheet too before getting onto the bed, life would be perfect, but if he moved now he would break his concentration and possibly wake Brina up too - so he didn't.

He took a few breaths and focused on one single point on the corner of the wall and tried to duplicate the relaxed state, defocusing his eyes to snap into that mode. It was about two minutes before he got anywhere; not being a child anymore his mind was harder to fool, and was not so willing to accept something that it knew to be wrong. But eventually he was there with his face up next to the wall, and after a few snapbacks to normality, he was able to hold it steady.

Despite the effort, it was quite exhilarating both from the effect, and the fact that he had managed to achieve it. He could feel his heart speeding up, and the cooling effect on his face where he had started to sweat with all the effort of focusing. He also felt a tingling, energising sensation start to come up from the base of his spine; sort of growing with energy, and building all the way up, like a stimulating current flowing upwards, in a gradual wave of pulsing electricity creeping and flowing uncontrollably up the length of his spine. It slowly worked all the way up his spine in steps, gradual stages, in a twisting motion all the way up to his neck, and then into the back of his head, and in.

An intense yet oppressive 'room-pressing-in' feeling started to close around him, which was combined with a growing sense of being out of control with a mounting, seemingly oppressive, vivid déjà vu sensation.

Slowly everything else was shut out; no cicada noise, no touch of the sheets below him, no smells, just approaching growing visual intensity, and panic inducing expanding sensations into his mind. The same sensation as suddenly receiving anaesthetic gas or an injection, with that moment after the first breath when your body reacts to the lack of control, a sense of detachment, adrenaline careering through your veins and body. That fainting, disengaging feeling, with a racing loud heartbeat and sudden oppressive closing out of your senses, where your brain focuses inwards on itself, desperately trying to work out what is wrong in this unknown territory.

He moved his eyes around but had no peripheral vision. It just seemed that everything he looked at was close up. The sharpness and depth of field hurt the muscles in his eyes.

If that had been all it wouldn't have bothered him, he would have just closed his eyes and drifted off to sleep, but there was something else. There was a sense of lack of connection and control. A feeling that something else was going on that was stressing him intensely, and something that couldn't be described or identified.

He began to sweat, hard.

He tried to relax, forcing himself to breathe and regulate his panic. He had been on the usual range of stress management and mental discipline courses, so he used the tools he had learnt. He knew that if he just let the feeling happen, stayed in control, it would gradually become less acute and intense, and eventually he would get back in control.

But now he could sense a direct lack of feeling in his body, and his legs and arms disappearing and numbness filling his head, like taking in more anaesthetic gas.

It was working against him with every breath, distorting, numbing and shutting him down systematically, all in slow motion, and gradually he was losing himself.

He felt as if he was moving in on himself, trapped and held somewhere between asleep and awake. Trained to manage his mind in stressful situations, he stuck to his meditation tools and mind disciplines to keep himself conscious at some level. In some control over his instincts, not to panic, to focus, to concentrate.

He was still there, in charge, as it all slipped away with closing-in mental numbness until everything was gone. No senses, just his mind; but not in any state he had ever known. He went through intense feelings from absolute fear to total and complete and utter limitless bliss, love and elation, naked of any self. Small, like a lost child in the wilderness.

Then suddenly it was all gone in an instant, and there was no emotion at all. Nothing. No feelings of fear or happiness; it was just completely dark and empty with no other sense of anything.

But he was still there, not asleep or unconscious, just in an empty, stark, intense black void of endless nothing.

The effect was that of deep, full breaths of pure oxygen, floating in the air in a starless, lightless, limitless space. Yet he was there and fully conscious. He was able to see, but all he could perceive and sense was an endless nothing all around. But he didn't know where he was. He was somewhere else completely, and yet he hadn't moved.

The intensity was overpowering. His brain was racing to adapt to the strange perception of what state he was in. It was racing to cope and interpret, yet without letting fear take him, for he had no fear, no emotions at all.

In fact it all felt natural or normal somehow. All the processing power normally set aside for the use of his senses was inquisitively looking around for something to do - to see, to feel, or hear, or anything to latch on to.

Occasionally shimmering walls of presence would appear above and to the side, and would then close in on him only to disappear as his mind tried to create something to get some form of depth or perception of where he was, before being dismissed as fake or illusionary by his mind that was not easily fooled or hypnotised.

He knew his eyes were still open, and that they were working hard to try and visualise for him, but his mind had detached itself from them, and from the rest of his body.

All he was 'seeing' was just a black nothing.

Gradually he could feel himself calming down and gaining control, so he continued to send slow, deliberate messages to his lungs to breathe; even though he couldn't feel any part of his body he sent the signals anyway.

Just breathe and relax, he thought to himself, *just bloody breathe*. But he had no idea if he was breathing or if his body had just stopped functioning in his absence.

He had no sense or feedback from his body at all, but he became aware that it was still there somehow doing what it was supposed to, delivering blood, adrenaline, oxygen and energy.

It was doing its job, every cell working away in its self-preservation mode. The force now was incredible, the energy intense, as if everything were focusing through a single point of stress.

His body knew that there was something very wrong, and it was trying to convey that to him, but his mind knew that he was quite OK, in control. Feeding a signal of panic back to his body would do him no good. His mind was on fire now, racing on its own, alive with freedom, uninhibited, detached and unrestrained outside of its device and normal programming. He was in a limbo state, still in control, but outside and detached from everything. He could sense that he was still in his body and he could sense the background around him; the wind and the birds outside the room, but without actually hearing, seeing or feeling anything. It was a weird duality.

The initial sense of foreboding was diminishing, and was now replaced with heightened, intellectual, emotionless thinking, processing dozens of complex thoughts all at the same time. Without the sensual distractions it was doing a whole day's thinking in a few microseconds, with intense energetic currents and flows. It was thrilling, unbounded and unrefined, combined again with the occasional intense sense of déjà vu.

Yet he was completely rational and self-aware. This was not dreaming or a state of unconsciousness - this was very different. Conscious, clear and very immediate, there were multi-level feelings, thoughts and emotions flowing in like strong waves. He was in control and could make rational choices of thought in a streamlined way.

He could now optimise his own thoughts at many levels, computing via conduits at astounding speeds without distractions. It was a feeling that he wasn't able to relate to anything he had been through before, everything seemed to be happening instantaneously. It was all new and thrilling, quick and highly refined, yet intangible.

Everything seemed to make so much more sense here and was so much clearer and faster, meaningful, and he was able to now resolve thought in abstract and multidimensional ways like there had been a release of pressure and constraint. It was all pure and uncluttered and whatever it was, he was just in it.

Then everything stopped in his mind. He diverted his attention outwards. Again it was pitch-black; depthless, quiet and still, empty, unimaginably vast, like floating in deep space, but with no stars or light anywhere. This was not like being in a deep black room where you can somehow sense the walls even in the complete darkness. Here there were no walls, nothing. Just a total, endless black void. Yet that void was intensely clear and hard.

He was still totally self-aware, calm, rational, and yet emotionless. It was just his mind here; no body or eyes or hands. He seemed to have lost his identity too, his own self, and he had no feel of who or what he was. All he had was curiosity.

Slowly he became aware of something in the blackness below. Something indiscernible and vast began to appear from the darkness and was now coming up towards him. Impossibly far away but there, flat and shimmering in the dark, using up all of the down space, miles away.

It was a floor, like a flat, black ground or terrain coming up from the depths. Right on the limits of his visualisation, but there, discernible and everywhere below. It had taken his full attention because it wasn't coming from him, he was sure of that. It was vast, black, massive, and occupying everything downwards like a dark plain or sea below him.

It was cold and vivid, enigmatic. It was completely without emotion. It was just practical, matter-of-fact. It was just there, as if it always had been, unearthly, shimmering, on the edge of vision, and he didn't know what it was.

He wasn't afraid of it. It was just a flat lightless terrain surface, coming up from below from the impossible depths that hadn't been there before.

He now felt cold, and sensed a vibration - but that may have been a part of his brain reacting to its association of where it thought it was - the distance telling him that it should be cold up here, telling him he must be somewhere up high in space where there was no light or heat, just void and an unnatural, uncomfortable space. This was definitely no dream.

He instinctively looked up but there was nothing. It wasn't windy either as he had no body to feel wind against, but it seemed as though it should be, there was a kind of background faint roaring noise like strong wind makes far off high in the air.

There was a deep, low-frequency, vibrating sound too that he could somehow feel but not hear. It was fascinating, enthralling and obsessive; but he had no emotion so it was just translated into passive interest.

As he concentrated, more detail became evident, and directly below him he could now make out massive matt black pieces or tiles that formed the terrain. They fitted together, interconnecting as giant jigsaw pieces, moving and floating as if slightly separate, and yet integrated, making up the entire surface far off below.

The edges of the pieces shimmered being on the very limits of his perception, his mind's eye straining to create form and contrast to them, trying to create discernable edges.

More pieces became identifiable as he looked around below. He knew it was a representation of something; a translation of a thing that existed that had no visual form.

It was manifesting itself in this way to give some form of reference, so that he could visualise it or interpret it in some way, but with associated rules, laws, and constraints. He was sure he wasn't creating it; it was just something expressing or representing something to him in a way he could relate to or comprehend from this point of reference.

It seemed quite stark, harsh, hard, and almost brutal. Of the two dozen pieces that were now clearly visible directly below, each piece, or tile, was linked four ways to other pieces just like a normal jigsaw, but it was vast.

He wasn't sure if it was meant to be that way, or if his mind just presented it like that to make sense of the information, or to represent connectivity, as any other completed jigsaw would be.

Each piece was flat and many miles across. The map went on further to the horizon, but he could perceive that it wasn't endless and that there was an actual horizon.

That feeling of expression became stronger now and it was apparent that this was something he was being shown because he wanted to see it, desired it, needed it, and yet he felt no emotion.

He was still totally awake and very conscious. That feeling was also combined now with a sense that he was no longer in as much control as he had been a few moments ago.

There it was too, a feeling that there was something else there next to him. But not something he could see, just sense, or feel, like when you know someone is watching you, or the change in air pressure when someone comes into a room behind you.

He knew it was there and yet it felt quite natural and somehow normal. It had a sense of being just very practical, and emotionless; something doing its job in the dark with him or part of him. The presence was not threatening, imposing, or dominating in any way, nor with any deity-like charisma or feel.

It was just there like some sort of emotionless friend or helper, yet definitely male.

He didn't feel surprised at it being here, strangely, like a friend he had known for a long time, and was almost expecting to be there. He felt almost bland acknowledgement, just impassive with a 'nothing to say' feeling.

Looking down again he tried to come to terms with what he was looking at, and what this jigsaw puzzle meant.

Immediately, and as if in response, the answers came to him; but not spoken or written words, but as a direct relay of information, a feeling, a recognition, a statement of thought passed directly and instantly into his mind.

He experienced the answer and understood it at once rather than something actually being said. It was a statement, a picture of knowledge, an expression fed straight into his brain, a pure information transfer. It also seemed subdued somehow as if it were tired or weak. He just asked in his mind, and it gave him the answer back in instant thought relay in a completely matter-of-fact way.

What he was 'told', if that was the correct definition, was that what he was seeing was a map of knowledge of everything. Structured answers to every conceivable concept and question, laid out in integrated pieces. A vast, consolidated, integrated knowledge base of total information. It manifested and presented it in its most perfect, resolved, and integrated, correlated form.

At that, the dark pieces then started to take on more texture, meaning and form, with shapes appearing in them with dynamic elements and motion, but still maintaining their vast original structure, coherence and blackness.

Looking at each piece individually he could feel or sense what that element was about, somehow, like an index page. Some concepts were massive, complex and awe-inspiring, and yet at the same time they felt like normal, almost every day things.

Each component piece contained a distributed network of consolidated mass structured data. Some pieces were abstract and obscure in content, or in some cases just blank or seemingly deliberately hidden.

He formed the words as a thought in his mind to make contact with what was next to him, *what am I seeing ?*

The answer again came back as a thought, rather than a reply in words, together with images, feelings and impressions, but all happening in an instant directly into his mind. There was a sense of straightforwardness about it all, one of emotionless practicality and indifference, like serving a function, allowing him access, or sharing a conversation. It was as if that was what it was there to do, an interactive librarian; just a guide willing to answer questions, there to help.

Somehow he knew what to do and what these things were; he was drawn to the answers below. He wanted to explore and know more. Now he also felt as if some sort of guard or fail-safe had been removed, and because whatever was next to him gave no warning or caution, he assumed it was alright. There was no indication of danger, it was somehow 'OK'.

Sam's mind was a lot less emotional than it should have been and was behaving in a very practical way. He wasn't afraid, but he was disciplined and conditioned by the need to learn things, and his thoughts indicated that this situation was safe, and that he should learn.

He was also sure that the thing that was communicating with him didn't feel like any sort of god or anything dangerous, sinister or powerful, so it was all OK somehow; it was just natural curiosity. Besides, his mind was highly trained and disciplined, so he was sure he would be fine. Anyway, this was exciting and new, interestingly powerful and enthralling.

Sam was keen to find out what was inside the pieces, but rather than move himself to the pieces he decided to try and move one to him. He chose a piece below him at random and changed his virtual vision and depth of field to be closer, as he had just done in the bedroom, until it came close to him.

Shrinking as it came nearer, until only a few feet away, it was now only several yards across. Then he went into it, and he was part of it, and it filled the space all around him.

There was a sudden, massive parallel pulse of instant understanding, experience, thought, logic, and knowledge imprinted into his brain all at once, like a dimensionally independent array of images; a mass of visions.

No feelings or emotion, just a rush of complex information, a mind-blowing dimensional mass of indescribably perfect knowledge. Thought, logic, integrated concepts, and beautifully represented rationale all happening at once like being given a 'plug-in' to the brain.

It was direct, hard and intense, and definitely not coming from him. It was so completely and utterly different to anything he had every experienced before. It was indescribably exquisite, intensely articulate, and it all made perfect, profound sense instantly, and continued to expand and elaborate in all directions. All the time it was completely open, expansive, and everything was immediately obvious in every sense. It was vast, like being inside total understanding of everything.

The sensation was like nothing he had had before and was totally indescribable. It wasn't just like having something explained, or knowledge shown to you, it 'WAS the explanation' and the 'knowledge' transferred en-masse directly with all its splendour and associated feeling, context and grandeur, instantly into your mind along with a blissful, euphoric feeling.

The physical sensation was like grabbing two metal bars with either hand through which an electric current was flowing - not enough to electrocute you, but enough to switch everything on in your body and mind all at once in vibration until you let go.

However, instead of electricity it was limitless information and data delivered in an instant. But it was also capable of being explored, navigable, and instantly understandable in every concept; massive awareness and a limitless cosmic conscious understanding.

There were the answers presented in majestic, perfect, obvious splendour, without the limitations of speech or sight, or speed of learning, but at the same time exquisite and simple, efficient and beautifully eloquent and articulately presented in a refined way that didn't require the need for explanation, with all the context and endless correlated logic already there in instantaneous enlightenment smashed into his head all at once.

It was like no book, film, or lifetime experience ever could be. He was *inside* knowledge, but perceived in context that was all the parts of everything at once in a way that was far more than the parts themselves.

The physical sensation had the same intense feeling as standing with your face a few inches from an express train as it rushes past, together with the nervousness you would have if someone else had their hand pressed against the back of your head at the same time. The rush, the power, the speed, and the intensity, but without the physicality; just pure knowledge energy.

Now he was in the piece he understood. All around him it was obvious, the arguments, the logic, the evidence, the rational explanations. It seemed to be explaining that there was no God.

He understood it all, and could experience it all now in every way, all the thought processes, all the arguments, all the explanations, reasons, logic, physical evidence data and history. It was just practical logic; the reasons for the mental crutch being there, the human nature aspects, the needs and evolution of its concepts, the analysis of evidence, the archetypes, the science, and the complex analysis reinforced with the injustices. Why the ideas were there, and what had caused them.

Every conceivable scrap of information was there in the piece around him; he had been imprinted with the overall answers and concepts all at once. If he needed to explore other factual component elements, they were all there in intricate and regal detail, laid out around him and manifested in perfect, eloquent, exquisite logic. It was all just a misunderstanding, a breakdown of communication, a misrepresentation of the mind.

Yet there was something not quite right. There was more, another level of perspective that initially seemed to say the same thing, but then in argument for there being one, 'a god', with reference to the previous, and then links off into other pieces, giving greater depth.

It all culminated in what seemed to be a confused mess all in the space of several seconds. It then seemed to convey three different concepts at once.

He knew everything, he was inside knowledge, but it didn't

seem to integrate somehow, like being given every answer before knowing what the problem was.

He seemed to have been passed through a vast knowledge journey in a few seconds but there were things missing, or rather not there, but this was all totally impossible to explain.

Reacting more from the shock than anything else he moved it all away in his mind, and he was outside, and above it all again. He looked down on the dark shadowy pieces below, from the peace and stillness of the black empty void.

It had been an instant massive revelation, a completely mind-blowing experience, but at the same time emotionless, practical, hard, immutable and very direct.

It was also exhilarating and combined with a sense of achievement and enlightenment. Somehow it felt as though his forehead should be sweating, but here he didn't seem to have one.

He tried a few more. One was the start of the Universe and its evolution, and lifespan to date. Now he knew how old it was, its development, structure, and so much more; all in instant, magnificent representation. He was in the Universe.

He experienced it, knew it, and was part of it and everywhere in it all at the same time, like being inside the knowledge of it, and merged with it. The timeline of the Universe wasn't a number; he could feel it represented, as an existence, something that was inside in his mind as an experience, looking back in the same way that you could equate or feel the time between now and when you started school. That was how it was presented, that massive timeframe - as a feeling of vastness, a lifetime.

But he was able to translate it in his own mind to a real figure of nearly fourteen billion years. The information was bounded though, and limited, so he couldn't see anything before the start.

Coming back out he noticed some pieces below were now more intense, enhanced, or appeared to be larger somehow. The subjects of these he hadn't previously had a clue about, or had ever been interested in.

Inside were concepts you couldn't put into words, visions and images you could only experience and see in your mind, not on paper or in film, represented in an indescribably elaborate way.

It was all dancing around and combined with thoughts, perfection of form and representation, but not visually; it was represented as parallel thought. The balance, the symmetry and the complex interaction imprinted itself in his mind like no movie or book could ever do, but with perfect efficiency and dynamic, blissful complexity.

While in a piece he could explore, navigate, like progressing through logical integrated network, and at each point masses of additional knowledge would come in, all with relation to the next context, as if exploring a terrain of concept. It was enthralling, and all so clear and obvious now, just being inside knowledge itself.

Having lived your life in four dimensions, to have your mind experience the concepts, feeling and reality of several more was awesome and exhilarating. The feeling came that there was one dimension more than there should have been; more than the ten or eleven that were thought, and then it was gone. Inside and around real atomic and subatomic structures. In and around energy flows and dynamics.

Hundreds of particle combinations with fields and waves and interaction that came with explanation, of understanding without text or needless metaphor or mathematical equations. In a way no magazine could describe in diagrams or a lifetime of lectures could explain or define.

It was a rollercoaster ride of everything instantly. It was being inside the understanding and having thoughts, experience and knowledge context already in your mind at the same time. Like having the combined brains of all the experts in the world on that subject instantly, already integrated, and yet seeing it in a fantastically elaborate way that was new and perfectly presented.

Integrated concepts of time, dimensions, and quantum mechanics came through to him so he was able to gain perspective on things instantly, even seeing how things actually were in true form, compared to regimented theories that had been developed already - all to help put perspective on the final picture.

It grew and grew in complexity. Everything now built into spheres, bubbles with surfaces spinning around, then grouped inside larger ones alike, in and around. Each spinning to different sets of rules, and contra-spinning in balance, in an ever expanding hierarchy of spinning things.

He moved out again, up into the void. He then quickly went into other pieces that related to other topics and thought formations. Concepts such as aliens were presented and elaborated on, then explained through history with examples.

Logical explanations of mind attribution, understandable fear causing imaginative constructs, balanced out with natural scepticism to a point of resolution that there had been none, and were none. For the first time there was a definite sense of emotion there, and one that he couldn't express or compare with any that he had of his own, he could sense it, but it wasn't coming from him. These explanations went on into other pieces.

There were vastly more complex and integrated symmetrical biological understandings which linked off into other directions and pieces to help explain other concepts; how the brain worked and linked together, cells, neurons, human development, and DNA integration.

From that he was led onto obscure concepts like ghosts. Now he knew what they were caused by, and how it worked, and how the information in static mass was perceived, stored, projected, and interpreted. All of a sudden it was obvious. They were quite simple and not confusing at all. It was just all data, information management and storage.

Then into water and its information properties and how we perceive it. Hills, cells, evolution, perception, geology, and body energy and biomechanics. It seemed to be speeding up.

Facts were just conveyed as direct information with no associated feelings; cold, hard, mind flashes packed with understanding - like the 546 years that humanity had left, accepting the information all in the same way, without emotion or feeling, just with a matter-of-fact placidity.

Subatomic field communications between us, explaining all sorts of previously mysterious happenings, and imaginative mystical psychic abilities, linked back to other pieces in practical ways. It all became not so mysterious, and all quite obvious.

The direction wasn't structured, he just seemed to drift from one experience into the next, or so it felt. The key was not to question it or halt the flow but to just go with it and accept it as a passive observer, along for the ride, not stirring or panicking, just accepting the rush, but with some selective choice.

When he pushed the pieces away, the intensity of what he had experienced diminished dramatically. He still had the information in his mind, but there were no links with it as before, the mapping and navigation had stopped, so recalling context and structure was difficult and faded in intensity quickly. Like pausing a hundred films that you were watching all at the same time, each of which interrelated to the others - you could remember the films to some extent, and the conclusions, but the cohesion and the interaction stopped immediately.

He still had the answers though, and most of the information, but the beauty, depth and elegance was not there; he couldn't articulate it or navigate it in the way it was inside the piece.

He knew that he knew it, and the intense feeling was still there, and raw, but now he relied on his brain connectors to integrate the elements together to allow him to recall and remember the information.

It was a struggle fitting together the information and how it worked. He hadn't lived through these experiences of knowledge or built them up gradually in a structured way, he was just being left with dozens of encyclopaedia volumes of data but no indexes.

It was like opening up a computer cover and throwing an encyclopaedia in and expecting the machine to read the pages and store the data. So, somehow, there was a big difference between his memory and his mind, and how the information was stored here and how it was represented.

Some pieces were obscure and almost useless, the layouts and structures of cities for example; what they looked like, and how to navigate them. They were just like a mental picture, so he didn't venture into those.

Obscure things like how to maintain a forest, and utility type knowledge, vibrational movement, and some that seemed to have no context or value at all from his perspective.

It was all very different to how you would learn or remember things in real life though. The data and understanding weren't linked together with connections as you would for experiences on say, a holiday, with the journey, the sites, meals and events all giving you a set of memory pegs.

This was all flat and factual with none of the emotional links, just the keepsake holiday snaps and videos without the feelings or a three week guided tour round an historical city, but instantly in a few microseconds, yet in fantastic glory and brilliance and context all thrown at you at once.

A few of the pieces that were previously dark now began to change and have elements in them that he could see. On entering one it became clear that he could only see this knowledge because he was now able to put it into context because of what he had already been shown elsewhere.

That made sense. Before then it would have been meaningless so there would have been no reference. He could also go back into previous pieces and get more of it in context; like now knowing what the Universe was for and why, which seemed to cause some confusion.

There were also things that raised questions in his mind that he couldn't answer for some reason, as if he had gone into things he shouldn't have, seen too much. The key though was not to stop before something happened.

He understood what destiny was now, but it still left quite a few missing pieces that were unnerving to him somehow, a disassociation, lost elements - things that should be there that weren't.

It all began to gather pace.

On the next piece was a simple flash of lightning on a scene, just an impression, and didn't seem to register anything at all. Which is when he became aware that he was still in his body somewhere, and he was receiving warnings from it, something wasn't right, and his alert emotions began to make an appearance.

Panic and pain messages were coming from his body, real stress. The last two pieces he had been in had caused him direct pain somewhere, and somehow he knew that, and he was responding to those priority interrupts overriding everything else to get to him.

But those insights came now with his own desire and instant addiction, and he wanted to know more; having tasted so much knowledge, he couldn't resist it. It was a pure and perfect drug. Instant doctorates were a thrilling overpowering temptation, and it was enthralling and intoxicating. He wanted this more than anything - it was overpowering, the desire, the need, and yet he knew it was going to kill him.

He was definitely going to die, and he couldn't help it, and somehow in this place he didn't seem to really care, it was just the way it was.

To experience and understand these awe-inspiring things was worth it, even for an instant more. The pain was acute now, and his perception grew numb along with a humming, ringing, like the dull loss of sense after an explosion, the emotions were rife.

He ignored them now, set on a fixed path, and the consequential matter of death wasn't a problem. He was inside another piece, he wasn't even sure what it was for, and it felt as though every cell in his body was screaming questions and answers through him; it was intense, a point of absolute extreme pressure, a criticality of stress, a single point integrated at many levels with him in-between.

Now it was all coming from around and below on the absolute limits of everything, a reference point, it was too much. He came out again into the void.

Then, for an instant, he felt something come from his very cells, communicating with him somehow with whatever was around him, below and then through him.

He perceived it and took it in; it was different and out of context with what was going on before. He had no reference or explanation or relation to it, but it was no matter, he was now on the edge of death, he knew it, and everything started going on all at once beyond any control.

Everything happened at every level very fast - a mass rush of information. Something was not right. Something had gone drastically wrong in so many ways.

Then suddenly a real voice spoke as if from somewhere else.

He latched on to it, connected to it, and everything stopped still. Dead calm.

He was transfixed in a motionless state, paused in the void, with just the intense humming feeling remaining.

Again the voice came, and suddenly there was a hand in his hand.

The hand was there, he knew it somehow.

He couldn't feel it, it wasn't pressing his skin, but it was just there. And now he sensed another hand, on his forearm, but that wasn't really there either.

The voice had spoken his name and everything froze around him waiting for something to happen, like the silence in the aftershock of a shell exploding, with his ears singing, and time and motion at a standstill. In the background was a dull, vibrating tone and a deeply oppressive feeling, which somehow he knew represented pain in his head and body.

"Sam." A change in tone this time, a real pressure on his hand. Feeling, life, air. He thought of the great pain and sadness he would cause to others if he didn't return. The feeling of responsibility was being put into his mind.

But the lure and hunger for the knowledge drug, of carrying on in here to see everything was intoxicating, and totally addictive, and inescapable. He had already bound part of what he was to it, and leaving here intact would be impossible.

The voice was female. Was love. Someone caring, feeling, wanting him, drawing him, pulling him out with need. It was a long way out of the narrow deep mineshaft he was in though. He heard it again, locking on to him, binding with him.

It had directness and feeling, and an inverse polarity to where and what he was in. He was on a boundary, a decision point at the knife edge of reality. "Sam, come back!" a request... of urgent feeling...a command.

That was it. That moment, right then. He chose. He waited for a moment dwelling on the place he was in for a second more just to remember it, and then followed the voice. It needed him, loved him, wanted him to return, so he had a duty, a responsibility and now a directed purpose.

There was no emotion here - he could see that now, in direct contrast to the human voice. Here was just cold logic in the depths, a dark library, stark and basic, and with this new perspective he knew it just wasn't right, he didn't belong there.

He no longer wanted to be left here in the void.

So he chose love. He could feel the hand on him now, and his body, things around him began to fade in perception. The presence he had communicated with now went. He could feel it move away, just diminish and be no longer there, no longer needed.

There was a rush out of the dark.

He became more aware of his body, and the temperature in the room, the voice, the air and the light, like waking from anaesthetic, although he had been totally awake throughout.

His open eyes began to give him perception of light, yet out of focus, and sight of images again, but slowly.

Feeling of his body came back.

Gasping for air and breathing hard he became aware of a pain in his head that was unimaginable, like no other pain he had ever known, like nothing you could describe, beyond any type of hangover.

Parts of his body were numb and immovable.

He was soaking wet and lying in cold sweat, his face hot. He tried to move but was all over the place; rhythms of nervous electrifying vibration going through his body, his left leg and arm were weak and unresponsive. His mind was on fire. Everything in the room moved, vibrant and sharp, alive with an eye-opening intensity, colour, contrast and auras that made his eyes ache.

The hand held him down on the bed gently, and concerned eyes looked straight at him from a pale, worried face. It was difficult to focus. His mind was hammering to try and make sense of the physical world around him and the mental convoluted mind storm going on in his head.

His heart was beating heavily with the panic from the numbing fiery pressure pain in the temples of his head, especially at the back of his neck and skull.

The air was spinning around him. He was suffering the effects from a sapping marathon of the mind and body. He could only focus on things a few feet away so the walls were blurred, and his peripheral vision was all over the place.

It felt like he had been there for several hours but in reality it had probably only been twenty minutes at most. So much information and knowledge in such a short space of time. The feeling wasn't odd though. It felt bland, like he had just simply been down the library and picked up and read a few books, as you do.

Despite the panic he was immediately aware that he was now very different. His perception on life had completely changed along with everything around him.

It wasn't so much the new found mass of knowledge and vision that he now had, it was more the perspective that he now took on everything, powerful and encompassing revelations, a completely different understanding, a new way of seeing things. His senses were alive, and now his mind worked in a different way.

What he now had in his brain, although very mixed up, was earth shattering; a mass of information that wasn't there before.

He would no longer be able to see the world in the same way again. He could sense it all still there, like implanted packets of data flashing back at him, but not naturally or logically structured, just there, unlinked in different locations. It hadn't gone, it was all still there, distributed throughout his head.

Unfortunately along with it came a very real and ominous impression that somehow a mistake had been made. A breach of protocol, an error, as if something shouldn't have happened, or that he had seen too much. He was also confused as to who or what had communicated with him in the dark, it was all very real and clear and imminent.

He hadn't been asleep or unconscious. He hadn't travelled off somewhere or been imagining it; it had happened. It was very, very real, and direct and clear, hard and precise.

A critically important chain of events had occurred that shouldn't have happened. Yet most importantly, somehow, he knew that all the jumbled complex knowledge still in his head, even though scattered about and vast, was way too much, and not supposed to be there.

He looked directly into Brina's blue-grey eyes as she looked down at him, her face still anxious and scanning his features.

His mind was working to make sense of what he was seeing in the room, trying to reconceptualise everything, and relate everything, switching back slowly from parallel to serial.

"Are you OK?" she asked clearly and slowly.

He nodded.

Her face immediately relaxed slightly, but her eyes were still searching his face for information.

He tried to form words that came into his head, but his body behaved as if it had been rescued from a frozen lake, shaking and in shock.

Slowly he placed his right hand on her cheek, and he was able to try and speak despite the nerve driven electric spasms his body was making.

Fixing her with his eyes, very slowly, and with spasms in his breath, he managed three coherent words,

"I...   Know...   EVERYTHING."

CHAPTER 2 - THE BEACH

He woke up with his back pressed flat against the coarse dark sand of the beach dune looking up into the grey sky above. He hadn't been aware of drifting off to sleep again, and the salty wind on his face was uncompromising to his desire to stay that way.

Grasping at reality, his eyes darted about the clouds trying to sense where he was, gathering perspective for his mind, which itself was lumbering out of the starting gate of sleep. He could feel his lower body vibrating in the sand.

It was unnerving and he couldn't work out what was going on. After a few seconds his mind automatically did the science and the maths for him and relayed the obvious; it was just his mobile phone in his back pocket humming away. It was obviously a text from Brina, who was now he assumed, leaving the supermarket in town to pick him up.

He knew he had been 'looked after' by her for the last three days but he couldn't recall any of that time, it all seemed to be voided. He felt clean, shaved, and pressed, but it was either thanks to his own system autopilot, or Brina, that had been doing the driving for him as far as his body and his welfare were both concerned. He wasn't starving and his shorts had been ironed so he had a fairly good idea which one it was.

He slid his hand behind to pull the phone out, but only succeeded in putting grey gritty sand in there instead. He flipped over on his side, and pulled the pocket liner out to get the phone and the sand out. He slapped the pocket lining to get the grit off like some waving, beached seal on its side, with little regard to what he must look like. He picked the phone out of the sand, rolled over onto his back again, and placed the phone in the sand next to him so he wouldn't forget it.

As she was the only one to have the number it was either Brina, or something free he couldn't survive without from some enthusiastic telecom company, so rather than looking at it he just he left it there in the sand without bothering to check it.

Sitting up he noticed that there were now a few more people on the beach walking dogs or collecting drift wood. Fortunately he hadn't yet been classed as a suspicious washed-up dead body on the shore. This was probably as he was too clean looking and a little too far up the dune to qualify.

There was a clear stretch on any beach where you could sleep peacefully. If you were too close to the sea or too far inland, you always ran the risk of being resuscitated by some well-meaning unattractive passer-by, regardless of whether you were dead or alive. Although the sandflies currently biting his bare ankles were clearly not that fussed either way, capitalising on his sleeping insensitivity.

Smacking them off he was amazed just how something so small could inflict so much pain; little black flies the size of pin heads but clearly with fangs that a rattlesnake would be proud of. Smears of blood and black bits of fly were now all over his ankles, so he rubbed sand over them as he had nothing else to use. He had to remember to put something on them when he got back or they would itch like hell for days.

He had learnt that the hard way in the first week in New Zealand. He got angry with himself for forgetting to put insect repellent on, then he remembered that a few hours ago he could hardly remember his own name, and then he got angry at Brina for not looking after him properly and not remembering for him, which was rapidly followed by guilt at even thinking such a thing.

Over the last long three days, the pain in his head had given way to numbness. It had been working flat out doing something. It felt as if it was busy processing, converting, interpreting, but oddly it also felt as if he wasn't involved.

There seemed to be a sort of parallel-to-serial conversion going on of mass interpretation, piecing together shredded magazines into readable pictures and comprehendible messages. It was mostly all beyond him though, and it was a slow process that he knew would take a long, long time, and a lot of mental glue; one that was preferably alcohol based.

He had regained some energy now although his feet and legs and one arm were still nervy and tingled with occasional pins and needles and a lack of sensation. The cool sea breeze had made the muscles at the back of his head and neck become almost totally locked, and his shoulders were so stiff they would have foiled even the strongest Thai masseuse.

His body still seemed to be vibrating slightly, resonating as if in some aftershock. He could feel tingling energy in his arm and especially in his hands and the tips of his fingers. It felt as though if he were to put his hands into the sand it would all vibrate around them. He tried it, but it just seemed to have the opposite effect of stopping the vibration altogether.

It was quite therapeutic somehow though, so he left his hands moving around in the sand for a while, sensing the rough and smooth textures and the heat.

He wasn't used just doing nothing, just sitting there waiting, without anything to do and with nowhere to go. He always had to be doing something, working on something, thinking about something all the time. So getting into the habit of stopping, not doing anything, and being unable to do anything, felt very awkward and alien. He felt like a little boy lost and alone, spare and disjointed, as a single tall poppy in a field of wheat.

He also had doubts in his mind about what he had really experienced days earlier. He knew so much now, all that knowledge was there in his head. He couldn't determine where had it all come from and where it was all stored. Was it just his mind playing some highly elaborate trick on him? He was smart enough to know that the experience, feelings, and flow of information had all been within his own mind. The bandwidth required for the data flow ruled out any other option. No field could cope with that level of information transfer at such speed, even though there was a field-traversing or navigational feel to it, but that didn't account for where or how it was there.

He knew that he knew all these things, all the knowledge was all still there, and that it was correct, vast and complex. It hadn't been there before, but was that in itself just a trick of the mind? Something deep inside himself told him it wasn't. He was OK. He wasn't ill or at risk, and from his training and experience, the one thing he needed to do was keep his head down until he knew more about what was going on and why.

His perception of everything seemed so different again; everything was so vivid, vibrant, and clear. Everything took on a clarity he had never seen before but he couldn't explain it to himself as to how. It was as if he couldn't remember how he used to see or experience things before. He was also aware that, all by itself, his mind would now automatically try to pull things together so that he could see or sense and could correlate things into some wider integrated context or meaning.

It was a good job there was nobody to talk to here, as he had no way of explaining how his mind was working - it was just *different*. Whatever had happened to him had had quite a profound transformational effect on his mind and body.

There were just too many things in his head that would be impossible to explain to people, or even articulate in any form. With his 'manager' head on, he thought about a whole range of things that would have to be in place just to build up a picture or plan to explain it all; like a series of projects to show how it all fitted together. Each small piece or concept he had seen, and now understood, would be a massive undertaking in its own right to conceptualise, convey, or show with evidence. It was just too much. Too many complex things all interrelated. The problem was just too big. So he would just leave it all alone for now, step back, and try not to think about it and concentrate on himself.

There were obviously many things troubling him, but he was still too much in 'shock mode' to think about it all logically, and as soon as he started to try to work things out his mind started firing off again in many directions at the same time.

It would just stumble and blunder into large blocks of knowledge that had been left there for him to rediscover, so he just tried to think of nothing for a while.

He had always been very much an atheist from an early age. From the age of about eight years old onwards the ideas of God and religion had seemed illogical, childish, unjust and unscientific to him. Large gaps in the blind logic required 'leaps of faith' that seemed like a cop out to his young mind. He had combined this with the lack of any physical evidence, and the steadfast 'head in the sand' mentality of others that ignored the lack of proof and scientific fact.

He had not been impressed with religious behaviour in general either, and the lack of responsibility, or accountability of any god that they claimed to believe in. Knowing and allowing so many unspeakably evil and unjust things to happen, even to total innocents, did not make any logical sense to him.

What he knew now seemed to go way beyond all of that, and yet was remarkably simple, clear, and obvious, yet also at the same time highly sophisticated and complex. It was as if something had dumped the entire library of human knowledge onto his carefully blanked out piece of paper mind, and somehow he had to make sense of it. Yet he still had no explanation for what had happened, and it also seemed emotionally distant, detached, so he just decided to not think about it for a while until he had physically recovered, and let whatever was going on in his head have time to do what it was doing.

He was learning to follow orders now though, something previously he had been very bad at. Brina had taken control and managed him over the last three days, telling him what he was to do, with no leeway or quarter. In his current state he was very happy to comply with this, and simply did what he was told, following it to the letter.

Having someone to think for you, and do for you, was a wonderful new experience for him and he had closely bonded himself to her in that short time. Giving himself totally into her care, being reliant, and in someone else's control, was not something he would have ever dreamed of letting anyone do before now.

Being the archetypal control freak and slightly arrogant it was not in his nature at all, but he somehow liked and needed it. It also made him aware of just how madly in love with him she was. She had come out of her shell, exposing that love in a completely devoted and committed way. He knew he had played her up quite a bit, and got her to do trivial things that he was quite capable of doing, like fetching a glass of water, but it made her happy, and he was happy being pampered.

They both knew it was just a way they could communicate how they felt. He was totally surprised. He never had any idea she felt so deeply about him, and she seemed so content to take care of him and to look after his welfare.

He was also aware that she wasn't the most tolerant of people, so he had to be careful not to let it go on for too long. In another couple of days the novelty would probably wear off, and he would need to be either completely better by then, or really dying.

Looking around the beach now, Sam noticed that it was still hazy and dull and that there weren't many colours here.

It was quite stark and bland in the grey clouded sea mist; just lots of different shades of grey and green, interspersed with the occasional black rock.

He remembered that yesterday he had ventured out for a brief walk in the garden of the house and had been confronted with a mass of vibrant colour in intense resolution from the exotic plants, flowers, and trees that had been planted there.

It was as if someone had just swapped your old little black and white portable TV for a new plasma, widescreen, colour, high definition 3D one, and turned all the levels up. As if coming out from a dark cinema into a bright, busy sunlit street.

That, coupled with enhanced smells and sounds, was what, he assumed, an LSD trip must be like, although he couldn't really say as he had never 'done' drugs. His mind was at the same time trying to correlate everything.

Too much information was coming in all at the same time which he couldn't deal with or describe in real terms, so after fifteen minutes he had gone back inside to rest again, closing his eyes to stop the process.

He looked down again at the mass of seaweed and vegetation on the sand several feet down the slope below. A picture came to him from a few weeks ago in Arrival customs at Auckland Airport, of a large middle-aged lady having a heated debate with an official over being fined for bringing an apple in her hand luggage.

The young official was strict but firm about the tight rules on what could and could not be brought in to the Country, and how they had to protect New Zealand from diseases and parasites. She was equally adamant that she had been given the apple on the plane, and as a result it 'shouldn't count' in her loud, pseudo upper-class, 'Don't you know who I am?' voice. She wasn't going to pay the associated fine, and that was final.

The discussion wasn't really a debate as neither party seemed to be taking notice of what the other was saying - they seemed to be almost following separate scripts. He and Brina had just looked at each other and moved sideways to another queue, as it was obvious it was going to take a while. Life to Sam had been very much a case of standing back and looking at the bigger picture of what was happening all the time.

He remembered the discussions in the other queues in Customs with the same conversations happening over and over; the officials all trying to make people who couldn't speak English understand what they were talking about by simply saying the same words, but saying them slower and louder; people from other countries looking bewildered as to what was going on as there were no translations into their language on the plane they came in on, and they simply did not have a clue what was being said.

Everyone just trying to do their jobs. Everyone just trying to get somewhere and everyone standing around waiting and getting annoyed with one another. Step back, look at the bigger picture and see what is really going on and what is actually happening, what needs to be done, and what the end result needs to be.

He visualised now the same gloved official standing on the shore having the same debate with the sea, accompanied by a vast pile of penalty fine notices to cover the array of insects, spiders, seeds, fruit, nuts and small furry animals it had imported. What would the woman say if she saw all this in contrast to the apple?

He thought about the insects and spiders clinging to the vegetation across the treacherous voyage, through the surf and rocks, over the hot sand, and finally up over the dunes and into the bush. Then coming head to head with the hostile natives, not to mention the small furry animal language barrier problem, and also trying to communicate with the hard working customs official who was unable to see things from their point of view.

It brought a smile to his face, which was a relief as it was something he thought he would never do again. It was all so simple really, just about making things work. Stepping back and seeing the bigger picture and managing things to achieve benefits for everyone. It wasn't difficult, it had all just got a bit over-complicated, and just a bit muddled over time, but then we were good at doing that. It's what life was all about.

He leant backwards at an angle on the sand, resting back on his elbows. He looked at the sand, the loose rocks, and the bleached grey driftwood around him in amongst the rough grass. Further up on the dune he noticed some ants darting about around a hole.

They had clearly spent some time doing reconstruction work, clearing up around the entrance to their nest after the storm. He guessed there must be a few hundred in there; they were quite large ones, about an inch or so long each, long legged and fairly fast.

He remembered there was some algorithm you could use to estimate the numbers based on how many went in and out over a minute but couldn't remember the exact multiplier, so he guessed. He always had the same problem with working out the time and distance of a lightning strike, from the time it took from hearing the thunder, to when it had actually occurred. In any case it didn't really matter.

He wasn't sure if these were native ants or alien imports but, as he wasn't an expert on ants, he was in no position to judge. The reason it caught his eye was that several of the ants were trying to manipulate a large dead insect into the hole. Because it was so much larger than the entrance, perhaps a couple of inches long, they couldn't squeeze it past a stick that had been blown into the sand blocking part of the entrance hole.

He watched them for a while trying various options, taking off the wings, trying to move, or cut the stick, in different directions. They were certainly determined and getting quite frustrated, or so it appeared.

Could he be bothered to get up and help them? It wasn't his problem after all. Would he be interfering with natural selection and the way of things? Would they die if he didn't and were they supposed to be there anyway? Trouble was that he had seen it now, and it was in his head, he now had responsibility, compassion and visibility. If he didn't do something how would he feel? Would he worry about it? Would it stay in his mind?

"Sod it" he said, and got up on his feet and walked the few paces to the nest, carefully moved the stick away and watched.

After a few moments of nervous defensive actions the ants settled down to their job and manoeuvred the bug into the hole, and they then all disappeared. However they didn't seem very grateful.

He walked back to the spot where he had been before and rested back on his elbows again. He decided not to lie down again and get caught sleeping as Brina would be arriving soon, and also he didn't want the ants nest to suddenly decide that he was next on their list. He thought for a while as to why he had just done what he did, instead of just ignoring the ants or going over and filling in their hole. It was just in his nature, it was the human element. That's what he was, and the kind of thing he did. He was a good man, and it was just 'the right thing to do'. Just as well nobody else was looking though, or he would probably have been laughed at, or labelled as mad.

Besides he had nothing else better to do.

After a while he heard the hire car pulling up into the long gravel car park at the back of the beach beyond the dunes. It ground to a halt in a purposeful way close to where she had dropped him off. Rather than jumping up he waited for the door to open and close, and then a few minutes later her head appeared over the dunes. She had become quite assertive over the last few days. After the 'Episode', as she now referred to it.

Unbeknown to him at the time, after his 'Episode' Brina had tried to get out in the car to get a doctor out to him but when she got to the car she found that one of the tyres was flat. She had then tried to call on the phone but the one in the house was disconnected. As there was no mobile coverage at the house she had walked into the village and found a payphone but that was out of order too. It was all very odd.

So she had changed the tyre with the spare, and had gone out the next morning to get it replaced before discovering that the doctors' surgery wasn't open that day. Luckily on returning she was relieved to see that he was much improved, and had decided to get him checked over when he was well enough to get out.

She walked over to him on the beach and sat down beside him, looking at him, inspecting his eyes to check for any indication of problems. She was wearing his sunglasses on her head like an Alice band, which looked great against her straight blonde hair. He wasn't sure of the reason, maybe it was having a part of him she could take with her, something subconscious. Or she may have just left hers in the house, and it was just handy for keeping the long hair out of her eyes. Before he would have been indignant, and told her off, but now it just made him content.

At thirty she was a good eight years younger than him, but they were well matched in life skills, experience and maturity. She knew how to look after herself, and her body, and made every effort to be aware of what she looked like and was mindful of her attire at all times. She was smart, with a degree from the 'University of Life', and had an exceptional empathy with a wide range of people, adapting herself quickly to communicate on their own terms. She was also far more tolerant of fools than he was.

There were a few things that he couldn't 'get' about her, like why sometimes she would take hours to get ready to go out and yet other times she could be ready in five minutes and yet still look the same. She had a few mental battle scars though, mainly as a result of being kind hearted to the wrong people, and quite often you might open an old wound and she would react swiftly without warning.

She never seemed to wear that much makeup or perfume, or perhaps it was just very subtle. Things like that with her were very much superficial to life. She was far more interested in the 'doing' and 'seeing' and going places. Clothes, makeup, perfume, shoes and accessories were there to serve functions rather than to be the be-all and end-all, as with many women. Yet oddly enough she managed to look great all the time, and to dress appropriately with a subtle air of breeding.

It was as if she had been in every conceivable situation, location, and environment already and always knew which right outfit to wear. She could get it to look right too in a moment's notice, with a few changes here and there, but in a practical rather than a 'dress up' sort of way.

His mother had told him to look out for a girl that other girls loved, and at the same time loved to hate. He understood this, but knowing his mother, he was never sure if it was a deliberate misdirection or not. Certainly Brina fell into that category, and probably several other categories that his mother didn't know about. Although she had been born in London she had a few Eastern European features about her with blue-grey eyes and a slightly hardened edge or tone here and there.

When they had first met he had been impressed not just with her looks, but also with the immediate confidence she had with everyone. She always seemed to make a point of shaking hands with people at the same time as looking them straight in the eye and smiling.

People seemed to like her straight away, and would immediately be inclined to confide in her. Most of all though, she was kind and caring, and in the last few days he had seen through so many of her protective covering layers to her spirit and soul underneath. More than that though, somehow, it seemed that he had always known her.

Today she was wearing a smart, light blue, knee length dress that was one of her more empowering, confident outfits. She had kicked her shoes off in the car, and was now sitting barefoot next to him, indifferent to the marks the sand may make to the back of her dress. She was flicking the sand with her toes slightly impatiently and had a smile on her face, so he knew she had been up to something and was waiting to tell him about it.

Brina stroked the palm of her hand along his bare lower arm reassuringly. It was lovely being touched by love, a caring intimacy that meant so much, so different from anything he had known before. His perception on everything had changed, not least the fact that he was just happy to be alive, anything after that was a bonus, and so he just appreciated everything, and loved her for it.

After a few moments she helped him up, which again they both knew wasn't necessary, and they walked together back to the car with her arm around his.

Once he was safely in the car, she sat in the driver's seat. She turned sideways to face him, shifting her backside in the seat and folding her legs underneath with her arm supporting her against the seat. She told him that while she was in town she had called in to the local doctor's, and had arranged a private appointment for him in an hour.

He was quite taken aback for a second as he wasn't sure about involving other people just yet, but it was clear that she was still concerned about him, and so he wasn't able to argue or come up with and adequate reason not to go.

So they drove back to the house and Brina unloaded the food from the car into the fridge, and left him in the passenger seat with the music on. She came back out ten minutes later with some shoes and socks and some trousers for him as he was still barefoot. She put them all on him, which was just an amazing experience, and of course made no sense as he could have walked the few yards into the house and got changed there.

The town was just a single main street, with several small rough track side roads coming off it. There were around two dozen wooden framed, single storey houses down each one, and some dozen or so of the normal range of shops and businesses along the main street. There was quite limited traffic flowing through, and only twenty or so people around. The air was a little dusty as most of the side roads were rough unsealed tracks.

It clearly served as a local hub for all the houses in the area as the number of shops and businesses there were too many to be supported by so few houses from within the town itself. A couple of the buildings looked to be significantly older than the rest, and were built from stone and brick with tiled roofs, whereas the rest were built around twenty years ago with mainly painted wood cladding and coloured metal roofs in line with more earthquake-friendly building standards.

The surgery, however, was surprisingly modern looking, single storey building, clad in red brick, it had a coloured steel roof with ample well laid out tarmac car parking spaces outside. Brina parked the car eventually after a few attempts, then stepped out and came round quickly to the passenger side. Sam had already opened the door and was trying to get out on his own. She put her arm under his unnecessarily and helped him up.

They walked together through the sliding automatic doors and into a small modern air-conditioned reception area that was empty of people. There were some dozen seats and a children's activity area, all new and pristine with plush carpets and furnishings. Even the walls looked like they had only been finished and painted in the last few weeks. Nobody had even had time to put up any of the normal array of information posters. So clearly this was a leased building, and a leased reception setup and facilities too.

Brina motioned for him to sit in one of the seats by the window, and she stepped over to the empty reception desk and rang the bell. A nurse appeared at a few moments later, and indicated from her expression that she recognised Brina. She ticked a notebook, and spoke to her briefly before Brina directed the woman's attention unnecessarily to where Sam was sat.

He stared out of the window. He liked staring out of windows, not so much to see what was there but to just stare and think. Even as a young child he had spent a lot of time staring out of windows. His teachers, the ones that noticed, kept telling him off, and even commented to his parents about this.

It didn't seem to stop him knowing everything though, it just seemed more interesting in his imagination rather than concentrating on what was going on in the classroom, especially when the teachers just seemed to be just repeating themselves. His dreams and imagination were so much more vivid, intense and exciting than mundane reality.

Since he had met Brina though, things had changed. He still liked and wanted to stand and stare out of windows but every time she saw him doing it, she would find him something else to do, something to keep him occupied, rather than doing 'nothing'.

Standing around doing 'nothing' is one thing women can't stand.

Looking on the information panel on the wall next to him he saw that there were four doctors listed at this surgery, which seemed a lot for a town this size, so he guessed they may be covering the wider area. The magazines on the table in front of him were fairly limited to cars, home buying, sea fishing and interior design. The car one looked quite promising until he picked it up and realised it was just on V8's. So he scanned through the sea fishing one for a few minutes, then got bored and put it down. He couldn't see a clock anywhere so he got out his phone from his front pocket and in so doing released some sand that had still been there from when he had transferred it from his shorts. The sand fell onto the new, dark blue carpet tiles on the floor behind his seat. He looked at Brina for a second but as she was now busy reading he just put the phone back. He wasn't very good at relaxing, or not being in charge.

A minute or so later a grey-haired man wearing a tie and jacket appeared from around the corner, and checked over at the reception counter. He then looked over to them and smiled. He called Sam's name and gestured towards a side room, and they both got up and went in. The treatment room was pretty much the same as in the waiting area, but much smaller, and aside from a desk, a computer, and two chairs there wasn't much else in there. Sam wasn't a great fan of doctors in general and had managed to avoid seeing one for over five years.

Brina started the conversation and explained as best she could what had happened and this was followed by a few questions and answers before the doctor concentrated on Sam and asked him for his perspective. Sam didn't go into much detail of what had happened during, just the situation beforehand and his symptoms afterwards. Notes were typed into the computer as he spoke, and Sam noticed that the doctor wasn't looking his way at all. A few obvious questions were asked like "Had it had happened before?" to which he gave the obvious answers.

After he had taken his blood pressure with some strange electronic band, the doctor gradually started treating him more and more like a child, explaining simple things to him and various facts he "Must understand and come to terms with at his age." At the end the doctor said "Well I am sure it is nothing to worry about. You have probably been overdoing it and may be a bit stressed so I will give you something to help you relax." He typed something on the computer and stood up and went to Reception, and returned with a small piece of paper that had been churned off the printer.

He pointed in the air in the direction of the local chemist and gave Brina a few instructions. Looking at the prescription Sam saw that it was for a mild sedative. Sam looked back at him, and raised his eyebrows, "Are you sure you don't want to prescribe me a course of antibiotics too?"

The doctor looked very confused and indicated that he didn't understand the context of the question. "It's just that you seem to be used to talking to people of either a young age or of limited intelligence, and since I am neither I thought I would offer you a second opinion" said Sam. The doctor's expression was still confused and so he asked Sam if he "Were medically trained in any way?" "No, my mind is my own" came Sam's curt reply.

Sam couldn't believe how angry he was getting. It was the doctor's attitude that really got to him. "You just haven't listened to what I have told you. You haven't done any cross checks or given me a proper diagnosis, or offered to refer me to a specialist. Basically you have just fobbed me off with some useless drug." He handed back the prescription and walked out of the building and got straight into the car, leaving a confused Brina to sort out the bill and to deal with the situation.

He was surprised at himself once he was back in the car. He was not normally like that at all. It took a lot to get him angry and that situation was nothing. He shouldn't have behaved like that - it was all because he was angry at something in his head that was troubling him - not at what had actually just happened. He felt insecure and vulnerable, defensive and under attack.

His mind flashed back to just before his fifth birthday when he had to undergo a major operation in hospital. He hadn't been aware of it at the time, but the operation was the first of its kind, it was life threatening, and there were a lot of professors, senior surgeons and consultants that had been brought in to watch it being done. As a small boy though, all he remembered was being taken from his mother in the large Victorian hospital, and being put on a wheeled bed, all the time trying to be brave as he had been told to be.

As he thought about the memory it became quite clear and vivid, and he remembered the nurses that walked alongside his bed as it went through the corridors; they held his hand and were kind, he even remembered what they had said to him, and how they were dressed, the style of their uniforms, and how they behaved. It was amazing how much you could remember from a stressful or panicked situation, it was as if the adrenaline forced your mind into permanent record mode.

He had arrived in the preparation room, which was full of equipment and other people, and that was where he started to get really nervous, and seeing this they tried to reassure him. He was OK for a while there, and seemed to be coping, up to the point when he had to have an injection, and that pushed his bravery too far. He was shaking and sobbing now looking around and they had to forcibly hold him down to administer the anaesthetic jab.

That stress, that sudden panic and uncontrollable fear overcame him, and as he gradually faded, the room drifted, yet he had fought and tried to stay there, frightened of what was going to happen to him. The last thing he remembered was the face of the young blonde nurse who was holding him down. She was probably no more than twenty, but to a five year old she was just another adult.

She continued to talk to him, calmly looking into his eyes, reassuring him, but he couldn't hear her in his deaf panic, he felt her pressing her hand to the front of his shoulder, holding it down to the bed. He saw her blue uniform, white cap, the upside-down silver watch on her breast pocket, her face that looked as if she was about to cry, and he smelt the smells in the room. He looked straight into her eyes. She cared for him, she was responsible for him, and she was doing her job, even though at that moment it was breaking her heart.

He never saw the crowded operating theatre. He was never

there, he was out of consciousness. He never felt the repairs to his body, never felt the blood given, the skill, and the simple miracles. He never met or knew the people that had saved his life.

Twelve hours later he woke in a ward bed and knew nothing of these things. Just a long scar on his stomach, tubes and a drip by his bed, faces he knew, needed, and a large, carefully wrapped box with a dark green big metal truck inside. It was amazing what we could remember.

A minute or so later Brina got into the car with the receipt and prescription in her hand. He didn't say anything. She looked at him like he was a sad puppy, put her seat belt on, and drove to the chemist's.

She was in a very determined mood, and was empowered by her new control role, and he was still too stuck in his 'hard done by', 'old dog' mode, to say anything else. She popped into a few of the other shops while she was there to get a couple of things that she hadn't managed to get at the supermarket. He was left sat in the passenger seat alone while she went around, which made him feel like a spare part.

He watched all the people going by, and they too all seemed different now, all had a new context; what they were buying, how their faces looked, how they behaved. A couple of middle aged Maori women walked past with a pushchair with a small baby inside that he assumed must be a grandchild. It seemed to be eating something blue on a stick.

They just ignored Sam as they passed the car. *Blue food?* He didn't remember having blue food when he was young. It was the sort of thing you gave to rodents, not people. His mind flashed back to about six months before when he went to a nephew's birthday party at a nursery. There was a blue iced cake, with blue sweets on the top, which was among the offerings laid on for the small children.

The previously quiet and happy four-year olds were later bouncing off the walls and attempting to kill each other. He had been talking to one of the assistants and she explained "Well, it's what they want these days, and they all have the same, so what can you do?"

At the time he didn't really think about it, but stepping back and looking at it from the outside, it was totally barking mad. Why give a child something artificial that it doesn't physically need, that will turn it into a hyperactive maniac, just because you think it wants it? Who was in charge in that situation? Who was in control, and what would be the long term consequences?

He remembered back to his time at university when there had been an Open Day. The Food Science department had laid on some demonstrations for food tasting and one of the displays was about the colour of food. There were five cakes – they had all the same ingredients but had been dyed different colours- and you had to choose the one that looked and tasted the best. Of course nobody chose the blue one, and this was because, as they explained, that you didn't get blue food occurring naturally for some reason and so your body and mind was telling you that it was wrong, and that you wouldn't like the look or taste of it, and they were right. *There was blue food everywhere now! How the bloody hell did that make any sense?* Sam thought to himself.

The drive back to the house was only a short trip but he wasn't at all comfortable sitting in the passenger seat. It wasn't right somehow. He didn't talk to Brina as she was concentrating on her driving. Even though they drove on the same side of the road in New Zealand as in the UK there were a few odd rules over priority at junctions that were a bit strange, and she was in 'care' mode so he didn't interrupt or break her concentration.

She had taken her shoes off to drive, and had hitched her dress up slightly which left her legs bare which were now quite tanned from the sunbathing. They were also toned up with all the activities and walking over the last few weeks. She caught him looking at them and smiled. "Feeling a little bit better then?" she asked. But it would be a long while before he felt 'that better'. His eyes were still writing cheques that his body couldn't cash right now.

Brina hadn't been happy at all with the holiday home that they had been staying in for the last week or so. It was large and sprawled over a wide area across different levels on the hillside with ample gardens and a pool.

It was quite an old building in New Zealand terms, and was unusually built of solid stone rather than the usual modern American-style wood stud walls, plasterboard, insulation and lap cladding. The stone was dark, and probably originally volcanic, but looked like thick slate and was densely pressed with quartz elements.

The floors were mostly flagstones but with carpets in the living rooms and lounge. It was unique and there were quite a lot of individual touches and bespoke follies about it. This was probably why it was set aside as a holiday let and why it wouldn't ever feel like anyone's real home.

Brina was convinced that the house was haunted, and late at night when they were alone in the large house together, she was sure there was some sort of presence or 'feeling' along the top corridor.

In the room they had slept in for the first night it had felt odd and cold, and she was convinced someone had died in there in a dramatic way. She had a dream of someone being strangled or smothered that night. Sam hadn't felt that but agreed to move rooms anyway to a lighter, airier, warmer one. She wouldn't go back in the room and had shut the door on it.

There was something odd about the back corridor though, a cold feeling that you weren't alone, and he was sure he had seen a shadow out of the corner of his eye on more than one night up there. From then on it drew his attention, and scenarios or situations would go through his mind of what may have occurred there.

But now he knew what it was all about, and what people sensed when they saw a ghost or had a spiritual encounter or sensed something and he knew why it was there.

It all seemed a bit obvious now, but at least he wasn't troubled by it any more. He decided not to explain it all to Brina as he wasn't really ready to deal with long, complicated explanations. He didn't want her to think him mad, and besides, she had been a lot more 'cuddly' in the evenings as a result.

He slept well that night. The air had cleared, felt fresher, and it wasn't as warm and close and humid as it had been.

His eyes opened to the bright morning sun and he was immediately aware of the smell of bacon.

His arm had flopped out of bed and he was hanging half out of it, face down, with the sheet over his lower half and his face pressed against the bedside cabinet. One of those true-to-life sexy poses that you don't tend to see in films.

He lifted his head up and away from the wood, and squinted around the room. Brina wasn't in the room and he assumed she must be getting him breakfast. He felt a lot better even though he had just woken up, his mind was more alert, but that could have just been the bacon triggering his major key brain functions.

He fell the remaining part out of bed and knelt up and wrapped his dressing robe that was on the end of the bed around himself.

He went to the bathroom and ran his fingers through his hair to get it slightly less sideways, and washed his face in a handful of cold water and pinched it back into shape. Then finally he began automatically brushing his teeth.

He remembered that he was just about to have breakfast about three seconds after he had already started brushing, he stopped, and then decided to finish as he had already started. Besides he would have to work out what to do if he stopped now, and it wouldn't feel right just interrupting the process for no good reason.

He went into the kitchen to see Brina. She had cooked a full English breakfast for him; eggs, bacon, beans, toast, marmalade and all the trimmings. It was all laid out on the table with napkins. She was already showered and dressed in jeans and a checked shirt and she looked fabulous. It was a real 'Beauty and the Beast' moment, although he would have preferred the term 'handsome'.

She smiled at him when she turned around holding a metal spatula, but was busy so didn't hug him, just gestured to the seat at the table. As he sat down she brought a plate over to him, and a few moments later she joined him with her own.

She had made a real effort to put all the things he liked on the table; it was wonderful that she had even managed to get hold of some decent coffee.

Sam drank loads of water with it all as he just seemed to need it. He guessed he must have been quite dehydrated. The drinking water there in the house was collected from rain off the roof into a large tank outside and filtered so it was pure enough to drink.

It also had no added chemicals or residual ones from the ground. Sam was always dismayed at the way tap water at home smelt a bit like swimming baths with all that chlorine and fluoride or whatever they put in it.

That is why he only ever drank bottles spring water normally. This however smelt much better than the stuff that came out of the taps at home, as long as you didn't think too much about what was in the gutters or the water tank that is. They sat and ate and talked about day to day things, it was good, natural somehow, it was if they had always been together.

After breakfast Sam took a shower and whilst he was soaping himself all over, he made up his mind that he was going to buck up and move on. Rather than dwelling on all the things he now knew about, and being a grumpy sod, he would just get on with things for now.

For some reason he always had all his best ideas and thoughts in the shower or bath, and was able to see things clearer and with more perspective.

It was only now that he knew why, and it wasn't just because it was warm and quiet. It was all very well knowing all of these things, but everyday life still went on. You may know a load more about the world, some of which was disturbing or depressing, but you still had to live in it, and exist, and carry on with responsibilities and duties. In some ways it was a bit like the purpose of taking a shower, you may be able to put up with yourself but it didn't mean that everyone else had to.

As he stood there under the water his mind wandered. It was going to be a long shower. He had always thought that the Romans had the right idea about living. With their numerous bath houses, fountains and aqueducts, fed from fresh springs, heated naturally and washed away with clever engineering; all integrated and public with pools and social interaction, all part of the ethos.

He wondered what they would think of us using chlorine and

fluoride? But then they used lead for pipes, so that at least was one up that we had on them.

There were even communal group toilets which he remembered seeing in Rome several months ago when he had taken Brina for a week's trip there, and the expression on her face when she realised what they were.

He didn't think Brina or her mother would have coped very well in Roman times, but then ultimately women seemed to cope very well with anything, far better than men did. So maybe Brina would have been fine living back then.

He wasn't so sure about her mother though.

The time he and Brina had spent in Rome was very rewarding for him. He always loved doing things for other people and sharing the excitement with them in showing them things he loved. He had been there before a few times, and was able to show her around the archaeological sites in a structured order, backed up with some detailed knowledge.

He was careful to make sure they had spent some time shopping, and had included a few romantic evening meals too. She had loved it all, and was suitably impressed, and interested in his 'guided tours', although he wasn't sure how genuine that interest was, or if it were more directed towards him, but it didn't matter either way.

She had taken a lot of trouble in what she was wearing, and as always seemed to have the right footwear for the long walks. That was something he was impressed with, her practicality. Silly girls, in silly shoes, were very annoying, and she was neither.

She could not work out how he knew where he was in the city all the time, which way he was going, or which direction the various archaeological sites were, or down which roads. It was almost as if he had a map or GPS built into his head.

She was very tolerant of him, even when he turned down a side street, and was confused when it turned out to be a dead end, which from his expression 'never used to be there'.

The only time she had a problem was at the Coliseum. He had managed to get a VIP pass to avoid the queues, but walking out into the middle arena her bright mood changed very quickly, almost as if she were being affected by some sudden illness. She had started off being very interested and enthusiastic in his descriptions and stories, excited and awe-inspired by the scale and grandeur of the place, but after thirty minutes there she seemed to go pale and lifeless, as if all the energy had been drained from her.

She looked uneasy, off guard, and finally, highly agitated. He took her out quickly, and found some shade in a nearby café. She had clearly been suffering but hadn't said anything to him, not wanting to spoil the experience for him.

She described the feeling to him as a great oppressive negative pressure, as if she was somehow sensing the echoes of the violent deaths, or the presence of the souls stored in the towering walls all around. It was like an ominous resonating evil sensation in the silence. Like being in a giant grave, with the only signs of life the grass and plants growing in the exposed holding bays of the arena lower levels, or with the occasional cat searching for dead birds.

He didn't admit it to her, but he also felt the same, something he hadn't felt the previous time he had been there and it had left him feeling depressed and sad. Probably some echo from the many violent deaths in the distant past.

He gave her plenty of time to recover, which she did after a few drinks and a rest, before he began route marching her off to see the other sites. He loved that about her, she was always willing to go that extra mile to make him happy, just in the same way that he did for her.

However, she seemed to also want to make everyone else happy too, and make everything right, and she would always give far too much of herself. He could see this trait being taken advantage of quite frequently by some people who clearly didn't deserve it.

As he was thinking of all of these things, complex thoughts started to form in his mind, linking concepts together. This had been happening quite frequently and seemed to be bottling up.

So to try and keep some order to his thoughts he decided that he was going to write the information and facts down, so that they didn't keep going over and over in his head, and in his determined mood he made a start that morning.

He just jotted some of the key points down on several pieces of A4 paper, but it all initially looked a bit disjointed and rambling, and to someone reading it he would probably come across as mad. So he just stuck to short statements, and kept them all a leather folder that he carried in his case.

He didn't want to use the laptop for it as it just didn't seem right; it didn't seem to be able to represent what he wanted to write or draw somehow. So he just rambled on paper, it helped to gain some sort of control somehow, like putting a stake in the ground to get some order, even if it was only a tiny fraction of it all. More of a statement of intent, rather than anything else.

They still had another three days left in New Zealand before they were due to fly back. Brina wasn't going straight home. She had arranged to stop off and visit some girlfriend in Sydney - someone she knew from a few years back when she used to work in London, who had subsequently relocated with work to Australia. Sam was going to go along, but as her friend had become recently single, and as Brina pointed out, that would mean he would have been a bit of a loose end, and in the way of any juicy gossip.

So he had decided to go straight back on his own, and to leave them to it for a week. It had been a long holiday already, and he wanted to get back and get things sorted for work.

The whole trip here had really been planned on the spur of the moment, coming at a convenient time with him finishing a work project for his company, and her new client delaying a start date by six weeks for a new contract. So rather than looking into the best options for price and luxury as he normally did, it was more down to what was available, and what they could get to see in the time.

So they had booked flights, a few hotels, and this place, but everything else was just made up as they went along, which had actually worked out quite well, allowing them to change where they went and what they saw depending on what they found when they got there.

When they had first arrived in Auckland they had stayed in the city centre for a few days to see some of the sites in the local area, and to get over the jet lag. The air was very fresh and clear, and the sun very harsh and bright, with a bluish white intensity that was in stark contrast to the beige soft, damp, overcast beige in the UK. The hotel was the best one he could find but it was just about OK for Brina.

She was a bit fussy to say the least about what she considered acceptable, or what she could relax in, the standard of the bathroom, the size of the room and the decor.

Once she had checked it over and was settled it was fine, it was just getting over that initial barrier, that defensive 'making sure there was nothing wrong' thing she had. He couldn't imagine she had ever stayed in any rough hotels in her life, so he wasn't sure why she was so sensitive.

He was much less fussy - as long as it had a big bed, and it was quiet he was happy, oh and cotton sheets, soft pillows, smoke free, good TV, and spa facilities with of course a Jacuzzi bath, just the few basic essentials and he was just fine. He had stayed in quite a few rough hotels in his time, when he had been on his own, mostly his own fault. It was different when you were on your own, you didn't spend any time worrying about if everything was alright for the other person, so you just got on with it.

You didn't have that 'to and fro' bantering to see if everything was working. He suspected that if she were on her own, Brina would survive quite well enough in the middle of nowhere with just a tent, sleeping bag, and a bush.

She had that hard survival edge to her, an adaptable 'Just watch me' persona. Mind you, he was sure as hell not going to find out, she may be able to survive, but he was fairly sure his life would made very difficult as soon as she got back.

On the second evening they went for a meal at a restaurant by Auckland Harbour which looked out over the massive array of boats and yachts. They seemed to span the whole area between the city and the giant Harbour Bridge, and off to Watchman Island a mile or so off the coast.

The food wasn't good at all. It was obviously what the chef had read about in a magazine or seen a TV cook make on an afternoon show – it was laid out in a 'Nouvelle Cuisine' style but without any of the taste or fresh ingredients. The idea being it was OK as long as it 'looked' right.

It was at that point that he became aware that a lot of the women around seemed to be very interested in him, smiling at him whenever he caught their eye. It was very noticeable to the point where Brina became quite annoyed, especially when she had returned to the table from visiting the bathroom to find a woman chatting to him, leaning over the table toward him. Sam was tall, dark haired, and reasonably good looking, but he had never encountered women behaving so openly flirtatiously with him before, as was the case here and now.

Brina assessed the situation in a blink of an eye and immediately 'saw her off'. The two women exchanged a glance and it was clear that a mass of protocols, standings and assessments took place in that instant. It would have made good viewing on any soap drama or natural history documentary. Brina collected herself in a heartbeat as she sat down, and smiled at him, replacing the napkin on her lap.

On the way back to the hotel he had dragged Brina into the casino, which she wasn't keen on at all. It just wasn't her thing. The place was much larger than he had expected and seemed to be full of Asian men and women, all with incredibly miserable looking faces.

It was a peculiar environment, stale, smoke-filled and dimly lit. He would have expected to see a lot more happy faces in a place designed to provide entertainment. He placed a few bets on the roulette table, and offered some chips to Brina but she wouldn't play at all.

He could see she was quite uncomfortable, so they left and went up the Sky Tower to see the city lights at night from the top which he thought was quite romantic but it wasn't as much as he had hoped, they were both tired, and so after they went back to their room early to just sleep.

The following day they had set off up north and once off the main motorway immediately hit the traffic jams on the windy, single-lane roads through little towns with weather-boarded shops like something from the 1950's.

There weren't that many road warning signs, but instead they had signs flashing up the number of traffic fatalities that month on that particular stretch of road.

One sign even displayed a big smiley face declaring that '0' motorists had died on that particular road that month, and Sam wondered if the face turned to a 'not-smiley' one when someone died to make it clear how you should feel. The important road signs were fairly sparse, but they clearly meant what they said.

The ones for 'sharp bends' usually had deep densely vegetated ravines associated with them, and if you slid off the road into one then it would probably take many months before anyone found whatever was left of you.

They followed the tourist path to the Bay of Islands to see the dolphins on a boat trip and explore the area. He noticed how much hotter it was up there, almost subtropical.

On the boat trip they were lucky enough to see an orca whale, and a large pod of dolphins including a baby which Brina was thrilled about.

They stayed up there in a self-catering luxury apartment for three nights to allow enough time to do all the tourist trips. They also managed to get a bit of scuba diving in at the Poor Knights islands for one day which was great , although surprisingly cold in the deep, and the boat trip back was a little rough, and left them both feeling seasick.

He had always had great sea legs and was confused at feeling ill. He had dived in many seas and oceans around the world and was usually fine on boats, so he just put it down to the jet lag or being upside down, or the change in the gravitational field or something.

That was the other thing he remembered, since arriving 'Down Under'. He had lost his sense of direction. He had always had a sixth sense as far as knowing which path or route he needed to go in or where he had come from, so that when driving around he knew which way he had to go to get to a destination.

It was like an in-built satellite navigation or compass, so he always knew which way was North or South or whatever. When walking into strange towns he could always find his way back to the car, or in woods he could track his way through with no problem. It was just a feeling a sense of right, where he was, where he had come from, and where he needed to go.

His ability amazed Brina, but he wasn't sure if she was really impressed or just placating him. It also worked at night so wasn't anything to do with the sun. It was probably just to do with a throwback to when we were hunter gatherers. He commented to Brina that he was sure most women had the same ability going around shops, it was just a shame it didn't extend to them being able to find their cars in the car park afterwards, but she didn't find it funny.

It was just a survival thing he supposed, and probably something we had and just forgotten or evolved out of. He couldn't remember when he started to be aware of it but it was when he was between seven and ten years of age. Something migrating animals used all the time with field sense and movement through the lines around the earth.

But here it was gone, or he had lost his bearings or reference to it, so it must be to do with being in the southern hemisphere, and the change in the field.

Mind you it would be interesting to take some birds that were just about to migrate for the winter and fly them down to the Southern hemisphere and see what they did, and which way they went.

They would probably just stay put he thought. *Lucky he had a map.*

They spent the following day sharing the driving down to Taupo and Rotorua in the centre of the North Island which was dramatically different with its high mountains and rugged terrain with volcanic evidence, past and present, everywhere.

The whole area was alive with various mud pools, geysers, and volcanic lakes. Brina wasn't impressed with the continual rotten egg sulphur smell, but there was a lot to see and do, and they stayed for three or four days.

He had wanted to go up the Ruapehu volcano to see some of the location from the *Lord of the Rings* movies, but as it was summer the ski lift was being serviced, and so they were only able to drive up half way and park. They had spent a few hours walking around and taking photos of the views, bleak and rugged slopes of sharp dark rock with ancient lava fields spreading off in all directions.

He remembered returning to the car, and parked next to theirs was an English family in a small hire car with the doors open, having a blazing row. The dark haired woman, in her late twenties, was stood, arms crossed, with her backside resting on the front bonnet of the car looking into the distance.

She was sulking about something, which was clearly one of the limited number of mental functions she was capable of. The stressed husband was busy ranting in the front seat about a wide range of meaningless issues, which were about where they were going and what they had to see and why. Strapped into the back in a baby seat too small for her, was a small girl about four years old who was mithering and had a large packet of 'glow in the dark' hyperactive crisps in one hand.

Behind the back of the car was a boy aged about seven who had a plastic elven sword, and was busy bashing the boot of the car with it, and anything else around, while deftly from the other hand drinking from a straw of a fast food bottle of something coloured and fizzy, probably to wash down the chocolate that was still partly round his face.

His name seemed to be 'Nayfan' and was reminded of this at regular intervals by his 'possible' father, which was accompanied each time by various meaningless and unheeded instructions. The whole thing seemed to infuriate Brina, yet up until then it wouldn't have been something that Sam would have noticed or taken the time to think about, and would have just ignored.

On the way back up to Auckland to catch the flight to the South Island they had stopped off at a nature reserve which was away from anywhere else. It was a beautiful, fresh sunny day and they walked together along the rough paths of the tree lined bush. The exotic birdsong from high up in the balcony of the trees was so different to anything he had heard before.

There were streams and banks crowded with ferns, and exotic flowers and shrubs with occasional information signs here and there. They just walked slowly together without talking, just soaking up the rays of sun as they filtered down through the branches. It was idyllic, tranquil, and soporific, a slow drug relaxing the tensions away. It was a shame they were so far south down the Island now, he would have loved to have gone back there.

Then for the remaining week before coming back up to Wellington, and then to here, they had flown down to Queenstown in the South Island. Sam had planned to see most of the South Island while they were down there but they ended up just staying in the surrounding Queenstown area for seven days.

It was a shock to discover just how far the distances were, and how remote everything was when they got there; distances that looked like a few minutes on the map actually took hours, and the few roads were very winding.

The landscape was truly dramatic, stunning, 'awesome' was the overused adjective, but probably the only place in the world where it was allowed to be overused. The ski lifts there were fortunately in operation to go sightseeing up the mountains despite the lack of snow.

The tourist operations were in full swing and there was a great supply of activities to fill your time, from jet boating, exploring, gold digging, and sightseeing flights. They stopped off at the bungee jumping bridge which he had read about, but they both decided to give it a miss, it just seemed to be too commercialised now. So they had flown back to Wellington for their remaining week or so, and now had just three days left before they were to fly back home again.

It was good not to have to go anywhere that day so they just spent it relaxing about the house and by the pool just recovering. It gave them a chance to actually talk about themselves, and learn about each other, rather than talking about what they were doing or where they were going, as they had been for weeks. So at the end of that one day, he had learnt a surprising amount more about her, and himself.

On the day before they were due to fly out he felt that he had recovered fully, and they drove into Wellington to visit the shops and the museum.

They also had time to walk around the city, which was surprisingly cosmopolitan. The outdoor precincts were very well laid out, if a little windy.

His impressions of New Zealand were very different from the impression people had given him. He somehow had the idea from people that had visited the country that it was 'still like it all was thirty years ago', but this didn't seem to be the case at all.

There were clearly aspects of life there outside the cities that resembled more the farming village environment, both in attitudes and hard practical working life structure and psyche, but it was adapting fast to a whole range of global influences as best it could, and yet maintaining and preserving its beauty and character, despite the usual pressures.

They grabbed some sandwiches and coffee for brunch and sat on one of the benches in a small park in a sheltered spot out of the wind. Brina was much more talkative today, and led most of the conversation, saying how glad she was that they hadn't used the ferry to the South Island as the sea looked very rough in-between the two islands.

She also talked about what she was planning to see and do when she visited her friend in Sydney. She was so animated and alive, he had obviously done something right somehow. She was clearly very much in love with him, and it showed in her face and words, and even the way she sat and focused on him.

He tried to remember to sit up straight and look interested in her too; he just wished he felt better than he did. He knew he did love her too, but even after a few hours walking he just wanted to go to sleep. But he wasn't going to let her know that, so he finished his coffee, and looked keen to get going again.

They walked to the Te Papa Museum which was impressive for such a small city, and it had an extensive Maori history section. It was good to see that even in a very young country they were keen to preserve any history and culture that they had, unlike many older countries that had become indifferent to what they had.

It had all been very well thought out and planned, even the building itself was earthquake proof.

He became very aware that he seemed to be very interesting to many people as he and Brina walked around. At first he thought he had something wrong with him, like his flies were undone or his shirt hanging out at the back. They seemed to be smiling and looking or trying to work something out or if they had seen him before.

Quite a few women smiled at him again, and looking back at them after they had passed, and he noticed that some of them had just stopped to look at him directly. It was quite disconcerting as it had never happened before, and he was quite sure he had looked in better shape, and certainly better dressed, in the past.

There was another thing that had unnerved him that day. They had gone into a large book store to get a guide book for the city and some new novel for Brina. Sam had been wandering around, and was drawn to the Science section, just because it was still in the back of his mind what he had experienced.

Something seemed to be telling him to ignore the books but he had nothing else to do so he picked out one on the 'String Theory', and he flicked through the pages with diagrams and equations and glossy diagrammatic images to explain certain theoretical concepts in a more bite-size, *Readers Digest* fashion.

It was odd - his brain seemed to be collating everything he was seeing without reading it in detail, building it in his mind like a house of cards so that the picture formed and he could see what was right and what worked, and what was wrong or unstable. It just seemed so simple and clear, what was right and what was wrong, and yet weeks ago if he had read it, it would just have been a mass of unintelligible words and equations that he wouldn't have understood, and would have had no interest in at all.

He was still not able to understand the mathematical equations in themselves directly, but somehow that didn't seem to matter. He just knew it. He put the book back on the shelf.

Late in the afternoon they visited the city zoo, which was Brina's idea. She thought it would be somewhere quiet and easy and safe. It was a small old site that was a bit tired but it was pleasant and quiet enough to walk around together, although it felt wrong to be looking around a zoo in another country. He was almost expecting to see a fox or a badger or a Yorkshire man in a flat cap to show you what strange creatures there were in the countries on the other side of the world.

There was one animal that Sam hadn't seen before, a Sun Bear, which had a peculiar marking on its chest and a furrowed brow which made it look depressed in addition to it's obvious boredom, and Sam wondered if it knew something that the people around here didn't.

It stuck in his mind - the image of it standing on a hillock in its enclosure just rocking back and forth on its legs, giving a comforting rhythm to itself like a baby trying to pacify itself in some way in an environment that was alien, mindless, and insane.

Driving on the way back out of the city Sam looked up and was surprised at how many houses were perched on the sides of the steep hillsides, and how narrow the gap was between the cliffs and the sea through which the only road and rail line passed.

In a place so concerned over the threat of earthquakes, and being the meeting point of two fault lines, it was perplexing how people could not see the obvious, and how they were influenced by the 'here and now' and the cost, rather than the 'maybe'.

On the last day they woke up early and set off to Wellington Airport, arriving mid-morning at the hire car depot to drop the car off. It was quite a small airport compared with Auckland where they had arrived, and as it was quite windy, he was glad that they were taking off rather than landing. The airstrip was fairly challenging to get a plane down on between the hills and the sea, especially in the wind.

Sam watched one small aircraft coming in to land from the observation area, and the plane had swayed around so much, it looked like the wing tips would hit the ground.

Brina caught her flight to Sydney and they hugged and kissed before she left, like they weren't going to see each other for a year, rather than just a week. He supposed it was because being abroad and separating wasn't the same as saying goodbye at home.

It was an hour before his connecting flight left to Auckland for the on-going flight to Singapore so he had a little time to look around and reflect on what he had seen, and to look for some mundane, innocuous magazine to read on the flight.

CHAPTER 3 - BUBBLE IN THE SKY

Having waited so long in the departure lounge in Auckland following the short hop from Wellington, it was a relief to finally get on the plane. It was the usual 747 on that leg to Singapore. He was so accustomed to the layout of different planes now that he knew each plane like his office or home. Consequently the hand luggage he had brought with him was minimal and efficiently organised.

He always felt when flying, that it was always more sensible to fly over as much land as possible. At least, he thought, that way you have a better chance of surviving if you went down. The other route option was going via LA, over the expanse of the Pacific. Somehow the idea of going all that way over such a vast unending area of water was unnerving, it could be many hours or days before help arrived. Besides going this way round the planet gave you one long night or day, rather than two shorter ones.

He was in the habit now of taking jet lag relief tablets for long haul flights, which for the last several flights had worked well. However with the delays in the departure lounge he was already into his third round of pills, and so felt somewhat odd getting onto the plane. He sat down in his seat in Economy Class.

He would have begrudged spending so much on Business or First, not because he couldn't afford it, but because most of the people in there weren't paying for their seats themselves; they were either on business, were civil servants, officials, or were military types. It just grated on his nerves.

Being able to book his own seats in advance meant that he was usually able to get a spare seat next to him, or in this case, three in a row all to himself. However, rather than feeling smug, he was just glad for the space and solitude. It was a relief, being able to lie down and sleep in peace. So as soon as he could after take-off he did so, which also selfishly meant that he didn't get joined by any talkative company.

He wasn't normally that overtly selfish, he just didn't care at that moment. After about fifteen minutes had gone and everyone else had finished either moving or deciding they were happy where they were, he sat back up to go through the on-board entertainment. There was a choice of a few hundred options for film and radio channels, and a meal menu which had a choice of just two. He noted for later the two films he hadn't already seen, and the non-veggie option, and listened to some music before the meal arrived.

He had travelled with this airline quite a few times, and the service and meals were very good in comparison to others. He had probably built up enough points with them to travel Business Class next time which would be OK, allowable somehow, as it was free. He had a glass of something alcoholic, described as white wine, but which tasted like plastic, with his meal. That was alright though, as the alternative was beer which, he knew from experience, tasted like warm watery aluminium.

When she picked up his tray he asked the stewardess for some ear plugs and an eye mask, which she duly brought back politely a few minutes later. He had always been impressed with the staff on this airline at how smart, well presented and efficient and polite they were, and continued to be despite working for such a long time. Combining the roles of a waitress, nursemaid, hostess, and safety supervisor was no mean task for twelve hours on your feet.

Like them, their uniforms were efficiently designed and well made, and seemed to offer the right signals rather than the wrong ones; smart , neat, constrained, and yet beautiful without being overtly sexual. Each of them had gone to great lengths to get their jobs. They were highly conscious of their role, responsibilities, and duty, unlike many others he had seen on some airlines. All the makeup and hair was immaculate, and all done to regimented and guideline specifications. Oddly though, this time, each one of them in the cabin had stopped to talk to him and smile.

They seemed quite flirty which was a little curious, more so as each one of the three had almost repeated the same behaviour just minutes after each other. It was as if they had mistaken him for some famous actor, and had gone to check him out. It happened in sequence several minutes apart, one after the other, and then they all met up at the other end of the corridor and started talking and looking in his direction, until a more senior stewardess came in from the forward section, and then they suddenly looked busy.

So, feeling sure that a tray wouldn't be dropped on him, he replaced his fold-down table, took another jetlag tablet, and pulled his blanket around himself and popped the earplugs into his ears, which took a little effort, to cut out the background low level roaring noise to a dull hiss. He played around with his pillow and position across the seats before finally putting on his mask, followed by a few adjusting fidgets before shutting himself off from the world.

It was warm, cosy, black, and hopefully free from any possible interruption for the next ten hours, if he wanted it to be. Getting completely comfortable took another ten minutes, especially with the folded up arm rest in the middle of his back, which required a repositioning of the blanket to compensate. There was always something digging into him and he just had to adjust the comfortable things around him to make the best of it so it wasn't annoying in any way, but after several minutes he was good.

Paradise is being alone on an airplane in a space in your own world. Silence filled with a background hum, sensory deprivation and all distractions compensated out. Total blackness, low air pressure, air flowing over you so you can't sense anyone around you, snug, warm and cosy in your own bubble of void. Aside from scuba diving at night nothing else came close. This was warmer, drier, and had the main advantage in that you could drift off to sleep, and have a reasonably good chance of waking up.

When he moved his head slightly it broke the seal in the plug in one ear and it made a surreal background noise, up and down, a two tone deep hum, changing subtlety as in the film *Bladerunner*, when Rachel was being interviewed by Dekkard whilst taking the eye-reaction test in the dim light in a palatial room open to the night.

The two androids, both of whom thought they were human, clinging to important emotions from lives that weren't even theirs. The ambient humming sound, varying in and out with different pitch, volume, and then back again. He could control it with a small movement of his head, and it was highly therapeutic. He concentrated on emptying his mind, slowing his heart rate down, relaxing the muscles in his shoulders and legs. Using the meditation techniques he had been taught he was able to go off to the place where he was calm and safe to reach his level. Whatever that was.

He recreated the music in his head from the movie to go with the ebb and flow of the dual tone ambience; it was as if he was actually hearing it being played. The soft gentle notes and slow peaceful, radiant melody filled him with emotion. He had not been able to do that before, it was a new experience, and it seemed to originate elsewhere. This was a much better idea than falling asleep with headphones on - he always seemed to wake up with a headache when he did that.

There was something about music, something very important, but he didn't know what or why. He hadn't encountered anything in relation to music in the event that happened days before, and there was no piece for music or anything that related to it.

Why did music mean so much to so many people? And why did some music sound good, and some just awful? Why did our taste in music change, and why collectively does it instil so much emotion in us? It makes us feel so much more intense about other things; love, sights, places, people, and feelings by association. How was it that these harmonies do things to our minds in that way?

He had no idea. No understanding. He hadn't been into that piece in his 'experience' but there were so many relevancies to it in others that he knew that it was very crucial. But he didn't know how.

He was quite glad in a way that he didn't know. It was intriguing not knowing, and yet knowing it was important. He had experienced so much and understood so many things that it was quite good to have a few things that were still a mystery. It also meant that he could still enjoy it, appreciate it, without having the concept and the mystery of it spoiled.

His mind drifted on now, becoming more detached, unfocused, slipping into the state between sleep and wake. Thoughts came without direction, control or structure - he was safe in that comfortable dark womb-like cocoon. Just good to let the thoughts take their own path undirected, no 'snap back to reality' issues, pressure to resolve a problem, or guilt forcing him to think about the need for planning. Just drifting, letting all the spare mental capacity usually allocated elsewhere on senses to rest, and be forgotten, and to explore their own direction.

Thoughts from the past came to him. Flashbacks of holidays, social events, good and bad, even some from school. Even the odd turbulence the plane encountered was just part of the background now, it wasn't sudden enough to distract him or even make him think of it, it was just there, like being rocked.

The thoughts remained surprisingly platonic considering how relaxed and calm he was, and even with the proximity of the attractive stewardesses, and the memories of women he kept having, it all stayed away from the top shelf. He put it down to 'still in recovery mode' from days before, and so that was OK, he was still a real bloke, and the odd platonic fantasy 'sex-free' dream was acceptable, as long as you didn't discuss it with your mates. Besides, he would be better soon.

A vision of the advert he had seen the week before came to him of the man walking up the beach in swimming trunks. 'Togs' as they were called in New Zealand, or 'budgie smugglers' in Australia, in their usual subtle way. With the man walking up from the beach, over the dunes, and then onto the beach road, then into town to the high street. The question being posed by the advertisers was 'At what point do they change from acceptable swimming wear on a beach, to unacceptable underwear in public?' With the expressions of people changing as he walked along. Going from beach hunk to streaking weirdo in just a short distance, with the parents covering the eyes of their children in the street, so they didn't 'see' the terrible sight.

He felt a brief smile return to his face. Wasn't it strange how people's perception can change so quickly and be controlled by stereotypes and each other within groups, countries, and cultures? Then gradually the gentle smile faded slowly away as he drifted peacefully into a dreamless sleep.

As a child he always had trouble making sense of the world. It just seemed so illogical, irrational. He was bright, he understood things quickly, and he was a few years ahead of the other children in his class. They all seemed to be so immature to him, and the teachers just behaved like older children.

He picked concepts and facts up quickly and could see things in a very different way from others. As a young boy he played well with others, and joined in games, and was happy generally. Up until the age of twelve he had played a lot of chess, even to National level. He had loved strategy games like that but wasn't up to ever being a Grand Master; you had to 'live' it and be a dozen moves ahead. To get that obsessed, and locked in to one thing was not a healthy thing to do, nor good for meeting girls.

By the time thirteen came along he had become very much more isolated and alone, not introverted, just different, with only a few friends who had also been classed by the mainstream boys as 'fringe'. He was not much good with girls even though he was tall, and reasonably good looking, fit, strong and well-built - he was just too nervous and shy. He just didn't know what to say to them. Also every time he tried to help anyone it seemed to go wrong or backfire or he would get blamed for problems that weren't his making.

By the age of fourteen he spent a lot of time watching television and playing simple computer games, which were very limited then, or fantasy roles playing games with the few friends that were of a similar ilk, and intellectual level. However, like him, they were also somewhat socially lacking, which didn't help.

He had an incredible imagination since he was five, and could create entire worlds, races, dungeons, and monster adventures in his head with no trouble at all.

His dreams were vast, colourful, elaborate and unbounded. Things that didn't make sense to him or that were irrelevant didn't stay long in his brain. He had always had a remarkably high IQ but he didn't ever make a thing of it,; he wasn't into joining societies for it or getting awards, he didn't want to be labelled as 'nerdy', or 'more nerdy' than he already was.

By the age of sixteen he had surprisingly been involved in a lot of sports, but that was mainly due to his height and physique and reaction speed. The sports staff preselected him for set roles and allocated them like sergeant majors. If you were tall you played basketball, if you were big it was rugby, quick-footed it was football, and if you were fast, and it was dry, it was athletics. So because he was stereotypically ideal for many of those he did a lot, other than football, but he wasn't sure why, other than that he had the right physique.

So most days, including weekends, he would have been doing something sporty, which was good for him apparently. He enjoyed the social interaction of the teams he was with, even though he wasn't really part of it, he was liked, but not accepted. He was still treated as an outsider even though he was part of the team, and so was still subjected to the occasional ridicule by them, mostly due to his non-stereotypical character and personality.

Girls were still a problem. He was really bad at the problem of girls, cringingly awful. Girls were really interested in him, apparently. However there were just too many barriers, like actually having to talk to them. Girls, he discovered, were pretty merciless, and unless you were 'Mr Confident' it was a one-way battle for which you would be given no quarter.

Unless you had all the right skills, like being able to hold a conversation about something interesting, or look them in the eye when talking, you were just toast, outgunned. Your performance scorecard, and anything you said, would be passed around the 'girl network' as a warning and for general amusement. Girls just wanted to have fun, but it was hard to be a fun guy when you were terrified, and didn't understand the game. Parties? Well they were just things other people went to.

He never had the opportunity before the age of seventeen to know a girl just as a friend; he was too socially inept, and there were well defined defensive walls in place in such a large school. At seventeen though, he changed, and was able to concentrate on a smaller set of subjects which he enjoyed in the senior school and also the numbers in the school were a lot less, and just the brighter ones remained, so the levels and barriers changed. Being a 'senior' meant he wore ordinary clothes and a casual jacket rather than a uniform, so he was now accepted as a senior boy, and therefore viewed differently by everyone; teachers, parents and girls in the year below. Most of the people who had given him grief had now moved on, and the whole ethos felt different, even though he was still the same underneath. Everything around him had changed and he was now able to slowly evolve into something else.

Things began to make more sense and people began to become interesting, understandable, and more adult around him. He carried on with his sports, he was sort of tied in now anyway, and set in the routine. It was from around that time that he also had some odd experiences, sort of déjà vu instances, where he would go to a place and be absolutely convinced he had seen it before, or knew the smell of somewhere in the past. It was quite profound and he could almost feel when he had dreamt it in the past even though it hadn't registered at the time, or seemed important.

Thinking back he realised that he had actually had his first example of that when he first joined his school at twelve. He had been out on the school playing field and looked back over the sports pitch to the building, and he knew he had seen that exact image years before, and from the same angle in a dream, with everything in it. Even though that was the first time he had been there. At the time it had been quite disconcerting and confusing, but he didn't have any more until he was seventeen, and then he had many.

He wasn't affected by them now though. They didn't happen that often anyway, and they weren't as intense as the first ones he used to have. He was now taking on a more adult perspective, dismissing, ignoring, and accepting things more easily.

So at seventeen he began to do very well with some subjects, and mixed a lot better socially. He made more friends and even managed to get to be invited to some parties, although not the 'interesting' or 'eventful' ones, but it was a start. So after a lot of hard work, change, and learning, he managed to get a long term girlfriend, i.e. one that had actually had a name and called herself 'his girlfriend', and stayed with him for more than a few hours.

He had worked hard at school, had one or two more girlfriends, and eventually gravitated to a good university. There he opted to study Robotics and Computer Science, which curiously wasn't his first choice. Much of which now was a distant memory.

He remembered recently discovering some of his university final exam papers in the attic and looking at them intently; he knew he had answered them correctly in the past, but now he couldn't even understand the questions. But the important thing was that he had passed, proved that he was a bright spark, capable of achieving, even though the academic demonstration had given him very little of use and had exhausted his best years.

That was the trouble with the academic structure. It looked after itself, ivory towers, stovepipes of control, without the accountability and relation to needs in society. But who would bother to change that system, what incentive was there? It was self-perpetuating after all.

However on leaving university he got a good job, and had progressed quickly through various demanding technical jobs into positions of seniority, way in excess of that normally attributed to his age.

He had hit the business at the right time, the boom years for computing, writing operating systems, office packages and secure defence system applications.

Then he had moved on to consultancy, contracting, and owning his own companies, branching out into new directions and senior management consultancy.

This is how he had met Brina.

He remembered the first time he had seen her; she seemed to have a glow about her, a welcoming smile, a sort of presence that was addictive and made you want to confide everything in her, which in fact most people seemed to do. People just wanted to be around her, tell her all their secrets, and all of their problems.

He couldn't remember what she was wearing when they met, or what he had said, or when it was, even though apparently he should. However he remembered her like he had always remembered her, and it all seemed a long time ago, and yet he could remember her as she was then as if it were yesterday.

Six hours later he woke up briefly from a dreamless sleep. There was a smell of food cooking which he assumed was the cause, and which he also guessed, was dinner on its way, so he emerged from the cocoon and quickly got his seat ready and put his tray down. The stewardesses with the serving trolley were only a few aisles down and were making steady progress. He didn't really need dinner but it was included in the cost. Even with all his money and lifestyle, he always had a 'thing' about making sure he had everything he'd already paid for, even if he didn't actually want it. It must be something in his genes.

He ate his pre-paid meal accompanied with a whisky this time, and squinted at the screen in front in the low light which showed the plane's location. They were still flying over Australia. He went to sleep six hours ago, and they were still over Australia. It was kind of hard to get your head around a country that big.

There were still hours to go yet, so he finished up and laid back down into the cocoon again, trying to get back into that same exact comfortable position.

Settling down took a while, he was quite fidgety now and probably needed some exercise, the whisky and the monosodium-glutamate in the food didn't help. Eventually he got back into the zone and settled to sleep again.

The whisky reminded him of the holidays he had had in the Scottish Highlands; he could smell and taste the Laphroaig still on his lips. He could see the dark peaty lochs, cold and flat, reflecting the mountains around them in their waters. They were stunningly beautiful, but harsh and stark in the cold winter. He imagined the dark water, close to him now, on its own in blackness.

He could just visualise the surface of the inky dark water, with ripples on it moving in slow motion, caused by giant drips falling into it slowly from above. The circular ripples moving perfectly symmetrically outwards away over the surface into infinity.

Water. Water was important. He could now recount some information of the piece he had been into which was all about the memory, energy, and information in water. There was so much in there, and it seemed so clear at the time, but now it was just pictures in an album, from a holiday he couldn't recall actually having ever been on.

He remembered a TV documentary he had seen about the floating Water Bridge experiment between two beakers, and water memory that couldn't be explained by science. He couldn't remember the specifics but it related to information, or something in the water, carried over a line of static water between two full beakers. He had seen that in the piece too in a microsecond, and had seen the answers, which was simple in context with other pieces he had been in, but there was so much more behind it; it was to do with information storage, communication at the subatomic level, like a blueprint of energy.

He had also seen how it related to homeopathy, and how that worked with the transfer of information with the information signature of different poisons that the body would react to, without having the poisons themselves, through repeated dilution. It was all just information, and data transfer. Simple really, as was everything when you thought about it. In the same way as when you injected things into the body too, and how it reacted to heavy metals like mercury.

Even tiny bits of 'information' could have drastic effects in different situations. After all, everything was just information from one perspective. The connection with water in the body was there too. How it was affected by things put in it or near to it. But more puzzlingly, and more importantly, why weren't people more aware of it all? It was all pretty obvious really, what was stopping people seeing it?

As he allowed himself to drift more into his thoughts, he was able to correlate it all a bit more, and to somehow make sense of some of it. However it was nowhere near the level, clarity, depth, and context of the original experience. It just wasn't the same. Very much like showing Neil Armstrong a picture of the moon, and asking him 'What was it like?'

He tried to concentrate his mind on the water subject, trying to focus his thoughts in one direction rather than letting it fire off at tangents. Perhaps it wasn't just water. Perhaps it was a capability or a capacity in everything. It's just that water was pure and simple, so it was easy to get simple, uncomplicated information into it, rather than so much complex information in everything else.

Maybe it was just that water was particularly important to us; it is what we were made up from in the most part, so we have an affinity to it, and relate to it so well. *That's probably why*, he thought, *and probably why we can find it easily if we need to, by using our subconscious minds by various means as with all animals.* Then a picture of a man with a set of divining sticks appeared in his head. O*dd how little study had been done on all that, and why things like homeopathy and divining, and things of that genre, were ridiculed, and even more so recently. These lost or redundant skills, which are or more likely to be 'conveniently' forgotten with more modern, 'better' methods.*

There were so many other things, about water, that were important and he tried to get into that depth of integrated understanding again. In the darkness of his imagination they started to appear as paintings, masterpieces at the end of a corridor. They were visible up close before, but now were just tantalising glimpses. He remembered the experience of being up close to them, the intricate brush work, colour, the smell of the oil and texture, together with the light and exquisite artistry, matched in context with the other paintings in all their emotional grandeur. He visualised the hallway and the picture at one end. He started walking down the corridor. Then nothing......

He didn't remember going off to sleep but he was suddenly woken with a hand on his arm, and he jumped. Lifting his eye mask up in a cold sweat, he tried to collect his exhausted mind together, lumbering back into reality. His bleary eyes met with the stewardess's a few feet away. She was saying something to him but he couldn't hear anything with his earplugs in.

She smiled and reached across him to open his window shade. Her breast brushed against his chest as she did so, but it felt intrusive rather than arousing, as if his body was on the defensive. She stood back up and smiled at him again, and walked to the rows behind him, continuing the procedure of opening all the shades. He assumed from this they were only twenty minutes away from Singapore. He was meant to be belted up, and so got up slowly and put his belt on and sat still for a few moments to get his mind working again. Looking around at the rest of the cabin he saw that he was the last to wake up; everyone else was already preparing for landing.

Arriving at Changi Airport was always a strange experience. It was all new, and vast inside. There were expansive lounge areas, with wide high open spaces, and an elaborate range of new, immaculate shops, carefully positioned around the plush, tree lined atriums. From all of the many airports he had been in around the world, this was the cleanest, most automated, well serviced, and best architecturally planned that he had visited.

There were even areas of 'tranquillity'; restful massage areas, places to sit with exotic plants, orchid flower gardens, water features with fish ponds, and recorded electronic birdsong.

Even the toilets were immaculately clean, they even worked and the doors to the cubicles were actually attached. You could get a proper shower, a massage, a sleep, have your nails done, a pedicure, albeit not all together at the same time. It was also the most commercial and artificial of environments possible, with walls of plasma information, chrome metal, carpets, conveyors and sad faces. All there for your 'enjoyment' and pleasure- which was 'nice'. The first few times he had been there the airport had been a pleasant surprise, but now the fixed smiles, the artificial commercial virtual world, was now, frankly, getting on his tits.

The glossy new veneer disguising the hard edge commercialism, the information they think you need to know fed from a flowchart or leaflet. The convenient lack of understanding. The wall of strict law and autocratic officialdom was just a wrong turn away. You buy from the glossy front door, the smiling happy face. However try taking anything back, even with a receipt, and the door changes to a rough back street one, the face to the hard edged market trader, and you quickly realise that you aren't in smiley town anymore.

After a few minutes in the terminal he had a text message from Brina to say she had been "Thinking of him all the time he was on the plane." She had been resting at her friend's house in Sydney alone, and she was just making sure he was 'OK'. Ten seconds later his phone beeped again and a there was a message from Singapore network inviting him to be happy and 'enjoyed', followed by another trying to sell him something that he couldn't carry, or take with him, let alone fit it in his hand luggage.

There were still two hours to kill before his next flight left, and he had had his shower, and used the automated driverless inter-terminal monorail, again, because it was there, and free.

So he sat at the end of one of the seat rows in a main concourse opposite a long line of shops, empty of customers, with beautiful, yet bored, looking assistants; immaculately dressed suited women in short skirts and wearing too much makeup.

There were very few people around at that time of day and this looked like the least busy terminal atrium area. To the right of the long rows of seats, about a hundred and fifty foot away, an escalator came down from the level above. That was where the stopover transit hotel was, which is where he had previously had his shower.

He had discovered the facilities there from a tip on a travel website a while back and he had tried it out on another trip. You just went in and paid a few dollars to use the facilities rather than actually staying there. There had been two dozen people in there using the lounge, showers, gym and sauna, all getting free coffee. There were also two or three staff members in there, who looked perpetually confused as to why it was so busy in that small area. Why weren't all these people in the shops? It was a big mystery to them.

He pulled his laptop out of his bag from the seat next to him, and rested it on his legs to do a quick e-mail check. He wasn't normally that 'sad' but the text message reminded him he hadn't checked in for quite a while, and anyway it was something to do. He felt very relaxed, tired but essentially happy, but not quite up to the level of 'enjoyed'.

Looking up from over his screen he noticed an Asian air

stewardess and male colleague. They were standing about fifty feet away at the bottom of an escalator, talking to a yellow jacketed airport official who had a phone to her ear. He didn't recognise their uniform but he guessed the two must have been from a local regional airline. The official was a middle-aged Asian woman, also quite large, and she was wearing a suit beneath the oversized yellow-green reflective jacket.

Aside from the three of them there was nobody else around in the vast concourse seating area. The air stewardess was a beefy, officious type, probably in her late thirties, about five foot of bossy attitude, with hard nails painted with industrial grade nail polish. She was in a debate with the female official about something, while the young male looked as though he didn't want to be there, and was looking around for anything interesting on the floor. She waved at her watch and pointed down the concourse to the official, so he guessed that they had been given wrong information by someone.

After a few moments the official nodded to someone on the phone, put it away in her jacket, and then relayed some instructions to them both. She then said something, and pointed back down the other way with a definitive gesture. The pair then headed off past Sam, dragging their regulation small, pull-behind-trolley bags with them. The male keeping a few paces behind leaving the female official just standing there holding her phone.

Sam wondered what it must be like married to something like that, and it was clear that the young male wasn't going to allow himself to get into a situation where he might end up finding out.

By this time the official had walked over to the shoe shop about fifty feet in front of him, and was leaning forward to look at the display in the window, which from his perspective was now almost fully eclipsed.

Looking towards the top of the escalator something caught his eye. A small dark haired girl, about seven or eight years old with a small trolley bag, was stood at the gap between the two hand rails looking downwards. She looked obviously lost and distressed, and was scanning around the area below on the Ground Floor.

After a few moments, he could see her make a decision and she stepped hesitantly onto the top step, and it started to bring her down with her bag held carefully resting a few steps behind.

When she was about a third of the way down, a woman in sunglasses appeared from the glass edged landing further around at the top, and called out to her daughter below. The girl now looked wildly left and right, trying to work out where her mother's voice was coming from. She then suddenly realised she was going the wrong way, and immediately panicked. Seeing her mother she turned around and tried to climb back up the descending escalator, still holding onto her bag. She tried to push it up the steps in vain, and eventually fell over it and onto the metal moving steps in a heap, her hands clawing at the edge of the steps. Her bare knees began scraping along the sides, as she was dragged down. Finally frozen in fear, she clung to the metal steps, and let out a single scream of terror on her way down.

Sam leapt up from his seat, and at the same time instinctively shoved his laptop back into his bag, and placed the bag onto the seat next to him.

In a few seconds he had raced over to the bottom of the stairs. He couldn't see an obvious 'Stop' button. By this time, her mother was at the top of the stairs and was now descending fast, two steps at a time. However she was more focused on getting to her child rather than thinking of looking for a 'Stop' button up there.

The girl was almost at the bottom, and he reacted quickly, ran up the steps and grabbed her with his hands around her waist. He lifted her up like a doll into the air at arm's length, and clear of the metal stairs. She was still clinging to her bag with her hand, and it dangled in the air next to her. He allowed himself to be carried down backwards, stepped back off the step at the bottom and calmly lifted her, with adjoining bag, to safety. He then placed her gently on the floor in front of him away from danger.

Her face had gone grey-white; her eyes were wide open and wild, just staring at the bloodied hands and knees in front of her, the adrenaline already starting to make her body and limbs shake. He mother arrived in a blur a few seconds later, grabbing her up into her arms, and pulling her close to her body, and placed her hand behind the girl's neck. The blood from her daughter's knees transferring to her long cream coat in long smears. There was a rapid exchange of information, at which point the crying started.

Instinctively her mother carried her away from the escalator area, to the far wall further behind where there were some seats and shelter underneath the concourse above. Sam carried the girl's bag over to them, and rested it against the seats. He looked at the girl's hands and knees, and was relieved to see that they were only badly grazed with bleeding surface cuts, despite the hyperventilating and crying.

He recalled while on holiday in Turkey some twenty years ago, some other holiday makers telling him a horror story of a little girl on an escalator at the airport, who had her foot was nearly severed on a faulty step. There was some ensuing drama due to the escalator being in-between Customs and Passport Control, and none of the officials wanting to take responsibility, or even making any effort to help, as it wasn't in anyone's 'jurisdiction' or authority.

He really bloody hated that sort of mindless bureaucratic, incompetent injustice. The desperate father having to eventually get to some US military hospital to get her stitched back together, after several hours of literally banging his head against a wall.

Sam pulled some tissues from a pack in his jacket pocket and handed them to the mother, who, with trembling hands, duly placed them over the bleeding knees. "Can I help?" he asked, but the woman didn't seem to register. Either she couldn't hear him or wasn't able to understand. She was too busy checking over her daughter who she now had standing up next to her as she sat on one of the seats. She looked European but he couldn't be sure.

The daughter then started talking very quickly to her Mum in a language that he didn't recognise. From the pointing, the girl was telling her that she thought her mother had already gone down the escalator. He let the situation calm down for three or four minutes until she crying stopped.

He took out the last tissue from the pack, and folded into the girl's left hand, closing her fingers around it to stop the bleeding.

The mother who was crouching down, looked at him, and turned to him sharply and her demeanour suddenly changed. "You doctor?" she snapped at him as if it were an accusation rather than a question.

He stepped back and smiled defensively "No, no, not a medical doctor, no" he stammered. Her face became different suddenly, and changed from worried and defensive to aggressive. "Well should you do that? Is no right, no?" and she waved her hand at him like she was telling off some stroppy waiter that had just served her latte instead of a cappuccino. It was a shock, and it caught him off-guard, being attacked for trying to help.

He took another step back, and looked from the mother to the girl who was still white as a ghost and in shock. "I will get someone to help" he said. He straightened up and turned away. He knew it was just a reaction thing, her looking for someone to blame, to react against for her anger and guilt, but he wasn't expecting such an illogical outburst, it really shocked and upset him.

As he turned around, the previous two flight attendants walked quickly past again a few feet away, in a hurry, going back the other way again. They both looked briefly at the dramatic scene, but carried on past down the aisle, it not being 'their problem'.

He looked around again, and saw the yellow jacketed official still stood where she had been. However, now she had her back to the shoe shop wall facing him. She had her phone to her ear and was talking; clearly having seen what had happened she was obviously summoning medical help. He waited for her to finish her call as he walked up to her, and then breathlessly attempted to convey the information to her of what had happened, even though she must have seen it already.

Sam pointed to the escalator and the area underneath where the woman and child were now sitting. She nodded and smiled back to him, but her expression didn't match what he had said, and her smile disappeared too quickly. She smiled again and pointed down the aisle again, and gestured at him to move on, and looked at her watch.

She obviously couldn't understand English, nor anything of what he had said.

Her eyes turned right, and he looked far off down the wide corridor to where two security guards were walking quickly towards the bottom of the escalator. He decided to have another go and backed up the slow, simple explanation with gestures of height and movement, and pointing. Just at the end her eyes briefly looked at something for an instant over his shoulder, behind him. That was the 'mistake', and it took him a few moments to pull the pieces together and register what was really happening. As she looked back to him her expression was totally without emotion.

Sam looked right to where the security guards were coming from. It was no surprise to see them walk straight past the end of the escalator, and right past the woman and her daughter.

Sam turned and walked quickly back to where his flight bag had been left on its own in the middle of the row of seats. He heard her calling to him from behind, her English having improved dramatically, but he ignored it, his own 'understanding' suddenly going downhill at that point too.

Initially he was worried that she would follow him, but she was clearly stuck in place by her procedures, waiting for the guards to arrive in the location she had given them. He picked up his bag without hesitating, and walked off quickly in the opposite direction from the guards, ignoring everything. He turned around briefly to see them reaching her but turned forward again before any interchange started.

He walked another hundred and fifty feet or so in about twenty seconds, and turned into the nearest large shop, which was a designer clothes shop. Inside, he grabbed a jacket, and walked straight into the changing room at the back, closed the curtains and hung the slim fitting woman's leather jacket on the peg. Several minutes later the door opened to the shop, and then closed again after just a few seconds.

Three minutes later he came out and replaced the jacket on the rail. He picked up a black men's belt and bought it from the assistant who didn't seem bemused by his actions at all. She just took his card, processed it, wrapped the belt in tissue paper, and folded it carefully in a bag and handed it to him with a smile.

A minute later he stepped out of the shop and looked left again back down the corridor. He saw the official, and the guards, now walking back towards the escalator area where someone else official looking was standing with a large plastic first aid box on the floor near to where the woman and child were.

His heart was still beating rapidly but he was calm. He had seen it coming and felt it happening. He felt slightly elated that he had outwitted 'it'. Somehow he could see what was really happening and what was contrived. He felt the injustice of it too, like a wrongly accused thief - something acting against him.

'Outwitted' didn't seem the right word though, it didn't seem to have intent or will; it was just flow and direction without conscious thought. Even with everything he knew he couldn't work it all out. He knew it was there, something, but he didn't know what or where it was coming from or why. He walked down the corridor, the other way from the commotion, and went in search of a stiff drink.

The second flight, a few hours later, was packed, and the seat next to him that had been free when he selected his seat a few days before, was now occupied. Thankfully it was by a pleasant middle-aged Asian woman, who also thankfully just liked to read, rather than share her life history.

The only slight negative was that she had pre-booked some obscure Asian vegetarian dish, with a lasting odour that he couldn't escape from. Fortunately it was served long before his meal arrived so he wasn't put off his dinner. When his meal arrived, he asked if his beef could be 'extra rare', which the stewardess thought was politely 'amusing', but which his vegetarian neighbour clearly either chose to ignore or was too engrossed in her book to notice.

He locked himself back into his cocoon again, vertically this time, and eased his seat back slightly after checking that the sleeping occupant of the seat behind wasn't going to complain.

About two and a half hours from Heathrow his mind changed from sleep to half-awake state, brought on by a heavily muffled sound from the intercom about 'turbulence' and 'seatbelts'.

His seat was next to the window and he had his head resting against the side wall of the aircraft just in front of the window. The vibration of the aircraft was passing through his head. He thought he had put a pillow there but it had clearly fallen away while he was sleeping. Consequently he had a mild headache, was stiff, and ached from being in the same position for so long. He could feel that his feet had swollen up too, which would make getting his shoes back on a challenge.

Without taking off his eye mask, he felt around on his lap for his pillow until he found it, replaced it, and then the vibration stopped. He was dry in the mouth too from the air-conditioning, so he felt around in the pocket of the seat in-front of him for the bottle of water he knew was there. He took it out along with some mints without removing his eye mask in a well-practised routine, and settled back down.

He relaxed again and got comfortable, trying to get back to sleep after just a few minutes. It was at that point in the flight that there was a distinct feeling or sensation externally; that he was being checked over. It was just a feeling, like a caring ward nurse in a hospital at night casting her eye over him, making sure that he was OK. Then it was gone.

He lifted his eye mask up over one eye to bright sunshine and he squinted around, but there was no stewardess anywhere. Even the woman next to him was asleep, head back, mouth open, with her book still on her lap. The end seat just had another cocoon in it.

Her book was open on her lap with a bookmark in it. It was so tempting to slide the bookmark out, move the pages, and put it back inside in a different place, but he instantly chided himself for being so immature. He quickly looked around again, and then back at the book, and then did it anyway.

From the lack of motion and noise in the cabin, he assumed that everyone else was either still resting or watching movies. He wasn't able to settle down to the relaxed level he was in before; he was too uncomfortable, had too many toxins built up in his limbs and had too many distractions. So he relented and watched a short movie until breakfast arrived.

The stewardess delivered his breakfast onto his fold down tray, and he was yet again impressed at how immaculate she was after a dozen hours or so of serving, cleaning, preparing, walking, and organising. If it were him he would look like hell after all that, which he was probably managing to do anyway just sitting doing nothing in his seat. He felt his face and he was in serious need of a shave; he had had make do with the plastic disposable razor in the shower at Singapore which had not worked very well.

His breakfast had probably fared worse than him over the twelve hours, shut away in its little heated metal box. It was not appealing in any way now, especially after the three other airplane meals that he had eaten. He made his way through it though, and now the empty tray sat in front of him, with its lingering smells of sausage, beans and orange juice.

Even the plastic cutlery had a lingering air to it. It was ironic that you not only had to eat it, but you had put up with it sat in front of you for so long afterwards, patiently waiting for the rest of the plane to get theirs delivered, and then taken away.

On one flight he had selfishly asked for his tray to be taken away as they were still dishing them out to others so that he could lie down. This of course had caused chaos to the system, as the tray was passed around the cabin twice until someone found a spare seat for it to stay on until the trolleys were empty.

With all the various looks and comments he had received he wouldn't ever do that again. In fact Business Class seemed like a good idea right now for future flights, regardless of whoever else was in there.

The plane continued its descent down through rain clouds towards London. This heralded the usual accompaniment of babies crying with the rise in air pressure, and the last minute form filling by tourists.

Prising his shoes back onto his swollen feet he went through his 'getting ready' routine again. He was sad to be getting off. He enjoyed his own time and space. It had been both a virtual paradise and an artificial hell, but now he was going back to the real world, with real versions of both.

CHAPTER 4 - HARD LANDING

The only problem with windows on an aircraft when you are landing is that they allow you to see out.

Aside from the ultraviolet tinting, and the narrow angle, you get a fairly good true view on reality outside. You get a 'window on the world' you are flying above, landing at, and arriving into.

Unlike the little monitor screen in the seat in front of you, which just shows you what you want to see, and what you are meant to see.

The screen shows a sanitised, low resolution, perspective of everyone else's viewpoint, and what they think you need to know and perceive. Whereas in the 'good old days', when all you had was a window and a shutter and no screen, you just had one choice - to see everything for what it was from your own perspective, or to close it and just not look.

However there were certain situations when that choice was no longer in your hands, and you just had to see, and in this case get out and face it.

Landing in the grey rain gave him the same feeling as arriving in an office car park for work on a cold Monday morning in the winter. It always seemed to be raining when he came here, always overcast with heavy de-contrasting beige and grey effect clouds. Well, that wasn't quite true, once it had been snowing through thick fog. That was when he had only just landed in time before the airport was closed for three days.

Heathrow had always seemed a bland, dirty, rushed, yet puzzling place to him. It was a mystery why it always took at least twenty minutes to taxi the plane to the terminal after landing, and the same delay before taking off.

It was valuable time that could be spent queuing at check in, or waiting for your luggage to arrive at the conveyors. Still it was a consistent people machine, a working production line, and yet nowhere near as bad as some he had been to.

Passport Control was just the same as when he was here last; large, grimy, and dreary, with stale, stained, heavy duty carpets. The large area was still lined on one side with a temporary plywood wall while something was being renovated noisily on the other side.

They were probably building a few more shops like the several gleaming clean and bright 'in your face ones' that had confronted him straight off the plane. They would all be selling alcohol and perfume at 'Duty Free' prices that were slightly higher than those in the local supermarkets.

The queues were confusing though; things had been changed around during the renovation work and the queues didn't seem to match up with the signs above the gates. At first he thought he had chosen the wrong one, it was too long, and that the other queues were moving much quicker. However it became obvious a moment later that indeed it was correct.

It was just that a bored official had moved a rope across, and opened up another set of lanes further round, channelling people to just in front of where they all had just been queuing. Logical when you stepped back and saw what was going on, but it would have been useful if someone had explained it, or if they had put up temporary signs.

This, of course, was just to allow more people in the lanes. Jumping queues too quickly without fully assessing the situation was a classic error that he had made too often in the past. With a slightly impatient attitude, he would always jump queues.

However the new lane would always be the one with the granny in who had forgotten her PIN number in the supermarket, the old man paying in his loose change at the bank, or the middle-aged woman at the garage checkout with the declined credit card.

He was uncomfortable in his clothes now. He felt dishevelled, creased, and in real need of a shave, shower and change of clothes. He had swapped his shirt for a fresh one at Singapore, and had whacked some deodorant on, but he was fairly sure that it was fighting a losing battle now with his armpits.

His shoes were at least a size too small for his newly expanded feet, and the air around him in the concourse was chilly, stale and almost damp, which really didn't help.

He finally arrived at the desk and handed his passport over to the bored looking uniformed woman in front of him. She checked his face against the photo using her tired and bloodshot eyes. She passed the back of the passport under a scanner and then began to type into a keyboard in front of her.

Looking behind her to the back of the Hall he could see the central security kiosk with its one-way mirror, and an open door through which were visible two or three men in white shirts and ties leaning back on chairs looking at monitors. Another one came out of the doorway and down the steps and started to walk his way. "Sorry," said the woman in front of him "the system is running a bit slow at the moment" and she casually gestured with her eyes to the queue behind him.

Reaching the desk the other official leaned over it, using the chair arm as a support, and looked into the monitor. He then looked at Sam and then back again to the screen.

She looked at him again too, and he tried to not look guilty, even though he had nothing to be guilty about. The male official stood back up again, and then diverted his attention to the next desk at which there was a rough looking Eastern European man in his mid-twenties, dressed scruffily in jeans, t-shirt and a shiny quilted short coat.

He picked up the man's passport from the other desk, tapped it on the surface, and after a few words gestured the man towards a room at the side and they both walked off. Neither looked very surprised; it was clearly a regular event for both of them.

Turning forward again he was confronted with his passport in front of his chest on the raised plinth of the desk. She had clearly said something to him, but he had missed it, distracted by the events at the other desk. He picked it up and wished her a good day, but given the odds, there was probably a slightly better chance of her winning the lottery.

Walking along to collect his bags, the incident at the desk kept playing on his mind. Perhaps it was because he was tired, or felt uncomfortable and vulnerable. However, like the incident in

Singapore, it was almost like he was being attacked, or given a warning, yet not really, not directly or physically, but then he was probably just being over sensitive.

There wasn't the intensity of energy there in the situation that he had felt with the drama at Singapore. In this instance he could feel something going on, a focus, a sense of 'something strange happening' but it wasn't focused at him, he was just aware of it, as if observing a process or message.

After picking up his bags half an hour later, and going through Customs, he even felt guilty about going through the Green channel, despite not having anything at all to declare. He was probably just being over paranoid.

He was not into conspiracy theories at all, and in his experience and understanding, most, if not all, could be explained by circumstance; narrow minded bureaucracy, procedures, defensive legislation or plain greed. They usually went hand in hand with cultural paranoia, ignorance and certain geographical 'hot spots'. However, in reality, people were generally far too wrapped up with their own lives to put that much effort into other people.

Walking through into Arrivals he was confronted with a wall of people waiting behind a long, rail-lined, exit area. It was probably from watching too many films, but he always expected to see someone holding up a sheet of card with his name on it, or for there to be someone he knew just there to greet him with a welcoming smile. However there never was, and there wasn't this time either.

It was childish really, too many films with it in, or perhaps it was just that need for emotional help when you are tired at the end of a long journey. He pushed his trolley on through the Hall at a slight angle to compensate for the dodgy wheel which had a mind of its own.

He always took the trouble to check that the trollies worked correctly when he collected one, so it must have been something it had picked up on the way; some chewing gum in the axle, or just adding the weight of his case to it had affected the bearings. In any case he wasn't going to find out, pulling something sticky and unpleasant out from a wheel would only add to his troubles.

It was always an enlightening experience coming through the Arrivals gate at any airport. It immediately gave you a snapshot of the state of whichever country you were in, its culture, attitudes, racial mix, state of the economy, and the weather conditions outside.

Over the last twenty years there had been a steady overall decline everywhere on the Arrivals gate 'Happiness Chart', and some were now so bad that it would almost be preferable to just turn around and go back through the gate you had come out through- if it weren't for the ensuing security alert and the heavy fine.

Maybe it was just because travelling by plane wasn't that exciting any more - but then the people on the other side weren't doing the travelling, so maybe it was just the way life was going.

Occasionally you would hear the odd squeals of delight at the point of recognition, with hugs and long awaited kisses, but generally people just stood there looking miserable waiting to be happy. Or maybe it was just him, and he had come to see things differently over the last few years, growing into a miserable, grouchy old sod.

Things also seemed to be so much more detached now, and slightly misrepresented, like watching a black and white film animated on a screen in front of you, it was all there and moving - but it lacked something, and it all wasn't quite right. There seemed to be fundamentally exciting things missing in society now that were there twenty years ago. The thrill had gone out of life for everyone.

The damp, chilling air swept into his face and lungs as he walked outside, saturating his mind with oxygen enriched sensations. His senses filled with motors, rain, diesel smoke, a dreary beige light, grey dampness, and movement of sunless people everywhere. Reverting instantly now from a mode of 'catered for' contemplation and controlled flow, to one of brutal waking decision making to survive the busy environment.

Now he was caught in the rush, the race, preoccupied with the constant demands and needs. Everywhere were other people's views and ideas, work and processes. It dragged you in immediately. It preoccupied you with everything around, no time to stop and think, so many distractions, advertising, duties, must-do's, and responsibilities. So much going on all the time, keeping you busy, everything there to distract you, so that you can't see the wood for the trees with information overload.

But now he had a much wider perspective on the world, even though it was quite fragmented in his mind. He knew facts about so many things now, and had an understanding of so many concepts, and so much knowledge. Yet there were still so many questions, and links, and reasons that he wasn't sure of, or why, and many missing parts altogether. He wasn't comfortable with it at all, and like the cold wind in his face, the things that the knowledge brought with it were alarming.

The taxi dropped him off at his hotel near Hyde Park, which as he discovered on checking in, was also hosting a conference at the time. These things are never made obvious when you make the booking online.

On entering his room he was welcomed on his TV screen as 'Dr Sakomoto', so he had obviously been given the wrong room, or more likely, one not liked and swapped by someone else for some reason.

It would either have been non-smoking, or too far from the bar. It seemed fine to him. It had a bed, it was quiet and that was good enough. He switched the TV onto the BBC News channel to take it off the Welcome screen, and so that he could at least get some feel for what was going on in the world.

He had been pretty much out of contact with everything for a month or so. He sat on the bed and unpacked a few things from his case while the reports ran through. There was one on the progress of the clean-up operations, and aid relief after the Asian tsunami, and what had been done in the last few months.

Then it moved on to talking mainly about turmoil in the Arab countries and the political status there. There were different reports from several of them, comparing the situations, leaders and the manoeuvrings going on. It was odd how the impression of a country and its people was very different when you were there on holiday to that which was conveyed on the news.

He had been to all but one of the Arab countries they were reporting on, and he had a completely different perspective of them to what was being relayed. The next article was talking about the local UK elections coming up, and the ones that had gone on in the USA a few months earlier, and they were interviewing some people to get their views.

He always thought it was odd that there was no test that you had to pass before you were allowed to vote. You had to take one before you were allowed to drive. The same was probably true for politicians; just because you could smile convincingly or knew the right people, didn't mean that you should be allowed behind the wheel of a packed bus or airliner - *Let's all let nice, kind, little Jonnie have a go at flying us, he looks as if it would make him happy,* he thought.

Sam got up and switched the TV off. He needed some air.

He pulled back the long net curtains and tried to open the window, which ironically seemed to be jammed shut. He moved over to the other one which was marked 'Emergency Fire Exit' and got that one open on the second attempt and he leaned out. The window looked out onto the 'park view', which mostly consisted of a large tree with a piece of sky above it, but at least it was green instead of the red brick wall a few feet away, or an 'in your face' concrete office with mirrored windows.

There was a bird singing its heart out in the middle of the branches in the tree, just telling everything that it was happy to be alive. Then again it may have been singing that much louder and brighter just to stand any chance of attracting a mate in the din of the city. It was quite reassuring somehow, like a message that there was at least something living, and glad of it, even here. It was the first natural thing he had encountered for days.

Looking out to the side towards the hotel entrance was a banner on the wall advertising the international conference being held inside. It appeared to be for theoretical physicists of some denomination. He just stared at it. *What's the chance of that?* he thought. He pulled his head back in from the window and went to the desk. Sure enough, on the desk, was a colour brochure for the conference, in glossy expensive bindings, with timetables and impressive photos of the key speakers.

He had always been of the opinion that there was something fundamentally wrong with theoretical physicists; not just with what they wore, or their social skills, but that it just all seemed to produce very little of any use. Like one big scam.

They would lock themselves in their ivory towers or think tanks to develop theorems, or to debate ideas for years. These ideas were based, and built on, their colleagues' theories and ideas which generally lacked any actual evidence. Theorems that would be discussed, scrutinised, published and then presented at the annual get-together. This would all justify their existence, funding, and the occasional Nobel Prize or such like, which was of course the ultimate goal.

You could see the glint in the eye when it was mentioned, and of course something they would all be too willing to help each other achieve. There were none of those bitter in-fighting or bullying personalities taking advantage of their status and position. No behaving like back-stabbing old women, having childish sulking tantrums, and exhibitionism that you got in other walks of life, oh no.

These theories would then be followed a few years later with observational testing to prove or disprove the theory, which tended to conveniently crop up with at least one unexplainable phenomenon. Any evidence that supported the case would be published immediately and celebrated, and anything that proved it wrong would have its validity questioned and accuracy scrutinised, and new tests would be devised that moved away from that direction.

All of which gave credence and justification to yet more grants, and a bigger staff restaurant. Then work would commence on refining the theory into a more complete theory or an all-encompassing equation.

This process would then be then repeated until it was shown without doubt that the theory was in fact correct, assuming of course that the theories it was based on were correct too, or in fact it was all just a load of bollocks. In which case it would be agreed that everyone knew that anyway, and it would be filed in a dark room somewhere, along with all the restaurant bills.

There was this fundamental need to try and express everything in mathematical equations too, mainly because that is how they had been brought up, what they were taught, the way they had been shown to think, and all they knew. Theories that defined the creation of the Universe and how it worked. All based on other fundamental mathematical equations and understandings. Hiding behind walls of intellect and ivory towers in self-perpetuating institutions, which were impregnable to the masses that funded their towers of playing cards in amazed ignorance. Beguiled by the prospect of some magic solution to the world's problems.

However what happens when something fundamental, say with relativity, breaks down? That isn't quite right? What then, start from scratch? Think of something else quick with the 'Ah yes we knew that already, and didn't you know?' attitude.

You then find something that actually does go faster than light, or some extra dimension, or information travelling through time; in those cases what do you do? Do you publicly trash what has been worked so hard on for so long, or hastily hail it as an 'exciting new discovery' leading to 'a brand new series of lines of research and theories, and can we have some more money please?'

At which point, do the masses rise up and say, 'Well hang on, can we have a refund for the last forty years of funding and lunches we paid for?', and they will say 'Why yes of course, as long as you can show us the receipts', and the masses reply 'But you didn't give us a receipt', and they respond with 'Well you're paying us to be clever aren't you?' and 'Sorry can't talk now or we will miss afternoon coffee and cakes.'

This will of course lead to them being ridiculed in public with jokes like 'How many theoretical physicists does it take to change a light bulb? Answer four; one to come up with a theory and equation on why the bulb was broken; one to devise a theory on the best way to replace it; one to dispute and dismiss the theories of the first two, and the fourth to phone for an electrician.'

Then you could just take the approach used by most religions.

He stood there, still reading the brochure, all these thoughts going through his head. He didn't remember being this cynical before. Where was all this feeling and emotion coming from?

However the humorous thought seemed to help break up the pattern for a moment. It concerned him that he was getting so many negative thoughts.

It seemed that everything he saw would invoke a criticism or negative connotation, as if he was just looking for the faults in everything.

He looked at the back of the brochure and there was a picture of some guy wearing glasses, drawing equations on a glass sheet with a white marker, rather than using chalk and a blackboard like lesser mortals had to.

It was a shame that they were so obsessed with trying to describe everything with equations on two dimensional bits of paper or boards. Everything was not supposed to be structured around that sort of two dimensional minded thinking and so you just ended up with tribes of physicists in different camps all coming up with theories on quantum mechanics, dimensions and theories on how the Universe works, all with contradictory equations that when you brought them all together just didn't fundamentally fit or work together.

Nature and the Universe were all symmetrical yes, but they are also random, naturally selective, evolving, and unpredictable. That was its purpose. If everything in the Universe and nature could be mapped into a set of equations it would no longer be unpredictable, and therefore not be able to answer unsolvable questions in its own right, and hey presto there would be no point in us being here.

If it were totally predictable, like a computer program on error free hardware, you would already have the answers by extrapolation or simulation, so there would be no point to it. By being unpredictable that meant that it could be creative in its own right, and therefore have a purpose, have answers and knowledge, something that was new and different to justify its existence and to survive.

Maybe they could see things better by using different perspectives, like using 3D blackboards, or even using coloured crayons instead of boring white chalk, or introduce group hugging and meditation instead of mid-morning coffee and doughnuts.

A vision came into his head of groups of male physicist scientists being made to mix with a group of female biologists. One giant speed dating session in one large room, with an exasperated host trying to make all the matches work.

He was sure that with the right mix there would be soon new Laws of Attraction created; new theories of what was important. He understood why they had developed the way they had, it was just historical and for protection, but he just wished they could come out of that defined stovepipe and see it all the way he had.

He could see that eventually most things would get put into quantified equations of some sort where possible - but it was such a limited picture, like painting a landscape in oils on canvas. No matter how good the picture was it would still be without the sounds, the warmth, smells and the feelings of depth that encompassed everything.

Having an holistic perception, seeing and understanding things from every conceptual way, was not disconcerting but it was perplexing, especially when the world we have created drives us down such limited sensory pathways.

From Sam's perspective there seemed to be several things going on that were at odds with each other, and it didn't seem right. In the same way that universities were structured with departments set up and governed with set lines of study and thinking, to some extent the groups were in isolation from each other, and led to think and focus on viewpoints of the world in set ways like chemists or historians.

He shook his head. It was all too prescriptive and self-fulfilling, driven by the need to compartmentalise everything, in its place, all fitting into a piece, which in itself was a form of control.

It was time to snap out of his meandering thoughts now, and do something else, something to stop him thinking about so many things at once. Get back that reliable, positive mental attitude to move forward. Also he was worried about seeming mad, especially laughing at his own thoughts.

How mad was that? He thought, *worrying about being mad and laughing at yourself and having a go at people at a conference, when I haven't even met them.*

For all he knew, these people at the hotel could have discovered some great things and helped humanity on many levels.

Why am I being so critical of physicists? At least they were working, and doing something. Why suddenly pick on these people?

He could have selected other sections or groups of society that in effect achieved nothing at all, or in some cases just made everything worse. He shook his head to try and clear it again.

He had a shower, changed his clothes and grabbed a quick lunch in a café up the road. He then went for a short walk in the park to try and clear his head of the travel fatigue, and the effects of taking too many jetlag tablets.

They had worked well, but it still seemed as though he was floating, and not quite there. He wandered around the shops for a while and bought a few clothes to replace the ones that he had worn out on holiday. He also needed a new watch as his old one had stopped working and couldn't be repaired for some reason, but he didn't find one that was quite the same style so he left that for the time being.

Brina had made an appointment via a friend for him to see a specialist in the City the following morning, so he had quite a lot of time on his hands. But he wasn't very good at doing things on his own, he could never see the point, it was just filling time really. He didn't fancy going to the cinema, or catching a show in the West End, or going round a museum; it was like there was no point to just doing things in isolation.

He had felt so much happier in the last year doing things with Brina. Going to places on his own just seemed pointless. He loved her and missed her already, and he then told himself off for being so pathetic.

He found himself wandering up to the hotel again about 7pm, with no recollection of the previous two hours, aside from having grabbed a burger, which was odd as he never ate fast food. It was like he was lost and struggling to find a purpose or direction; just wandering around aimlessly. He even knew that he had been up and down one street three times.

Once back in his room again he made himself a coffee and sat on the bed with his back resting against some pillows. He almost decided to put the TV on but couldn't face watching anything. His whole life now felt as if he was watching a film, and that he had already been shown some short clips, heard all of the reviews, and someone had helpfully given away the plot.

Yet you still had to watch the whole thing through, mainly because there was nothing else on. The excitement and energy had all gone, but you felt compelled to watch it anyway, what else could you do? There are a few parts to the film you don't know, but fundamentally the story is there linked together as you imagined. It takes up your time and energy watching it, but even though you know that, you still see it anyway.

However that also puts you in a different position, a higher perspective, and in that instance something strange happens. There is an effect that occurs, because you now have so much more information before you start watching, that it makes you more involved with the plot somehow, prepared for what to expect and what to look out for.

You then start to look for additional clues, correlations and pick out events, that at the time, if you were watching it blind, would seem meaningless, but with your foresight you can see the relevance. With your 'precognitive awareness' you can put these clues into perspective within the plot, when otherwise you would have missed them, like another story going on underneath.

There is also an emotional tie having seen certain scenes before they are relevant to you, and you can relate to the characters and the music you have been introduced to already. So it is comfortable, familiar, and bonding, like a pair of slippers. It becomes more alive to you, with more depth than if you were just watching it without the spoilers.

You can see more of the overall picture and piece things together to make them fit from all levels, getting the plot before it starts. So the film becomes better, deeper, smarter, more interesting. If everyone did that, just imagine how good the films would have to evolve to be to keep up.

There was a film, he couldn't recall the name of, where there was a little boy who could see ghosts, and the boy went along to a therapist for some help.

It eventually turned out later in the film that the therapist was also a ghost. If you had known that at the start of the film you would have seen it in a very different way and perspective. You would be able to look for errors, understand the deeper meanings within the dialogue. You could see and understand things from the boy's point of view. You would be able to appreciate the cleverness of the directing, and the scriptwriting of the film.

You would appreciate a wonderfully clever film rather than just watching a good one, and experiencing the shock at the end.

Then again, you could say it was just wrong seeing it from the spoilt perspective, and that the naïve approach is how it is meant to be viewed to enjoy the experience.

It was starting to worry him, this knowledge and understanding he now had. He certainly had a very different perception on everything now; that was true, as if all things now had two or three meanings. The same as looking down a corridor and being able to see into an open room at the end. It could just be a good wall painting at the end of the hall, made to look like a room, or is the whole thing a dream?

So everything he saw now was tainted or spoilt to some extent, the uncertainty gone partly. But not quite everything and that bothered him. *Why didn't he know everything?* It felt like he knew so much, but when he thought about it they only related to logical things, or scientific information; he had no artistic or emotional or socialistic information.

There was also the sense of detachment, a disjointed feeling that he wasn't meant to be seeing the world this way. A cold, lonely, uncertain feeling of being on your own with no guide to right or wrong, or of what was real or virtual, or how to correlate the two.

Correlation. That word was important somehow and related to something he had seen or 'experienced' in the last few moments of the 'Episode'. It was how the information had been collected and managed that was important, but why?

How could he go back to what he was before knowing what he knew now, and seeing things from such a perspective? Do you carry on with your job of washing the windows on the office block knowing there is an earthquake coming next month? You could be wrong anyway, and besides they are still dirty, and need doing, if only for a month.

So the way he now saw it was that he had three options. The first option was to do nothing. The second was to try to ignore what he knew now, forget it and carry on as before. Thirdly, get it all down in as much detail as he could over the next few months, and find someone to talk to about it, to try and get answers to some of the missing elements, and to see if anyone else had been through the same, or experienced anything similar.

He looked out of the window again to the main street further to the right below where it was lit up with the street lamps.

He noticed a pigeon pecking away at a piece of bread or something in the centre of the road, indifferent to the people walking around it, indifferent to the perilous situation it was in. It would deftly move out of the way of the occasional car or van, knowing it could adequately respond in time.

You play the game of life, you follow the Laws of Nature, and you exist in a symbiotic state with everything else, give and take, win or lose, live or die.

So if that pigeon was suddenly a cow, it would be immediately highlighted as a problem, and would either be moved or minced.

The experience that he had that day a few weeks ago was of an overwhelming sense of power, mass, a mechanical monster, an unstoppable speeding train with no concern if you fell into it or under its wheels or not.

The thought of having to deal with it would be the same as reaching in through one of its windows to pull the stop cord, or of standing in the middle of the tracks with your hand up.

He made his decision.

He was going for the second option. The third choice was just too much, he felt too alone to take all that on, and battle his way to somewhere he didn't know where, and risk all he had.

It should have been exciting, a new purpose and adventure, a gauntlet to pick up, but he didn't want to take it on; it didn't feel right somehow. It also felt as if something was warning him away, and urging him to take the safer option.

So he made plans in his mind to forget it all. To do and see things together with Brina, see the world that he hadn't seen already. However he would try to write down on paper as much of what he had experienced as he could over the next few months, but only for himself, in case he forgot the facts or concepts. But that would be it and he would just file it away and not show it to anyone, not even Brina.

It would just be a reminder to himself of all of the amassed knowledge so that it wouldn't keep nagging at him, going round in his brain; so that he wouldn't worry about it, or try to do something about it, or doubt himself in the future.

Also writing it down meant it could be filed somewhere else rather than in his head. Yes it was probably selfish, but he didn't care. If he hadn't been so alone at the moment, and could have talked it though with someone, or have told a friend he could trust, he may have felt different, but he was isolated and vulnerable, and didn't fancy taking on the thing on his own armed only with a pen.

'You have to look after yourself for once in your life' he told himself.

Besides what was wrong with the philosophy of just wanting to be happy and making someone else happy too? He was only just getting serious with his relationship with Brina, and he didn't want to risk that, or waste time.

Maybe other people had been to the same place and seen what he had seen and knew what he knew, and then tried to do something about it, only for it to go badly wrong. Something told him that he was just to keep it to himself now, keep his head down, and not to do anything about it.

Having been burnt in his career a few times, with ideas being stolen, or by being let down by misplaced trust, he was very much wary of impulsively running naked down the street shouting 'Eureka'. All his work, all his life, had been to do with management of information, programming, data management, intelligence processing and security.

He knew that a little knowledge could be a dangerous thing, and the dangers of too much knowledge being populated too quickly in an unstructured way.

He wasn't ready for any of that. It would all be too much; his life wouldn't be his own any more, and he would be subject to too much pressure, demands, not to mention abuse. To most people it would seem like an attractive proposition - fame, money, glory, and awards, but not to him. It just seemed like a trap waiting to be sprung in an elaborate game.

Before going to bed he rang Brina, it being early morning there. She was very pleased that he was safe somewhere now. She talked for a long time about how much she had missed him. She had been thinking about him all the time he had been flying and travelling.

She sounded very relaxed, and hadn't done much the day before apart from sunbathe and go shopping. He decided not to tell her anything about what had happened at the airports, and decided to keep it that way for now. He slept well that night.

Just as he was leaving the Hotel early the next morning to go to the specialist's, he picked up a copy of the lecture notes that were on the table outside the room for the conference that was going on inside, and he quickly scanned over the pages.

He had agreed with himself that that he would not discuss what he knew with anyone or share his understanding on things. But, just this once, he couldn't help himself, so he took out a pen from his jacket and added a dozen or so paragraphs and diagrams at the end, with explanations. He then left it on the table and checked out of the hotel. It was a statement somehow.

The visit to the specialist was uneventful; after two or three hours of scans, tests and discussions, he showed no signs of having had any brain damage, stroke symptoms, or any residual neurological disorders. The only thing they could find was a tiny gap going down the middle line of his spinal cord in the centre of his neck, called a syrinx.

It was very small though, just over a centimetre long and a couple wide, and so they didn't think it worth bothering with. It had probably, they thought, been there for some time, probably since he was very young.

He was given advice on posture, and caring for himself, and was told to take it easy for a few weeks. He was then given an appointment for a further scan in the afternoon, and 'would be called at home' if there were any problems, which, he was told, would be unlikely, and which thankfully turned out to be the case.

Five hours later he was on the train home.

He went First Class this time. It seemed the safer option.

CHAPTER 5 - GAME CHANGE

Switching off had been easier than he had thought it would be. It had been over three years now since 'The Episode' and he was happy.

He kept busy with day to day things.

There was plenty of ongoing work and new projects, visits to relatives, events, and many holidays with Brina when they were both able to get away.

It all just seemed to pan out as normal, and just going with the flow seemed to work, and they got on with their lives.

As time went on, he thought less and less about what had happened and what he had experienced.

It worked well for him. He just maintained a positive attitude, doing the right things with his life, and with Brina. He wasn't walking away from it, or pretending it hadn't happened - he was just getting on with his life and his responsibilities. As the years went by it just became a memory.

There were a few lingering changes - he did notice that people seemed to treat him differently somehow. Friends and people would come and go, and their views and opinions would influence his own thoughts and opinions, as if he were in some sort of play or process, being 'shown' things and getting 'messages', but he just ignored it generally, and kept himself busy with a fairly strict daily routine, up at six in the morning and so on.

Brina too kept him occupied with lists, jobs, and things to keep him busy. He knew she was doing it subconsciously to stop him from being idle. It was a sort of control thing, but he didn't mind.

Sometimes when he did have time to himself he would be able to recall the pieces, and see them in the dark when he closed his eyes, usually at times of peace, or when he was just going to sleep. It was like it was still there somewhere in his mind, an afterglow, yet still stark and cold and hard. But it was only occasionally.

His relationship with Brina had grown very strong now, and he was even thinking seriously now about making plans to take it further, and to settle down permanently.

She had already moved in with him in his house in the country.

He was a bit of a romantic if he were to be honest with himself. He loved the idea of getting married, and the joy it would bring to Brina. Especially the wedding, which seemed to be all girls were focused on these days.

She never mentioned anything to him about the idea, in her eyes it wasn't the correct thing. However he was sure that somewhere she had already started making lists, which was her way of dealing with things like that, practical, organised, and prudent.

He wasn't so romantic about the words 'settling down' though, it sounded 'nice' but he was sure he wasn't 'old' enough, maturity wise, for that yet. Like an eighteen year old being 'put out to pasture'. It was an ongoing dilemma between exciting and scary.

There had been the odd day, here and there, when it hadn't been easy at all to forget what he had experienced, or to put it out of his mind and move on.

He was only usually reminded when he was on his own for more than a few hours with little to do, or it was triggered by an announcement in the news about some scientific discovery or event. There were oddly suspiciously coincidental documentaries on something on the TV, or someone else's findings put into a paper or book that he would stumble across.

He still suppressed the urge to 'go and tell everyone'; after all there were plenty of other things going on for him to distract himself with, or come up with something to focus his thoughts away. It was almost like he was protecting himself from a process that was slowly happening in his mind, and that needed time to work through without being prodded.

There had been two instances over those three years when he had been in a similar situation, and set of circumstances, to when it had originally occurred. In doing so he had almost returned to the same 'place' or state again. However, in both cases, he had managed to control it, pull back, and restrain himself.

He wasn't sure if it was fear or if his system had stopped him from a safety point of view.

It was a weighed balance between absolute knowledge and power, and fear and caution. Again he had been relaxed and stupidly allowed his mind to experiment again, wandering around, and then felt that change in sensory perception, and level, followed by growing panic.

In both cases he had an overwhelming feeling of déjà vu. As an analogy, it was like going from a quiet empty street and walking into an abandoned secret library that he hadn't been into for a very long time. It was if he had forgotten all about it, but suddenly having the same feelings, sensation and knowledge as before. With the same sensory changes of smell, cold and dark.

At the same time it was exciting and addictive knowing what was there, and what you could learn, combined with your existing technical knowledge.

But in both cases fear, trepidation, rationality, and common sense had stopped him going any further than a few feet inside the 'library' before walking backwards out of the doorway and onto the street again. Still clinging to that residual sense of perspective, danger and consequence.

I have responsibilities now and I have made my choice. I'm not going there again. Not for anything, why should I? He thought. He had fulfilled his promise to himself of writing all the facts and knowledge down in summary form. He had now put it all into one of his thick leather management binder zip folders, and a year ago he had placed it in his safety deposit box where he also kept some of his other papers and a few family valuables.

It felt strangely correct that he should be doing this. Something in his mind was telling him that he was doing the right thing, and that keeping his head down was correct. He would be happier in the long run, whatever that meant.

Besides, every time he let his mind wander back to those events or dwell on the issues or contemplate some of the scientific announcements in context, he would get a feeling of paranoia, or persecution, with odd events or circumstances that would go against him, or sap his energy. It would depress him, and force him to work harder than he needed to.

He knew these feelings were coming from within himself somehow, it wasn't external. It was like he was protecting himself, refining his programming, changing to the situation that had occurred, using his skills and experience to adapt to it. But there was a sense that there was something outside of him that was also there doing something.

It wasn't obvious or malicious; it was just there, something tipping the balance towards the busy, the preoccupied, the compliant, and the happy. Like a tree being bent in a specific direction with slight pressure over time, or with wind or sunlight coming from one side steering the direction of life.

If he just got on with things, life seemed so much easier, better, and was more rewarding. If he stopped to think about the way things were, or got 'down' or depressed, he would find that things would go wrong. Things like buying shares that went down in price, or having workmen around that seemed to do more damage than they fixed, or buying things that either didn't do what they were supposed to do or just didn't work at all. They always involved other people rather than being natural events.

Keeping his positive mental attitude worked well though and now things were 'OK' and he was happy in his relationship and with his life in general.

However one day, that all changed.

Many peculiar circumstantial events or situations had occurred over that time, and he was able to accept them as 'part of life' and the ups and downs of living.

However, on this day, it was different.

It was a warm July Sunday morning, and he was enjoying a lazy time on the patio in the garden of the house. He was sunbathing with Brina and he had just finished reading the magazines and the Sunday newspaper. He couldn't recall if it was something he read or something she said that started him thinking again.

It dawned on him how much he was being manipulated by fear and steered by conditioning. Brina had asked him for the time, and he had looked at his wrist out of habit, despite not having a working watch for well over three years now.

He had grown used to his old watch and when it stopped working he just couldn't find anything that he liked to replace it with. That seemed to be the case with everything; over the last few years he had subconsciously removed things that he could be attacked with. Any possessions he had previously been emotionally attached to he had now either given away, or had not replaced when broken or lost.

He had bought a few things in that time but they just seemed to either arrive not working or break within a few weeks, rather than the usual few days, just after the warranty period had expired. It had made him angry at the time, but rather than getting into a battle getting them replaced or repaired he had just got his money refunded. Aside from Brina and the house, he didn't really need or want anything.

He had put all his money into safe bank accounts now too, rather than high rate bonds or shares. He had also automated all the bill payments and accounting stuff so he didn't need to worry about all of that. He took steps to consolidate what he had, and minimise the risk to it all. Subconsciously protecting himself and Brina from anything that may 'get at them'. It might seem like paranoia to some people, but it wasn't.

It was just cause and effect, sensible management, as in any situation where you would try to control and manage your life.

They only had a few close friends now too, which was mainly due to a combination of them being so busy, and being a couple, rather than 'one of the girls', and a 'mate'. They were very happy with each other, but it seemed that the more time they spent with other people, or got involved with them, the more hassles they seemed to have.

Everyone seemed to want things from them; time, energy, help, money, but nobody seemed to do anything for them, at all, apart from a few minor exceptions. It also seemed the more they gave, or tried to do for other people, the more it seemed to backfire on them.

As he relaxed in the sunshine on the lounger, it seemed to be more like a game of chess but in reverse. The fewer pieces you had, the easier it was to play, and you were fine as long as you stuck to the rules. He could see the moves coming, and manipulate himself and the remaining pieces, to avoid any major issues. He was not playing to win, just playing not to lose, and doing the run-around. He had no idea who or what he was playing against, but the system worked; he and Brina were happy, so that was fine. As long as he didn't fall asleep and miss a move they would be alright.

Brina knew what was going on too, she could see it happening, and yet she was unfazed by it all; it seemed to be something she had been built for. She 'dealt' with people and situations better than he did generally, but he did see it sap her energy too from time to time, but she just bounced back. It was all part of a change in life that they were going through.

He had even taken to just wearing black clothes, rather than the colourful ones he used to like. It made him feel safe, and less conspicuous, less obvious somehow. He didn't know why, it just seemed a subconscious, evolutionary thing. He got bothered less when he wore it, people left him alone more, he got less grief, so that's what he wore.

It also made getting dressed in the dark mornings easier, and less of a concern as to whether things would go with each other. If everything was the same you didn't have to worry if it clashed. Brina said it was a 'slimming colour', but she said it with a smirk on her face.

Ironically, she had also taken to wearing similarly dark, or black outfits, and blue black dresses too, which he put down to a subconscious need to follow him, and match herself with what he was wearing.

Mind you she looked pretty amazing in anything, and some of the outfits she had were stunning. There was one thing that perplexed him though. He could not work out where all her clothes seemed to go. She had about thirty or so outfits in her wardrobe, however for the most part, they all seemed to be different from the ones that were there a several years ago when they had first met. It was an area he wasn't good at remembering.

What also confused him was that when they went shopping they always seemed to come back with a least a few items for her, which she needed, were in the sale, and fitted beautifully. They were always a 'bargain', compared to the non-sale price. The conversation would always be directed to the saving, rather than the cost. It was one of those magical things you didn't question.

The only area he was able to give advice on, other than what she looked like in things, was boots. He was always keen on quality made shoes, and good craftsmanship, he never minded spending a lot of money on something as long as it was well made, a good design, and made to last.

He hated spending money on poor quality things that you had to throw away. It was an understanding and opinion in him that she latched onto very quickly. She had several pairs of handmade black and brown calf length boots now, kept properly in their boxes along with several formal and everyday shoes, all from the same supplier. He had no idea what had happened to all the old ones, he couldn't even recall what they looked like now.

Another skill she had was that she could tell him what they were both wearing at every event they had been to together since they met. It was as if she had a photographic memory. She could also remember what other people had said any time they had met anyone, and what he had said to them.

It was almost like every time they went anywhere or met anyone she had an automatic video camera in her mind that recorded everything for use later.

He thought about continuing it backwards in time, and asking her what dress she had been wearing at functions they coincidently both been at before they 'got together' say five years ago. He could then catch her out and ask what had happened to that dress. However he couldn't be sure if some of the specific work events were before or after they started going out, and he may have been getting into some dodgy ground, especially if he had been to them with 'someone else' so he just dropped the whole idea. He wasn't that fussed.

Anyway she had taken charge of his wardrobe too now, and it was in a much better shape than he could remember, so it was probably best not to try and fix or meddle with something if it was working.

When they went shopping, on the basis that he needed some new trousers or shirts, they always seemed to come back with two or three items for her, and nothing for him, and yet somehow things would appear in his wardrobe and drawers that were for him, and in his correct size, and looked good. It was all magical.

These days when they went out to parties or functions, she would take great care to ensure he looked 'the part'. He was groomed, straightened and brushed, shoes polished, and wore a tie if he was supposed to.

She made sure that she 'matched'. It was also very odd, when she entered the room with him, everyone seemed to light up and want to talk to her, and be with her. Like she had some sort of charismatic power or energy. Yet if the two of them were separated in the room, she was very wary of what he was doing, especially if he was talking with other women.

Jealous? No, perhaps 'watchful' was a better word.

He had never really noticed himself being attractive to women, but when Brina was with him it was very different and noticeable, and he could almost sense women wait for her to move away before moving in to try and 'steal him'.

Nature was an odd thing.

Where had she been when he was seventeen?

He felt very comfortable being looked after and managed, and he could see that Brina was loving it. She was very happy doing things for him and being his soul mate.

She put him first in everything, and was always highly defensive of him to her friends, and even to her mother, which was saying something. But he still couldn't get that thought out of his mind that there was something wrong in the background, a nagging doubt, a slight vibration on the steering wheel of life, a feeling of something unimaginably powerful and immense that was there just under the surface, but asleep.

So now, although a while ago, he had surrendered and waved the white flag, decided to play along and to steer away from the knowledge he had seen. Whatever it was that was there still wasn't leaving him alone, as if he was subconsciously being gently steered and manipulated.

At that moment a large cloud went in front of the sun. He opened his eyes and felt the warm glow on his body change to a cool chill. He didn't know what to do now. He had also had too much sun, and had fallen asleep, face down, on the lounger. Now his back was sore and his neck ached.

For some reason he hadn't been able to get to sleep the night before, which is why he was so tired, and why he had fallen asleep. He had gone to bed as normal that night but something had bothered him, and after a few hours of trying he had been relegated to the spare room by Brina so that she could get some sleep.

Lying awake in the night in the spare room it was deathly quiet, no wind or noises from outside. In fact it was so quiet that his ears had constantly searched for something to hear. The air was too close and it all made him feel quite vulnerable, as if something were going to happen; every occasional noise would be analysed by his brain into any conceivable threat.

It was a feeling as if someone was about to break into the house, or something ominous was going to happen, like someone close to them had died and the phone was about to ring. Just a feeling of being exposed or open to attack. He had finally dropped off to sleep about 5am and then woke up a few hours later, laying on his front in an awkward position, with a stiff neck, exhausted.

The sun didn't look like it was going to re-emerge now, so he decided to go back inside the house, hoping to get some sleep on the sofa. However as it appeared that he was no longer 'doing anything', Brina decided to have a nice 'Sunday afternoon out' at the supermarket, the idea of which he, of course, 'loved'.

He particularly liked the idea of sitting in the car with nothing to do waiting for her, after having navigated around the stupidly designed car park and manic, old, short-sighted drivers with defensive 'it's your fault' attitudes and limited spatial awareness. With everyone trying to park as close to the main entrance as possible. *Why did these people who didn't work have to go to the supermarket at the weekends?* He thought.

He picked up his keys and threw on his t-shirt and trousers, irritably. Perhaps the sun would be back out when he returned.

She had been inside the supermarket for about ten minutes when he closed his eyes to relax for a rest in the car. His back was still a bit raw and his neck still ached so it wasn't that comfortable in the seat, but he tried to ignore it.

Despite the ache he realised that he hadn't been this relaxed for a long time; he felt warm, cosy, comfortable and safe in the car. It was as if his body was still glowing with the energy his body had absorbed from the sun.

He was parked directly in front of a wall with one of those large revolving advertising signs on rollers. It mechanically whirred round every twenty seconds, showing you a new printed advert, and then whirred round again to show you the previous one again. 'Whirr', stop, 'whirr', stop, over and over. He remembered hearing that same rhythmical repetitive deep sound before, but he couldn't remember where.

In the rear view mirror he could see a small car slowly pull up, and then position itself ready to park in the space next to him. It appeared to have a very old man in it, he was probably in his eighties, sat with his head a few inches in front of the steering wheel, and just able to see over the top of it.

He slowly went back and forward a few times, the engine revving hard each time. Then he backed up slowly at an angle, straight into the rear bumper of Sam's car. Sam went forward and up in the air slightly, as the old man continued to rev his engine oblivious to the reason why he wasn't going anywhere. It was one of those moments where you couldn't react; your mind wasn't believing what was happening. You shouldn't need to sound your horn as you were 'parked'; you were safe in your car.

After a few seconds the old man stopped, changed gear and went forward again a few feet. He then slowly reversed again into the space correctly this time, got out, and walked into the supermarket carrying an old brown bag.

Sam just didn't react, he was in shock still. After a few seconds he managed to wake himself up, opened his car door, got out, and went round to the back of his car. Luckily the car was solid and there was no damage, just a slight black rubber mark.

Sam decided not to go after the old man, who by now was heading through the supermarket entrance. Another car that had been waiting behind the old man's while it parked was still there. Inside was a woman Sam's age, and she was looking right at him.

The woman gestured with both her hands in the air to question if everything was alright, and Sam returned the gesture, and nodded to indicate that it was, and that it was OK for her to drive on. But instead she got out of her car, and stood in the space between her open car door and her seat.

She had very long blonde hair, and was immaculately dressed in a summer dress and high heels; she looked as if she were on her way to something formal rather than calling in to do the weekly shop. "I saw what happened, are you OK?" she asked, and Sam nodded. She walked over to him, and put her hand on his arm. "Are you sure?" she said, and started to rub his arm up and down whilst looking straight into his eyes.

"Er, yes" said Sam a little confused. "It can give you quite a shock, that sort of thing. Honestly, they shouldn't be allowed out" she continued. She looked him up and down, and smiled at him. "I think you will be OK though, a big strong boy like you" she said continuing to stroke is arm, and waited for him to say something in reply.

"Would you like my name and number in case you want to make a claim?" she continued. "No, it's OK" said Sam "There's no damage done, it's fine thank you." She looked slightly disappointed for a moment.

There was a sound of a horn from a car that was waiting behind hers, and she turned and her face blushed. "Must dash…" she said and walked backwards towards her car and got in. As she drove slowly off, she wound her window down, "Nice meeting you, we will have to bump into each other again sometime" she said, and laughed as she passed.

Sam stood there for a few moments, bewildered, and then went round to the back of the old man's car to see if there was any damage, but there were so many dents and marks it was impossible to tell. He tried to just calm down, still very confused. He got back in the car and closed to door, only to be confronted with the advertising sign again in front of him going through its whirring loop up and down.

Grumpy, and irritated by the repetitive noise, he gave up, and got out of the car again, locked it, and folded the wing mirrors in from the key fob. He then went into the supermarket to look for Brina. It was still cool inside, despite the early afternoon sunshine, and it looked like it was going to be another fine and warm evening so there should be plenty of time to top up his sunburn later.

Supermarkets were amazing places. All different strands of humanity, from all walks of life, pulled together, rubbing shoulders, or trying to avoid doing so; all doing the primal hunting and gathering, but within a well-defined etiquette.

You had to adhere to the personal space rules, the behaviour. The experience was accompanied, and managed, with suitable marketing and suggestive colour schemes.

It was an encyclopaedia of human behaviour; you could see the different approaches to shopping, the techniques for going around, the different speeds, and manners. How people would select queues for the checkouts and their techniques for getting through them as quickly as possible.

As they went around you could compare the politeness, the rudeness, and the different attire. It was also a flirting ground, a place to attract potential mates. But not for him. Not today. Not for Mr Grumpy !

He stood for a while at the magazines section and had a quick scan over the wall of glossy covers. His eye was caught by a copy of *New Scientist* that appeared to have a gap on either side of it, away from the other magazines, as if it was some 'odd one out', that the rest of the 'chat' and 'TV' magazines didn't talk to.

The headline on the cover had something that he latched on to, and he picked it up and flicked through the pages. Reading through an article about subatomic particles and quantum mechanics brought his mind back again to the 'real', and he could feel his brain pulling information together for him as best it could.

Looking at the article more closely, Sam could see that things were now moving on and changing in those particular fields;

people were desperately seeking answers, and were employing astoundingly imaginative new ideas and concepts.

They were trying to fill the gaps in more and more complex ways and yet it was troubling. Something in there was not right, one specific aspect in it was going the wrong way, he couldn't describe it; a manipulation, a 'never getting to the bottom of it' feeling, but one that he already had seen the answer to, or had already made sense of. It was very bloody odd.

He placed the magazine back on the shelf, and picked up a 'lads' magazine with a picture of tanned buxom blonde wearing just a swimsuit on the cover, holding some new gadget up in a suggestive manner.

He was for a moment temped to flick through it, almost as a 'so there - I can if I want to' gesture, but he didn't. Instead he just placed it back on the shelf right next to the *New Scientist* magazine; they overlapped, paired up. It seemed necessary somehow. He shook his head to clear it, turned around, and jumped with surprise.

Surrounding him were over a dozen people. They had all appeared quietly from nowhere during the several minutes that he had been reading. They were all no more than six feet away in a semi-circle, blocking him in, standing, reading, talking to each other, or holding on at arm's length to trolleys which blocked the aisles. He had no way out.

Beyond the six feet it was empty, nobody, it was as if a light had gone on in a room full of moths, or a group of zombies had all shuffled towards their live victim, dragging their knuckles along the ground. He just stood there frozen; it wasn't even subtle, it felt as if at any moment he was going to be pushed backwards into and through the wall of magazines. They all seemed unaware of what they were doing, or why they were all there.

A man was even reading a broadsheet newspaper a few feet away, arms wide facing him as if he were holding up some sort of barrier.

If anyone were to look at it from above, or on the store security monitors, it would appear like a 'pacman'-style computer game; the idea being to avoid being trapped and eaten, but he had taken his eyes off the game, and was now surrounded, with no magic pill around to protect him and turn the tables.

He stood there for another minute while nothing changed. He could have said "Excuse me" or rudely barged his way out, but he didn't. He wanted to test it, see how long it went on for, how obvious it was. At the point where someone started to back into him he decided he had had enough.

He stepped sideways and pushed apart two trolleys that had been parked lengthways in the middle of the one aisle blocking it, while their two female owners carried on a conversation in the middle of another.

As Sam moved, everyone stopped and looked at him, and as he moved the trollies to get through he heard one of the women say to the other "Honestly some people are so rude, he could have just asked me to move it." Sam just ignored it, and carried on walking out into the free space. After twenty or so paces he looked back to see the group start to dissipate and find more interesting things to occupy their minds.

Escaping from the 'Twilight Zone', he eventually found Brina at the end of an aisle looking at some 'special offers'. Her trolley was about half full, and parked at the side of the row out of the way.

On seeing him she smiled, and immediately made him busy with an errand to fetch some organic apples that she had missed from her list. So he duly went off to get a pack, and returning from a successful hunt made his way back a few minutes later.

He was walking across the end of the aisles next to the checkouts, and could see Brina's trolley still parked at the end of the aisle; she had her back to him and was bending over the handle of it, putting a box of eggs in it carefully. She was wearing shorts, too tempting an opportunity to miss, and he had a sudden urge to give her a gentle pat on her backside.

He knew she would tell him off, but you had to balance up the pain with the gain, and this was worth it. He checked nobody was looking, and he quietly and quickly crept up behind her. Just as he was about to reach the back of her, as he was passing the open aisle on his left, something caught his eye.

A middle aged, red-haired woman was rushing down Brina's side of the aisle with her trolley, not looking where she was going, late for something, flustered. He stopped. His plan was foiled.

He had come to recognise that sort of thing; people not seeing, and so he stood still and braced himself ready to move out of the way, or to back up if need be in that split second. At that moment he was framed right in the middle of the aisle.

The woman who was looking to her left at the shelves as she went past, caught sight of Brina in front of her at the last minute, and swerved right to avoid her, but at the same time caught her foot on the back wheel, tripped, and fell forward hard into it, thrusting it forward and right, straight at Sam.

Prepared, he braced himself to move safely back behind the end of the aisle. He knew the game, so he had to wait until the last minute before moving.

He didn't see it happen, it was too fast, but Brina's hand, then her body, pushed him to his left, hard, and out of the way instantly. It was the same way he was preparing to go anyway, so he was moved quickly away out of danger flying sideways behind the end of the other aisle.

That was the moment. Right there. Simple yet profound. The action that changed everything. He saw it as he fell. He saw the woman's hand move on the trolley handle that she was still clinging to, it shifted position and caused the trolley to track his sideways movement.

It wasn't a natural change of position, not something you would do normally, or instinctively do in that scenario. It made the trolley veer slightly towards him, but not enough to get to him, before he disappeared past the end of the aisle. The shelves were empty at the top end of the aisle so he could still see through.

He then saw her hand slide back, and the trolley straightened up again towards whatever had 'saved' him, in this case it was Brina.

It all happened in an instant but the movements and intent were unmistakeable, and replayed in slow motion for his mind to reiterate the 'deliberate mistake in the live movie'.

He could feel a sort of directed energy associated with it, exactly the same feeling of intensity and sense of moment that he had experienced in Singapore years before.

He heard Brina cry out in pain to his side, and his head turned as he fell sideways, to see her hit in the ribs hard by the front of the woman's trolley. He broke his fall with his arm and grabbed instinctively at some boxes next to him, which fell onto his back as he hit the ground face down, the apples still held to his chest. When he got up he saw Brina kneeling on the floor clutching her side, groaning and swearing hard. He hadn't heard her swear before or seen her that angry. However even 'down' she was still looking at him, and checking that he was OK, and her eyes followed him as he stood up.

The woman's face changed expression a few times; from initial shock and surprise, to blaming anger, then the realisation of her error changed it to the apologetic, concerned look.

As he stood there power, utter power, surged through him, insurmountable rage, so much so he couldn't move. His whole body was shaking, building energy; his heart pounding with the adrenaline, pressure came from everywhere.

The red-headed woman was clearly mortally embarrassed, and was apologising to Brina profusely. She was almost pawing her hands all over her, trying to smooth the problem away.

It was just seconds before two shop assistants arrived followed by the manager. Sam was unable to move trying to take in what he was seeing and what had just happened. Everything seemed to shrink in perspective, and the scene moved away from him.

The red-haired woman half turned to look towards Sam, appeared to think about saying something, but stopped herself, almost as if sensing that somehow if she did, at that moment, it would be the last thing she ever did.

It all seemed to be virtual, surreal, detached somehow. The ensuing scenario just went in a blur, virtual, dreamlike; the forms to fill in, the drive to the hospital, the x-ray, the trip home.

It also seemed to the people involved around them that it hadn't actually happened; the management and staff at the supermarket, the nurses.

Even a bizarre situation at the hospital where a woman doctor tried to diagnose it as 'shingles', which was a little surreal considering the detailed explanation of what had happened. She had been very pleasant to begin with, attentive to Brina, and asking her about what had happened. She then examined her side, which by now was red and inflamed.

However she then just made a sweeping decision based on what she could see, as if she hadn't heard what Brina had explained to her, or registered the events that had occurred. Brina had just looked at Sam in disbelief when the doctor had actually said the word 'shingles', and he in turn couldn't rationalise what he was hearing.

He got more and more angry, just seeing it all unfold in front of him, like some badly contrived amateur stage play. He then took over the conversation, reinforced what Brina had said, trying to get the doctor to see the obvious, until he eventually ended up shouting at the doctor.

He tried to remain calm and polite, but it was impossible, and he said several things loudly that were very much out of character. It was as if they were either trying subconsciously to pretend that it hadn't occurred, that it wasn't important, or that it didn't matter.

For some bizarre reason people around them just couldn't see that the event had taken place in their minds, or that Brina was injured. It was as if something was now trying to cover up or erase what had gone on, and make out that it hadn't happened.

Sam in the end just grabbed a specialist, and insisted on paying for an x-ray before allowing her to be discharged; for once Brina was in too much pain to argue with him.

Unlike most people who held doctors in high esteem, he didn't, he saw them more as car mechanics or plumbers, and was only accepting of them when he found one who seemed to know exactly what they were talking about, and who really knew what they were doing, in which case, he had the greatest of respect for them.

However knowing a lot about 'cars and plumbing' meant that he was frequently disappointed.

Fortunately there was nothing broken, there was just very bad bruising of the ribs and hip bone, and a torn muscle. However she would still have to be in bed for at least four days. They finally came out of hospital just over five hours after it had occurred, and all that time just seemed to pass in transience.

It was as if it was all being managed by him, the situation, but not with him there. When they finally arrived home the whole thing seemed like a detached scenario that had never happened, aside from the evidence of the large bruises and the crippling pain. The idea of a relaxing afternoon sunbathing was now just a distant forlorn memory.

The sleep helped her.

The following morning realisation returned. To Sam this was a whole different game now. The rules had been broken. In fact there didn't seem to be any rules, or at least none that he thought that he had been playing to.

He was in shock, and with a real sense of trepidation, a change from a gentle, virtual surreal, honeymoon life, to a cold stark oppressive grey reality. He could deal with things happening to him, but having people he cared about being attacked was something else.

He could no longer live the way he had, and he now had to get to the bottom of what the bloody hell was going on, and why.

His focus and perception on everything around him had been altered. Just like being alone in a dark forest experiencing all the smells, sounds, fresh air, and life and then hearing a stick break in the blackness behind you; your mind translates everything to the negative, and all the positive sensations are gone, replaced with warnings, threats, and with all your senses now on the defensive.

Now he felt as though he had just wasted the last few years.

Time he could have spent working out what was happening. Something he hadn't bothered about, and had been trying to avoid, had just come to call. He had minded his own business, but now something had changed that with a rude awakening, and stepped over the line.

I have done as I was 'told', so why was this going on now?

He had to work it out, but he wasn't going to rush into it like a bull in a china shop. He knew he had to be careful, take little measured steps without waking 'IT' up. Whatever 'IT' was.

He was at home now for the remainder of the week looking after Brina. Thankfully he had enough project work with him so that he could get on with it without going back into the office. She was on painkillers and so slept quite a lot of the time anyway. He thought he was very good at looking after people; he made her lots of cups of tea, heated up lots of things for her to eat, and even got the dishwasher to work.

She was not a good patient and kept getting out of bed to get things like books. However, they still enjoyed being useless in the wrong 'roles' together.

While she was asleep he used a lot of the time to scour the Internet for people who had come across similar ideas and concepts that he knew, or had experienced the same sort of thing, whatever it was called. Just anything to get some idea of what may be going on and why.

He had always made sure that his laptop was very secure with all the browsing protection and firewalls in place. Being in the 'business' made him very conscious of what information could be collected on what you were looking at, and by whom. So he knew what to do and what to use.

He tried different searches with different keywords, which with ones like 'enlightening experiences' yielded some very exotic answers and showed websites that he wasn't expecting at all, but at least he learned something there.

He narrowed down some definitions of the experience he had to a very specific type, and its representative description in various different religions. Cosmic consciousness, Brahma or Kundalini. Indeed, that specific experience seemed to be the root source of most of them, and he could understand why. But nothing to the degree that he had experienced, or even any description of the experience itself, just references to the after-effects or change, or in a few cases the transformational effect. Most of the knowledge that people in history had experienced they just could not explain, describe or remember.

He supposed it had something to do with what was there in the first place, what they knew, and what opening the 'door' revealed in the inner collective mind and beyond. What other people had been describing seemed much more gentle, colourful, soft and fluffy. With dreamy references to levels beyond levels of 'oneness', and blissful transcendental enlightenment. All to the highest imaginative extent of whatever they knew or had been told already, which was probably quite limited.

There was nothing about knowledge transfer, or the brutal 'hard core' effects he had experienced. He suspected that his mind had seen past all of that and was able to translate and interpret what was really there in a form that was much more technically defined. He was sure that he couldn't have been the only one with his level of intellect and background to have had this experience, and if that was the case, where were they?

Eventually with some careful refinement and work, he narrowed his search down to someone reasonably local. He came across a guy, well a professor, by the name of Stevens in the UK.

Stevens had come up with some interesting theories several years ago, but they lacked specific substance or evidence, and much of what he had written was not linked to the references he had and none were available on the Internet; it was all written in 'in the club' academic papers, or had since been deleted.

After a few more days investigating, he called the man's College research department office, and spoke to an elderly lady there who was obviously holding the fort during the summer holidays. She was very chatty and gave him lots of useful facts that he needed to know, and quite a few that he didn't, about the Professor.

She was clearly desperate for an interesting conversation with anyone, having nobody else there. It turned out that he had lost his wife in a car accident four years before, and he had retired two years later after meeting another woman. They had both moved to a village in the West Country to be closer to her friends, who were members of some 'group' down there. He had sold up everything and had bought a large old manor house in the area, and was going to become self-sufficient with growing vegetables and keeping animals, and she went on, and on.

Sam pretended to be an old friend of his, and implied that he wanted to send a letter to him. At first, with procedure kicking in suddenly, she was reluctant to give his forwarding address and offered to forward it for him, but in the end she relented; by this time Sam knew most of her life history anyway.

She then started on about the new woman he had met and quickly married again. How odd she was, her strange attitudes, clearly not liking 'her', or what she had 'done' to him by taking him away to a 'happy life' somewhere else.

She then mentioned that the department hadn't heard from him for a while, but apparently that was 'nothing abnormal for professors', and she laughed. There were also apparently one or two others, who worked just up the corridor from her that she hadn't seen for years either. Desperate to get off the phone now, Sam made up an excuse to leave saying that a courier just arrived, said "Thanks" and put the phone down quickly.

Doing some more checks he found that there were no phone numbers listed for either the Professor or for the address she had given for him. He had no choice but to get in the car and drive down to see him, a good three hours away in Somerset. So he set off early in the morning the following day.

That was the day Brina's 'mother' was due to come in to notionally clean the house and tidy up, so he left her instructions for looking after Brina, as a joke, which when he re-read the note looked a little stupid and obvious, but at least it was a start. He was sure there would be very little cleaning and tidying going on, but quite a lot of talking, especially with him not there.

The motorway journey was uneventful, and he used the time to work out questions in his head and how to approach the subjects he wanted to discuss without getting too off track.

He arrived at the address at midday, finding himself in a quaint, quiet, old Somerset village. The sign for the house led him along a short gravel road off the village road, which then led to open gates with tall stone walls surrounding the grounds. It was indeed an impressive house; old yellow-grey stone, in an imposing grand style, Georgian or early Victorian, set in large grounds with uncut long grass, with, what looked like, assorted allotments and vegetable areas that were now abandoned.

There were also a few empty chicken huts and pens, all dotted around what had obviously once been formal and impressive organised grounds and buildings.

There was also a fully fenced hard surface green tennis court, which looked well used with the net still taut. Around the front of the house quite a few wind chimes hung aimlessly, and there were numerous odd looking water features and blocks of crystals set on top of tree stumps. There were also carved blocks of wood here and there, together with a few stone Greek statues covered in moss, which had clearly come with the house. He parked the car on the weed covered gravel driveway in an area in front of the house next to the triple garage with wooden doors, and walked up to the entrance porch.

The front door displayed a couple of brass plaques which referenced some organisations or companies, but he couldn't work out what sort they were, or what they represented. He sounded the bell, and a few moments later the door was opened by a bizarre looking tall, late middle-aged woman with bright crimson, bulky, tightly permed hair. She wore a long, flowing, garishly coloured patterned dress, with various bangles, coloured stone necklaces, and earrings. He noticed that she was barefoot and that her arms were mottled with large freckles, as was her pudgy face, which was pale white and had clearly been kept hidden away from the sun.

Her eyes were black and cold in stark contrast to the beaming fake smile she presented him with. The whole impression was a little alarming to Sam; somewhat unexpected and confrontational. She was very different from the description of the Professor's new wife that the woman on the telephone had given him.

He returned the fake smile, and explained that he was looking for 'Professor Stevens', and combined it with a querying look.

Without changing her expression, the woman explained that he no longer lived there having died some four months earlier, taking his own life with an overdose of painkillers. That was it - she stopped right there mid-sentence. Nothing else followed and she then just folded her arms.

Sam was caught off guard. He wasn't expecting that reply at all.

He didn't expect him to be dead, and also this woman clearly wasn't his wife. He didn't know what to say, he was lost for words. He also didn't want to give away anything that he knew, so he just thanked her and left. It was a bit of a surprise to say the least; he had just thought that the Professor would be the one to open the door.

Lost and confused he sat in the car for a few moments trying to think as she still stood in the doorway watching him. He drove down the drive, and out into the village in search of a shop for some food for lunch.

However he was not able to find anything suitable there, so he stopped at the next village and pulled up at a petrol station which had a small store attached. Having filled up with petrol and grabbing a few bags of crisps and a sandwich, still in a in a blurred, lost state, he went to pay.

The young lad at the till was obviously a student working in the holidays as he was absorbed in a book that was resting on the till area. With only four or so customers an hour it was a good job for him, and clearly studying at the same time helped stop the boredom.

The credit card machine was taking ages to verify the payment, so in that time, Sam struck up a conversation with him about the local area. He mentioned the village that he had just come from, and the boy's face gave away a smirk when he mentioned the house.

From him, Sam learned that there was some sort of cult group in the village, and that the lad had heard the news about the Professor from reading the local paper. Apparently the Professor's family, who lived in Shropshire, had all been down for a number of days a few weeks after the Professor had died, asking lots of questions.

It was something to do with a dispute about the Will, and about the family taking the 'cult' to court over it. The boy thought that the Professor's new wife was still at the house from what the report had said.

He didn't know much about the group other than that it operated in several other places in the country, and around the world. Something to do with healing, group meditation that sort of thing, he waved his hands in a generalising motion. Sam gave up waiting for the machine and ended up paying cash, and left the lad a large tip. He was always happy to pay for useful information, and to pay people who took the time to read and learn it.

Returning to his car he ate his crisps and sandwich slowly. Then after a few minutes he went back into the shop to buy a bottle of water which he hadn't thought to get the first time.

Twenty minutes later he was back parked in the driveway to the house. This time he stopped by the open gateway rather than just driving straight in. By the side of the entrance gate he now noticed a plastic leaflet holder with a number of flyers in it. He got out of his car and picked one out and studied it. There were lots of green mystic symbols on the front; stars and ancient font letters, and the whole thing was clearly produced on the cheap.

There were several washy, fluffy minded paragraphs inside, and on the back. He read the words and in his mind he translated what it was saying into a translation in his own words as :- *are you sad, lonely, unloved, misunderstood, lacking purpose, direction and meaning? Then come and join us and we will extract you from the system, lock you away from society, give you something to waste your time believing in, re programme you , take all your money, and get you to suck in similar non-functioning highly suggestive people.*

He was ready for this.

He waited for his heart rate to slow down, drove up the rest of the drive, parked, got out and rang the doorbell again.

The same woman opened it. "Sorry to bother you again," he said before she could speak "but I should have explained before that I was looking for Professor Stevens as I represent the estate of an old colleague and friend of his who passed away last month. His colleague left part of his estate to the Professor in his Will.

Having checked with the office and it would appear that he remarried, and as a result his new wife, who we have in our records as still living at this address, would be entitled to benefit from the Will. Is she here at all?"

Sam had no idea if this story would equate logically to her or not, but he made it sound as convincing as possible. The woman seemed intrigued and confirmed that the wife was indeed there and guardedly showed him inside.

The house made him feel uncomfortable. There were lots of odd things that had been placed in strange places and they didn't quite work. Also the furniture that was there didn't suit the grandeur of the house or its age at all.

There was a small table, with a lamp on it in the hallway, that had a broken leg. He noticed that instead of it being glued or replaced, someone had taped it together and had shoved an old, curled up *National Geographic* magazine under a leg to balance it out. He walked past a doorway and looked into what appeared to be a dining room, with a grand table and chairs covered with dust sheets, on top of which were piles of magazines. In the corner were several piles of modern books in front of an empty wall of shelves. There was a distinct smell of patchouli oil and burning incense sticks, which brought back memories of his University days.

The smell was pleasant occasionally, but having lived along a corridor from someone who practically bathed in the stuff, your nostrils were very quick to baulk at it again. He had a similar problem with Southern Comfort but for completely different reasons.

It was quite shabby inside, and the minimal cleaning was clearly done as an afterthought. The carpet runners were old and Persian style; threadbare in places, covering the dark oak floorboards below. There were little copper bowls filled with water and flower petals here and there, and another joss-stick burning in a holder on a table at the end of the corridor.

He also noticed a picture on the wall of a large group of people standing next to a wooden log house in the midst of palm trees and bushes. It caught his eye as the trees were very similar to the ones he had seen in New Zealand three years back.

Sam recalled a conversation he had had with a guy when he was over there; a Kiwi friend of this man had gone over to the US to work for a few months and she had met, and married, a man there within a very short space of time.

They both returned to her native New Zealand to live but when they got there, the new husband kept 'disappearing' for holidays on the South Island – leaving his bride for weeks at a time. It turned out that she been completely 'taken in' by him and all he had really wanted from her was to get a visa to live in New Zealand.

She eventually found out that her new spouse was part of one of these cults, and he left her permanently a few months after arriving back and went to live with his 'group' and filed for divorce. Then the 'cult's' lawyers took her for half of her money and she had to sell her luxury beach-front house to pay it off and ended up living in a one bedroomed flat in the town.

He couldn't understand what it was about 'cults'. How they were able to bring in the vulnerable people with suggestive minds? He supposed it was only obvious to people on the 'outside' as to what was wrong with it. People on the 'inside' had been through a process, a 'path of enlightenment', designed to lead them into willing programmed subjugation.

He wasn't an expert, but he knew that there was a wide range and type of cults and spiritual groups, ranging from good to bad. Just like basic training in the armed forces, you are signed up and then indoctrinated into their way of thinking, behaving; taken down to the lowest level and brought up again in a controlled way as a follower.

However it all depended on the 'why', the 'what,' and the 'who' that was doing the controlling. That was the key.

He knew that the people who ran those things also varied a lot in personality type and belief. Usually, or in most cases, you are dealing with an individual, or a couple, and occasionally there is a group with a doctrine. Some highly sophisticated, with highly developed mind tools and rationale.

In all cases, the thinking and belief is on a very shallow level, focusing on the wrong ways of the world, the direction of peace, love, companionship, shared emotion and regime. It was all usually fairly harmless; using the need in people to get together with others, and to find an answer to things. Things that they can see aren't right, and helping them to find some higher placatory meaning.

Sometimes, however, they are sucked in to someone else's answer based on limited perception and determined blind belief in their own righteousness and 'highness' and overinflated pompous status, with selfish personal subconscious ambitions. Yet in some cases they were not so harmless for either the individuals involved or the wider perspective.

So people with need are given what they want to find; a different answer, or pathway, from that which has failed them so far. Through a process of rewarding conformance and hypnotic techniques, they eventually, through conditioning, have what they believe they wanted in the first place, and have given away everything that they originally had. All of which they have been shown to be the cause of their problems.

The individuals, couples or groups running these things are in general quite unpleasant characters. Usually with very forceful, yet deficient personalities, who may have very enhanced skills in persuasion due to their personality type. They need to control, influence; your archetypal playground 'bully'.

They are driven by their own fixed views, and are very closed people. Usually trying to bring people into their beliefs to put weight to their own position and perspective, and in so doing justifying it to themselves. This would then allow them to expand out into more and more bizarre concepts from their more stable position.

Conditioning was clearly a very powerful tool with cultism, and to see this conditioning at work, and the results, made Sam think about how much we are conditioned already in 'normal' life, and how hard it is to change from that back to 'normal' again.

But why are these cult figures there? What is their purpose? Were they just there to soak up emotional misfits and naïve people looking for answers and help? These were the more interesting questions.

He had to stop this negativity. He was feeling it everywhere he went; it was not good for him, not to mention a distraction. He had come here for a reason, he just wanted some information, and not to start righting the wrongs of the world.

He realised he had been staring at the picture for quite some time, and he turned and caught the woman's eye again as he looked away from the picture.

Their eyes. You can tell from their eyes Sam thought.

Sam didn't really have time for this, but in this case he needed to get through to something they were hiding. She quizzically gave him a false smile again and gestured for him to follow her down to the end of the long corridor.

Walking through to the back he found himself in a large plant filled conservatory with more oak flooring. It was decorated with crystals and wood carvings on bits of wire. There were three or four wicker chairs and two light brown leather sofas that had seen much better days. Several people were on them either reading books, or were sat on rugs and throw cushions on the floor meditating or talking.

The air was very heavy with the smell of oils, incense sticks, and body odour; it was all very 'ageing 60's'. Atmospheric forest and birdsong music was coming from behind one of the sofas, with the occasional sound of waves and whales thrown in. The ages of the people in the room ranged from early thirties to late fifties and he noticed that there were eight women and two men.

Sam was introduced to the Professor's widow who was sitting on one of the sofas. She was in her early forties, had long dark hair, pale, very striking, and from her face he deduced that she was probably 'on' several drugs. Sam had seen very similar looks on his travels.

He noticed that her hands looked older than the rest of her and that she wore a non-descript white blouse and a long denim skirt. A range of coloured beaded jewellery hung from her slight frame. He sat down next to her on the sofa but she didn't seem to register him at all; she was clearly 'off with the fairies' somewhere.

He introduced himself with the name he was using, and talking to her left side, he explained why he was there, giving the same story that he had told at the front door. He was aware that the woman that had brought him in was still standing in front of them so he looked at her and waited. "Can I get someone to get you some tea?" she asked. "That would be lovely" he replied.

When she had gone he fired off a set of questions to her which was hard going as the answers seemed to come back only as single vague words. So he just asked lots of direct questions looking for 'yes' and 'no' answers.

Despite her state he was managing to get quite a lot of information quite quickly, and when the tea arrived, he gratefully accepted it and placed it on the table by the side of the sofa. He turned to the Professor's widow again and said, "Just so that we can double-check your identity, can I view your passport please?"

The woman looked confused and looked at the red-haired woman for guidance, who then looked flustered for a moment. Then with a nervous laugh she said "Ah, I am sure we can find that somewhere" and walked off.

Over the next several minutes Sam discovered a lot. After the Professor's death she had by default inherited everything, and then given and signed over everything she had to the cult, including the house. Then she had burnt or destroyed everything of his, including his notes and books. She was told that they 'weren't true to the faith', and so it all had to go.

Months before he died, he had tried to get her to leave the group, but failed, and he eventually had got depressed and had taken some pills.

When he died her friends in the cult had moved into this house to help her out, to 'support' her in her 'time of need'.

It was sad hearing these words and he could only imagine the heartache that the guy must have been through; to have fallen deeply in love with this beautiful younger woman only to be tormented by her puppeteers in his old age. Manipulating him through her like a rag doll. *Why hadn't he just taken her away?* Perhaps he just ran out of energy and will.

It was clear now that everything of him had been removed, taken over, or deleted, and 'they' had covered themselves very well. He was really now just talking to a shell of a woman, a pawn, and he wouldn't get anything more from her, or anyone else here. It was very frustrating.

He left his sweet smelling herbal tea untouched on the side, thanked the woman, and got up and walked out. In the corridor he was met by the red-haired woman who had shown him in and she looked expectantly at him, clutching her hands at her stomach holding the passport.

She handed it to him, and he examined it. "Is everything in order? Do you need anything else?" she asked. "No, that all seems to be in order, I will go through the details with my office and we will get the paperwork sorted in the next few weeks" he said casually and handed it back.

He walked with her to the front door, and was just going to walk straight out, letting her think she had 'won', but somehow he couldn't just do that. His mind remembered the Professor, and the people he had seen there in the conservatory, and it made him furious. The more he thought about it the angrier he grew.

Even as he turned his back to her on his way out he could 'see' her in his mind, just standing there in the doorway, smirking behind him. Another thing he didn't like was that she smelt odd. He felt like turning around and just punching her in the face. Instead he began to just visualise doing so in his mind. All of a sudden an image of Brina came into his mind, looking concerned, almost intervening. He was still angry though, and he felt renewed energy pulsing through him, fuelled by adrenaline. He decided that he had to do *something*. He couldn't just walk away and not do anything like some coward.

As he walked out onto the gravel drive, he turned to face her as she stood in the doorway behind him. Her plump features were blank, characterless, indifferent and almost feral.

He fixed her directly with his eyes, and looked straight into the depths of her soul. He saw everything she was, his bright dark green eyes burning into those cold, black, dilated shark eyes. Within a second she realised he was a 'fake', and her expression changed from a sudden shock to a 'so what are you going to do about it?' smug smile.

Then a few seconds later, what colour there was in her face disappeared instantly, her smile went, her eyes widened in fear, and she 'knew'. She could not look away, her jaw slackened and it only took a few seconds more, but it was done, whatever it was that needed to happen.

Something in him had taken over, like a program, he had communicated something.

She blinked once, and then he turned away.

He walked purposefully to his car, and he could still feel the woman staring at him as he drove off down the driveway. He left with a cold feeling in his heart, and a bitterness in his soul.

He didn't know what had gone on between 'him' and 'her' but it was necessary, and very much one-way.

A little knowledge could be a dangerous thing in the hands of fools, but with it comes responsibility, and accountability. She may have naively been doing what she thought was right, or felt justified in doing. All of which were all in line with what she thought were correct views and beliefs, but he saw it differently.

Anyway she seemed to have 'got the message', whatever that was, and whatever went with it.

On returning home that evening he spent several more hours on the Internet again, and he worked into the next day. This time he was being much more methodical and selective. He concentrated more on the scientific side, looking into more research papers and academic discussions over the last fifty years on the psychological side from people such a Jung, stemming into more modern day theories and concepts.

It was all very interesting, but lacked any substantive evidence or direction, like a join-the-dots puzzle with only half the dots. Good ideas would be mixed in with other things from the spiritual, or the occult, to just plain weird. There were plenty of references to 'strange things and happenings' that couldn't be explained; abilities that some people had, and things that had happened in the animal world.

But nobody seemed to have had the sort of experience that he had had first-hand recently. There were plenty of websites which encompassed a whole range of spiritual and paranormal phenomena, from UFO's, ghosts, enlightenment, to crop circles. Everything seemed to be sort of superficial and all held varying opinions, attitudes, and religions.

Enough 'stuff' to fill a million computer hard drives. There didn't seem to be anything on 'relaxing quite happily on holiday one minute and twenty minutes later being pulled back from near death by your girlfriend, with the answers to Life, The Universe and Everything smashed into your brain'.

Probably not interesting enough, he thought.

It was like discussing the idea of 'burning coal in a fire' to someone; trying to work out how fire worked. Explaining it was hot, what it looked like, what coal was made from, and how it burned, and the sensation. Or discovering the quick answer by having your face shoved into the burning coals. The words to describe the experience just aren't there.

The reality of it made him quite angry again. That was the difference, there was a substantial gap between what he was reading and what he knew and couldn't articulate. One was safe and soft, and the other was hard and not. All these soft theories and conjectures were just that, with very little real evidence, or of being capable of taking that next step, the 'what if it's actually true, and the bloody hell consequences'. With what he knew he was able to eliminate a lot of the chaff; things he knew were total rubbish. Not that it was related to what he was looking for but, 'crop circles' - he had even met the guys that did some of them in a pub in Norfolk a few years back, they had used simple wooden boards to make them, and were in partnership with the farmer to charge tourists to see them.

Ghosts? Well he knew what caused that, but it wasn't what everyone seemed to be thinking, and it wasn't weird at all, quite obvious really, just information, and not at all 'spooky'.

There were so many 'unexplained' things that he now had explanations for in his head, and they were mostly fairly simple and obvious when you knew the answer. He had links and structures in his mind, and was able to contextualise them with other concepts, and the science to explain the connections.

What he was more confused about was why not more had been done or was being done investigating certain things, and why people hadn't explored the commonality between these 'unexplained' events. Like for example 'seeing' ghosts; there were many debates about whether they existed or not, and millions of stories, but nobody seemed to have taken it a step further and looked at the overall picture to build up a detective profile of the where, the when, or the who, or to ask the very obvious questions.

If several complete strangers can 'see' the same ghost in the same place, doing the same thing, time and time again, why weren't the alarm bells ringing with the Army? Why aren't all the top scientists called in to try to work out what is going on, test it out with every medium and spiritualist on the planet to build up a complete picture with theories and possibilities?

Why had there been no psychological tests and profiles of all those who had seen them? Why do people never see ghosts in colour? Why are they always by something solid like stones or ground or buildings rather than high in the air or far out over the sea? Exploring the link?

But no, the information is just swept into the quirky filing cabinet, with the odd photographer always trying to capture something that is impossible to do with a camera, the odd sensationalist documentary, and scientists looking in the wrong direction.

Sam now knew that ghosts were just shared information associated by surrounding reference matter that your brain and body could sense and convert into an image or feeling or motion scene. It was just information and energy stored as a snapshot from a previous time event, dramatic or not, lodged or associated in what was around it with time dimensional independence, with the information projected through its point of origin.

A resonance wave of the energy and information stored. Many number of things could cause it. Some people were very sensitive to it, or that specific collective signature, and others were not. They could receive the information in and their brains would fill in the gaps with sights, sound, or other senses; even though these in themselves weren't picking anything up.

But surely someone else must have worked that all out by now or at least come up with that concept even though it was impossible to test yet? It was obvious that something definitely wasn't right; somehow there was something odd going on, stopping the obvious from being worked out. But why?

There were a lot of books to sift through that showed wide ranging ideas on the spiritual to the psychic to the scientific, psychological, and nature. Most of the book summaries that he read pertained to a lot of different ideas, and suggested concepts that hinted at possible directions.

However they mostly spent a lot of time elaborating on the unexplainable facts, linked through to other peoples work as reference, and then they came up with some loose theory that guessed at a possible solution to explain the phenomena, only to miss pulling the rip cord before hitting the ground.

He did get some ideas that helped, but in general it was all quite loose and lacking real direction, like reaching for a bubble in the air only for it to always move out of reach.

It was like individual academics or groups thereof had pieces of the picture in their own fields, which they clung to protectively, and went into great detail and complexity in that area when they published their books, but no more; no joining the dots.

Some people had tried to connect a few pieces to form a coherent context of how something worked or what there was, but that always seemed to leave other areas unexplained or lacking in definition.

There was no overall complete picture, no cohesive workable model or solution that made sense. Nothing answered all the questions, solved the big problems, or accounted for what had gone on in the past. But working through the different areas, his mind would start to connect what was in his head and integrate what was there into a more rational and technical picture; one that made sense, although very complex and vast.

It was useful, at least he knew where he stood and what was going on, but he still didn't have anyone he could talk to that would be in the same place or level.

He had to stop early in the evening; his head was starting to ache and he had a pain at the top of his skull, he felt like Isaac Newton when the apple had landed on his head - although in his case, it felt more like it was a thick metal rod balanced end on.

Brina was still out of action. He tried again the following day with a more positive perspective, and looked at shared dreams and experiences. Most of the academic work was very high level, and mixed in with other concepts.

He tried listening to some of the audio discussions, but found that they were just rambling for the most part, self-important pompous academics, fond of using unnecessarily long words. They just seemed to be competing with one another, trying to grab credibility by including as many concepts into one as they were able to get away with.

So he concentrated on looking for people who had been commenting on discussion groups, and asking questions and looking for answers in the same way that he was. Not the 'I have had this strange thing happen to me', 'I have seen this ghost,' 'My dog does this - what does it mean?' types, but direct, knowing enquiries focused on 'why?' rather than 'what?', and those with an edge of panic in them.

That was when he stumbled on a German guy called Max Ehrlichmann.

He seemed to be asking very in-depth questions, similar to the ones that he would have asked. They were from several years back, and given in quite a reserved, cautious way, yet very specific and informed, as if he worked out something and was trying to see if anyone else had worked out the same thing too.

The questions ranged from psychology to spirituality and religion. The answers that he had been given were very general and were full of ramblings, or they took religious slants. He had seemed to be getting more and more frustrated and then it had all stopped about two years earlier.

However the questions he had asked seemed to imply that he knew a lot more than he was letting on; it seemed that he had just been trying to work things out or find others who knew what he did but at a much deeper level.

Sam did some more searching for his name and eventually found a news article from a local German paper in Ehrlichmann's home area. Sam used the browser tools to translate it, and managed to roughly work out what was being said in combination with his limited ability in the German language.

There was an article relating to a house sale which Max had

held where he had tried to auction many things off. There was also an earlier article condemning a new road bypass, and it referred to Ehrlichmann and detailed what had happened to him as a result of a compulsory purchase of his house. It mentioned the situation with his English speaking mother that he was looking after, and the fact that she had to go into a care home, and he had been diagnosed with Schizophrenia a long time ago.

There was also some mention of problems with his company or business but it was hard to understand it all. He was clearly quite affluent, and was probably in his late fifties and had never married. Then the information just dried up abruptly, and stopped altogether.

Not knowing very much about Schizophrenia, Sam looked it up on the web and looked at in in some detail. *How strange that it was such a difficult word to spell.* He was concerned for a while that he may be suffering from some form of it too at one point, but was quite relieved to find that he wasn't after looking at the symptoms and condition. Despite having all the tests a few years back for everything, it was the first time that doubt had entered his mind, but he was sure that he wasn't bloody mad, just bloody angry.

There were several variances of schizophrenia too, from paranoid to delusional, and there was lots of information on diagnosis and treatments, but not too much on the cause. However, it did highlight some interesting points, and they related to some concepts that he did know the answer to. The common treatments used to help with it raised a few hairs on the back of his neck when he read them.

Sam decided to go and track Ehrlichmann down. He did some more research and made a few quick phone calls to the estate agent in Germany, and eventually finally got his location pinpointed to a PO Box address in a remote village on the East coast of Paxos in Greece. It seemed that this was definitely where he now lived. Aside from this he seemed to have totally vanished from the face of the earth.

The next day, having been away for three days, Brina's mother came back again by taxi. She had arrived on the train some half an hour earlier and Sam had forgotten to pick her up from the station. She didn't seem too upset but went straight into the house and let Sam pay the driver.

She had been a model in the mid-60's and had moved to the UK from Slovenia to take on work for an agency in London.

This is where she had met Brina's father at some party. She was tall, slim and elegant with an air of breeding, 'posh spoken', but it was all put on, which showed through when she was either angry or had a few drinks, and had relaxed.

She loved a drama, but not a crisis, so loved the idea of being able to share such with Brina, and fuss over her, as long as she wasn't actually really ill. If Brina was really ill, then 'her daughter' would be 'annoying', 'inconvenient', and it would be too awkward for her to look after at that particular time.

Brina had not spoken much about her father. Sam knew that he had died many years earlier. He had owned a large estate with a few farms which had all been sold off, and divided up between the family when he died.

This had left Brina's mother comfortably well off, but not as comfortable as she would have liked. They had clearly been very much in love, and her mother spoke very fondly of him when he was mentioned.

All Brina would say about his death was that it was the insecticide sprays that killed him, something to do with heavy metal poisoning. It was an area that Sam was aware she was very sensitive and defensive about, and so he didn't ask too many questions.

'Her mother' was obviously keen to get Sam out of the house as soon as she had arrived; she was and always had been, quite flirtatious with Sam. She was the sort of person that was OK if you were alive, happy, rich, good looking, and interesting, or if you were dead. But not so good if you were in the middle somewhere, or heading downwards. Then she was very busy.

Being nice to her didn't seem to make any difference; you were either what she wanted, or in this case what she wanted for her daughter, or you weren't.

It was very obvious, and very unambiguous.

Luckily for Sam he was in the clear.

CHAPTER 6 - THE HERMIT

Having booked his plane ticket to Athens, he packed a rucksack with a few clothes, his leather organiser and a few other essentials. Brina, despite her discomfort, had got out of bed and checked off what he had packed, and then added twice as much in other 'essentials' that he hadn't thought of. It was an indication of how absent-minded he had become, and how preoccupied he was with thinking of other things rather than of day-to-day living.

He had always had a lot of common sense, and was quite used to being efficient and self-sufficient, but lately his mind just kept wandering off, and he would spend several minutes just staring out of the window; which is what he was doing now.

He had even forgotten some simple basics like sun tan lotion and his razor. It was just as well then that Brina had remembered to put in a battery operated shaver and a 'hand-luggage friendly' sized liquid sunscreen. She had become very attentive towards him now, checking him over, and surrounding him in a protective, mindful focus, like he was her responsibility or ward.

He continued to stare out of the window at the early morning sunrise. Just thinking, letting thoughts roll in and out of his head. He heard a gentle cough behind him a few minutes later; Brina had been watching him, but hadn't wanted to distract him.

She just was trying to help remind him that he had to be on his way, and that she had sorted everything out for him. He smiled at her apologetically. "You know you are behaving like an expectant father, don't you?" she asked and she handed him his flight rucksack with a smile.

He did remember to kiss her as he left the house, which in his current mind state was good, and she acknowledged his departure by brushing his jacket lapel free from hairs with the palm of her hand. She hadn't really asked him about what he was doing or where he was going, she just knew he had to do *something*, and she was sure that it didn't involve any other women so that was 'ok'. Just so long as he was safe.

He took a taxi to the airport. He would have normally have driven there, and parked in one of the remote outdoor car parks, where the planes nearly skimmed the tops of the cars as they landed. Where occasionally, if you were lucky, the shuttle bus picked you up to go to the terminals, if it wasn't raining.

However he didn't want to have to think and drive, or worry about where he had to be, so he took the easy option.

With just hand luggage it was much easier to hop around and about, and before long he was on the plane. The trip seemed to take no time at all and was uneventful. Then onto Athens, which was hot and dusty and the air was very short on anything useful, and full of plenty that wasn't. From the Arrival gate he went straight to the travel desk, and looked at the ferry timetable to Naxos as he had originally planned.

The whole setup looked quite complex, more so than on the diagram he had seen on the Internet, and there seemed to be quite a few cancellations and delays being shown on the board. The ferry that he had wanted to catch was not even listed.

The alternative was a local flight with Olympic Airways, but that wasn't until the morning, so he booked a slot on the first flight out in the morning, found the nearest local transit hotel, and checked himself in.

He had forgotten to pack his alarm clock despite Brina putting it on the side for him before he left. He must have forgotten to pick it up, so in the end he had relied on the hotel wake-up system to get him up early, which failed to work.

Luckily his flight wasn't until later in the morning so he had enough time, but the shower and coffee were a bit rushed. The whole thing was frustrating. He had just assumed that everything would be easy and simple for him to get from 'A' to 'B'.

He hadn't done enough checking or working things out and had left in a rush, and now he was paying for it in lost time and hassle, which was very unlike him.

With all the long haul travelling he did he was very much used to just being in big planes so the short thirty minute hop to Naxos was a novelty, as was the plane, with the turbulence and exotic landing adding to the 'excitement'.

By the time he finally arrived in Naxos he had already decided that going back on the ferry seemed like the more favourable option. Getting out of the small plane out onto the open airfield, he was instantly confronted with dry, hot, richly scented air from the olive trees, plants and herbs.

In Athens it was hot and dusty and just somewhere to travel through, like most cities. Here though, he was at an end point of a journey, so his senses gave him all the information on what was here, smells, noise, temperature, so that he could assess it all. A sort of 'right you are here now so take it all in and work out what is going on' moment.

He had been to many of the larger Greek islands before, but always on holiday, and had been relaxed rather than on a mission, so it caught him off-guard, this sudden unexpected transition in a small plane, and the feeling made him disorientated as he made his way to the small terminal block along with the other passengers.

Unable to get a hire car from anywhere, he eventually managed to pick up a dusty old taxi with an elderly, equally weatherworn, driver. He was grey-haired, unshaven, with a sweat stained grey and white shirt and brown trousers that were too short, and battered old trainers.

Sam remembered to sit in the front of the taxi so that he didn't get ill on the winding roads, and also so that he wouldn't get treated as a tourist. The driver seemed adamant that he was going to be a tourist anyway, and pointed out all the features along the way with rambling well-worn anecdotes and historical facts obviously cribbed from a tour guide cousin.

All the while the array of objects dangling from the rear view mirror, and the ornaments perched along the dashboard, swayed to and fro with every hairpin and pothole, up and down the narrow mountain roads.

The landscape was very beautiful with picture book blue sea and white beaches on the coast that contrasted dramatically with the steep angular hills, rough terrain, and olive groves inland. On this particular journey he wished he had been in the boot instead of the passenger seat so that he didn't have to watch the driving, or listen to the Zorba style 'music for tourists' on the heat-stretched tape grinding its way through the cassette player.

The driver pointed out a number of the ancient sites, and the mountains and cave where Zeus had been when he visited the island. Zeus had presumably, very sensibly in Sam's opinion, abandoned it and left long before taxis were invented.

Sam couldn't quite work out why the German guy had chosen to come here. Yes it was very remote, but quite touristy none the less. If he had really wanted to get away from it all Sam could think of a lot more suitable places; maybe it was just somewhere he had visited when he was a child when it had been less busy, and he had just wanted to get away safely somewhere to a place he knew he had once been happy in.

The Germans tended to be a lot more intrepid in exploring than other cultures, but it did seem odd.

The taxi pulled up to the village on the East coast and the driver worked out the cost on his antique calculator. There seemed to be a lot more button pressing than was really required, and Sam guessed that the figure would be based on his appearance more than the numbers on the screen, if in fact the thing had a working screen, or indeed any batteries in it at all.

The village was small; around fifty houses with just two shops visible, both of which just seemed to be for the tourist buses that stopped twice a day. There were the usual assortment of standard village constituent elements; the dog asleep on the dusty path, a couple of signposts that contradicted one another, a few advertising posters on walls with graffiti scrawled all over them, a mailbox and telephone, but not much evidence of actual people.

His driver hadn't driven off after he had been paid. He had just stepped out in front of the taxi in the layby, and was now sitting on the bonnet putting a roll-up together, ready to light up, in no hurry to get back.

However he may have just been waiting on the off chance that Sam had suddenly realised that he had come to the wrong place. Sam looked around and over the rugged land to get a feel for where he was. There were a few olive groves on the hills and odd shacks here and there, along with a few dirt side tracks.

There was one main road going down the slopes of the hill to the sea a mile or so away which had a beach sign alongside it that was pointing downwards to the ground.

It was very hot now, and humid, and the cicadas were in full harmony in the trees and bushes.

He walked around the back of one of the tourist shops to the narrow street behind in which there was a small rough general store which seemed to incorporate the village post office and everything else that the locals may ever need. Considering the space inside it was quite well organised and functional; outside was laid out with boxes of brightly coloured fruit and vegetables on racks.

However, unlike the tourist shops, there was no air-conditioning, so the smells of the food and herbs were quite prevalent and it all made him quite hungry. At the back of the store was a small counter, and a mail office section, with some parcels piled on the floor and several padded mail bags.

He couldn't see any sign of individual post boxes so he guessed they must be either elsewhere or that it was all just treated the same in one pile and given to someone to deliver.

There was a dark haired Greek boy of about seventeen, dressed in a shirt and trousers, who was sitting at the counter tapping messages into his mobile phone with one thumb with practised efficiency. The rest of his body looked very bored, and slouched back into the wooden chair, while his mouth chewed on something absent-mindedly.

Sam picked out a small bottle of water and shoved a few apples into a paper bag. He stepped up to the counter and placed them down. The boy took his eyes off the mobile, did a calculation in his head, and said something in Greek.

Sam knew a reasonable range of Greek words to get him by but he didn't understand, so he explained in Greek that he was English, and that he didn't understand.

The boy brightened up immediately, and sat up and asked him in perfect English for the four Euros. Then he went on to explain he was studying English at college, which was going to enable him to help run his father's tourist business in the area. Then he went on to tell him more about his life, ambitions, his girlfriend, and what he wanted to do with his business in the future.

It was quite a pleasant surprise to Sam; this kid was surprisingly articulate, motivated and smart. His initial posture and attitude seemed to be completely at odds with what he was talking to him about now, it was a complete transformation of character.

So much for first impressions, thought Sam.

It was great to see a lad with so much enthusiasm, even if it was being used mainly to just practise his language skills. So unexpected too, not the usual response of not being bothered with anything or the 'whatever' attitude, which seemed to be the 'norm' these days.

Playing along with his enthusiasm Sam got into an extended discussion with him, eventually explaining that he had come to visit an old German friend that he knew lived in the area, but he wasn't sure of the address, just the PO Box. He expanded that he was supposed to meet his friend in the village but that he had arrived several hours early.

Sam went on to describe his 'friend' from the description and picture in the paper he had seen and the boy's face flashed with recognition.

"Yes, yes, I know where he live, he live down on coast on his own, I drop his food and letters to him each week with my brother, we not much see him around the village. He very strange man, the people in the village they call him erimit."

"Erimit?" asked Sam.

"Yes it same in English I think, erimit."

Sam thought for a second – 'hermit' - it suddenly clicked.

"Can you show me where he lives and I can go there rather than waiting until later, I am happy to pay you say twenty Euros?"

After a few moments the boy opened the back door of the shop and shouted up the stairs, and then had a shouting match with what Sam guessed sounded like his sister upstairs. Eventually she came down still shouting and waving her hands at him. She looked to be about fifteen, but could clearly fight her corner like someone twice her age. As soon as she saw Sam, she stopped shouting and smiled at him, and pulled her long black hair away from her face. She nodded to him, smiled again and said 'Hello' politely in Greek, and then turned to her brother and laid into him with renewed vigour.

Sam was sure that in a few years she would make someone a 'wonderful wife'. A few moments later the boy said "Come, we go" and walked to the door. The girl, now sulking, planted herself in the chair along with her storm cloud face.

He led Sam up the street at the back to a small, white, rusty van, and gestured him to the passenger door. Sam opened it and waited for the boy to pick up all the larger items that were filling the front seat and throw them into the back, before getting in.

It clearly didn't matter if you were young or old, the driving here was pretty much the same, and Sam held on to the strap above the side window to gain some sort of futile reassurance.

They headed off down the rough side road in a bouncing rumble surrounded by clouds of dust.

On the way the boy explained that the 'erimit' had had a special house built a few years ago that had been delivered in four large truckloads and a couple of containers.

All of it had been put together by a team of German builders in just two weeks. The team had been in the village several times, and in the shop, and he had heard that the house was specially designed to be made without metal in it at all - not even any nails - just wood and glass and stone, but apparently they had done a few over the years, and they just took longer to put it together as they had to use wooden pegs instead of nails and that sort of thing.

It was refreshing to see the boy talking to him as if he had known him for years, and his grasp of the English language was amazing especially with some of the more technical words. He just needed more practice to improve the flow and structure.

Sam had found that generally everywhere you went, if you could get over that initial barrier of being tagged as a tourist by the locals, you would quickly find that people were very much the same underneath in the way they interacted with you.

You almost had to break the spell of people 'acting' for tourists. Make them see that you were a normal person. That they didn't have to play the tourist music, show you things they thought you might want to see, feed you the food that you were supposed to eat, or try and fleece you at every opportunity.

But then in some countries that was just a way of life. It was a ripple effect too - as soon as you looked like you were talking normally to someone, and you didn't look like a tourist you suddenly weren't.

However in some places, looking and behaving like a tourist also had it advantages, at least you could escape without having to listen to a whole list of their problems, which usually started after about twenty minutes when the pleasantries were out of the way.

After driving for about a mile they turned off the road onto a rough track to the right which went over the brow of a hill and down to the coast the other side. It descended through an olive grove, and then wound down through bushes and trees in zigzags to the rough coastline below.

The road then turned into a winding grass pathway just wide enough to get the van through, and then out over a field that had a herd of goats in it, where they stopped in a cloud of dust next to a water trough at a gate at the far side.

Getting out, they climbed over the locked gate and walked down the track on the other side which opened out into another grass field which had circular tracks all over it, to a fence and gate with woods on the other side. Looking around and down over the trees he could see that beyond the woods was a large peninsular out into the sea with a rough rocky coastline around it.

There were a few signs on the gate in a number of languages warning of **'Dogs'** and **'Private Land'** and **'No Entry'**, in both Greek and English.

There was also a large American style mailbox on one of the fence posts which looked very out of place, it had a small red plastic flag turned up, indicating that there was something in there that needed posting. Below it, and on the other side of the fence, there was a large dark green cool box with a couple of rocks placed on its lid.

The boy pointed to the cool box. "On Wednesdays that is where I leave the food and the other things on his list which he leaves in the mailbox the day before. My brother picks it up when he delivers the mail, then he gets his bill every month in the mailbox, which he pays by cheque in an envelope. We sometimes see him walking about, but he doesn't talk much, he often uses the shed in the wood there."

Sam looked to where the boy was pointing down the dusty track, and saw a large sturdy wooden shed with piles of logs stacked against the side in the dry grass, and a few other items that he couldn't see clearly, set into the woods. Sam gave the boy thirty Euros, and said he would see him later.

The boy gave him a small card with his mobile number on, and told him to call if he needed anything, again Sam was impressed.

He was the sort of lad you would want to hire on the spot if he were back home. The boy tucked the folded notes into his top pocket, got back in his van and drove off up the hill, followed by a long billowing cloud of dust. Sam looked back at the scene below him down the track, taking it in, and deciding what he would do next.

Getting over the gate was not as easy a task as he thought it would be. There was barbed wire along the top, and the fence either side was waist-high in barbed wire as far as he could see. It followed along the open fields, and probably went far beyond to the rocky cliffs. By carefully positioning his feet and placing his rucksack over the top he eased himself over without causing any permanent damage.

Instead of taking the obvious route down along the disused track, he picked his way through the woods to the shed. The door was securely locked with a heavy padlock and so he looked in through the window at the side of the shed. Inside there was an assortment of woodworking tools and a couple of axes, an old metal stove , some rusting fire irons and a whole selection of other metal objects.

Even on the wall on a board there were things like scissors, fish hooks and blades. It looked very practical and organised, and what was there was quality, and all the best German brands.

Sam remembered his conversation with the boy about there being no metal in the house, and realised that this was clearly where the German stored the essential metal items in one place, away from where he lived.

Walking down the track, the trees stopped as he ventured downhill to an open grass ridge line with steep rocks on either side stretching out to the sea. The track followed the thirty foot wide ridge for around thirty yards before opening out again to form a large peninsular, which was almost an island in its own right, in front of him. There weren't any beaches that he could see and it looked pretty inaccessible from the sea, rocks on all sides, and just this one track.

The woods he had been through covered about three acres and the island peninsular in front of him covered about another five or six, with a couple of small rough sharp edged hills in the middle surrounded by rough, rocky landscape.

He could see the house in-between the two hills, single storey with a long pitched roof. He hadn't been too sure what sort of house he would find there; in his mind he had envisaged something ranging from a gothic mansion to an eco-mud mound with a single door, like something suited to a *Hobbit*, which probably stemmed from an image in his mind generated of the schizophrenic Gollum.

What Sam couldn't work out was how the hell they had managed to get the trucks and equipment and lorries down there and along the ridge, but then he knew from some of the commercial infrastructure projects he had been involved with that these guys were pretty good at getting things like that done, it made things more exciting, and generally they wouldn't have even started it if they knew they couldn't do it.

He walked on further just to the end of the ridge and stopped in his tracks as a dog ran out of the woods. It was a large, mixed breed type of dog with brown and black markings. It didn't bark but ran straight towards him and fixed its eyes on him.

Sam looked around for a tree, but there wasn't anything close by that he could climb up. He knew not to run, so he stood still and tried to not to look threatening, or like lunch.

As it approached, the dog slowed down and stopped, went down on its haunches a few yards away, and waited, focusing on him.

So they waited for several minutes just looking at each other, like a Mexican standoff, the only motion coming from the dog panting in the heat.

Two or three minutes later a tall, well-built man appeared from the track through the woods up from the peninsular, carrying a shotgun in front of him.

He stopped about twenty yards from Sam and the dog looked back at him to check with his master.

Sam recognised the man from the photographs he had seen, but he seemed much more weatherworn now, older looking, and bent with rough hands, grey hair and a beard. He was wearing a lumberjack style shirt and thick brown trousers, a wide brimmed black leather hat, and was, oddly, barefoot.

The German said several words in Greek and pointed his gun at Sam and waved it in the direction of the track back up the hill. The dog looked back at Sam to see what he would do, it was on its guard now, and didn't move.

Sam had excellent eyesight, and he stared closely at the gun, and noticed that something that wasn't quite right; the barrel was too glossy, as if it were painted, and the holes at the end seemed to be blocked a little way in, ending just a few inches inside. Sam walked several feet up to the dog and put the back of his hand to the dog's nose.

The dog smelt his hands for a few seconds before rolling over on its back to allow him to rub its tummy, to which Sam obliged.

The German shouted again this time in German and then in English too. But Sam ignored him and concentrated on the dog, and then said in German "He isn't a very good guard dog is he? It's as if he knows I am OK, and that I am here for good reason." Or at least that's what Sam hoped he had said. His German wasn't brilliant.

"Who are you and what do you want?" came the reply in perfect English, which indicated that Sam's German accent and vocabulary wasn't up to having a further conversation in it.

"Max, I have come to talk to you, and to get some answers from you. Maybe even provide you with some too. You aren't the easiest person in the world to find you know?"

"What did you do to my dog? He has never done that before" Max asked.

Sam ignored the question and walked over to the German who raised his gun at him.

"I don't think you will do much harm with that, unless you intend to hit me over the head with it. It's made of wood isn't it?"

The German stared at him for several moments and then lowered his wooden replica gun.

"Who are you?" he repeated. Sam introduced himself and shook Max's hand, and then went into some detail about himself, about what he had read and why he was there.

As he went on he could gradually see the man's posture relax and his face started to look more interested. After twenty minutes or so, he had changed into a different person, his persona had altered completely; he was now warm and pleasant, and to Sam it now almost felt as if he had known him forever.

The German then unexpectedly shook Sam's hand again and gestured towards the house. As he turned he said something like "Useless" in German to the dog, and he waved his fist at it and the dog lowered his head and looked suitably embarrassed.

Sam followed Max along the path through some sparse trees and into an open, dry, rough grass area of about two acres that had been cleared of trees. Sam saw that there was a well and a dozen or so large vegetable plots, a few goats and some pigs in a sty. There were a couple of very small fields that had been fenced off which seemed to include a variety of young fruit trees that didn't seem to be producing much, and some crops, most of which had died off having presumably been planted in the wrong soil or in an incorrect climate. There was certainly no sign of fruit.

It was like a miniature farm, or one he had created from ideas in a book rather than a practical working one. So the self-sufficiency drive was a 'work in progress' but explained the continuing need for the cool box of food.

In the middle of the cleared land was the house which was very impressive, angular and modern. Built obviously from factory-made wood panels, expertly finished and assembled in tinted glass and stunningly beautiful hardwood beams.

He wasn't sure what type of wood it was, but it looked as if it would be there in another hundred years. The roof was long and pitched almost to the ground with the ends open in glass walls. It looked state-of-the-art with beautiful architectural features all around.

There were two brick chimneys coming up in the middle and a large concrete water tank in the ground at the back presumably to collect rainwater from the roof. Through the window at the end he could see into a large, tall, open living space that led to further rooms at the back, and he could just make out an upstairs too. Inside he could see a range of furniture, some very large garish modern art oil paintings, and a mixture of bookcases and other wooden objects.

There were a few things with the house that didn't seem right though, but he couldn't quite put his finger on it or work out what they were from here.

The boy in the shop was right about the metal. There was none here. It was all kept away in the shed. Everything had been well thought out to avoid the need for it. On the sunny side of the house there was a stone patio area with a wooden table, chairs, and a lounger.

To the side of the patio was a large brick built stove or oven, like the ones bakers used, with a white chimney. Next to it was a worktop with a cupboard underneath. It had a dark marble-like surface with a square ceramic sink built into it, but there were no taps.

It wasn't what Sam was expecting at all. In his mind, hermits lived in caves or little shabby wooden shacks, or in mud thatched huts; they had hair down to their knees, limited interpersonal skills, and questionable hygiene habits. If this was life as a hermit, it had been seriously undersold.

The German walked up to the house and swung aside a big glass wood-framed door on plastic runners. He then gestured for Sam to go in. It was surprisingly cool inside and fresh, light and airy with a warm, calm feeling and it was remarkably quiet.

There were plenty of heavy thick books along the walls in tall, carved, oak bookcases; several hundred at least, not the sort of well organised leather bound, uniform height and antique effect ones you would normally expect; not ones that were just for show, just there to impress; but a random mixture of hardbacks, tatty paperback loose magazines, academic papers, and several with covers missing or sticky notes stuck to them.

This was clearly a working library, with a mixture of fiction and heavy duty spiritual, religious, both Western and Eastern, and psychology literature, and all in various languages.

He scanned some of the titles but they didn't make a lot of sense to him, although a few of the authors he recognised vaguely, including some German psychologists.

Looking about the open plan room, here and there were oddly combined mismatching pieces of wooden furniture, including a rocking chair, a few coffee tables, a writing desk, and a couple or ordinary wooden fiddleback chairs which had various papers stacked randomly on their seats.

It was a bit of a chaotic mess, with loose magazines and books everywhere on the floor. There was also a jumble of ornaments, small cardboard boxes packed with items brought from somewhere else, all now with nowhere to go.

A healthy layer of dust covered things here and there, especially on the 'not walked along' pathways and on some of the other shelves.

In the middle of the room, around the fireplace, was a comfortable looking pair of old, dark brown leather sofas. The fireplace was stone, built with a brick chimney going up through to the timber roof at the top, with piles of roughly cut wood in stacks to the side. It looked as though it hadn't been used for some time and was probably only needed for a few weeks in the winter, if at all, and was probably built more for effect than for practical use.

The walls were cream coloured, rough and unpainted, and had the occasional expansion crack running down to the floor which was made from heavy, solid, hardwood boards. They looked as if they had originally been sanded smooth and waxed, but now were quite dull in the main walk areas from dirty feet.

There were no curtains or blinds in the house that Sam could see, and with the large expanse of windows this made it feel very open even though the windows were heavily tinted to help reduce the sun's glare.

At the back of the room there were three entranceways on the ground floor, and two upstairs on a landing at the top of the wooden stairs in the middle. It was certainly very well designed, and the quality of the craftsmanship was outstanding.

However the modern design of the house was at odds with the old rustic look of the furnishings and everything else that was in it. Looking through the doorways to the back of the house, the rooms at the bottom appeared to be very basic; one with a big farmhouse style solid wood table and bench and a tiled floor, and from what he could see, shelves stacked with food items.

The other was a washroom with a toilet in it and a couple of filled plastic water buckets on the floor. The rooms upstairs, he assumed, were the bedrooms, but he couldn't see up and in from where he was standing.

Completing his first scan around, and having decided how much he liked the place, he now set about working out what was wrong with it. Having been forewarned about the lack of metal he was now looking for anywhere where there should be some - fireplace, hinges, joints, handles, wires - just out of curiosity. But there was none.

At that point he also realised that there were no electrical sockets at all either, no electricity and no lights. There were wooden candle holders here and there on small tables and shelves and a few more were randomly fixed on the walls. There was no TV, fridge, stereo, washing machine or dishwasher.

He smiled quietly to himself as he visualised Brina's mother being shown around here, and being introduced to it as her new home, and he pictured the look of sheer horror and disgust on her face as things slowly dawned on her.

He followed the German through to the back kitchen room with the large table and benches. It was much cooler in here, and darker, surprisingly so. The food on the shelves looked to be mostly fresh, in containers or covered, but there were several packets, bottles, and boxes too. There was a preparation table in the corner and there were also several dozen bottles of wine in racks.

The door at the back led out to another small patio area with several more raised vegetable and herb beds and some more fruitless trees. The dog now came round the side of the house and parked itself by the open back door, in what looked like a well-defined spot.

Max gestured to the seating bench at the table and walked over to the shelves. "You want a drink and some food?" he asked. "Yes please- anything you are having is fine" said Sam. Max took out a couple of wooden plates from a cupboard under the table and put a few bits of bread on them, covered them in olive oil and then added a couple of pieces of fruit and some cheese.

He grabbed two mugs and took a half empty bottle of wine off the shelf, took out the cork that was half in, and poured it into them. Sam couldn't remember ever having wine from a mug before, and as the German placed them on the table he saw Sam looking at them. "Sorry about the mugs, only the dog knocked the glasses over outside on the patio, and they were smashed."

The dog looked sad and guilty again at Sam, and then flashed his eyes left to the food shelf and back again. The dog hadn't tilted his head or raised his eyebrows, or made any noise, but Sam got the gist of what he was thinking.

Within a few minutes of meeting Max it almost seemed to Sam that they were lifelong friends, just having met up again after a few years apart. He could sense an underlying sadness and hardness with the German, but this was combined with a matter-of-fact strength of character, a grit, a forced transition of life sustained by a stoic, flexible soul and a strong body.

Sam politely tucked into his food and wine, which was surprisingly good. "So what do you do for a corkscrew around here?" he asked. Without pausing the German replied "They do make plastic ones, I probably should have bought more than two though, as I broke one four months ago and when I eventually got the cork out, the wine was off anyway."

Sam looked at Max but the German wasn't looking at him as he spoke, he was just concentrating on his food as he ate and spoke, a bit like a little child does.

Sam couldn't work out why Max had an issue with metal. From all the things he now knew he hadn't come across anything that suggested that metal might be a problem. Maybe it was just that Max was worried about being attacked, or that he had just read something about it. Sam didn't want to get into any debates about it at this stage, so he let it drop, and finished off the last of the white wine from his mug.

"You fish?" asked Max, standing up abruptly. Sam looked puzzled and said nothing.

"Do you know how to fish?" Max asked more deliberately and slowly.

Sam nodded, but he clearly wasn't able to give the correct inter-bloke affirmation messages quickly enough to get away with the lie. Even the dog looked doubtfully at him.

Max went out of the back door and walked the few feet over to one of the raised beds and scraped the leftovers from the plates into it and covered it all over with soil, and then came back in again.

He then walked into the other side room and there was the sound of ceramic on ceramic, and then a bucket of water being poured, then the washing of plates and hands, and water draining away. A minute later he came back in and placed the 'bloke clean' wet plates and mugs back in the cupboard. Drying his hands up and down on his shirt, he then gestured with his head to the open back door.

"We have about six hours before it gets dark" he said, and then turned around to get a plastic box of something from under the bench.

Sam stood up and left his rucksack by the side of the table. Max led him around the side of the house where there was a rack with four fishing rods and a tackle box up against a small shed some yards away.

Max handed him a rod, the tackle box, and then took a rod for himself, opened the shed door up, took out a wide brimmed hat from a hook on the back of the door, and placed it on Sam's head. He then picked up a small cool box that had a very distinctive fishy smell to it, indicating that it was something you wouldn't want to open in a confined space. It was a well-practised routine, and everything was where it should be for just picking up and going fishing, which from what Sam could see, must happen almost every day.

There was a rough grass path that led away from the back of the house, wound around the small hills and down through more trees to the shoreline. Max was still barefoot. Sam thought that the soles of Max's feet must have been like tough leather to be able to put up with the stony ground.

The dog decided to follow them down the path some yards behind, having made a mental percentage calculation on the interest balance levels between the men, the box, and the food in the room that was now the other side of the back door that Max had closed.

After a hundred yards or so through the trees, the narrow path dropped steeply down to the rocky shoreline below. The path zigzagged down over boulders and rough crags steeply to the sea. At the bottom the German had built a platform of rocks and concrete just above the high water line on which to sit and fish from.

There were a couple of wooden seats and a small table all weighted down with a large rock. The clear, sapphire blue sea was some fifteen feet away, and it looked as if the tide was coming in. There was a slight onshore breeze so the waves were about a foot high.

The setting was picture-perfect; a clear, blue, gentle sea with minimal clouds and dramatic scenery, opening out so that he could see the whole coastline of the main island stretching around to the horizon. This had to be the most ideal fishing spot in the world, but then that probably depended on what your view of what 'ideal' was.

They set about preparing the lines and Max took the bait out from the cool box, and put some more seawater into it to keep it fresh. He then expertly baited both hooks, as it was just easier that way. Sam noticed him take some gloves out from the tackle box to handle the metal hooks and the reel. Clearly there had to be some compromises.

Although Sam could cast his line out with the rod, and 'look' the part, he had no idea what to do if he actually caught anything. He was sure he could reel it in and land it OK, but no clue how to get it off the hook, or gut and prepare it.

He decided to cross that set of hurdles when he came to them, and just hoped the hurdles weren't too large, or armed with big teeth.

The dog walked onto the platform and looked at Sam, and then at the chair he was sitting in, and then back at Sam again, in a 'I think you'll find that's my seat' way. It was incredible how expressive this dog was.

After a few moments pause for dramatic effect, the dog gave a sigh, and walked around and flopped onto the ground in the shade behind the other chair. This was followed by a couple of positional adjustments to emphasise how uncomfortable he was. Then backed up with the occasional reminding sigh just to let him know that he was still there, and that he was suffering in silence despite the injustice of it all.

Max left the platform, stepped down, and walked the few feet over the jagged rocks to where the waves were and stood there for a while inspecting the sea. Max was still barefoot, and Sam was sure he would come back with his feet in shreds.

The dog seemed to be happy to let him go on his own. Sam remembered back in New Zealand how most of the children he had seen went around everywhere in bare feet all the time, it was just something that you got used to.

It also reminded him of a woman alternative therapist that he had met through a friend at a party in London, who had turned up to it barefoot; she said that she could only help and connect to people if she was connected to the earth.

At the time, which was a year or two after he had left

university, and still in his arrogant, intolerant, youth, Sam had made a joking comment about it not working well through the carpet and underlay, which had gone down like a lead balloon.

Now though, with what he knew, it all made sense, and it was all fairly obvious. In fact he wasn't sure why someone hadn't invented shoes that just let the positive energy and information pass through them rather than not wearing any shoes at all - then you would have the best of both worlds - not to mention a great marketing opportunity and fewer trips to casualty to get the thorns out.

Sam looked at his sturdy, rubber-soled shoes that were now covered in a thick layer of dust and a few scuffs from rocks along the paths.

He had moved away from wearing leather soled shoes in the last year, it had been a subconscious thing, just preferring the style or the feel to the old look, but now he thought about it more he knew why. Anyway, at least he had been right about the rubber underlay.

He decided to take his shoes and socks off now though. It seemed the right thing to do.

"So not tempted to go for a walk on the rocks then?" asked Sam looking down towards the dog. The dog ignored him.

"Just think of all those healthy free radicals you are missing out on. All that earth energy and the feeling of seaweed between your paws." But the dog was only interested in anything that was food related, and there was no likelihood of that here, so with zero enthusiasm, all the dog could manage was a disparaging sigh.

He rested his jaw on his paws and settled down for what would be a long day before dinner.

Sam had owned a similar dog in his teens when he still lived at home with his parents. He had built up a really close bond with it straight away from when it arrived as a puppy.

The dog was so linked in with his routine and his emotions that it seemed to know just what to do and where to be. It got quite obsessional sometimes, even to the point where it was able to manipulate him, and could sense when it was going for a walk even before Sam had decided to go.

Sam's Mum had commented several times how she knew when to get Sam's dinner ready, as the dog would go and stand by the front door ten minutes before he arrived home, whatever time that was.

During the summer they would go everywhere together in the fields and woods; quite often the dog would run off for half an hour or so but would always come back, and always seemed to know where Sam was.

His Mum had suggested that he rename him 'Shadow' but Sam didn't like the name. It sounded like the sort of dog you would get in a Western movie.

When Sam went away to university the dog just seemed to switch off, and would just lie around the house all day. His Mum had got quite worried but after a few weeks it seemed to get back into some routine. But when he returned home for the holiday breaks, although the dog was pleased to see Sam, it seemed that they never quite had the bond that they used to have before he had left home.

Several months later the dog died in its sleep of old age.

Sam thought that he would be able to sense it when it happened, but he didn't. He was extremely upset though for weeks, which was odd as it was close to the end of term and he hadn't seen it for months.

He had almost forgotten about him and hadn't thought of the dog for some time with so many other things going on.

When he died, Sam just felt a little loss for the good times that they had shared together, the memories, and the sad feeling that they could never come back, but that was all.

Two weeks later when he got home at the end of term, he went straight to find the dog's gravestone in the garden.

His Mum had left a few flowers from the garden in front of it. He stood there for several minutes before kneeling down onto the grass, and then he began to cry; tears just flowing from his eyes onto the ground, with a feeling of such sorrow and a pain that he had never known before.

CHAPTER 7 - DUAL PERSPECTIVES

Once they had settled comfortably in their seats, holding their rods with the fishing lines out, Sam knew it was his lead to start the conversation.

He waited a few minutes to allow the 'silent pause' effect to sink in, to feel the environment, and be aware of the space. It was important to sense that moment of peace between them; it was a bloke thing. There was plenty to communicate, in silence, in the time before any words needed to be spoken.

It was a very difficult thing, trying to start a conversation on the spur of that moment, in that situation. Neither of them had ever met each other before, they both came from different cultures, had different lives, and knew very little of each other.

 Yet they were trying to broach a subject that they both knew was vast and complex, and had so many dimensions to it. With a situation like that, where do you start?

With men, of course, what 'didn't need to be said', and the time taken not saying it, was as equally important, and as necessary, as that which did.

Unlike with women of course, he thought, where short spaces in the conversation were simply opportunities waiting to be filled. Just gaps in the conversation, that if went on too long, became uncomfortable, and 'awkward.

Conversations between 'blokes' tended to be in series; sequential shared journeys, travelling from 'A' to 'B' with many convenient stops along the way. Time was taken to reflect and take in what was said, and to also put those things in context, the view, and what was going on around them.

Women's conversations however, always went off in many directions, down cul-de-sacs, did thirty-three point turns, worked in parallel, and had no plan or idea of where 'B 'might be, or even where 'A' was, and certainly no idea of how to get back there.

Women would just form projections of consensus, using some form of magic, rather than a lateral sequential logical process.

Bizarrely though, both mechanisms achieved the same result; they were just different ways of getting to the end point. Both achieved the same objective, with just different ways of doing things and different perspectives and priorities along the way, with neither 'side' knowing how the other worked.

Sam opened up awkwardly with a 'rough history of his life' thing; what he had done, achieved, studied and worked on. Essentially all the things that seemed important to him or what he thought may be of relevance to Max.

It was a little mentally exposing, but it seemed necessary somehow. He had to establish that he wasn't an 'idiot', that he was successful professionally and wasn't prone to 'loony fringe' thinking. Also that he wasn't the 'growing his hair long and wearing New-Age hippy clothes' type.

He just laid his cards on the table, a little like a personal job interview, going through his résumé, all of who he was, and what he had done. He talked, uninterrupted, for about twenty minutes, which seemed a lot longer than it actually was, and when he had finished he felt a little more comfortable in that he had somehow established his credibility.

He then carried on talking for about half an hour, describing the 'experience' that had happened to him some years back, as best he could, and included by some of the key events that had gone on since then.

He covered some of the information, knowledge and answers to things that he had in his mind, but without going into too much detail. He didn't expand on the things he wasn't sure about. He just kept it all general, open ended, and left out what he didn't know for sure.

Then he went on to outline his actions and decisions in getting to where he was now. He deliberately left specific references to other people out of the conversation as it just didn't seem relevant.

At the end of it all he realised that he had been talking for about two hours, just downloading his soul. In that time he hadn't heard anything back from the German, aside from the occasional confirmatory grunt or nod. Sam stopped talking. He was about to go over what he knew about Max, and his background, but he decided not to for some reason. He waited in silence.

Max looked at him sideways for a moment, and then back at the sea, a range of thoughts and emotions flowing over his face. At one point it looked like the German was, uncharacteristically, going to break down and cry. However he recovered himself with practised ease, and left his face expressionless. He just scanned the fishing line in the water for any sign of movement while he worked out what he was going to say, and how he was going to start.

"She will be OK you know?" he said abruptly "I found a good Home for her. One that will care for her, and she can make friends and be happy. It is all paid for, so she won't have to worry."

Sam didn't say anything; he just assumed Max was talking about his mother. Max had just taken for granted that Sam knew all about him, and what his situation was, which of course he did to some extent. But Sam didn't want to interrupt him so he just let him continue.

"I ask myself every day, why me? What have I done? I didn't ask to know, I didn't want these things, I didn't want to be this way, it's so completely unfair" he said.

Sam was very keen to not seem like a psychiatrist by staying silent, waiting for it all to start coming out. He made a humming sound that was somewhere between a trained professional 'hmmm' and an embarrassed cough, as a mate would give in an awkward situation, which of course sounded stupid, and made Max shut up for another minute before he said anything again.

"Your 'experience', that you had," he said "it's called a 'cosmic consciousness' experience, although that is somewhat of an outdated and culturally specific term. It's very rare you know?

"And equally rare for anyone to recall and retain any specific knowledge or details from it. I have some books on it back at the house if you want to read some more, including some examples of people who have had it in the past, although that may give you a somewhat…" he paused trying to think of the word and chose to use a couple of others that were close enough, "arbitrary, broad brush, or limited perspective. In your case you seem to have handled it well, considering.

"You have seen too much, far more than anyone should have to. Remember, 'ignorance is bliss' but blissful ignorance is not something you can go back to once you 'know' and 'see'."

He turned and looked at Sam closely, examining his features.

Now the ice had been broken they were both able to relax a little and 'see' each other a little clearer. After a few moments Max looked back at the sea again. He took a deep breath of air in and sighed. "I knew you were coming", he said "does that surprise you?"

But Sam said nothing.

Then it all started to pour out from Max; his life, his work, his views. He had developed Schizophrenia a long time ago in his early twenties, and had managed it all well for many years with help from his widowed mother, which is where his fluent English came from.

The condition had made it difficult to maintain relationships with women or friends though, and so he had become quite isolated. However he had worked hard, and despite this, he had set up some successful businesses, and made a good amount of money and achieved a good lifestyle from it.

His symptoms had got slightly worse as he got older, and he seemed to have quite a few recurring visions with each attack. It was at this point that he had tried to get some more professional help. His doctor had prescribed him some medication which had initially helped him considerably. He had also suggested that he attended some group meetings with other sufferers, to see how they coped and to share experiences, and other various psychiatric therapy sessions.

He also used the Internet, which at that time, was just getting started. He had discussed his treatments, and shared his feelings with others. It was then that he realised that he was having the exact same visions as many other sufferers, in particular one vision involving a cave in which he would enter it in his mind and write on the walls and he would use pictures and writings of the same type as other sufferers. This retrospectively wasn't that unusual; but what he was actually seeing and drawing in them though, was, and very confusing. He also had no control over it, or the attacks, and he had subsequently been moved onto a different medication.

This had helped with the intensity and frequency of the attacks, and the experiences and visions had also subsided. He had taken up painting and sculpting at that point too, as a way of expressing himself and relaxing.

This was also quite common, and it was a way of trying to articulate or represent a lot of the things he had seen or experienced - most of which were quite negative and dark.

A few months later he had been sitting in his study drawing a picture with charcoal, using a wide easel at an angle on the desk in front of him. Suddenly he had had an attack, and had visualised a scenario in which he was in the same cave again; he was writing things on the walls, just random text and pictures.

When he had woken up he was surprised to see that he had actually written down many words on the paper in front of him where he had slumped forward but had still been holding the charcoal. He had obviously broken the charcoal pencil at some point as the words stopped half way through. But for some reason Max wouldn't say what the words were.

In an attempt to try and get some deeper answers Max had searched the Internet again and had done a great deal of reading on the subject of Schizophrenia, anxious to research more about his condition. He had joined more discussion groups and a few societies. This was before the days of online social networking groups.

He had also started studying psychology, and a whole range of other subjects and religions. He had given over his business to be managed by a family friend so he could spend all his time on it.

One of the areas he had focused on was the commonality in the way that sufferers got hallucinations, weird visions, and people in their minds 'talking' to them, or those that had multiple people, or even plants or animals, in their minds giving them advice.

He had even read poems that many people had written. He was looking at how people were trying to express themselves in the same way, but it was the correlation of the information, and what it was saying, that he was interested in.

He had even got a group of specific Schizophrenics together, getting them to relate to what they saw in one group, and what they had experienced. He tried to correlate and compare, and then map out a picture of what was being described, why their brains were trying to make sense of something, and how they had been treated by society.

What they saw or experienced wasn't logical, or easy to express, and came out in the various forms of art or writings which took a great deal of interpretation and gathering of information. He had given them all specific tasks or work to do including correlating experiences from wider groups, to try and somehow make sense of it all as groups, rather than individually.

What Max was saying was all coming out a bit piecemeal, as if he was just dumping the information out in whichever order it came through into his brain. It was clear that he wasn't that used to talking to people either, so he came across occasionally as being slightly aggressive, harsh and direct.

"Let me tell you," he went on "these things can be very disturbing and frightening and even harmful. Obviously the person involved does not comprehend what is going on, and has no control over it, and what they see can be very depressing and vivid and can possibly even lead to suicide. It is seen as an illness, different from 'normality', debilitating, as it affects their ability to integrate into society, to work, to socialise to actually function.

"Quite often this condition is brought on by illicit drugs, or alcohol, or it may even be hereditary. So this implies that something has triggered or enabled something in the brain, which changes the perception or switches into something receptive. You are tuned into some other wavelength if you like, or other parts of the mind, stuff that it isn't supposed to be accessed normally.

"So you get these instances where the brain is switched into this mode and it receives different information. The problem is that it isn't structured in a way that can be interpreted logically somehow by putting it into some rationalised perspective.

"You see, you can look at Schizophrenics in one way, and you can see people, not with a disability, but with an ability to link into visions or experiences. To tap into or connect with other information, and then be able interpret it from a new perspective. Just because they are able to see things in a different way from the 'normal reality', doesn't mean that the 'something' that they are trying to interpret isn't there. The information must come from somewhere."

Max was trying hard not to get angry; however at some points in the conversation it was clear from the way he was clutching his fishing rod that he was quite frustrated. He also switched frequently between the 'them' and 'us', subconsciously trying at points to disassociate himself from the condition.

"I began to notice though from my studies," he went on "that from the descriptions of the visions and the nature of the locations within them, that there were very strong commonalities. This was the same for the art and poems. The same places, the same way things were represented, and the same sort of messages. They don't all make logical sense unless you correlate the information and the way it was being seen.

"You had to apply coordination to it all in some way. Even with the ordinary dreams people have. For example, did you know that the third most popular dream people have is of their teeth falling out? How peculiar is that for goodness sakes? Did anyone think to ask why that is or how so many people have the same dream when it is such a strange thought to actually have in the first place?"

After he had worked out what was going on, Max had wanted to go back to the groups to explain to them what they are seeing; to help them come to terms with it, and to not be so depressed or confused; learn to ignore it if possible, but at least realise it was something special, and give them hope and realisation and support.

But from what he knew now, he was too scared, and in any case, it was too much for him in his situation to do by himself. He had so many other things to deal with, and with all his other responsibilities and problems it would just have taken too much time and energy.

"You see, you get a scrap of information, an idea, or snapshot of something and you start to add them together, and build up a picture in your mind of what is going on. Like you would if you were creating a painting in real life; you give it colours, shape, structure; it has depth style, and brush strokes and size.

"After a long time, and a lot of hard work, you build up something that starts to make sense. You may even have several of these paintings that fit together, like a mural or movie that also tries to express something, like cavemen used to produce on the walls of their caves to represent something that was going on. You then speak to others who have also done the same and you realise that what they have produced is very similar to your own; there are consistent commonalities, the same messages, the same thoughts.

"They may have used different colours, shapes, interpretations and style, and have applied more emphasis on certain things, but at the end of the day, what is being depicted is the same thing, it's the same story, the same image, the same result."

In learning more about what was happening he had stopped taking his prescribed medication, and had even strapped a pencil to his hand to try to repeat the episodes. He didn't have great success with it at first, and for a while things just got worse.

However after several months of perseverance he was able to duplicate it. After a few more months he had got quite a lot of information written down. The other strange thing that he had noticed was that he was writing with his left hand, and normally he was right-handed.

Over the next year he began to decipher the 'messages' until he gradually became aware that there was a lot more coming out, and that it was getting quite worrying.

He then went on to explain that it was also then that he started having things go wrong, events that seemed to go against him; telephone lines being cut by a digger in the road, and not being fixed for four weeks. People making his life hard. All sorts of external events that weighed on his mind and got in the way of him actually doing things, as if he were somehow being attacked.

"The episodes have nearly stopped altogether since I've been here. This is good, and perhaps I should have done it long ago."

Sam was still aware that Max was assuming that he knew everything about him; that he knew all of his past history and what he had done, and about his condition. This was suddenly alarming, as really he knew very little about this guy or about his mental stability.

Max looked at Sam again, and held his look for a few seconds longer this time, before looking back and squinting his eyes back towards the sea.

A few minutes later Max went over in detail some of the things that had happened to him after that. About how he had lost his business after a strange series of events and how he had been repeatedly let down by people. About weird circumstances and all the problems with the house and road plans, and concerns about his mother. All about her stress and people not doing things for her. How his house had been broken into twice, and tradesmen who had come in to repair the damage had ended up making more problems than they had fixed.

Even silly things like a washing machine that was delivered broken, and the endless problems he had had getting someone to collect or fix it. Max started to get visibly agitated even talking about it all, and even small things, which on their own wouldn't bother anyone, seemed to press on his mind like a vice.

Everything that he was talking about seemed to have a very consistent theme, always involving someone else who had control over him, with a ridiculous set of coincidences or a chain of events and bureaucratic red tape. They didn't seem to happen all at once but sequential like bullets, or Chinese torture; like a slow wearing pressure.

A doctor would describe his behaviour as being paranoid, or say that these things were only coincidental and would prescribe him some antidepressants, but standing back and looking at it from a different perspective you could see that it didn't add up, and something was definitely going on.

It was a measurable force of some kind, always pushing against him. There was no direct or obvious attack. It was uncomfortable listening to it, and Sam could very much relate to what he was saying.

Max hadn't been assaulted or physically threatened or arrested or been in any serious accidents, but Sam could see that he had been through a constant battle; it was a relentless steady pressure on his mind and life; one that kept the bearing down on him all the time, sapping his energy, occupying his thoughts and time. Just stuff wearing him down, trying to avert him or test him, or maybe tell him something.

At that moment Max's fishing line snapped taut, and the reel on his rod gave a short whizz. Max pulled sharply on his rod, but from his expression it was clear that the fish had come off the hook already. The line went slack, and on pulling it in it was obvious that the 'catch of the day' had made off with his bait.

After he had re-baited and cast his line out again, Max broke off and went straight off on another topic, and in doing so jumped several levels of understanding in his own mind, to where he assumed Sam understood 'what was going on'.

"I have found," he continued "that the best way to see the way things are, is from an outside perspective. The collective subconscious mind is just a merciless uncaring animal. You would perceive it as a nest of ants on a small oasis in the desert, with us people just treated by it all like worker ants.

"As there are no predators to the ants in the oasis, it grows into sub groups who try to take control of the nest by either force, subterfuge or by giving misinformation to the workers. But all these ants and the groups believe they are thinking for themselves; either the happy, hard done by ones, the little workers or the dominating elite.

"When in fact the nest itself has developed in parallel its own hive mind long ago, and is subtly in control of everything but not in a conscious way, just a directing influence driven by need and nature, it is evolving, refining, adapting and experimenting in parallel with its own surroundings, capabilities, and knowledge developed by its ants.

"It all subconsciously follows the Laws of Nature, fitting in with what works and what doesn't for survival. So the ants may see their world, if they stopped to think, as illogical, mad, unfair, chaotic, but to the hive mind it is all logical and makes sense. The ants are just part of its body that does different things as it grows and develops. That's its nature; it just does what it does, but with subtle, subliminal control looking after itself.

"So you see what is happening to us, and if you look back in history at what has happened you can see most things that go on are as a result of evolution of our own collective hive mind. About twelve thousand years ago, when there was great hardship around the Mediterranean area, everyone got together and 'civilisation' was kicked off - that was really when the hive mind came into play.

"That was when we started cultivation, working, gathering collectively, fighting and using resources. Civilisation experiments then evolved - Mesopotamian, Greek, Roman, Chinese, Byzantine, Persian et cetera, down through to more modern times, with developed politics, war, communication and religion.

"You see psyche groups vying for control and historical inheritance adopted into in the minds of people. Everyone playing politics and fighting anyone who may compete in their virtual battles, in a virtual world that subtly impacts on the real one.

"This is what I was seeing in my visions, and the words I was being given to write when I worked out what it was 'saying' by a process of correlation and interpretation.

"Even though there are leaders controlling the governments, banks, and religious groups, all of whom think that they are in control, in fact they aren't in control at all. You can go on about religious groups having control of the banks, or the influence of criminal heads, politicians, or even whole countries, all with their own agendas- in the end these are just meaningless when you realise that they are just being driven by our collective subconscious mind, which itself is just busy sleepwalking."

To Sam it seemed as if his Max's mental download had all come out as a bit of a mess. It was unstructured and jumping around all over the place. It was as if Max was some sort or oracle or visionary who had been given a series of messages or pictures, and was being punished by something for either having that knowledge or for trying to do something about it.

It was also evident that Max hadn't been made aware of some of the things that Sam had seen; all the knowledge, perspective, and all the information. What Max had seen or had gained was an emotional perspective of what was happening, and what he believed was going to happen, very much from a negative emotional point of view expressed as similarities or analogous to other things, and primarily focused on the injustice of it all.

Sam's perspective was much more detailed, precise, logical, and rationally balanced. He had knowledge of the technical how, the what, the why, and the cause and effect. However despite all that, he hadn't experienced it, or appreciated it, from Max's point of view. Sam had also come up against it hard like Max had, but not over such a long period.

He also didn't have the voices, the repeated episodes, visions, and elements in his psyche communicating and translating information to him. Max clearly knew there was something going on outside of himself and what it meant for everyone, however he didn't know how it was working, or why, or what it all really meant. He was just filling in the gaps based on his own life perception. He didn't have an overall complete picture.

Sam knew a lot more, but none the less it was from a practical point of view. From this emotional angle, it made him feel quite anxious to have it exposed like that, with feeling and pain. To Sam it almost seemed as if something was protecting him from it all to a large extent in his life, in a way that Max didn't in his.

As they sat there in silence, a train of thought progressed in Sam's mind. He worked through all the new objective views from Max of what was going on. He then built onto that all the things he knew to map it all out objectively, fill in the gaps, and complete the picture.

Max continued to explain how the human race would continue to fight, use up all available resources and then feel bad about it. It would continually battle between religions, cultures, and countries, all attempting to dominate one other. It would poison the seas and our bodies with chemicals and develop more and more sophisticated drugs to fine tune the evolutionary capabilities of viruses and infectious diseases.

He believed that there was nothing that the human race could do in the future that would change the ending; so it must be something that has already been done or not done. Something set in motion that cannot, or is not letting itself, be changed.

His guess was either something in the sea or antibiotics or chemicals that have already created a viral development process. He believed that it would eventually evolve into something that would be untreatable as a pandemic.

Slowly but surely, it was all being subconsciously directed or self-directed along a path of self-destruction which it cannot get away from a culmination of waste, toxins, resource plunder, pollution, over-population, and so on.

Max then went on to talk about 'messing with genetics', sidestepping natural selection, chemical pollution, medical and medicinal over-exposure with antibiotics causing out of control viruses, toxins in the seas and land again.

"We are gradually killing ourselves. Easy to ignore though when there are so many things filling our minds with immediate needs, environmental blocks, not to mention media and electronic interference and devices."

He then started talking about more social problems and attitudes.

"The Internet has become the new religion for young minds with its belief structure, their faith in it and the hypnotic mechanisms it uses. The unregulated, uncontrolled social network churches for virtual people, with idols with millions of followers, adoring believers. Places where all your questions are answered, all the support you 'need' from ill-informed, self-qualified people.

"All from the comfort of your own bedroom. Creating a surreal identity, and existence, in an out of body virtual world for their alter-egos. It's addictive, all encompassing, and just another form of control, using up all your time, life, and energy. Their hands clasped all day in addictive prayer through their electronic devices. All these things there to save you time and energy to enjoy your life, but in effect, do the exact opposite.

"People need to get outside, meet people and communicate with one another, face to face rather than sitting with something that restricts nearly all of the bandwidth. Do things that really communicate between people; talk, kiss, love, hug, play, and resonate with the right sort of people directly. Understand that these devices are just tools - they are not your life.

"It is difficult to see these things happening when you walk through quiet woods or rambling open hills on your own. It is also equally hard to see what is going on when you are in the busy city streets surrounded by towers of steel and concrete. But put the two together and it is not hard to see the truth.

"It is not anyone's first priority to care for the world when you are focused on your own survival. With your mind forced to think of working, self-preservation and family needs. You may do occasional guilt placated token acts of recycling or planting trees but in the end we are all driven at the collective level by the need to survive; to eat, to control, to be safe."

Sam was trying to piece together what Max was trying to say, what he was trying to represent, but at the moment it seemed to be just a list of complaints, problems and 'what was wrong with the system' rather than a specific definition of the 'system' itself. There was little substance to the view. What he was saying was correct - but it was not very constructive.

"Politicians are driven by popularity so they give people what makes them happy, so difficult decisions and changes are rarely made. The tide flows along the easiest channel, the silt sinks to the bottom of the lake. We avoid things that are too hard. We have a world full of injustice, corruption and bureaucracy, all paid for by a society that is overworked and underpaid, and it had always been that way.

"But in the last twenty five years it has all changed. There is now a fundamental shift in perception, and in the level of information and communication, and it is getting worse. There is just no top-level real strategic management going on. Everyone is just competing with everyone else; it is just a downward spiral.

"Even during the Second World War people had hope for the future. It was bad but people bonded together, pulled along by your 'Bluebirds over the White Cliffs of Dover' spirit.

"Now people can see very little promise for the future, and we all have too much information. The world has merged into one and it doesn't like itself very much but can't do anything about it. We only deal with the crisis as it confronts us, but we don't deal with the crises that we can't see, or those that are a direct threat. When it's out of sight, it's out of mind, and so it is these crisis 'tigers' that creep up on us and eventually get us; by which time, it is all too late.

"The best thing that could happen to us would be an alien invasion like we see in the films. We would bond together to fight the common enemy, and stand together in the future knowing that we are not alone and that we must be strong to survive in this harsh universe. We would then grow strong, develop technology, move out into space, explore, conquer and eventually create a galactic empire, and eventually be back to square one!

"So," sighed Max "that's not going to happen. So what do we do? We are fundamentally flawed and we can't get around it. Collectively we are doomed.

"Gone is the energy of the people with the strength, force, influence and charisma to bend the future around them that we had in points in history. We now just exist on a narrowing path down a hill. The life force and energy of the youth is gone, spent now on virtual worlds and filtered through controlled pipes of communication.

"Heroes are now clowns, actors, and entertainers. Leaders are puppets and sycophantic 'yes men' shaped by media, popular opinion, money and corruption.

"Religion has done its part in destroying life, change, hope, empire and strength. We escape the bounds of one, only to be overrun by another.

"This is the control of the self-controlling machine, narrowing the path, and emotional depression focusing on the cogs and wheels of the machine as it unknowingly and subconsciously moves along its blind path of oblivious self-destruction."

Sam stood up abruptly at that point to stretch his legs.

The conversation had got very one-sided and his mind was having trouble staying focused. He rubbed his legs to help relieve the stiffness, which wasn't necessary but it helped prevent him seeming rude or bored to Max. Sam wanted to rub his head it ached so much, but that would have given completely the wrong signals. Max just ignored him and carried on talking.

"Try and do something about it, or let people know what is going on, and you just become open to attack like everything is working against you. You try to mitigate all possible things that can go wrong, or get at you, but somehow things still manage to bite you.

"Things get at you; events happen as a chain of consequences to stop you in your tracks. They don't just happen in threes either. Also if you are aware that they are not just happening randomly but in direct consequence of something reaction to you, then by knowing what is going on you can actually measure the events happening, and predict them. This will usually be just as you are trying to do something, or just relaxing.

"These things will always happen at a point of change, and will always involve someone else. They usually stop you doing something, and the scenario contains an element you have no control over. It usually involves money, or loss of value, and at a point when you say you are 'happy' or something like that.

"When you are aware of 'IT', know that 'IT' exists and that 'IT' is working against you, you plan everything you do from then on; leaving nothing to chance. Everything is carefully thought out for the next day or so, and you minimise everything you do. Somehow, even then, things will conspire to work against you, odd events will happen.

"Even with the small number of things you do, somehow some part will be ruined, usually by somebody else or by something that you had no control over.

"You will think – 'What are the odds of that?' and you then invoke the same scenario, and time and time again the same thing happens. In scientific experiments, the odds would be so infinite that you would say that it was impossible; impossible several times over. In fact, if you set up the situations and manage the windows that you are open to attack from you can actually control when these things happen, then the odds in the end become irrelevant.

"IT is designed to move your thoughts away from where they are going, using natural selection to filter your thoughts to other things, and 'punish' you for thinking or doing the wrong thing, or exposing IT, making IT obvious. Yet, these are not conscious thoughts; they are natural forces with no self-awareness behind them, keeping the 'slaves' oblivious."

This was the first time Max had referred to 'IT' as being something; not a person or a thing, just IT, some undefinable loose collective entity.

"Then again you may try and not think of 'IT' at all, just think nice positive thoughts all the time, live your life like in all the self-help conditioning 'habits' books. Be happy and think as all those 'know-it-all' types tell you to behave. Or, you could have part of your brain removed and live in ignorance and bliss.

"But when you know what is going on, you just can't help thinking about it, like an itch you can't scratch, nagging at you. Once you know 'IT' is there you want to get to the bottom of what it is all about, and why. Even though the way ahead is a complex minefield, a jungle, a hill covered with a mass of kids on motorbikes."

Max stopped and looked back inland up the hill with anger on his face. *Clearly,* Sam thought, *there had been some sort of attack going on even here.*

He didn't understand the reference, but it was obviously something important to Max. He looked back at the sea again and gave a long sigh.

"You eventually hunger for a detachment from reality, shut yourself away, and try and hide from it as much as you can" he said almost under his breath, and he then looked back at Sam.

"Following realisation that this subconscious collective thing exists, and the subsequent analysis, there is a sense of loss of perspective of the real; a disjointed feeling, a lack of purpose, a feeling of lethargy and loss of sense of direction. You are clearly not meant to know IT is there. Which is what you would expect.

"Normal life should consist of learning, playing, working, and competing - all based on need and self-preservation. When you are being attacked it suddenly becomes difficult to drive yourself forward, gain enthusiasm, or enjoy life any more. All your energy goes.

"It's like a sense of being removed slowly from the game. It's like running a marathon race only to realise that you are on a wheel in a hamster cage, turning a cog in a machine; you get food and water provided, you meet other hamsters, but at the end of the day there is no reason to carry on and you curl up and die.

"Unless, of course, you just become a hamster with a hamster mind, a hamster brain, and hamster habits, in which case life is great being just a hamster.

"With these things going on, you start to make less sense to people, you seem odd and they try to fit you into their pre-defined holes and roles, but can't. 'Why aren't you that', 'why aren't you this?' All because your perspective is different. You lose interest in talking to other people, the conversation being a little redundant in 'light of new information'. You cannot start to talk about what you know, or feel, without sounding mad in the first sentence.

"You see too much of the negative side of people; the ignorance, the stupidity, the useless, selfish, lazy side. All achieving nothing and only really busy when it comes to reproducing more hamsters. Why is that? Why are we becoming more stupid as a race? What is driving that? We should be so much smarter.

"You ask yourself how the system got itself into that state? You try to ignore it all - get on with your own life. Which I did, until it comes after you, in which case you become a total hermit, which I had to in the end, as clearly just ignoring it wasn't enough." He then gestured dramatically around in the air encompassing the island and sea with sweeps of his hands.

"So eventually you turn into a recluse like me, and lock yourself away in what feels like a cupboard. You don't speak to anyone; you waste yourself away and lose your appetite for life. You don't care about your appearance or about any social graces. In the end though, despite all your best efforts, you eventually go away, fade completely, wiped away from existence like an annoying error or a wayward ant."

He went quiet for a few minutes again, trying to calm down.

"I am trying to be self-sufficient, here on my own, and keep myself to myself, but even here it still won't leave me alone, it still keeps attacking me occasionally. I just want to live in peace and quiet with my dog.

"People just don't realise or care how much some things they do affect and influence you. People just don't care anymore; they just have no responsibility or interest in others' lives. Of course it's fine if you are doing what IT wants, and working in blissful ignorance; but try and push against IT, and it will crush you like an ant."

There was a pause.

Sam waited and thought for a few long moments. He wasn't sure if Max had finished talking or not. After several more seconds Sam said "You are all right here though, you know, on this island, in this environment?"

Max thought for a moment,

"Well yes. As much as is possible I just cut myself off from the world and protect and isolate myself as best I can. I own this land and house, and have enough money coming in from savings to pay for all I need until I die. I get the odd trespasser now and again…" he smiled at Sam, "and I have trouble with a couple of kids on trail motorbikes.

"They use the field at the back there as a race circuit, just the other side of my fence, which makes the most unimaginably stressful noise as they have no silencers on them. It's the vibration or the frequency of it - I just can't stand it.

"So when they come, which is usually at a weekend, I come down here with some earplugs, and just fish or read. Anything to stop me hearing and thinking of it. I confronted them once but it just seemed to make them worse.

"They always arrive just as I am settling down to relax. But it's manageable I suppose, anyway I have nowhere else to go."

Sam hadn't the same perspective on the darker side of life that Max was pertaining to. He didn't have the same negative 'this is all bad and the world is going to end horribly' view.

To Sam it had just been given a date or timescale of when it would happen. He had worked out the date or duration in the 'Episode' only because no information was coming back after that time.

There was no why or reason or cause that he knew of, or that he could work out. There was no feeling or sense of what was likely to go on in that time, going into the future, other than that practical fact of the end time.

The other thing Sam was aware of was that talking with Max was starting to have quite a negative effect on him. He felt quite down now; sad, depressed. It was also probably a real and viable reason as to why the fish were staying away.

Sam looked sideways at him. "Yes," Sam said "but looking at the bright side, we still have quite a few years left to go, you and I, and there are still plenty of fish left in the sea."

It created a lightness in the conversation that Sam needed to make, however he was also aware that with all the things Max had been through, that in his own situation he was very lucky to still be alive.

Then again, so was everyone, when you put things into perspective.

In Sam's case it was some information, or thing, or situation, or key element that he had, that Max didn't.

CHAPTER 8 - MEN AND FOOD

Later in the evening, when the sun was going down, they walked back to the house, fishless. The wind had picked up making the sea too choppy to carry on with lines out, and the spray from the cool, onshore wind made it a little too uncomfortable to carry on just sitting there.

With the sun now behind them, and casting shadows on their backs from the trees and rocks, it was getting cooler too. The temperature was still that of a warm summer day at home, but with it being so hot earlier and the temperature having dropped by ten degrees or so now, it felt cold in comparison.

The male body always adapted quickly to changes in the environment. It adjusted to fit in with what was there in the surroundings and simply made the most of it.

It was only logical, and natural, that a mind should do the same; adapting quickly to the pace, the depth, and the range of subjects covered in a new situation. Such was the case with Sam. Within a few hours Sam had totally relaxed.

He had become mentally and physically acclimatised, ready to explore and hunt barefoot through an olive tree jungle, and adapt to any subject of discussion as required.

It was never easy though, to overcome subconscious feelings or thoughts, in any situation. Primal attitudes and drives were always there. So walking back from a 'hunt', not having caught and killed anything, ached in their inner stomachs.

They felt the air of 'failure' hanging over them, like two schoolboys returning home from a day by the stream with empty jars. You couldn't get away from it even though there was nobody at home to apologise to when they got back.

They walked back in silence. They were both a little weary, and the breezy sea air had made Sam feel slightly drunk or bewildered, especially now that he had begun moving again, using his stiff muscles - which wasn't easy after sitting still for so long. The air was windless and still just a few yards inland, and the noise from the sea died away quickly, replaced by the clicking sound of cicadas as they passed through the rocky grassy banks and into the thinly wooded areas again.

The dog followed them all the way to the house, where Max dropped the fishing gear off at the place he had picked it up from. They went through the back door and into the kitchen area and the dog resumed residence outside in his usual spot.

It was so quiet and peaceful here, almost painful on the ear. Sam had now gotten used to having so much noise all the time everywhere; from outside, and background house noise, the TV, radio, even the fridge. Here, as soon as you stopped moving, your ears were busy searching for any sounds to latch onto.

Several years ago he had gone out into the desert in Egypt, and he had encountered the same depth of silence. Far out in the ocean of sand at night, his ears almost aching trying to perceive something, anything. It was just a void; nothingness, dead still, not even wind passing through or over anything.

You could even start to hear your own body, and the slight hiss of the blood flowing in your ears, with your mind trying hard to work out why you had suddenly gone deaf. He liked this place more and more by the hour.

In the kitchen Max got a couple of mugs and filled them with some white wine from a newly opened bottle. He lifted out some plates from the cupboard and set them on the table. He collected some bread and cheese, and sat at the table with them, handing Sam's to him in a functional, non-ceremonial, manner. Without making eye contact both men sat without talking.

It was definitely one of those 'Where's the beer?' moments. Beer would have been perfect, not to mention essential, at that instant given the lack of fish. But Sam worked it out straight away, of course, no fridge, cans, or metal bottle tops.

He didn't say anything, it was just not right though. So they ate the bread and cheese, and drank the warm wine, in silence. There were some sacrifices that, in some circumstances, were just a little hard to bear.

With a few hours left before it got dark, Max offered a tour around the peninsular. He wanted to show Sam some of the things he had done, and changes he had made to the landscape of the island. As they walked away from the house, Max pointed out pathways he had put in, and rock walls that he had built.

It didn't seem very much, but just one man on his own working by hand could only achieve so much in a few spare hours each day. Also working in the intense summer heat limited even those hours to non-arduous tasks. Aside from the area around the house, there wasn't much useable land either, it was all fairly rugged and rocky and there was very little topsoil around.

Even the seashore was just jagged rocks and cliffs with no beaches to speak of. However he could see why it was attractive to Max; it seemed highly defensible, cut off, isolated and less likely to attract unwelcome visitors, boats, or lost wandering tourists. Equally it was easy to see why the land hadn't been bought by anyone else.

As they walked along, they talked, and Max changed tack on his previous conversation to a much more philosophical perspective. He began pointing out his feelings on changes that had happened in the world over the last thirty years in human values, and the positive elements of which that he felt were highly important fifty or even eighty years ago that were no longer as visible. Things like virtue, honour, honesty, chivalry, loyalty, wholesomeness, courage and trust.

Concepts that, in his view, seemed to be almost redundant now. He used the term 'shining light in men's eyes' which seemed odd, and it brought back images to Sam of old black and white photos, where people seemed to literally have brighter shining eyes although this was probably more to do with the photographic technique, the paper, film, and lenses of the time.

Sam also thought of the race of men in the *Lord of the Rings* books, the ones that came from the North, that had the same shining eyes; but he couldn't remember the name of them. It was odd how when people mentioned things or ideas, other thoughts just popped into your head from nowhere.

As they walked through some of the wooded area that they had been in earlier, they looked out at the sea once more, and stopped.

Max seemed a lot more relaxed now that they had been walking; he seemed calmer and was talking more freely. He seemed comfortable, and spoke normally, expressing himself with his hands and using body actions. He no longer seemed as though he was falling over what he was trying to say, but was now able to just talk.

"You look about you in society," he went on "and these values are so rare these days, suppressed by the natural evolutionary move towards pathos, laziness, lack of virtue, doing what's needed to get on. There's just too many bureaucrats, bankers and lawyers.

"Too many people not doing anything productive or constructive in real terms, just pushing paper around. We are gradually slipping slowly into a grey world of mediocrity. We are being led by media, public favour and lack of accountability or responsibility.

"Young people see no future or 'point', their energy and hearts have been taken away – eroded. All they see is a life of no hope, and no chance of even buying their own homes, lives of massive debts and of just being exploited.

"The cost of living is too high for them, yet most have been brought up in a good lifestyle, unlike their grandparents' generation, they are used to having everything that they need provided for them, fast food, fast information, all their needs and emotions catered for and pandered to.

"So moving out from that comfortable environment they expect to continue that lifestyle; to borrow what they want to perpetuate that existence. It's just human nature, but they get further into debt as they feel they 'deserve to live like that'.

"Why should this be, and what purpose does it serve? It's obvious that this isn't what people really want, so what is happening? We are pushing against a tide, swimming up a river. Always pushing the envelope of what we can get away with. Seeing how low we can sink, with more and more limits broken, lowering the levels of gutter media to give the public what they want, with no regard for what is right?

"So again collectively, there is a big loss of any sort of integrity, responsibility, accountability and regard for life itself.

"People are also no longer in touch with nature or able to interact with the land, the forest, the ebb and flow of the seasons, with the plants and trees, or have any understanding of the ecological values and symbiotic living that we once had, and needed to survive. We have become detached from it. No longer integrated by our nature, we have evolved away from it, and each other.

"In so doing so, we have lost much of the value and understanding of it; why it was important, together with the pure wholesome reflective effect it had on us. We are sanitising and virtualising ourselves away from what we are, and where we came from, becoming inhuman, lifeless, programmable machines."

The conversation made Sam think back to his childhood in the 1970's and 80's, when things seemed so much more simple and straightforward. Everything used to have that 'hope for the future' perspective, that 'exciting brave new world' feel to it.

But these days the world just seemed to be just fighting itself, inwardly, with everyone just trying to get on as best they could, despite everyone else trying to make it hard for themselves and each other.

There was just something missing, something deep. People used to be so different with each other, the music, the attitudes, the mentality of everyone. Of course it could have just been his young naïve interpretation of the world then, and just lack of global understanding at the time, but he looked at young people these days and they just didn't seem to have the same fire and enthusiasm for real life that he had then.

Where had it all gone, and why had it changed? He thought.

"And so the children…" Max went on, and Sam snapped back to listening again, "…of the future that we are creating, will store all of their emotions online, with controlled, managed virtual lives. More and more you will see children who are locked into television, existing online, playing games on computers, and fulfilling channelled academic pressures.

"They live their life through created drama, social networking, online chat, texts, and studying the wrong things, eventually having electronic communication permanently integrated into their bodies.

"Excitement and imagination is fed to them on a plate, so they are left with none of their own. Games that thrill, numb your senses and dull your feelings. Television to make you behave and think in certain ways, at their own demand. Children become the zombie army of the future. All communication becoming slowly totally electronic, and minimised.

"We will no longer have, or need, face-to-face interaction, and will subsequently have limited experience of face-to-face feelings, expressions, and emotions. So eventually we will all be unable to deal with it, and become socially dysfunctional, and rely more on chemical drugs and alcohol to plug the gaps.

"Even sex and relationships seem so much less emotional and much more practical, just driven out of necessity rather than emotional desire and true love. Stereotypical images and role models of what is expected of people; the look created by films and magazines and television. Pornography desensitising natural thrill and exploration and replacing it with unrealistic expectation and dissatisfaction with reality.

"Relationships become difficult to sustain with stress and pressure, and added unnecessary demands of life.

"Things used to be so much simpler, yet now we have made everything so complicated, busy and involved."

It was all a bit rambling, but Sam agreed with everything he said. It was much better and calmer than the conversation he had had earlier in the day and it was clear that letting him just vent his frustrations was helping him to try and structure what he felt.

It was almost as if he had a list of complaints or problems or issues in his mind that he had to somehow offload onto Sam. He often seemed to repeat himself just to make sure he had said something, and it was as if he couldn't move on to the next stage until he had completed it, laying out all the issues up front. It was still unclear to Sam why he was telling him all of these things.

Sam could see that he was trying to get things out that he needed to say, so he didn't interrupt him.

The stability of the German's mind was something Sam hadn't

had any real time to stop and think about. He had been in such a hurry to get in contact with him and to speak to him that it hadn't occurred to him that this guy might actually be unstable, and he had no idea if he was capable of anything sinister.

From Sam's perspective he was more inclined to give people the benefit of the doubt rather than making assumptions based on stereotypes.

He knew to some level of detail of the nature of Schizophrenia; the presence of multiple personalities, and the various psyche forms. However he was no expert on it, or indeed on the nature of how the system worked in the mind, and how the collective information in everyone's mind was processed from that perspective.

So he couldn't really put himself in Max's shoes or understand his mentality, as obviously he wasn't Schizophrenic himself.

The wine had released something in Max, and his emotions had been opened up, but calmed slightly, like a release of pressure.

Sam was glad that they both had only had a couple of drinks. Alcohol always made Sam quite relaxed, happy, and pleasant to be with, but he didn't like the effect it had on some other people.

There was a definite occasional undercurrent of anger in Max still there; a bitterness, a frustration, that welled up now and again. He had a lot of sympathy for Max and his situation, but he wasn't about to put himself in the firing line of uncertainty, he still wasn't able to trust him.

About ten minutes later they arrived back at the house again. Max set about getting the patio area around the outdoor stove ready. He picked up some chairs, a small wooden table, drinks, plates, some large candles lamps, and some plastic cutlery. It was a secluded area just to the right of the house with several bushes and trees giving some protection from the cooling wind that had now got up.

It was paved with close fitting, square terracotta coloured tiles and was surrounded by a waist-high stone and brick wall, against which the dog had positioned himself near to the stove. Max had given Sam the task of lighting a fire in the stove which took an embarrassingly long time to get going.

He knew how to set up the logs, and the kindling, and even managed to find the fire lighters that were at the back of the cupboard under the domed oven, however he couldn't seem to get enough air flow to get it going well enough.

After about twenty minutes he realised that the flue wasn't working, and stood up on top of the brick stand to look down the chimney. Instead of the metal baffle on top that was meant to keep the rain off, Max had stuck what looked like a wide round cork place mat there instead.

This clearly wasn't much good at stopping the rain getting in. It was propped just inside the flue and from the ground you couldn't see it at all. Sam lifted it off, and released a plume of smoke. He looked back to the house to make sure Max hadn't seen him making what was an obvious blunder for a 'bloke', and got back down quickly.

Within a few minutes the fire was roaring away. He wiped the blackened underside of the cork mat on the grass, and placed it behind the oven out the way and hoped Max wouldn't notice.

Max arrived about ten minutes later with wooden tray full of food. There was a lot of food, probably enough for six people. There was an assortment of meat on wooden skewers, a large bowl of salad, bread and potatoes.

They didn't seem to go together; it was all just grabbed out of a cupboard and thrown at random onto a tray, with no finesse or style of presentation. It was just a pile of food ticked off a list. Stuff you ate. There was a bottle of olive oil, but no other extras - no salt, pepper, or sauce.

Food was clearly there as a function to him, not something to be enjoyed. There was no grill on the fire either so he placed a couple of logs either side of the burning wood and coals, and balanced the long wooden skewers with the meat on them across them to cook.

He used a stick to turn them occasionally, to stop the wood cindering too much, even though they had been sensibly soaked in water beforehand.

The food though was good, fresh, and full of flavour and aromas, which mixed with the evening scent coming from the bushes and trees around. The meat was a mixture of blue rare and well done charcoal, but Sam wasn't very fussy. It looked OK to him.

Again they ate in silence but it all seemed more relaxed now, Max was clearly becoming more at ease with the situation, and at having someone like Sam around to talk to.

The dog hadn't made any fuss either; it just lay next to the wall with its eyes half closed, clearly banned from begging when food was being consumed. But when they had both finished eating, it sat up, its eyes clearly focused on the leftovers with a newly interested demeanour.

The sun had completely set now, but it wasn't quite dark. The air became filled with the sound of cicadas and a few birds singing evening songs away in the woods. The wind had dropped off and the temperature had settled to a pleasant eighteen degrees.

There were a few stars appearing in the sky above, and these were occasionally joined by floating sparks from the fire lifted by the heat and smoke. Sam helped Max clear things away to the kitchen and piled the plates into the sink in the other room.

They returned with another bottle of wine and some mugs to sit outside with again, and Sam added some more logs to the fire.

After a few moments Max began talking again, carrying on from where he had left off much earlier.

"If you look at society today," he began "you can see where this is all going, communities vanishing. We are becoming much more individualized, everyone focused on their own needs rather than others, yet we are fascinated with what is happening with other people, news, what is going on in the rest of the world, facts, figures, profit, who is doing and saying what, gossip, trends, fashion, films and so on. Yet overall there appears to be no emotional coherence.

"We have just evolved into functionally limited and emotionally weak individuals. We have voted for governments without feelings or strength of character. Strong individuals, kings, emperors, dictators, have all been superseded with democratic governments or military states.

"So by removing the need for individuals, we have done away

with the random emotional element. It is no longer logical. It is ineffective and irrelevant.

"Thus we have been evolved into a more emotionless world, less religious, at the higher level. No Crusades, wars, the 'Glory of Rome' stuff.

"We really just can't be bothered any more, and no more of your 'Once more unto the breach, dear friends…'" He finished in a 'put on' English accent and gestured with his arms in dramatic fashion before taking another mouthful of wine.

"We, as individuals, can see how important emotions and feelings are. Or at least we believe them to be important. Love, hate, greed. So why are we creating a world now where these things are being supressed or generated artificially? It just doesn't add up.

"So stepping back, I eventually figured out what was going on and why. We have formed this collective mind, a joint integrated subconscious, that has evolved with us, of which we are all part of. Not just the collective psyche structures in all of us, that Jung and other psychologists have correctly defined, but something operating in its own right in macro form, a hive subconscious mind, of which we are all part of to some extent, and subject to.

"IT also has a collective shared knowledge database, built up of all our combined knowledge, filtered and mapped and correlated to form clear pictures, and logical analysis of everything we know about, yet also interpolated from its own perspective.

"IT holds this information in our minds collectively, in the minds of everyone, like a distributed network database, so that in our minds there is our data, our individual knowledge, and also our collective knowledge and thoughts, but coordinated in its own right.

"In the same way as bees in hives, or wolves, develop a collective awareness and operate as a whole or as a group, so IT has developed or evolved to operate and think on a collective basis, but at a much more sophisticated level, a general will, all communicating at a subatomic level, passing information between each other as a field, refining direction and decision based on need and supply and demand. Taking care of threats, making use of resources and driving us to build up its knowledge base, to learn and discover, explore and find, creating need, and at the same time improving its integration and working mechanisms that are made up of psyche groups within IT."

This was all now starting to get interesting for Sam. Max was now moving on from the negative perspective he had been going over earlier, and was now able to start defining what 'IT' was, and how it was structured and operated. Much of it was making a lot of sense to Sam. Max had obviously had to get over the hurdle of his anger, frustration and perception, before he could start to get to the heart of what he had worked out from it all. What Sam didn't know though was, which parts were correct and which bits Max had just assumed.

"So," Max went on "that's why we have such large parts of our brains that we don't appear to be using very much. Our brains have become a massive biological multiprocessor system with distributed shared collective knowledge, and decision making systems with a dynamic knowledge database. It is referred to as Akashic Records in some cultures. It has become so sophisticated that it is now very adept and smart at directing attention away from its existence. It is natural for IT to be hidden from us by natural selection and evolution, after all nature favours the group rather than the individual.

"IT even makes it hard for people to be able to describe it, or identify it, or define it.

"The problem with describing and articulating what you perceive is going on, or what it's all about, or what you have experienced, and what is being 'shown' to you in real day-to-day events, is a very difficult thing to do from many aspects. How it all works, what IT is, and what is happening, in real 'down to earth' terms.

"It's not just being able to find the correct descriptive words to encompass the experiences or feeling or concept, but also elaborating it in terms of analogy, feeling, and relationship terms to the world we see and feel, and the concepts we understand and can relate to. So the obvious is hidden from us.

"You can know a concept of something in your head that you

feel or experience, and it makes perfect sense, the perception is there, and at that time it feels completely obvious, clear and rational.

"You have a mass of understanding and thought processes are all going on, with how every part of it all works, along with context, and the feelings and emotions and sense of yourself. Like having that sort of 'Eureka' moment where you know everything and it all fits and makes eloquent sense.

"Then, at that very moment, you try to write it down as best you can, while it is still fresh in your head, even using examples or analogies to assimilate the context or relationship to something we all know and understand in the world we all see.

"You write down as much as you can. You read it back, and it makes perfect sense, clear and accurate as much as is possible to describe what is in your head, even though you have only captured a small essence of what you are thinking and feeling into words.

"Like trying to explain what a passionate kiss is like. The memory of it, motion and actions, the thoughts and sensations, and articulating the feeling of passion still in your head. So you write them down, you describe them, as best you can, along with the actions, and information from your senses.

"A few days later you go to read the page that you wrote. Now however it's not the same at all. It seems odd and not complete; the complexity, the feelings, additional context or reference that you had before isn't there now. It doesn't make as much sense. It is flat, boring, the intense feeling you had before for the revelation just isn't the same.

"You read some parts of it, and you aren't even sure what you were on about, or what it related to at the time. You realise then that there must have been so much more in your head at that time that you weren't aware of, or able to latch on to, something with a collective perspective, thoughts or concepts that just don't translate into descriptive lateral real world concepts or thoughts, like translating parallel into serial. Describing a kiss isn't the same as having one.

"IT is putting ideas or knowledge into my mind to help it work things out, perceive, and rationalise. Once the information has been processed, then it is pushed out. It is hard to keep it in mind or to articulate it, very much like dream information or structure.

"You know how hard it is to remember dreams? It is transient. Unless you are able to write it down, into say a journal, it will be lost.

"However if you are able to do just that, by doing so you can then also build up a much bigger picture of what is going on - a cross section objective view over time.

"We find songs are easy to remember, a series of links, a journey. You can write them down, remember them, and associate with them. Collective information doesn't work like that; it is very much parallel and state orientated, pertaining to a decision point and data coming together to form a focal point. It all has context and meaning when it happens but that is it - like travellers meeting at a crossroads.

"Some days your perspective or awareness is the same as everyone else's. You struggle to feel or see the way you did, losing sight of it all, surrounded by distraction and crowds, you are back to 'normal'.

"You then also realise that it's not just a problem with articulation or descriptive ability, it's to do with reference; you are trying to explain something that has many dimensions, or aspects to it, that are all interrelated.

"Things linked like a brain diagram, all relevant at the same time. Things that only mean something when they are put together at the one instant in time in your head. You can't describe it in totality in any order as it's all in parallel, and it doesn't make sense in any other way unless it is correlated, and then only in your head.

"Which is why you then revert back to analogies to try and create some sort of picture of it, as it is not 'like' anything you could envisage or draw a picture of.

"It is also apparent that people are only allowed or able to perceive and understand and 'see' what they need to, or are required to see on a compartmentalised 'need to know' basis.

"So you may try to explain something to one person, and they can see and understand and equate what you are trying to express, but someone else may not, or they only 'get' one part.

"People are deliberately kept ignorant and naïve, it is in IT's interest to do so. IT only needs some people to be aware of everything, or at least large parts of everything, so they can do their job or role as part of IT.

"This happens over and over again for lots of concepts that you perceive, or manage to work out - these revelations.

"At the time it all makes sense to you in your head, clarifying some part of what IT is how it works. However describing this concept to someone else who has not experienced the same is next to impossible, as they have no reference or way of conceptualising what you are saying.

"Often you don't even know where to start; it's like describing a musical concert to a deaf person. The capability of describing IT improves over time as we develop more knowledge and understanding and are able to describe IT in more informed, descriptive concepts, technical terms, or analogies.

"Then equally IT itself becomes more complex as you go on, evolving, keeping pace.

"It is then that you realise that this process is going on all the time everywhere, and that what is being translated through to the conscious part of your brain, or whatever or however you define it, over the long term, is a synthesised picture of something much more complex being correlated within our combined psyche underneath, and collectively all the time. Therein lays the fundamental problem, which in itself is a clue.

"The trouble is, if you don't write it all down at the time you end up with no reference information at all. Yet by building up lots of these concepts and visions or revelations you begin to build up a coherent set of pictures, snapshots, that eventually becomes a film of sorts, a different perspective altogether, as I said before.

"You notice too that by doing this you are also creating more concepts in themselves; interesting similarities or crossovers that were not obvious before that you can now use to relate to the others. You are now building up your own additional form of translation and perspective.

"Also, you find that things you wrote several years ago don't make as much sense now as they did then. You have moved on so much more in your understanding, the same as moving up rungs on a ladder. But they are still important as dated reference points, a diary, and an indication of where you were in the evolution of your thinking at the time.

"Each time you knew and understood everything in relation to that concept, and it made perfect sense, and it was correct at that moment in time; it's just that you have more of a depth of knowledge now, and can create a better level of understanding before going up to the next rung a few months later.

"Throughout history religions have changed in much the same way; they have evolved in complexity in line with human understanding, cultural bias, and global knowledge at that specific period of time.

"With what you know now though, you can see their flaws, the gaps in the logic and context. You can see where, and how, and by what, causes the religions were created in the psyche, and how they are reinforced and perpetuated by the collective subconscious mind.

"So in that respect they are important in that it is useful to see what is, and what was, going on at that point in history, and indeed now; for instance - examining the process of change and its mechanisms over time - if they weren't there we would perhaps be starting again from scratch, rather than avoiding reinventing the wheel, or going down the same rabbit holes.

"For example if you were to read the pages of your diary now from when you were eighteen, it would just look like naïve adolescent ramblings; and yet to an eighteen year old reading it, your words would make perfect sense, and mean everything, as it did to you then at the time. So you just have an on-going diary that only makes sense at the time you wrote it with no coherent overall statement or picture, unless you see it as a process.

"If you are smart, you question, you step back, and look at what went on before; the process, what was assumed. What does, and doesn't make logical sense. You use the knowledge of what we know now. You find others who have done the same thing, compare notes and share knowledge, put a methodology around it, test it, stage manage it; treat it like a business project if you like.

"You use your skills and experience to approach it objectively. Which of course is what you would do with anything, if you are wise.

"It's then that you see that other people have tried to articulate a small number of these new concepts more recently in the form of films or books.

"They seem to be trying to say something, or small parts thereof; something underlying, mysterious or secret, a hidden idea, ultimate knowledge, that sort of thing.

"This has happened much more regularly in the last few decades in certain science fiction and fantasy works; each just small pieces of an overall picture that you have in your head that is obvious, but you just can't describe it unless you were to take all the pieces together, and integrate them into one somehow."

At those words Sam felt a rush of tingling energy in his body, like a light going on somewhere inside. It was as if several things in his mind were suddenly switched on to work together, equate what was being said 'to' or at him, with what he understood, or had to work out. His mind started racing with numerous thoughts, all flashing up, and going off in different directions, and the muscles in his torso and back started to tingle.

Sam stood up, he needed a moment to think on his own without Max saying anything else.

It was getting cold now in the pitch dark and the fire was going out. The cicadas were singing loudly too, and Sam was sure that if he sat around for any longer his legs would start being eaten by their insect friends.

Max took the hint and they gathered up everything that needed to be taken inside and went into the kitchen to put things away, save for the scraps which Max slipped into the bowl outside the door.

The dog was pleased with the long awaited bonus, but not so happy when it looked into the bowl at the handful of bits. It looked up indignantly at Max as if to say "Is that it?"

The dog was clearly expecting a large steak instead of the morsels he received. It demolished what was there in a few seconds, sighed and then slopped off to its kennel just along from the back door. The dog already knew there was little chance of being allowed in the house, unlike the 'favoured' visitor.

After clearing up, they both went into the lounge with their mugs and a bottle. Max lit the candles in the room which gave an eerie light to the bookcases, comfy chairs and disorganised furniture. It was still quite warm inside so there was no need for a fire, but it did seem quite strange without one in the dim light and silence.

It almost felt as if there should be something, even a stereo playing some form of music. Sam wandered over to the bookcases with his mug, and looked more closely at some of the sections he hadn't seen earlier. There were certainly a lot of books. They were all neatly organised into a variety of different topics, fields, religions and reference journals, both fiction and non-fiction.

Max was sitting in what was obviously his favourite sofa. He waited for Sam to carry on looking until he reached a bookcase close to him, at which point he resumed the conversation.

"Certain films or books suddenly have hidden, single, indirect meanings or concepts in them that sort of make sense in one part of the context of what you perceive, but you are not sure if they were trying to say something or if something else was trying to get a simple idea across through them as some sort of message or piece of information.

"It's like something is trying to say something or explain something or describe itself subconsciously in a way we can't perceive. No other form of communication like maths or music helps with the problem. It's also not helped by a sort of collective subconscious hypnosis that makes it very difficult for people collectively to see or comprehend what you are writing. Just as in the same way as our own conscious minds shields or hides our subconscious from us normally.

"Even if you made it all into a play or a film or a book, they would not see the overall message, just the story.

"It isn't much help if the thing that is communicating with you doesn't know what IT is itself, or has very limited understanding of the context and perspective of what you are in. Like a vastly evolved and complex hive mind trying to define itself to a bee.

"You firstly can't believe what it says. How can you? If IT doesn't know what it is itself, and only has its one point of reference, i.e. itself, or limited context to describe itself with, you can only go on what it does, how it behaves, how it reacts, and what its priorities are.

"None of this is helped of course by you being part of IT. You have to build up a picture based on many methods, including a process of elimination as to what it's not, like twenty questions.

"IT may think it knows it all, has ultimate wisdom, ultimate power, will live forever, and is all there is, but then so do most teenagers from their perspective."

Sam sat down in the leather sofa the other side of the fireplace from where Max was. It was comfortable enough but not something you could fall asleep in. He leaned back and put his head against the back of it, and rested his mug of wine on the armrest. Max sat forward in his seat so he could talk 'at' Sam - to get another point over to him.

"If it acts like a teenager, thinks like a teenager, drives like a teenager, behaves like a teenager, thinks it's God almighty with little understanding of its own body full of teenage organs, all of which are getting stressed and confused, then it probably is a teenager.

"Of course teenagers these days don't listen and we don't understand them at all.

"It's all part of life, growing up, understanding ourselves, and not being able to understand anyone else. Equally you can't fall into the trap of defining IT as a teenager either, as by trying to evaluate IT by perception, IT then defines itself as such, like a self-fulfilling prophecy.

"You can only go on what IT is interested in, what subjects it focuses on, what it knows and doesn't, and work out why, and then cross reference it all.

"Like in any body, it's only when you have a problem or when things go wrong and something happens, that you become aware of what is there. Like your appendix. Normally you would never know you had one. If everything is OK and working well, is looked after, and is functioning correctly and you felt fit and healthy, you would never even know things were there.

"But when errors creep in, and it isn't managed properly, then things in your body go wrong. When pain, stress, and pressure come along that's when you see. The same also applies to the mind, and the collective mind, all in the same way.

"The trouble with the collective mind is that you may also run the risk of changing it by the very act of observation, as with many things, so you also have to let it define itself as much as possible.

"For example it may be a baby, or it could be several thousand years old. Stand back and wait, be patient, build up a perspective, cross check. But this of course is not easy considering the nature of what we are trying to describe.

"What you need is a fixed point of reference to hold onto in your mind; something that doesn't change, beyond the thing that is changing, a describing outside perspective. You must equate what there is against it, a sort of management perspective. This gives you something outside of IT to describe IT against, otherwise you are simply trying to describe and articulate something that you are not sure about, and being inside IT you have nothing to compare or describe IT against."

The words that Max was using now were surprisingly clear, precise, and well defined. Sam almost wished that he had been recording or writing down what was being said, but instead he just listened intently. He was a little sorry that he had the wine now, but then the situation seemed to be working as it was. He sat forward a little more in his seat and tried to concentrate.

"So when you have thoughts in your head, with a perception that is enlightened, and an experience that enables you to perceive in that respect, or that way, you can envisage all the thoughts and concepts of what is actually there; how it works, what it is, what is there, and then it makes perfect sense, it all fits together.

"But putting that down in written form or picture is not easy, you cannot describe it all at once like from parallel to serial, so all the context and meaning and expression cannot be incorporated at once.

"You even try to use multiple analogies to convey the series of recognisable 'pictures' in our terms of reference . IT will of course try to outsmart you, that's what it does, that's its nature; IT is diametrically opposed to us as individuals, and we to IT at the same time.

"It's also frustrating because you can't understand why people can't see what you see; why they are stuck in their 'religious' perception of life, and the way things are. Why they don't see the world, and life, the way you do and what seems so obvious to you is so farfetched to them, or appears mad.

"You kick away their mental crutches, explain things and they get upset. You rationalise every single thing that happens, and what is going on, and they sort of understand but they don't 'see' it. None of them have the point of reference that you have, well, all but a very, very few.

"Of course, these days, you get books that rise quickly in popularity that elude to a small piece of these hidden secrets; with the answers woven into subtle stories, pertaining to some 'big mystery' that they never quite get to defining in any detail, just pointing to many strange connections and letting you pull your own conclusions together, with weak unfulfilling endings.

"The trouble is that you see the hard facts and the level of complexity of what is really going on is way above all of that, and at far too complex a level to that which people can deal with.

"As a result, of course, the truth as you see it wouldn't sell many books, if indeed you were even able to describe something so vast and complicated. Not to mention the problem of actually trying to write it all down when you are living with the thing in your mind, day after day."

He paused and looked down at the ground. His expression changed and it was almost as if he had lost his place in the conversation. He was trying to convey an image of a picture to Sam and kept going off in different directions trying to express different aspects of it but was clearly frustrated with himself.

"In some respects it tries to categorise people into roles in the same way as we do into types of worker where people are naturally put into slots or functions. This is why we see people wanting to see other people settled into in set roles such as doctors, dentists, lawyers, bricklayers. We aren't happy unless we can label and categorise everyone.

"IT just operates like a robot or an operating system with a shared database of matrix neurology. It forms data collectively and generates natural evolutionary steps in its development. Like an operating system in a computer, with a highly complex Artificial Intelligence that is doing what it does within its remit; expanding, evolving, sharing, collating, adapting, driven by inertia and a need for survival and information.

"Yet, we ourselves do not all like the way the human race is going. We don't like the way we are, but we seem powerless to change the direction. That is because we are dealing with something that is operating at a subconscious level. IT doesn't 'think' or 'behave' the way we do. Although IT is a combined consciousness, IT is just operating on a lower level. It has a massive database of knowledge and is able to channel information very well naturally. It needs to operate at a lower, slower level like basic brain functions, IT is regressive to us, not as 'advanced'.

"Although we think and have emotions and brain structures at many levels, IT doesn't need to. IT hasn't had to evolve the way we have, or had to develop through complex evolution for survival. IT evolves for IT's benefit, biased towards its own needs and benefits, not ours as individuals. It has no other natural enemies, only failures within itself. So us trying to make sense of IT is very difficult.

"We can see ever worsening trends developing in the world with attitudes, culture and violence but we cannot seem to change it. We just do the things we can get away with, rewarding the wrong behaviour, gathering resources we don't need, and we keep pandering to the lowest levels even though we know it's wrong."

Sam stood up and walked around the room. He needed to stretch his legs again, they were starting to complain and he didn't want to start looking uncomfortable or appear to get tired or drift off to sleep. He gestured for Max to carry on talking, and wandered over to the paintings to look at them more closely for a few minutes as Max talked to him, before eventually returning to his seat.

Max continued "You can see traces of these collective reactions sometimes globally. Certain events can trigger something collectively, which bring on a common emotional response and reaction far in excess of the rational impact of the event. This is focused on by the media and is then reinforced.

"Take the death of your Princess Diana! That had a profound emotional effect on a vast number of people in complete disproportion to the event or the feeling people had for her just before the event. It was just a specific shock at that time that seemed to trigger a collective emotional reaction like being woken suddenly from sleep. Sudden bursts of adrenalin, a need for release, and to share mourning to overcome the hard need to mourn.

"The shocking destruction of the Twin Towers was another such event which, although terrible, was not on the geographic scale of, say, an earthquake flattening a city in Haiti. It was because it was on the live news, witnessed together by hundreds of millions of people, that it had such a dramatic effect that was transmitted and shared at the same time.

"It left you feeling cold; you could not understand what you were seeing, there was a massive collective shock as to what was happening; resonated and reinforced around the world, that invoked a collective response, much the same as an ants or bees nest would respond to someone visibly kicking it.

"So why would a collective mind allow such a thing to happen in the first place? Why does our God 'move in mysterious ways'? Well it's because it is a collective subconscious mind that doesn't think consciously, and IT is quite logical and automated acting on its own behalf. So the answer is that IT doesn't allow these things to happen consciously, it does not take conscious decisions, it is just a combination of basic functions, animalistic natural behaviours and subconscious influences. So all IT does is influence direction and goals and behaviour.

"For example, the Twin Towers in New York was an event resulting from hate – an emotion which IT doesn't work with. So '9/11' happened because it had no overall risk of effect on the direction or the operation of the machine, except that the emotional impact of what actually happened, did.

"The same happened with the death of Princess Diana and the subsequent illogical amount of collective grief afterwards. Not just in your country, but worldwide. Where did that come from and why? What caused it? Was the response needed somehow – a release that had to happen, a response in need for collective grief over anything?

"There was a collective need to grieve, triggered by news and visual press stimulus, and this was the ideal opportunity – the question is why? Why was there a need? What was the real underlying problem? Has that emotion gone now? The whole thing built up and up with people crying uncontrollably, yet before she died she was 'off the radar' for most people, nobody really took much interest, many people looking at the news could not understand what was going on, it did not make sense.

"The same thing with the Twin Towers; the event generated a shock wave, a collective emotion, produced by everyone experiencing it at the same time. So you see that sort of effect didn't happen in the same way historically when we just had newspapers, or depended on word of mouth.

"Also if you look around everywhere, we are, or IT is, trying to control, channel, and manage collective emotions and behaviour. It's all around us - television, entertainment, crowd control, sports events, concerts, live shows, festivals, and how or where we work.

"Why are we having our lives filled up with so many *things*? Why are there so many things to do, and why are people using up our time so much? We do not exist as individuals any more.

"Evolution has enabled some animals with the ability to utilise the subatomic communication field to improve their efficiency and survival rate; getting that 'edge' above the others. To know when you are being looked at is useful to a deer if being stalked by a wolf, and a wolf that can communicate with its pack as one is a more efficient hunter.

"That sense is non-directional - although you may feel that someone is watching you, you can't sense from where. You can't easily detect friends or close loved ones staring at you as you only react to strangers or threats. The same applies to close bonded people, twins, synchronised people who respond and think in the same way at the same time.

"Many types of dream occur and you can find thousands of people who can analyse the dreams you may be having. They can interpret them into a rationalism of emotional events or dilemmas you are facing in your life at that time.

"Your dreams are a way of attempting to sort out problems in your mind, with your rational mind turned off and with the logic disabled, you are left with our emotional core mind to deal with the problem in an emotional, irrational way, interfacing to the collective mind. If the problem does not go away then the dreams may re-occur, and in some cases be very frightening and vivid.

"There are some types of dreams that are very common and recurring, conveying the same message. How often do you hear people say 'I had a dream that I was falling?' So how does this involve a shared, collective subconscious? Well, for starters, people have already mapped dreams to specific problems so clearly that we know that there is some form of reverse logic going on.

"For example, if you have *this* problem then you need to have *this* dream. Before it switches off and implants a message with a dream template, the dreaming mind takes that template and weaves a dream around with its own interpretation of it and works it through.

"So why do we need to dream at all? What is the benefit, or are we working to interpret something? Surely we should have evolved so that we don't need to sleep or dream if there were no need to?"

At this point Max stopped and was now clearly waiting for Sam to say something, some affirmation that he understood and agreed with his point of view. Max had some sort of concept image in his head that he was trying to get Sam to accept, or at least see and understand, with analogy and examples.

However from Sam's perspective there were a lot of gaps in the picture. Sam knew that he could either agree with him, and let Max continue, and hope that the picture would become a little clearer, or stop him and get him to try and describe a little better, what he was on about.

The concepts that Max was putting across were starting to make sense in parts, although it was hard to try and visualise or perceive what Max was trying to convey. The picture that Max had in his head of what 'IT' was in comparison to the picture Sam had were similar but still very sketchy. So Sam decided to let him plough on, and gave a few reassuring nods and motioned for him to continue.

"So," continued Max "if you can't provide IT with what it wants then you are ignored, and you eventually go away, or do not matter. So by natural selection, you, us, people, over generations, evolve to be what IT needs.

"Conversely, if you think or try to go against IT, or try to change things, you will find things are made hard for you, and people are set against you, and strange odd coincidences happen and stop you in your tracks."

It was then that Sam thought of the incident with Brina at the supermarket. Something 'clicked' and he narrowed his eyes.

"The secret is to trick it into thinking that you are giving it what it needs, slowly and gently taking, but giving at the same time. In the same way as if you had to de-flea a wolf.

"You could also view IT as a machine, a program, following set rules and controls, and the Laws of Nature. But if IT is aware of you as a problem, and you identify yourself as a real threat to IT, whether internally or externally, then IT is capable of using that 'magic' to act against you via other people."

Sam could sense in Max the feeling of injustice, and the lack of control of his life that he felt he had lost. This was the thing that made him so angry and frustrated.

Max hadn't done anything wrong other than try to work out what was going on, and why. He had made himself out to be a threat and he had been picked on. He was unable to fight IT or have any recourse or help to get around that injustice.

"Oh and another thing…" said Max, turning as he was walking back to the kitchen, "IT can't read."

Sam was putting it all into context with what he knew and what he had been through, and he could now feel a growing anxiety building up from his stomach. He really wished that he hadn't had the wine. His head was trying to equate the consequences of what Max was telling him, or more to the point, what loose ends Sam was able to now tie together.

It was all so obvious. It explained so many things that were going on, the basic contexts, but beyond that it was still so vast and complex. With the knowledge he had he started to work through a lot of the unexplained connections, and it made his head spin.

From the conversation with Max, combined with the knowledge Sam already had in his head, he was now creating a very complex picture in his mind of what was really going on.

Probably far more complete and refined than the confused shape that appeared in Max's.

Max seemed to only cover certain aspects, but there were a whole range of other areas, disciplines, sciences, spiritualties and unexplained things that needed to be combined with it all to make sense of it. It was there in his mind, the picture, but it was impossible to describe it in totality.

Max pointed to the bookcases on the wall.

"It's like going into a library, where you have the opportunity to learn everything, but you can't possibly read everything, you just have to know what the library is, how it is divided into sections. You also stop to work out how the library was built, and why it is there, or who is the librarian and what they are doing."

Stepping back now Sam could see that there was a much bigger picture coming into view, and it had ominous consequences and implications. He now felt like a 'know-it-all' adolescent student thrown into the streets of a city and exposed to the harsh realities and dangers of real life.

Max came back in from the kitchen carrying a mug of coffee, and walked over to the bookcase and pulled out a modern hardback book.

"You see," he went on "there have been many people in the past who have experienced close interaction with the collective mind in many different ways. This has happened either as a result of how their mind worked, circumstances, accidents, drugs, or just random nature. It's a question of interpretation, putting what you perceive into words, and articulating what you experience based on what you know, and already understand."

Sam could read the author's name on the side of the book - 'Philip K Dick'. Sam had heard of him but couldn't associate a book with the name.

"Here," said Max "in here, this guy tries to put some parts of it down into fictional ideas, and he works it into a science fiction story.

"Vast Active Living Information System - VALIS" and Max turned the book to Sam so that he could see the cover. At this point Sam remembered a few science fiction films that he had seen and realised that the stories for the films had been written by the same author, but he hadn't seen that one.

Max looked at Sam. "Do the letters rearranged mean anything to you?" Sam thought for a minute, but at that point he was not really interested, he was getting tired and the wine was numbing his mind.

"Elvis?" he said finally with a slight shrug.

"Alice? Spelling was never my strong point…" and he smiled apologetically.

Max looked at him blankly. Clearly Max had the typical German sense of humour.

"No," he continued slowly without changing his expression "If you rearrange the letters it spells SILVA, and also forms the start and end of VANGELIS."

At that point Sam's now fuzzy and tired mind cleared instantly and he sat up and narrowed his eyes again. His mind jumped back to the series of personal development courses he had gone on many years ago at the suggestion of a friend in the early 90's for meditation and improving his mental abilities and health.

"You mean the SILVA method?" he asked. It was now Max's turn to look taken aback. "You know about SILVA?" he asked.

Sam went on to explain the courses in detail and of what he had learnt and used many years ago. Was Max implying some sort of conspiracy going on here ?

Sam wasn't into conspiracy theories. He had seen far too much of the realities of life. His work had taken him into the deepest, darkest areas of government organisations and establishments, and he knew that in reality the vast number of conspiracy theories were very much just speculation, or caused by the need to cover up incompetence, inefficiency, or job preservation, or for operational security rather than anything interesting or deliberate

As far as conspiracies went, Sam had a fairly clear picture in his head of how the world was run and operated, and it was not the usual concept that many people had of sets of hyper-rich groups controlling everything, feeding misinformation to the masses, and some underlying long term agendas of control.

Yes, there were groups in banking, and criminal organisations, media, and political organisations that exerted influence and control to meet their own needs. However, overall, there was nobody at the helm, no 'Men in Black', no groups of people that met in secret every month to decide on what the world was going to do, and what lies the media would feed it.

Much of the deceit and subterfuge and dealings were as a result of individual greed, political drive and selfishness; fear covering up incompetence, poor management, and good old bureaucratic red tape.

So the range of conspiracy theories that were high level were just that - people trying to make sense of the overall lack of logic in the way the world wasn't run.

Even organisations set up to make the world a better place were in effect powerless, as the countries and organisations who wanted to do something about it all were reluctant to relinquish true power to let it all happen.

The world had just grown too quickly and the mechanisms for running it hadn't been given enough time to evolve and expand with it. So there was no group in charge. No dark men behind the scenes making all the decisions for the world. Which on one level was good news, and on the other not so good.

So Sam knew where this was going. In most cases the theory arose from someone who was paranoid about something that they had no visibility of and that they were suspicious of, and with something that defied explanation. This in turn led to creative imaginations generating concepts of what *must* be going on behind closed doors; whereas the reality was somewhat more boring, with the individuals involved on the inside just doing their jobs, as best they could, within the constraints and limitations of the system they existed in. It was easy to create coincidence.

So he decided to interrupt the flow of the conversation. "You mean like a message from Elvis?" queried Sam smiling.

Max just stared at him, confused, and Sam returned the stare, and raised his eyebrows. They continued to stare at each other for a while, exchanging silent information, until finally Max walked over to his mug of coffee, picked it up, and emptied it in one.

"You see," said Max more firmly "this guy was writing his stories at the same time as these methods were being developed for the mind and body.

"It was a sort of coded message. He spent his whole life trying to explain what he had experienced, an experience similar to the one that you had, and he was trying to make sense of it and wrap anything around it that was going on to make sense of it all, as did many before him.

"But he just couldn't. He did a great job and worked hard, but he wasn't able to get close to working it all out. Lots of these people were schizophrenic or of similar mental situations, where they were influenced, in touch, and affected by, the collective parts of their brains, and conversely directly affecting the overall collective mind or psyche groups; some massively so, mentioning no names.

"People were interfering with the natural progression of things that they really didn't understand, which in itself is all part of the process; even more so in the last hundred years with the use of mind altering drugs.

"Since then it has all gone, what is that expression of yours? 'Tits up'." Max again used an English accent and smiled.

"You see," Max continued "there is a difference between

imagining what something could be, believing what it might be, thinking what it should be, and knowing what it is.

"When you '*know what it is*', you have responsibility, and then you have a choice.

"You can decide to do something about it, or not."

Then he looked down and his smile disappeared.

"It's all just too mixed up now, too complicated, too controlling, too difficult to understand.

"It's just a mess and there is nothing anyone can do about it."

CHAPTER 9 - WHERE THE HEART IS

Sam woke with the daylight in a place he was not familiar with; the sun streaming through the bare windows into a room of half empty packing boxes.

He was lying on a wooden framed bed, its new mattress still in its plastic wrappings. He was still clothed and he ached, and his back was damp with sweat from being next to the plastic. His head felt numb, not from a hangover, but as if he hadn't slept, like it had been working away all night in his absence. He sat up and his back complained at the additional burden it had to endure in addition to the brick hard bed it had already had to cope with.

He was tired, irritable and in need of a shower. His mind was busy processing things, thoughts flying around all over the place, pulling bits and pieces together from dreams and concepts that had obviously been working around in his mind in the night, sparked off by his conversations with Max.

The sounds and smells from the Greek fauna outside his window drifted in through the half-open windows and he slowly worked out where he was and why he was there.

There was quite a breeze blowing now, which seemed to have shut the cicadas up. He got out of bed, stumbled around in the room looking for his rucksack, pulled out a bottle of water and downed it along with a few headache tablets.

He then opened the door and made his way to the kitchen to find something for breakfast. The back door was open so he guessed that Max was already up and out walking somewhere.

Sam walked barefoot over to the fridge, which of course was only a cupboard with a cool box in it, and opened it, still bleary eyed and only half-awake. He lifted out the carton of milk which he found was empty and that it had a slightly cheesy odour to it. There were a few things he could not quite cope without, and breakfast was one of them.

It also had something to do with not having to wake up until the last possible moment, even if that was as you drove into the office car park for work in the morning. Breakfast was one of those automatic pilot activities, and meant that everything had to be in place beforehand to avoid having to wake up and think.

He closed the door and looked around the kitchen, and then just picked up an apple from the fruit bowl, and ate it standing in the open doorway.

There was no sign of the dog either so he assumed they must both be off doing some rounds somewhere. In any case he didn't feel comfortable any more, not just physically, but with the situation there; it felt odd, as if he had outstayed his welcome, even though he had only been there one day.

Before long there would be some personality clash he was sure, besides he could feel that the levels of the discussions were tough for the German to cope with, stress-wise.

He didn't want to push him too far, or force him to deal with keeping pace in discussions that put pressure on him. He didn't want to be responsible for a nervous breakdown or stroke - he just wasn't qualified to deal with that sort of thing.

He made his way to the bathroom with his bag and washed and shaved himself as best he could. He noticed that even the water pipes and the taps and fittings were all plastic - Max must have had some very interesting meetings with the builders in the specification of what was required.

Sam put on the fresh set of clothes that Brina had packed for him and then went back to the kitchen to wait for Max and his dog to return.

It was awkward telling Max that he was leaving. He felt as if he was abandoning him from one perspective. Max managed to look both sad and indifferent at the same time, weighing up his need for space and solitude and his limit of capacity for coping with company.

Max had spent part of the night making notes for him; books, people and things to look into, and he gave it to Sam in a folder with a couple of other thin books to read. After a few minutes of conversation they walked through to collect Sam's things and then out through the kitchen door again. They shook hands as they parted. It was as if they both knew it was the right thing.

It was OK, but a little awkward none the less.

Walking back up the hill in the early morning seemed a lot harder work than it should have been. He put it down to the thin air and lack of decent sleep, but it could have been that the drinks that the German had given him were still leaving residual toxins in his muscles. It was, in any case, better to leave now than in the intense full heat of the day.

He still couldn't get a mobile signal to ring the boy at the shop, so he knew he had a good half an hour walk to get back to the town and so he paced himself.

As he got to the top of the path the air turned quite close, and the sky clouded over with heavy grey clouds and Sam desperately hoped that it wouldn't start raining before he got there.

 He decided to stop and rest for a minute when he got to the entrance of Max's land. He sat on the cool box and realised, sadly, that it was empty, otherwise he may have been tempted to borrow a bottle of something cold from it.

Breathing in the dry air heavily, he closed his eyes and concentrated on not sweating too much. It was going to be a lot harder getting back up than coming down, and this wasn't something he had thought about, or planned for, in his excitement to get there.

Standing up slowly he headed off back up the hill, and traced the track back up to the road. It was very dusty and not easy to walk on but he managed it. The noise from the cicadas was loud now next to the trees, and made it hard to listen for approaching cars.

A couple of minutes went by, and a truck came down the road. Sam stepped into the grass verge, which was just as well, as the damn thing didn't slow down at all. It just gave a single blast on the horn and carried on at speed, followed by a giant cloud of billowing dust which drifted and landed over the already dusty bushes and trees, along with his clothes and rucksack.

He just couldn't understand the mentality of some people; it was blind selfish ignorance, they had no consideration for others, and it was all just a juvenile means of amusement.

About twenty five minutes later he arrived in the village. It was almost deserted and so he made his way to the shop again.

It was now getting on towards midday, and instead of the boy he had met there before, he found a smart middle-aged woman behind the counter. She was wearing a headscarf that covered her straight black hair. She seemed polite enough, and greeted him in broken English, indicating that he had become somewhat of a local news story.

Sam wandered around the shop, picked up a few bottles of water, some fruit and a few packets of sweets. While paying for them he asked the woman if he could get a taxi to the airport, and what the price would be.

He knew full well that he had just walked past a taxi with the driver asleep inside it, but decided that it would be wiser to get someone else to wake him up, and that it would probably be cheaper in the long run.

They both stepped out of the shop to look for a taxi and Sam stopped in the shade to let the woman go over on her own to wake the driver up. As she crossed the road a couple of teenage boys riding off-road motocross bikes came up from one of the side roads into the village, shattering the quiet.

They stopped outside one of the other buildings and got off their bikes. The noise, in stark contrast to the peace, had unsettled Sam. Quite why anyone would need to make so much noise and deliberately use something without an exhaust silencer was beyond him.

He realised that these two must be the same ones that went on the fields just outside of Max's property and had caused him so much stress. So he guessed this was no coincidence.

The woman was still talking to the taxi driver so Sam wandered over to the boys. Standing up straight and looking confident, he looked at them both. "Do you speak English?" he asked, and they looked at each other and then back at him and nodded slightly arrogantly.

"Do you ride your bikes on the land down there by the German?" he asked directly, backing up his question with points and gestures.

It was clear that they understood him, and that it was them, from their expressions. However instead of acknowledging it they just took on an air of petulance and aggression, a 'So what are you going to do about it?' attitude.

Sam pulled his wallet from his pocket and took out 200 Euros. "If you stay well away from him, the German, I will give you a hundred Euros each, and the same again in a few months when I return."

The boys clearly understood what he was saying, and checked each other before nodding to him. He handed them the money and then turned towards the taxi, in front of which was now a very interested woman and a curious taxi driver, and both were looking his way.

The journey back passed by without event. Mostly he had his eyes closed trying to get some rest. His mind was a bombarded with different thoughts and ideas buffeting around, in and out. The top of his head hurt too now, right in the centre of his skull, where his soft spot would have been when he was a baby; even the bone ached, and down into his head.

He rubbed it hard but it didn't make any difference, it just made the bone ache more. The front of his face felt cold too, despite the very warm air. At first he thought it was the air-conditioning in the taxi making his face feel chilled, but when he put his hand to check the vent he realised that it was not doing anything, the driver was obviously saving petrol by not switching it on.

It felt like the area above his nose, his sinuses, and the front of his forehead, was cold, like an ice cream numbness; a fresh, clear feeling, the same as you would get when inhaling frosty air, that spread like a pain up your cheeks, over your nose, up to the front of your head, and then into your brain.

Bizarre. He felt the front of his face and head with his hand, but it didn't feel cold. He wound his window down, and rubbed the centre of his forehead to try and get rid of the feeling but it didn't make much difference, he even felt as if his nose was starting to run. Perhaps he was reacting to some sort of pollen.

He was starting to feel quite sorry for himself, so he sent Brina a text to let her know he was on his way back. He just didn't feel up to calling, and the signal was too limited and erratic. So he just got himself as comfortable as he could and tried to sleep through the bumps.

He arrived at the airport mid-afternoon, and he now felt really very uncomfortable. He paid the driver and went into the terminal block to get the next flight which, luckily, wasn't full.

His onward flight from Athens was only another hour's wait, so he just wandered around the departure lounges and went in and out of the few shops.

People around him seemed like zombies, even a few stumbling into him like he was an invisible magnet.

The plane to Heathrow was half empty, which was a help, so he got a little sleep and freshened up a little before he landed. But going through Customs at the other end was like being on some conveyor belt, and all he wanted to do was get home and sleep.

Walking through the arrivals gate at Heathrow in the evening he just fell in line behind a group of students who had gone through Passport Control before him, when someone caught his eye to his left beyond the barrier.

It was the beaming face of Brina.

Her face shone out from the crowd like a beacon radiating some sort of aura. As soon as she saw that he had spotted her she ran to the end of the Arrivals channel and waited for him, just beyond the line.

It was very confusing for him, why was she here?

He walked up to her, smiled, and put his rucksack down. She jumped at him and wrapped herself around him kissing his neck. Lovely though it was, several things went through his mind, not least that he hadn't had a shower in days.

It was one of those things you see on films that happen to other people at airports or train stations, but it had never happened to him before. So he didn't know the rehearsed routine, so he just stood there looking pleased but dumb. They held hands, walked to the car which she had parked in the short stay car park, and she drove him home.

The following day, feeling more alive and a lot cleaner, Sam decided to take Brina out on the hills for a picnic. It was such a fantastically clear and bright sunny day and he just felt the need to walk and relax. He needed to get up somewhere high on the grassy hills which were about half an hour's drive away.

As a boy he had spent a lot of time up there, and he just felt the need to go somewhere that he knew, and where had been happy. These hills were covered in earthworks from the Iron Age and were very popular with walkers and tourists, but he knew where to go to find peace, and to get the best views.

Mid-morning they drove up to the car park near the top of the hill, and Sam got the small picnic basket out of the back of the car, along with a blue tartan blanket. Up there it was a beautifully bright, warm and windless, with a clear blue sky and an occasional light wispy cloud up high. They walked together up the gravel path that wound up and around the hill that was shrouded in trees.

After ten minutes they reached the part that was ridged with earthworks, and the grass path diverted around them to a gap in a gully, and then steeply up through to the very top. This was built to keep the Romans and other invaders out, but it was peaceful now; soft green undulating grass, traced with silent shadows and birdsong high up in the air.

The ancient hands and feet long ago, that had strived in the rain to move the earth into defensive ditches and build their simple houses were now long gone. The only things digging here now were the rabbits; the only things building anything were the birds, and the only residents were the overweight sheep that kept the grass down. All were blissfully oblivious to the fates of their hardier, yet still very tasty ancestors.

They found a quiet, flattish spot on the sunny side of the hill, and then laid the blanket down. Brina set the basket out as she had prepared it, and he knew she liked to do things in the right order. It was still late morning, so a little early for lunch, and they just had a coffee from the flask.

They both had the same type of coffee, and made the same way, so it made doing the flask easy. Well that was what he had told her anyway, he was reluctant to say anything else in case he ended up having to make his own.

Sitting up on the blanket, he looked out over the valley below and the hills further off in the distance. It was still very sparsely populated here, and there were plenty of fields between the villages with their church spires. He could make out the path of the river in the distance which wound through the floor of the valley it had created.

On days like this you could see for miles; so many things moving, things going on, sights to see. Having finished his coffee he relaxed onto his back and looked up into the blue sky above; soft white wispy clouds drifting by, with the occasional skylark hovering high above, singing away.

Twenty minutes later, Brina laid out the picnic and they ate their way through it. She had packed a small half bottle of wine for him, some orange juice for herself and a couple of wine glasses, which made him laugh. She asked him why he had laughed and she seemed quite 'put out' until he explained about the mugs that he had been given by Max.

The picnic was just crisps, sandwiches, and sausage rolls but it was great, and she had put in some strawberries and cream. He hadn't really eaten properly for days so it was just the best food imaginable. They packed it all away, laid the blanket back out, and laid down to relax and look at the views again.

He had always been interested in old hills and mountains; they seem to hold a fascination to everyone. They have their own life, a spirit, a feeling of presence. People love to walk on them, to climb them, to conquer them, to drink from their springs.

They seemed to capture and hold history around them, storing ancient events, emotions, and souls deep inside implacable stone and earth, massive and indomitable, silent and omniscient. What was it about them that gave us such an affiliation to them? After all, they are just landmarks that we see all the time. Just something you can recognisable from afar, like tall buildings in cities.

But there was something different about them that he couldn't describe; something that drew you back, more than any lake, river, forest, valley or sea ever could.

He was calm and happy. Brina had fallen asleep now, curled up to him, and resting her head on his shoulder. She had one arm on his chest, and the other tucked around her middle with his arm wrapped protectively around her in the warm midday sun.

In some way hills, and mountains, gave you energy - you could feel it within them. Lie on one on your back, and look up into the sky, and you can feel the heartbeat of strength beneath you. Maybe, he thought, it was the energy in the water drawn up through the rocks by its mass. Maybe it was that that holds the key to it.

Find a hill that is millions of years old, and has been fought over, and worked on for thousands of years, and you will see hundreds of people drawn to it every day. Yet find one that has been around or less than a few thousand years, like a volcano, and nobody will fight for it, or walk on it more than once, unless it is one that we have built ourselves.

He thought about the significance of this. It was interesting, but of course a lake or a sea wasn't stable, and couldn't hold the energy and information static. Seas and lakes were non-stable structures, not to mention polluted, so it was the combination of water and static structure over time that held the key.

Mind you, hills tended to be fairly inert and not likely to get up and change the world. But, none the less, something we could perceive a bit, he thought, like a gravestone with things written into it.

Basically though, on the whole, not much use really, apart from some good exercise and nostalgia and giving a good feeling. This of course depended on the hill. Some hills probably retained a lot of bad feeling and malice, and other things that you probably didn't want to know about.

He remembered what his Grandfather had once said about a lot of the Welsh hills having bad feelings about them, namely the Black Hills - they were probably fed up with all that mining. He said they weren't as welcoming as others so they didn't get visited as much, a bit like some people he knew.

Sam thought about his Grandfather now. He could see him walking the hills with his walking stick and flat hat, jacket and brown trousers and sturdy boots. In Sam's mind, his Grandfather had become almost part of the hills, and the hills part of him.

That feeling being carried forward of living on and around the hills, with the life and loves of many more, will continue to live on when we are gone, and our bodies are just dust and water in the ground.

His mind was really wandering now, daydreaming, resting, and not wanting to think too hard, or get drawn into too much complexity. Brina never worried about him daydreaming, it was just another opportunity to find him something to do.

If only she knew how much hard work it was, his brain working flat out, imagining stuff. Curiously she never criticised the dog for doing the same, but then again he was a devious git.

Insects though never had that problem, they were smart, they kept their brains limited in size so they would never get asked to do the washing up. He drew his thoughts back to where he was.

They just seemed fascinating, hills.

There was something different about them; it wasn't like going to a library to read books, or a gym to get fit, or to a concert to feel the emotion and energy. Yes, all of these other places will change you, and draw you back for more, you will feel a better person, but you won't feel part of them, the place.

You are a spectator at a concert, a user of the library, and a member of the gym. However they are not in your heart and soul. You may have a right to go to them, it maybe even written on a piece of paper. You can say you belong to a gym or a library, but it is not the same as this sort of belonging, not a 'sense' of belonging; something drawing you back in your mind to a place, like nature's migrating powers.

Perhaps that is why we build overly tall towers and buildings in cities? Perhaps cities without hills need tall buildings to make people feel that they have a hill - something to give them reference to and from. That's what they do these days, when there is no Rome to build or pyramids to create.

He loved these hills.

A single skylark hovered in the air fifty feet above him singing its frenetic song. In the high altitude and still air, it was shrill, and the only thing he could hear.

It was beautiful, and something unattainable in anything any human could aspire to create or duplicate.

He closed his eyes, and drifted off in his mind for a while, just letting the song of the bird and gentle breeze empty it.

After thirty minutes or so Brina stirred in her sleep next to him and he drifted back again to being awake, and he opened his eyes to look at her. She was dreaming and was twitching slightly, murmuring something, gently stroking her middle with her hand.

Immediately he understood. He knew. He could see. He held his breath. He couldn't wake her, nor could he let her know that he knew, besides he was sure it wouldn't be long before she told him; perhaps this was her subconscious way of doing so.

He smiled, closed his eyes, and slept.

CHAPTER 10 - MEETING OF MINDS

The following morning he woke up in their large, light and airy bedroom to sunshine flooding through the soft, cream, plush curtains.

Brina was still asleep lying on her right side away from him. He was curled up close behind her, on his side with his arm arched over her side and across her front holding her right breast fully in his hand.

He had his bent knees up behind the back of her thighs. She had her arms around his, and was holding his hand, and she had pressed herself tightly up against him, breathing softly and steadily in her sleep.

He could never work out quite how he managed to always wake up like that, the bed was massive, and yet they always seem to be clinging together.

Somehow it seemed right though, comfortable, and Brina always slept deeply in that position. He could feel her physically relax, and her breathing slow and soften, and she pushed herself against him, like he was some sort of protective shield along the length of her spine, defending her against something. It was so tempting just to lie there all day, but eventually something would force him to move, the spell would be broken, and the day had to start.

These days he always seemed to wake up mentally and physically tired, almost as if he had been working all night. He would struggle out of bed, and step into the shower. The hot water and solitude would allow ideas, thoughts, and knowledge to start flowing through his mind.

He had left himself a notepad on the side of the washbasin next to the towel rail so he could jot down ideas and thoughts after he got out, before the ideas went away. It was very annoying having ideas or thoughts, and then not being able to write them down somewhere, and subsequently not being able to remember them. It was at least something to get them out of his head in some form of scribble that he could try and make sense of later in his journal.

Brina's mother arrived mid-morning and it was fairly obvious that she was in on the secret that he hadn't been let in on yet.

She was just bubbling and busy and excited, and was far more overtly polite and interested in him than she normally was, even pinching his cheek at one point.

He could see Brina was very unsure about how to go about telling him, and had clearly wanted to do so before her mother had arrived, but she simply had not had the courage or opportunity to do so. So instead, before her mother got there, she had busied herself with tidying up and vacuuming to occupy herself mentally, as well as using up the available time.

She had always been that way. She would somehow always find things to do rather than have to think about things, or do the things she didn't want to do. In times of pressure and stress, things in the house became very clean.

He could see her suffering so he decided to make it easy for her to talk to him about it. When they were all in the garden he made out that he had picked up a splinter in his right hand, and asked Brina to come into the house with him to help get the splinter out.

She followed him into the utility room and got a needle out from the sewing kit. He held his hand forward and let her take it to get a closer look. It soon became obvious that there was nothing there, and she looked at him questioningly.

In that moment a wall of understanding passed between them, he smiled, and she smiled back. "It's a girl" he said, and she wrapped her arms around him and clung to him like there was nothing and nobody else in the world.

Some minutes later they returned to the garden as Brina's mother was not the sort of person that liked her own company, and was not happy for more than a few minutes on her own.

Sam left the two of them together and went to get a bottle of champagne from one of the fridges. If there was one thing that really amused Sam, it was Brina's mother after several glasses of alcohol. It was like releasing a dam of gossip, a flood of impropriety about everyone that she knew.

It was a game that Brina played along with, and knew not to interrupt, all the while now with her hand resting subconsciously on her middle and with the occasional look and smile towards Sam.

Over the next few weeks or so, Sam occupied his time with reading from the list of book titles that Max had given him.

He would often read until three in the morning, when the peace and quiet of the night gave him time to think. He had started making his own journal now, and kept it, and various notes in another black leather folder that he had used on one of his previous contracts.

It was just tidier than having lots of disorganised pieces of paper lying around, and meant that when ideas or thoughts came to him, he could just jot them down, record it, without then having to remember or think about it.

It was just the act of writing something down and it got it out of his head. It was reassuring too somehow, to get information and thoughts down in a structured way. It was something he had learned to do on one of those management and personal development courses he had been on years ago.

It helped to structure his thoughts, record things from a management perspective as he went along, so that things didn't get on top of him, so that at the end of it, somehow, it magically all made sense; a logical story or perspective was being formed in its own right.

Most of those sorts of courses seemed to have vanished now or morphed into something else, probably with all of the same concepts, just rebranded and polished.

It was the same with many things now, probably due to high demand or financial constraints. He tried to apply the lessons that he had picked up, the habits he had learned, but it wasn't easy these days with so much going on everywhere and with the pace of life being so much faster.

There was just so much to remember to do. Everything was so frenetic, demanding, and there was so much more information flying around.

It felt as if this was what he was supposed to be doing at the moment; reading and understanding. He was building up a more refined picture of what was going on, or more to the point, seeing above other people's perspectives on things. Most of what he read dated from the 1980's onwards, he wasn't drawn to anything else very much before then.

Weeks later, he had pulled together a set of names of people that he needed to speak to, mainly professors in specific fields or leading authority types. But rather than entering into discussions with them individually, he decided to get them all together at once to get an across-the-board perspective. He was fairly well used to dealing with academics and he knew from experience that getting into discussions or debates at a distance would be fairly non-productive and just time consuming.

So, after discovering that three of them were attending the same conference in London, he decided to get them together beforehand. He would pay for their time and, most importantly, offer them free food. Pressing the right buttons; paying and food always seemed to work well. He then used the attendee list of the conference to draw in a couple of other names, a biologist and physicist, until he had ten in total.

He had sent out the handwritten fax about eight days ago now to the ten people he had identified during his research and investigation on the Internet. They all seemed to be at the forefront of the areas that he was trying to focus on.

It was a difficult thing to approach, the subject that was so vast and subjective, but it was the only way he knew of dealing with it. He couldn't tackle each area in turn, that would take forever, what he wanted was a broad-brush perspective view.

He had carefully worded what he had to say without giving too much away. He had then faxed a dozen or so pages to each person and made it clear that no further correspondence would be made, and that they were to have no contact with him before the meeting.

He had arranged generous payment for their time and travel expenses, and he knew that what he had written in the pages was enough to get anyone more than interested.

He deliberately hadn't told Brina what he was doing, just that he was going to a conference and where it would be. He didn't want to worry her or involve her at all. He knew she would only insist on coming along and keeping an eye on him. In any case she should be resting.

He had used his normal contacts and channels to arrange the small conference room and facilities for the following morning. He had stored all of his slides onto a memory stick so that he didn't have to carry a laptop around with him or his bag, and he had just brought along the basics with some printed notes, and his black folder.

He opened the door to the conference room to find a debate going on which stopped the moment he entered. Ten faces looked at him from around the large table and the room fell silent.

Sam smiled and sat down at the head of the table and put his folder down. He had deliberately arrived a few minutes early, and the two catering staff were still laying out the cling film covered silver food trays, plates and tea and coffee on the side tables.

The younger of the two, a tall acne-faced lad in his late teens, left quickly, while the other, a dark haired girl in her early twenties dressed in a white blouse and short black skirt, was trying to quietly place the coffee and tea cups out from a tray.

She was obviously embarrassed by what was going on in the room and her face was slightly flushed. As Sam finished setting up, she politely made her way out of the room casting a nervous glace at Sam, who thanked her with a polite nod and a smile.

He looked around the room again. He noted that in addition to the ten that he had invited, there were three or four other fresh faced young individuals who had managed to get themselves brought along as bag carriers. They were all sitting together by along the side of the room. All of them had the same look of both being keen and intellectually arrogant at the same time.

Sam introduced himself to his 'jury' and began the meeting with a summary of what he had sent them a few days earlier, and what he wanted to discuss. He then went into some detail on aspects of what he had experienced, what had happened to him since then, what he felt he knew and his objective views on what he believed was going on.

It was a good hour before he finished his prepared presentation, and allowed them to make comments or to ask any questions. A pale faced, balding guy with rectangular glasses and unkempt sideburns coughed, and then said "Perhaps you can just run me through what it is you think you saw and what you felt happened in your experience again."

Sam recognised him as the Psychology professor he had invited, but it was a little difficult to be sure as he didn't look much like the photo on his own website, but then again it was amazing what you could do with photo editing software these days, even with photos that were well over ten years old.

So Sam spent another ten minutes going over again what had happened to him a few years before, and how it seemed to have opened up a sort of door to collective knowledge.

It wasn't so much the 'what he knew' that he was trying to concentrate the discussion on. It was the 'how he had come to know these things', and the ability to pull all sorts of knowledge and concepts together from seemingly nowhere, and with such depth and focus.

These were concepts of which he had no knowledge of before, and yet could now understand. How for example he knew about, and could relate to, the twelve dimensions; how we operate within them compared to what we can see and touch.

How information can pass to and from and along the dimensions, and how they are all interrelated. All this and more that he had no understanding of before his 'Episode'.

As far as he was concerned a few years ago, there were just the four. That was the sort of thing he was trying to convey, the 'how', rather than discussing the technicalities or specifics of the science. Also how it was ongoing, not just from the initial experience, but how it seemed to be a continuing process of knowledge transfer, where was it all coming from and how?

He, as much as possible, talked only in general terms, as it was very hard for him to explain such a complex experience perspective to people who mainly spoke in mathematical equations most of the time, besides he would probably just end up using the wrong words.

It was like trying to describe the experience of going to a West End theatre production, and just telling the story. How could you describe all the colours on the stage, the style of the backdrop, the shape of the props, the smell of the theatre, the noise from the crowd, the music, the shared emotions, the drama, to people who designed sets, did makeup, produced plays, and developed scripts but had never actually physically been to one?

Not easy.

He wasn't really making any impression on them. Their point of reference was not the same as his.

He tried another tack. "It usually helps if you ask me questions after I have described something. That helps some of the context recreate in my mind; like taking me back to the theatre in my head, recreating that moment and then asking me something more specific like 'how does the neutrino exist with both matter and antimatter elements within it?'

"But please don't start reciting equations at me – it doesn't mean anything to me. I can understand quite a lot of complicated concepts, but the way it works it doesn't see things in terms of equations - only mental constructs, or thought forms."

So the first question came in about subatomics. It was to do with the standard model, with String Theory, and the interaction with quarks within protons and neutrons. Sam was able to start reliving part of what he had experienced; the perception of which was almost like a play where at each stage the knowledge starting coming back to him with every step, interweaving the relationships, reliving what he had experienced as much as he could from the conceptual imagery and flows in his mind.

It was hard though, after such a while, to recount everything, like trying to remember every detail about being in a car crash.

He was gaining some ground now. He said that he could sense that there were around a hundred and forty-four subatomic groupings; that some of them had the state of being dimensionally independent in one or many aspects. For example there was one, or maybe two, that were time independent, and had no time dimensional effect or relationship. He was trying to put things over not so much as theories or ideas but with more emphasis on what went on, and how the information was represented, and the fact that previously he had no idea about any of it. However finding the right descriptive and technical words was difficult.

"I am interested to know," Sam went on "how this knowledge gets into my mind in relation to things that I haven't ever heard of, read about, or had any interest in. For example, biomorphic harmonics. I stopped studying Biology at school when I was fifteen and haven't read a book about the subject since then. Equally that applies to subatomic physics, psychology, spirituality, if that is the right word, or anything like that.

It's all there, and it all makes sense, it all forms a bigger picture of what's going on. When you start talking to me on subjects or concepts, everything you say makes sense to me. I can rationalise everything else I know about, and I can build up a collective picture of how that all fits together with everything else. It all makes sense, and it all happens in real time. I need to know how that is possible?"

His comments appeared to be met around the table with looks of scepticism, but there was quite a bit of interest in the actual concept that he was talking about. They clearly didn't believe him, but the story sounded academically 'very interesting'.

Sam was starting to think that he had made an error in getting so many of them together at once. It now didn't seem right or correct, using this approach. He was using a business type arrangement. The 'get everyone together for a meeting' thing that he normally did, but it wasn't working with so many competing academics; they just worked differently, and with a different mentality.

After another hour of discussions he realised that he was becoming frustrated with himself at setting up this meeting the way he had. It really wasn't working. He wasn't getting anywhere. There was nothing coming in from them in terms of advice or help, none of them knew where to start; they couldn't relate to him, or to each other, as to what he was trying to get across.

"Don't you all bloody well see?" he suddenly erupted. "We should all be individually far more intelligent by now. Collectively we can be so much more, but individually in comparison we are stupid, self-destructive, ineffective, inefficient, and going nowhere. Globally we seem to be so obsessed with finding things out; using all our energy and resources to obtain more and more knowledge, rather than consciously sorting out the global mess we are in …"

He suddenly stopped, mid-sentence, as he realised that he was actually shouting.

Then he became very aware of what he was saying and wasn't sure where it had come from. The statement was out of context with what he had been talking about – he had got angry and the words had seemed to flow out of him from somewhere.

He looked around the room and there were many open mouths and confused, shocked expressions. Clearly his attitude, and his manner, was not something that they were used to.

For a split second he wasn't sure if it was caused by the grandeur of the statement that he had made, or the casual statement about being obsessed with finding things out. For another split second he wasn't sure if he was going to be questioned further or lynched.

Then silence.

He felt something change in the room, and all at the same time, three or four of their faces changed to have the exact same condescending smile, followed by two others, who gave silent stepped exhalations through their noses.

It was if something had kicked in, a group shared program that had been activated. It was if something was now preventing them from seeing the things that he was trying to convey, or that they were no longer able to understand his perspective.

Somehow it was as if they were no longer 'allowed' to see what he was describing from their stove piped, hierarchical, defensive academic perspectives. As if some form of higher programming had blocked them; some failsafe mechanism or loaded function was at the same time operating to change their whole attitude, coordinating a group response towards him.

It wasn't right, something did not equate, it didn't seem logical.

He stood up, his eyes darting to each of them in turn. It did not make sense, something had changed them, and the situation was changing from a supportive position to a defensive one.

The mood in the room was artificial, and very different to how it had been several minutes earlier. It was very odd and he couldn't quite put his finger on it. He felt his self-confidence draining away from him, and he suddenly felt cold, and very alone.

He had made an error.

He was dealing with something at the wrong level. These people existed in comfortable protected spheres, in isolated systems of control and scope. He was trying to push them out of their bubbles, to come together, and it had sparked something that had reacted against him. He was going about this the wrong way, and he had stepped on something's toes, which was now fighting back, and putting these people on the defensive.

He didn't really hear anything after that for the next few minutes. He pulled his memory stick from the projector unit, and gathered his things.

 The next thing he knew he was walking along the corridor to the stairwell, still numb, his mind whirling.

His head was spinning as he followed his feet down the stairs and out through the door.

He didn't really know where he was, and didn't know where he was going – he just wanted to walk. It was cold and windy, and the streets were quite empty. The office was on a main street, and he found himself walking up towards a junction. His mind was still racing from one thing to another.

Even at the traffic lights at the junction of the main roads there were still only a few people about. He hadn't even put away any of his papers back in his folder which he still had in his right hand, he just clutched them to his chest as he held his jacket closed with his left.

At the crossing he waited for the green man, and then when he was about a third of the way across, a gust of wind caught under his jacket and blew one of the papers out onto the road.

Instinctively he stepped back, and leant out to pick it up – counterbalancing himself with his folder in the other hand.

The folder was ripped out of the air by a car, which he had neither heard nor seen coming. He turned his head to see his thick leather folder skidding along the gutter, and a glimpse of a blue estate car driven by an old man with glasses. The man clearly hadn't seen him or the red traffic light, or even noticed he had hit anything, and he just continued on his journey.

He stood in the middle of the crossing stupefied, until a sudden sharp pain in his wrist alerted him to its urgent trauma. Luckily his palm had been facing away from the impact, otherwise he could have lost a few fingers. As it was the side of his wrist ached badly, and there was a sharp pain in his thumb joint.

His papers were blowing in the air all around him, and everything to him appeared to be in slow motion, like a freeze-frame sequence in a movie. He found himself unable to do anything except stare at his folder in the gutter; the papers, and the car, disappearing into the distance.

Nobody saw him, nobody helped, he just stood there motionless, lost.

He jumped with a start as a car right behind him politely sounded its horn, and he span round still clutching his wrist, and instinctively hopped back to the curb of the crossing.

The man in the car gave him a puzzled, frustrated look, gestured irritably at the now green traffic light, and then drove on leaving him alone.

The street was empty of people and cars. He could feel his heart pounding, and the adrenalin pumping around his body, and a clenching feeling in his stomach.

He staggered a few feet over to where his folder was in the gutter next to the railings. He was giddy and the world was closing in around him. He put his hand out to the traffic light post, and dropped down to one knee, his head facing down.

Determined now, he was concentrating on not being sick or fainting. His face was flushed and sweat was pouring down his back. He lay down on the ground in a foetal position, all the energy now gone from his limbs, his head pounding, with weird flowing feelings of déjà vu and odd thoughts and visions filling his mind one after another.

He lost all sense of where he was or what was going on around him, his mind was disoriented and his vision spinning. He felt the cold, gritty pavement on the side of his face.

He smelt stale urine from around the metal post by the curb.

The flaking grey metal of the base of the railings, and black tarmac seemed to zoom in hard and fast, and then he blacked out.

CHAPTER 11 - THE SHIP

Sam opened his eyelids, just very slightly. The glare of the hot sun was bright and harsh on his waking eyes, especially as he had no sunglasses on.

His body was warm and relaxed on the slatted wooden sun lounger, which also raised his feet off the hot wooden boards of the ship's deck. The sea breeze gently flowed over his bare legs and arms. It was a lovely warm, relaxing feeling, comfortable, caressing, with that mellow 'under the duvet' feel.

He couldn't quite work out though yet in his mind what was going on. He just wanted to stay in that blissful moment wrapped in a soft, virtual, protective blanket of half-awake serenity. However something was nagging at his brain.

Disoriented now, he tried to gather his thoughts and perception to work out where he was. He didn't remember going to sleep, or of even getting here, or of wearing shorts and a t-shirt, or of being on a sun lounger. The sea air, and the ship - they were also things that didn't make sense. It felt normal though, correct, but a little like waking with a hangover with no knowledge or memory of the night before.

It was a pleasant feeling though, as opposed to finding yourself in the dog basket on the back porch with various complaining joints and bones, and a splitting headache, with a disapproving spaniel staring at you.

He could feel the slow rise and ebb of the ship beneath him riding over the gentle sea, and the vibrational throb of the engines deep down in the heart of the vessel. The railings, several feet in front of him the other side of the long deck, were the old fashioned type; thick cast iron, heavily painted in white and black.

Behind him was a metal painted, riveted wall, and several feet above was the slight overhang of the deck above, which may have been another walkway or possibly the First Class deck.

His head was still a blurred fog. He looked out to the sea, which was a deep pearlescent blue, flat calm, and giving off sparkling reflections from the harsh sun.

There were only marginal hints here and there of waves and foam. In the distance there were a few islands, hazy grey and dark green, and indistinct at this range. In the medium distance was a large flock of seagulls, some on the water, some circling lazily in the air overhead - probably attracted by an indicative sign of a potential shoal of fish beneath the waves.

It all had a Mediterranean feel to it with the heat and the colour of the sea and sky. Also the distant vegetation, with occasional scented aromas on the air, indicated that it was somewhere closer to the equator than anywhere further south or north.

His arms were balanced on the wooden armrests of the lounger, and he looked down his familiar legs to see his bare feet crossed one over the other.

He was still half-asleep though and the information coming in was difficult to process and correlate. Suddenly his phone started to silently vibrate in his back pocket. And then it vibrated again; someone was trying to get hold of him. Instinctively out of habit he leaned over slightly to one side, and reached behind with his hand and into the flap of the pocket on his shorts.

But there was no phone there; nothing in his pocket, and yet he could still feel it vibrating. Then a few seconds later it stopped, like some sort of phantom phone. He was still too sleepy though to process what was going on; he must have just imagined it or something - how could he possibly feel his phone vibrating if it wasn't there? It must have been some remnant of a dream still in his head, or some vibration from the ship.

Shading his eyes from the sun with his hand, he turned left and looked sideways. Brina was directly next to him on another wooden lounger. She was wearing a blue-black patterned bikini with gold metal circles on the waistband. She also wore a light blue and gold sarong around her shoulders and sunglasses shaded her eyes. She had one arm propped up on the arm rest, and was reading a book on a black e-reader that rested on her bent knees.

She had the other arm behind her head, supporting it, and also catching the sun's rays under her arm to even out her tan. Sam noticed a small white towel covering her feet to stop them from burning. Her skin was smooth, and covered in suntan oil, which smelt like all the good holidays he had even been on.

She had that sort of film star pose about her with her blonde hair efficiently tied back to catch the sun on her shoulders and face. She turned and smiled at him reassuringly, and then went back to her book.

She looked very calm, serene, relaxed and at home on board the ship, with no symptoms of seasickness or a hair out of place. She was still, relaxed, and not talking. Something wasn't right.

It was her all right, but he could sense straight away that she wasn't there physically; he didn't feel any sexual energy towards her. It was as if it were virtual; a sort of movie, real just not physical, but then again this was certainly no dream.

He caught a scent of her suntan lotion again and it immediately brought back a memory of the beach in New Zealand, like a code key, linking to and unlocking a memory function or data module in his head.

It was no good - he still hadn't got a clue where he was, or how he had got there. Brina's presence was stopping him from panicking, but with every passing moment the picture of where he was became clearer. The perception more defined, sharper. However that only made it more nonsensical, disorientating- it just wasn't right, he had no memory of how or why he was there.

He closed his eyes again for a moment, a little giddy now, but his other senses just kept on building the picture for him of what was there, with more sounds, smells, and feelings. It was like a computer program being developed, a stage play unfolding, or a film being written and produced in his mind.

He could feel his breathing speed up as the adrenaline started to flow, but was it real air he was taking in or just his perception of it? He could smell the varnish from the wood on the lounger still present in the air, it transported him to a moment when he was a boy gluing his model aeroplane together on a metal table in his bedroom; it suddenly brought it to mind in sharp reality.

It was a memory from his past that he had forgotten, but that link brought it out of lost storage into his present mind.

He opened his eyes again, and the harsh reality of the light drew in and the picture around him reformed again as it had been before. Brina, the deck, the rails, the sea, the old overweight couple walking barefoot along the deck in front of them holding hands.

Passing them now was a little boy wearing lederhosen; he was holding a blue balloon and walking past the end of their loungers, going the other way down the wide wooden deck of the liner.

Sam sat up, and turned to Brina, whose sunglasses now left the book and turned towards him once again. "Where am I?" he asked abruptly. She lifted her glasses from her eyes, and looked at him questioningly. "Where am I? How did I get here?" he repeated. Her brow furrowed, and she looked perplexed. "I don't know" she said succinctly, but she didn't look concerned.

"Are you real?" he asked her. He expected her to look affronted or confused, but instead she just calmly sat up on the lounger and put her e-reader down carefully beside her. She then looked at him, sighing with slight disappointment, and gave him the 'Don't be silly dear' look at the seemingly obvious question.

"You have created me in your mind to help reassure you, and to give you some reference here in this place. I am here in a way for you, I am protecting you, and doing my job, my role, and although I am not here in one respect, I am however communicating with you at some basic levels from where, and what, I am."

There was a pause. Even that didn't sound like Brina talking. That sounded like him explaining something to himself, or some sort of robot or program machine response. Yet he could feel she was there in some way, she had that knowing smile, and she seemed to know what she was doing, which was both reassuring and irritating at the same time.

He couldn't explain it, but somehow he knew she was there in a way, and somehow not. There was something of her there, but in his mind he was building an image of her to translate something of her. It was to make sense of what was there into something he could recognise visually. She was something to relate to, assimilate, a bit like the rest of wherever he was. It was like no dream though; it was very precise, vivid and clear, and yet not real, a sort of half-way house, or meeting place between the two, a hard 'out of body experience' world but with a surreal fictional nature to it.

That was it! He sat up abruptly and swung his legs over the side of his lounger. He didn't like 'not knowing' and that was enough to spur him into getting up and sorting out what the hell was going on. He stood up quickly, walked to the rail, and looked down along the length of the ship.

It was a vast liner, enormous, much larger than anything he had seen before; black painted, old style, heavy duty riveted metal seemed to stretch along for ever, and a long way down into the waves. Masses of painted metal lined with several layers of round portholes. The ship was making several knots along the water, which sprayed and lapped along the side as it went.

He looked back and up to see a few more levels above, and painted funnels with white smoke trailing up into the blue sky. He could make out many people moving about the decks, some leaning over the sides, some playing games or enjoying other types of entertainment. He looked back at the sea again and was now really struggling with himself to get a handle on what was going on, and his brain was very much at an impasse.

The hand on his shoulder made him turn around abruptly. Brina had come up behind him, her sunglasses now moved up onto her head, and her wrap now made into a skirt. She put her hand in his, and he felt her warm palm and soft fingers, which felt reassuring somehow.

He knew that talking to her would be of no use. He was now drawn to explore the ship and find out what was going on, where he was, and why he was here. It wasn't something he could wake up from. He was really here in some sense. It was an unnerving situation to be in, neither awake nor asleep, not in a dream nor in reality, and with no reference to how he was there or how to get out or off.

There were now more people walking along the deck. The embodiment of the scenario of where he was now became more defined, clarified and clearly described. It was like watching a storybook unfold in front of him, as if it were being elaborated on piece by piece. It was like building up a vivid mental map of a role-playing computer game as it was being played out.

The people were very varied, and seemed to represent just about every class, age, colour, and geographical culture going. It was almost deliberately so, like an example representative set, stereotypes all jumbled and interacting with one another.

He could easily recognise certain typical individuals or groups; Americans, Asians, Eastern Europeans, and all other cultural and religious orders. It was like a procession going past in both directions. There were quite a few individuals that he couldn't place, and some that looked like they were wearing very old style clothing, some even ancient.

Many looked as though they were unaware of their surroundings, or were oblivious of one another. Many seemed more interested in themselves rather than what was going on, and some just looked like zombies bumping into things. It was starting to look like something out of a Hollywood film set, where somehow, all the extras from various films had got free range of the entire wardrobe department, yet had no script, and were just milling around together during lunchbreak.

He was still barefoot and he could feel the heat from the wooden decking where he stood. He could sense the texture of it under his soles and feel the gaps in the wood itself with his toes. He steadied himself by holding on to the railing for a moment, warm smooth and vibrating. His head was feeling a little giddy, light and unfocused. In the shade along the deck promenade, he could make out a few doors into the interior of the ship; white, metal with glass windows, and, in front of it, a wooden stairwell going down to the deck below.

It all looked very new and clean, and yet very old at the same time. Now and then he would catch the odd whiff of paint, varnish, grease and coal smoke.

He was aware that he must have looked like some sort of drunk passenger, but the people moving around didn't seem to notice him at all. However he realised that quite a few seemed to stop and acknowledge Brina. One old lady paused to talk to her, introduced herself, and within a few moments began conveying her entire life story. She then started on her well-rehearsed personal problem list. Then she soon moved on to dramatic and interesting ones that had been extracted from everyone else's. She held onto Brina's forearm to steady herself, which also served to prevent Brina from getting away easily.

However Brina politely and kindly gave the woman her usual genuine smile and attentive nods at all the right moments, and looked as though she didn't mind.

"Well my dear, did you hear..." it went on, but Sam switched off after a few minutes, and looked out at sea again to try to find another form of reference. In the distance ahead was another island, and they would be going quite close to it, much nearer than the others he had seen. It would be a chance to see if there was anything on there that would give more of a clue as to where he was.

It was mostly sand, with a few dozen trees, and many rough bushes dotted around it. There were a few rocky outcrops near the coastline, but it was no more than half a mile across. There was nothing on there to indicate any buildings or inhabitants aside from a few nesting sea birds.

They were now just a few hundred yards away, and he was still none the wiser. It was at that point that Sam equated in his mind that something else was wrong; they were getting too close to the island. They weren't heading straight for it, but for a ship this size it was just too near. It wasn't as if the island wasn't easy to see. It was also broad daylight, so whoever the captain was he must be asleep or something.

Sam gripped the railing, almost anticipating the ship running aground. He wasn't afraid though, why would you be? This wasn't real. He shot a quick look at Brina who was expressionless, still being 'talked to', with one hand holding tightly to the rail, while the other was clasped in both hands by the old lady.

There was a lurch from the ship and the deck rose up and to the left. Many of the people walking along it seemed to lose their footing and stumble. The ship ploughed on, and veered off away from the island, the side-on gliding impact with the sand bank correcting the navigation error. It then sped on out into open sea as if nothing had happened. For some reason Sam wasn't worried or scared, he was still too confused and disoriented trying to work things out. He looked back along the deck where people were standing up or helping others that had fallen.

Some fifty yards along the deck a small group had starting fighting with another group, but he couldn't work out what the reason for the fight was. People looked quite stressed, uneasy, but after a while of collective reassurance they all just got on with what they were doing before. A few more minutes and it was all calm again, everything was as it was, and as if nothing had happened.

Sam looked around. It was just as if a needle on a record had come off and then been replaced. Surreal. He stopped the next person to walk past him by placing his hand on their shoulder. It was a bit rude he knew, but then he wasn't in a very civil mood. The man he stopped and turned around.

He was about three inches shorter than Sam, and was wearing what looked like white dusty sheets wrapped around him with a brown belt around his waist and a muslin shoulder bag; he had long, black hair and had old worn brown sandals on his feet.

"Right, who are you, where am I, and what the bloody hell is going on?" demanded Sam. The man looked at him and then blinked.

Then in clear, perfect English dialogue, he said, "My name is Gerald. I am an Atlantian. I represent a specific psyche group structure in the Western World. You are on a ship that is an analogy representing a conceptual interpretation between *your* mind and the collective mind. You have created this as an aid to provide an integrated communication mechanism between the two, and no, I do not know what is going on."

Sam blinked, and was suddenly wishing he hadn't asked. Again it was very concise and machine like, and clearly accurate and precise. "But…" said Sam "I thought Atlantis was …." And then he stopped himself.

The man looked at him again waiting for him to finish his

sentence, but after a pause, he just said "May I go now? I am late for a game of deck chess." Sam, open mouthed, lowered his hand away from the man, and the man politely turned and walked off. Then several paces on the man turned back "Oh," he said "don't stand too close to the rails will you? We had a big wave some time ago, and we lost quite a number over the side."

He turned to go and then stopped, and faced back again to Sam "Mind you, the ship was a lot smaller then, no more than a wooden boat really. Which I suppose is better than being on a raft, or just a mass of floating vegetation." He smiled, and then looked distracted for a moment, as if thinking of something else, and then he turned and wandered away keeping close to the inner side of the deck.

The whole thing was taking on more of an *Alice in Wonderland* feel to it. But rather than dashing off looking for more riddles and answers, as would be the norm, Sam stopped and thought for a while until the answers came to him.

He had learned that trick already; there was no need to play the game, if you could stand back from it, just 'see' what was happening or being 'said'. Like reading into a story; working out the way it was going, what the ending would be, without having to wade through the plot, and interact with all the characters.

It still didn't make much sense though, but he was slowly pulling the pieces together; working out what was around him, what he was being shown, and what he was trying to represent to himself.

The little boy with the balloon passed him again, this time holding his mother's hand. She was about thirty, blonde permed hair pinned up high, stunning figure, wearing a short, tight, bright red dress. She carried a matching clutch bag and wiggled along in designer heels.

Clearly the boy was a non-synchronous accessory. "Look Mummy," he said with a heavy North European accent "Stop! See those two lizards?" and he pointed with his balloon hand at two male lizards that were facing each other off, in the shadow of a large metal bollard next to the rails just along from Sam.

"Those lizards are fighting each other" he said with great

enthusiasm. His mother pulled his hand impatiently to move him on, but he held his ground "They must really like fighting," he went on, very excitedly "otherwise they would run away from each other wouldn't they?"

The mother was clearly 'busy', and rushing to get somewhere. However she stopped, then sighed impatiently raising her shades from her eyes to look. She was about to drag him off, but then saw an opportunity to explain something to her son.

She suddenly changed her demeanour from 'impatient bimbo' to 'caring and stylish mother'. She took a few steps back so that they both stood in front of the bollard, a foot or so away from where the lizards were now busy taking chunks out of each other. "That's what animals do darling" she said, in a New York accent.

She smiled at him, and bent down towards him slightly so that he could see her eyes and her knowing, caring smile.

"It's all part of life. It's just nature you see darling ?" She then stood up and moved forward, and, with the toe of her red shoe, deftly flicked both lizards through the gap next to the bollard.

The lizards flew sideways into the air, off the side of the ship, and down the long drop to the waters far below; both continuing to fight each on their way down, both oblivious to the flow of air and situation going on around them.

They were unaware of their situation, slaves to their animalistic subconscious drive to fight, and yet, dispatched in glory, by the one true, all avenging, red stiletto god in the sky. *What a fabulous story* they thought on their way down, *one that they would be proud to tell their children, and they to their children in turn.*

The woman straightened herself, repositioned her shades over her eyes, then gently pulled the confused boy further on along the deck sideways by the hand, as he continued to look back, and point - open mouthed. *Lessons for everyone there,* thought Sam.

He had seen her before. He recognised the walk, the confident, aloof, untouchable stride. It clicked after a few seconds; it was the *Woman in Red* from a film he had once seen, a program created in a virtual reality simulation.

The scenario was clearly there to try and tell him something, or to explain a concept; it was to do with the lizard brain, but he didn't get what it meant. The woman carried on walking down the deck with the little boy. Sam was expecting her to leave a line of sharp heel-shaped dents in the new soft decking as she walked along. But no, clearly here fashion statements overrode any boring practicalities like that.

The old lady had gone now, and Sam firmly took hold of Brina's hand for some reassurance. For a moment he felt just like the little boy. There were now throngs of people moving all along and filling the deck area. He looked at Brina and she was still looking in the direction that the *Woman in Red* had gone.

Both women had 'seen' each other for an instant, but had not attempted any interaction, although clearly some instant recognition or visual sparring had gone on. They had sized each other up in a single glance, but whatever information had been transferred, it was not confrontational.

Sam let Brina guide him and they wandered slowly along the deck until they came to some stairs that went up to the level above. As they walked he could hear snippets of the conversations going on from the groups that passed by. Some seemed quite animated, competitive, and in some cases aggressive, as if arguing over seemingly minor differences of opinion, status, or perception.

There was so much going on all at once, it was too much to take in. Then, as if in response, the scene and characters, or program constructs around him, slowed down to almost a standstill. He was now able to perceive what was happening at his own pace, before slowly returning to normal speed.

The whole thing was a mixed-up construct of collections of mind-sets, psyche groups, belief structures and historical legacy definitions, all defined within physical laws and manifestations. That was what his mind was telling him, it all got quite technical - the explanations, and the relationships. He shook his head again.

Brina led him up to the next level, and it opened out into a wider deck area with a similar number of oddball people walking about in various outfits. Several yards on from the stairwell was a set of wood and glass double doors leading to the inside of the ship.

In front of the doors stood a uniformed steward wearing a peaked cap and a white jacket. As they walked up Sam could make out the sounds of a string quartet playing inside. He had no idea what the music was, but it sounded like nothing that any self-respecting classical composer would feel comfortable putting their name to.

He went to walk through the double doors and the smiling steward politely held up his hand in front of him, the other tucked behind his back. "I am sorry Sir. This dining room is for First Class passengers only," and he then changed his smile to a more condescending one, and barred the way firmly. Sam wasn't even aware that he was a passenger, he certainly didn't class himself as that, but then he didn't class himself as crew either.

Without pausing, Brina came from behind Sam and brushed past them both. She went straight on in, but as she passed it didn't look like Brina. She had changed to a slim 'Marilyn Monroe' character in heels, with a close fitting, low backed, knee-length blue sparkling dress, "Don't be silly…" she said to the steward "he is with me", and she disappeared, wiggling into the darkness.

The steward gaped, and Sam could almost feel the gears working in his head. He slowly lowered his hand from in front of Sam's chest, trying to work out what to do. However it was enough of a hesitation for Sam to follow Marilyn into the room.

It took a few moments for his eyes to get used to the dimness in the smoky, chandelier-lit dining room. The room was exquisitely furnished in an Art Deco style. It had plush carpets, and was some three hundred feet across, much bigger than looked possible from the outside dimensions. The air was filled with cooking smells and rich tobacco smoke, expensive upholstery and overpriced perfume.

A few steps inside the doorway Sam stopped and stepped sideways along the side wall to let his eyes get used to the gloom. Further along the wall were several plinths on which stood some reproduction Egyptian granite heads depicting various pharaohs, with different styles of crown with snakes on their foreheads. Immediately next to him, against the wall, was a large fish tank positioned at chest height.

It was lit by a lamp behind it, and was filled with ornaments, pebbles, rocks, and artificial aquarium vegetation placed in amongst the bubbles. In the middle of the tank was a large, grey, and very bored looking octopus. Sam turned to face the tank and stooped down, looking closer inside through the glass. The octopus looked back at him suspiciously with one of its eyes.

It was busy playing with, what appeared to be, three or four large multi-coloured plastic Lego pieces. It held each of them in separate tentacles, each limb seemingly occupied in its own right with each of the toys independently.

It also had a small, round, rubber, black and white football, which it was passing between two of its other tentacles as if playing a game with itself. It reminded Sam of the octopus that he had seen on the TV that was able to predict the international football results with remarkable accuracy. He carried on watching it intently.

These were amazingly intelligent creatures. You could tell if you took the time to notice, as with many animals. It appeared that each tentacle had a mind of its own, and yet acted as part of the whole, negotiating and coordinating with the body. It moved and played all at the same time, and yet all the while its eyes were busy concentrating on Sam.

He wondered what must be going in inside the thing; all the negotiations, communications, decisions, feedback and signals. All those cells and body parts, busy working hard to do whatever was needed subconsciously, and its limbs still reacting with animalistic subconscious minds of their own.

He wondered how the limbs and cells would feel if they knew that they were just playing with bits of Lego, and helping at being a football oracle. The octopus moved a few more inches over to the glass, and lifted one tentacle. It unwound it upwards, which showed Sam its underside as it moved it forward and attached itself to the glass.

This was also something else that he was being shown- something that he had to work out. It was to do with this animal being formed of independently operating and thinking parts, each in turn made up of individual cells. All coordinating and operating in harmony with some integrated communication and nervous system that learned and adapted.

In some way this was trying to make some representation of what was going on in the collective mind, some interpretation of an analogy or action that meant something that he was supposed to get. Parts within parts, cells within organs and within limbs. All within the whole, all acting, operating, negotiating and doing what they had to do, or were able to. All parts different, but one whole.

He was struggling to see what it was referring to. There were too many things trying to be expressed at once, too many concepts in one go, which was the whole point; it only made sense when you did that. He wished he had more time to think about what it was 'saying'.

Sam looked at the tentacle facing him against the glass. The word *suckers* came into Sam's mind. Sam snorted through his nose, "Very bloody funny" he said in a whisper. However he didn't think that it was worth explaining the joke to the octopus; it didn't look like it had a sense of humour. Unless of course it did, perhaps it was fully aware of the joke, and was in fact demonstrating its superior satirical wit.

Sam would then retaliate by pointing out the fried octopus on the starter menu, followed by a suitable comment like "You didn't see that one coming did you?" But he didn't. It was too easy to get drawn into beliefs and meanings that just weren't there, and taking too much account of reading of situations that really didn't mean anything at all. *It was an easy trap to fall into* thought Sam, *not to mention how embarrassing it would be to get caught talking to an octopus.*

Sam remembered back to when he had been scuba diving at night in the Red Sea. He had been shining his torch around to see where he was going, and had inadvertently shone his torch directly at an octopus in the coral reef. It had reacted by covering its face and eyes with its tentacles in a coordinated response to an attack and a collective understanding of what needed to be done in response.

Now that this octopus had its tentacle raised, he could see that underneath the animal was a large metal bowl. Clearly it had made this its home, like some sort of comfort blanket that it carried with it, and just to prove the point, it started to move to the back of the tank, picking up the bowl underneath itself, and carrying it along with all its toys as it went.

It is just a baby after all, thought Sam. As it reached the back of the tank it tilted the bowl up on its side which revealed the base on which were written some words. Sam leaned slightly further forward and squinted.

He could just make out the words **'L'esprit de l'escalier'** engraved on the bottom.

He stood up, speechless. *Out-intellectualised by an octopus, the devious, spineless, little bastard!*

Sam looked sideways at Marilyn who was now bending over forward looking into the tank at some fish further along. His eyes strayed over her curves, and the large breasts with prominent cleavage that she had given herself. He was intrigued by the differences she had applied to her body from those of her own. Without looking at him, she stood back up, and scanned the room, "Don't get any ideas" she said, and then looked back towards him again.

She then smiled at him intelligently, and raised her eyebrows. It was an odd thing for her to say, he thought. Brina's own body was far more attractive in his opinion, but hey that was women for you. He looked back into the tank. He was tempted to lean forward again and whispered to the octopus "I bet you wish you had one of those to play with?" gesturing with his head in Brina's direction. However the octopus wasn't looking.

It obviously knows when it is beaten, Sam thought. So 3-2 to him.

Sam now stood back a few paces from the tank, and turned to the main part of the room. His eyes were now accustomed to the light, and he could see what was going on much better. The whole room was a chaotic mess. There were some fifty tables, many of which had been smashed up into bits, pulled together, and built into several different barricaded areas along the sides or in the corners of the room. To these had been added chairs, rolled up carpets and plant pots.

Each area had around thirty or so people entrenched within them, clutching lengths of wood and nasty looking kitchen implements. The string orchestra in the middle of the room was on a raised dais and seemed to be continuing to play despite the obvious war scenario being played out around them.

Everyone's attention seemed to be focused on the doors to the kitchen - the obvious source of food supplies. Oddly enough there were still a dozen or so tables dotted around the room, with people still seated, dressed in their finery, busily eating meals, seemingly avoiding or ignoring what was going on around them.

Just at that moment there was a shout from one side, and a group emerged from one of the barricades, and started running towards another set of upturned tables, clutching and holding up what looked like old books and sticks.

There was a volley of abuse and plate missiles were hurled at them from the defending group. As the group got within shorter range, these were replaced with a hail of kitchen utensils, assorted fruit, and bombs of curry powder. The attacking team retreated under the ferocious barrage, just in time to see off a sneak counterattack on their own patch from one of the other table camps.

The new group was headed by a tall woman wearing a long ball gown and tiara, who when realising her plan was foiled, hurled a spitting volley of words at the retreating group. They were very explicit, and not what you might usually associated with that sort of sophisticated look, accent, or demeanour. All the people in here seemed to be behaving very much like little children in a playground. There were even fights breaking out within the groups themselves, between individuals.

The whole room, that was once magnificent, beautiful, majestic, and refined, now looked like some seedy nightclub after a drunken brawl combined with some sort of idealistic company team building exercise that had gone very badly wrong.

Sam was trying to work out what he was seeing. It wasn't clear if it was representing countries, or continents, religions or cultures. There just seemed to be too many things added to the mix. Too many symbolisms and associations all happening at once. There were also many waiters and kitchen staff dotted around the room that looked more like androids.

However they seemed to be, for the most part, cowering behind curtains or desks or the bar, although some were making an effort here and there, dashing from behind large potted plants to help serve the trays and pick up the pieces of broken crockery.

There was too much information coming into his mind at once; too many messages, metaphors and analogies; too much knowledge all in one go. He started to feel dizzy and slightly panicked and fatigued all at the same time. The room started to sway about him. He sat down in a leather armchair in what appeared to be an area for smoking and drinking.

It was just an area with a few seats in it that was used before or after the meal. There was a small table next to him on which was an ashtray with a, still smoking, tipped cigarette in it. Sam now had his head in his hands and he was waiting for the dizziness to pass. The smell of the smoke made him feel nauseous. He needed some fresh air, and so got up to leave.

Marilyn helped Sam walk out of the room and through the doorway slowly. The steward opened the door for them as they went through. "Did you enjoy your meal Sir?" he asked, smiling politely, and raising his cap to Marilyn. Sam looked at him incredulously. He clearly had no idea what was going on in the room, or of the amount of time passing. "Err, Yes, great holiday…" said Sam cryptically "Thanks" still gasping for air.

Sam turned and walked further up along the deck past a few closed louvred wooden doors to individual cabins. He was just wandering anywhere, giving himself time to get the virtual fresh air back in his lungs. Brina by this time had changed back into herself again, and followed him a few steps behind. The change from Brina to Marilyn hadn't fazed him at all, it seemed only natural and necessary here, in fact when he looked around there were a lot of actors and actresses fulfilling roles.

Then again, all the real heroes and heroines seem to be actors and actresses or sportsmen, pop stars and the like these days. All being what people imagine they want, and are willing to pay for, reward, rather than what they actually need.

At that moment a famous Hollywood actor walked past, followed by a line of adoring women. Some were crew members, totally oblivious to the fact that they had left their posts and whatever work they were responsible for. It was an indication that something was very wrong with the system on board.

The same actor then changed his clothes, look, and demeanour into that of a singing 'Mr Darcy', which to Sam looked very odd, but the women loved it, one of them actually fainting. It was so effective that a few of the men close by started to behave and dress in the same way, at the same time looking like bewildered little boys, confused and at the same time grateful, for any interest the girls showed in them.

Clearly there were too many wrong signals and wrong influences going on here, it was almost farcical. In Sam's mind he started to expand the scenario out and imagined the whole ship full of people looking like Mr Darcy until that became the norm - all born and raised and encouraged to be that way, which was after all, successful. The women of the ship then having to compete, and find something more exciting to fall in love with.

It was quite clear too who was controlling and pulling the evolutionary strings; which from Sam's perspective wasn't exactly filling him with confidence. He was now almost expecting to see a seven foot tall famous celebrity teen idol with bright white teeth, in a glowing white captain's uniform with gold braids and medals, surrounded by an adoring entourage of 'followers'.

It was trying to show him things that were going wrong; the wrong signals of success, of love. Something was mixing up and confusing the 'recognising success' with 'amazing sex' messages for the wrong sort of blueprints of what was needed. The energy flows transmitting fake evolutionary needs, and direction towards visual entertainment and fame rather than survival.

He wondered how quickly things would change if a fully armed alien battleship suddenly appeared on the horizon. How impressed the girls would be with Mr Darcy's 'flamboyant' displays. He would confidently march up to the aliens and challenge them, with say a leather glove slapped in their face, or an offer of duelling pistols at dawn.

Perhaps instead he would call on some of his 'chums', challenge the alien side to a brutal game of football, gladiator style, with a rallying army of supporters, and show them what it meant to be in a real battle. In reality though, with the current situation, we wouldn't stand a chance. If one did arrive on the horizon Sam just hoped Mr Darcy could swim, but he was fairly sure he wouldn't know how.

Everything on this ship was there as some sort of analogy or representation. He thought about the boilers and furnaces deep down inside the bowels of the ship with all the men slaving away shovelling coal.

What was that supposed to represent? He thought *Hell? What would he find if he went down there? A demon bosun with a whip subjecting the poor unfortunate sinners to a lifetime of shovelling coal into the furnaces? Could he even find a way down there, or was it just a concept?*

Maybe the whole thing was just all automated now, diesel driven, or it could be nuclear powered for all he knew. It could all computerised now, or just a few people pressing buttons on their screens all day long. *What sort of life was that?* But then that was some people's idea of paradise.

Something was providing the energy to drive the ship though, so he assumed there must be something giving it power, even if it was just the power of fear.

They carried on along the First Class deck and walked past a ghost crewman that was busy swabbing the decks with a real mop and bucket. By the expression of people walking past him he was just seen as anyone else; ghosts were just accepted as normal on this hybrid ship. Sam moved around the wet area to avoid skidding on the slippery wood, clearly 'Health and Safety' on board was something you had to be aware of yourself. He looked back and noticed that the ghost was busy just mopping the same area again, as if it were a program stuck in a loop.

It was at that point that Sam caught sight of a little girl following them who seemed to be interested in what they were doing. She kept a good distance away, and everyone else seemed to be ignoring her, so he just decided to not worry about her.

Sam was not much good with determining ages but he would have guessed that she was between eight and ten years old. She had light brown, curly hair and an intelligent but determined face, and was wearing a simple checked blue dress. Looking at her again he noticed that she was carrying a small spiral bound notebook and a pencil.

They spent the next hour exploring different parts of the ship, well at least to the areas where they could get to safely. The Third Class sections were down below at the lower levels on the ship. They found the dining room, which resembled a soup kitchen set-up, where free fast food was being handed out to the Victorian-looking peasants, as if in an attempt to pacify them and keep them from mutinying.

They also appeared to have a whole range of simple facilities to keep them entertained, from pianos that played songs people could sing along to, to big TV screens, little electronic handheld devices, cabaret-type shows, and a whole range of coloured sweets and foods and pills.

All of the different sections and groups were kept apart from each other, compartmentalised and isolated, as if trying to maintain some order and control. Classic security protocols were used on the ship; locked doors, different levels, compartmental need-to-know systems, information corridors, and signage all over and inside the 'body' of the ship.

Well that was the idea anyway, but it was clear that on some of the decks that the system was being ignored and people were moving around inquisitively all over the place.

Coming back up another set of stairs they came across another room. It was just off from the First Class section and it seemed to be a sort of ship's Sick Bay, except someone had changed the sign to say 'Health Centre' instead. Brina stopped and was about to knock on the door when it was opened by an overweight middle-aged woman dressed in New Age style clothing. She walked out backwards holding a book, and she was talking to the man inside in a busy voice, all excited and full of herself.

The woman continued to talk about a range of subjects which seemed very spiritual or New Age. It was if she would never stop, every other word seemed to be either 'Me' or 'I'. Brina coughed politely and the woman suddenly looked confused, and she then turned and walked off.

Then in the doorway appeared a spritely man in his late sixties, Sam guessed, and he was about the same height as Brina. He had light brown, greying hair, and was wearing loose fitting brown and white clothes. Sam also noticed that he was barefoot. His face lit up when he saw Brina and she moved towards him and hugged him for the statutory three or four seconds of meme data transfer. Sam was quite taken by surprise; they looked as though they had known each other for years.

"Hello, so good to see you, how are you?" he went on, smiling in a welcoming, kindly manner, and gestured for them to go inside. As they entered, Sam saw that the small room was full of oddly coloured crystals, old books, metal bowls, wooden cabinets and tables, various religious objects, statues, and bottles. There were also various posters on the walls, and in one corner there was a table with a medical skull and backbone mounted on a wooden plinth.

It was a combination of things that you would find in a medical specialist's consulting room, a New Age spiritualist store, a homeopathic health shop, and a religious antique collector's room. There was also a small, white, glowing box on the wall that had a number of different shaped, size and coloured keys hanging in it.

It was clear that everything around the room were just tools; information devices that served a purpose to support what this man did. The important thing in here was the man himself, who seemed to have great energy and presence about him that was difficult to define or describe.

Brina introduced Sam to him, and Sam shook his hand. In that moment it suddenly felt as if he had known this person before, a long time ago; a very, very long time ago, but he couldn't describe where or when or how. It was as if he had always known him.

The man explained that he was there to make people better; to help people on the ship that needed him, and to do things he had to do. However he didn't go into details. He explained that his job meant that he saw lots of people who came to him for help and that, because of his role, he had been all over the ship and to every area, which had given him a very good idea of what was going on and what was happening.

He seemed to be a kind, genuine man, and was very specific about what he was there for, what his role was, and what he was doing. Sam liked that. On *this* ship, where most people hadn't got a clue what they were doing or what was going on, or even why they were there - this was good.

He quickly checked Sam over, moved a few of his limbs around, and then gave him a few tiny pills, and dropped something in his pocket, all in the space of a few minutes before Sam had any chance to question what was going on. He then gave Brina something to hang around her neck, but Sam couldn't see what it was.

As they spoke Sam started to remember things, things he didn't remember thinking or experiencing, as if there was a program in his mind that was communicating with something in the mind of whoever this person was, and agreeing things. It was a sort of resynchronising, remembering process, as if he was being helped to wake up in some way. It was all very odd.

Brina thanked the man, hugged him again, and then they left. Brina was quite a 'hugging' sort of person, and seemed to do it a lot with people. She was also into the 'kissing on the cheeks' thing, but he wasn't. This was obviously one of many ways of sharing information, or 'data', between people. The functions, or programs, in the devices exchanged knowledge and information with physical handshakes, and negotiated interaction protocols just as with kissing and hugging babies; which is why it is very important that you present them to the right sort of people - and this probably doesn't include politicians.

The corridors here were beautifully carpeted, and furnished with the same Art Deco style décor that Sam had seen in the First Class dining room. There were ornate side lamps and polished wooden furniture fixed to the walls. The ship had dozens of decks, and thousands of rooms; far too many for any real ship.

Some of the rooms opened up into massive cavernous spaces which were full of people doing research on science, or art and music. Some were just crammed with masses of people stood in rows like zombies going around in one giant loop. Each room seemed to represent different aspects of the world, cultures, academia, politics, geographic, religious and companies or industry. There were also some rooms that were definitely isolated or locked, and cut off from each other to prevent them mixing or communicating.

Normally a working ship like a military destroyer or a commercial vessel would be formed of a crew. It would be full of hard working people; organised structured and operational. They were all part of a ship's company, and the ship being part of what they were. Everyone on these types of ships knew what they were doing, what they were responsible for, their roles, how it was organised and what to do if something happened.

They had to be like that, in case they were attacked, or for safety, or for commercial efficiency. Everyone was organised, happy, trained, and everything just took care of itself, depending on the situation. There would be a captain in charge who guided the ship and who made sure everything was in order.

There seemed to be none of that going on here though - it was like a 'free for all', and very easy to see what was wrong all over the place. It was just mad, disorganised chaos, but then you can only see these things when you knew what you were looking at, and could apply your experience and knew the difference between right and wrong in context.

After a few hours of exploring, they eventually made it all the way up to the top deck, which was all clearly First Class, and very exclusive. They walked outside along the deck to the very front, and Brina led him up a short flight of steps, up to what, he assumed by its position, was the main bridge with its side lookouts, high above the front deck. Above them towered an enormous funnel steadied by guide cables stretching down to where the white lifeboats were suspended along the length of the side.

The Bridge itself from the outside was all white, with thickly painted metal bulkheads and square, thick glass storm-proof windows. Standing outside the side door to the Bridge was a man dressed in, what appeared to be, a bosun's uniform wearing loose white trousers and an open, badly fitting, blue jacket decorated with a row of gold buttons. He was in his late thirties, and had a thuggish, scruffy unkempt appearance, as if somehow he had acquired the uniform and job through ill means, and that neither quite fitted.

He was trying to look the part but was failing, and would have seemed more at home on a pirate ship. He had dark hair and eyes, was of medium build and wore an evil sneer on his twisted, pockmarked face. He also had a number of strange geometric tattoos on his neck and hands which looked artificial, like transfers.

As Brina reached the top of the steps to the lookout area, he eyed her up and down in her bikini. "Where d'ya think you're going darlin'?" he sneered in a rough, put-on, 19th century Southern England accent, and barred the way to the door. He seemed to have ignored Sam, and was concentrating on Brina, who for some reason he seemed to recognise in some way, not personally, but somehow by association, as if he knew 'what' she was rather than 'who'.

They continued the discussion without words in silence for another thirty seconds, and had reached stalemate until Sam came up beside her. The man's eyes switched from her to him, without changing any of his expression of condescending contempt.

He scanned Sam quickly, made a rapid up and down assessment with his eyes, and then switched back to Brina. She, in his mind, was the main threat and also now in his immediate view. Clearly Sam was not worth worrying about, or of any interest, and he didn't want to waste valuable time on him.

The silent battle resumed between them; vast amounts of information being traded between their eyes. Then for a split instant there was a slight look of uncertainty there, and a question in his eyes, and they flicked quickly back to Sam again.

He glanced to the top of Sam's head, and down over his torso, trying to work something out. Then back to his eyes again, and the colour began to drain from his face. He turned straight back to Brina, suddenly looking off-guard and losing his put-on accent, "But he's th ..." His words were abruptly choked off by Brina's hand snapping around his throat, and he instinctively grabbed at her rigid outstretched arm trying to release her fingers.

His mouth gasped for air, choking, and he struggled violently as she raised him clear off the ground by a good foot, in an almost mechanical effortless action, his feet kicking wildly. In one smooth motion she turned, and slowly walked, expressionless, several feet to the end of the lookout area with him writhing in mid-air. Then, without ceremony or emotion, she deposited him over the side. As he fell back, he clawed at her, trying to get some grip, some saving purchase, but he could only get hold of her sunglasses as he disappeared over the side.

There was no sound for five seconds until a deep splashing noise came from far below in the fast moving cold water. She calmly walked back to the door adjusting her appearance as she came, and looked completely nonplussed.

"It's alright Sam, he was just something bad that made a miscalculation of judgement" she said. "It's OK now, he will have a good long swim and will safely wash up on a beach somewhere in the morning - cold and wet but a little wiser" she continued in a straight, unemotional, dialogue.

She checked Sam over again and put her hand gently under his chin below his gaping mouth and closed his jaw for him, and then turned, opened the door and went in. Sam ran over to the side of the ship, and looked down but he could see nothing more than the sea flowing past far below.

He looked back in the wake of the ship and caught sight of a head bobbing amongst the waves, and after a few moments some arms starting to swim.

There were no calls of 'Man Overboard!' or anyone looking, or being even remotely interested. It was quite windy up here and he turned back to look over the ship. He could see above him some flags blowing in the wind attached to wires up to the smoking funnels, and he could see down on to the other decks with all the people moving around.

He was on his own now and felt quite lost, so he followed Brina in through the door to the Bridge, it was just the logical thing to do.

CHAPTER 12 - THE BRIDGE

As Sam entered the Bridge he saw that it was vast and tall, some two hundred and fifty feet long and eighty high like a cathedral. Again this room was massively bigger than it appeared to be from the outside. There were several large, important-looking male officers in various uniforms and costumes, who clearly represented the heads of certain groups or individual beliefs, all doing their own thing.

There were other figures wandering around, all busy with jobs and communicating with the rest of the ship using various means. They were responding to calls and messages coming in from lots of areas on the ship; all very efficient, important and busy.

In front of the windows to the front were many dials, instruments and panels. At the back of the Bridge in the distance was a vast, twelve foot high, marble dais or temple area, with many steps leading up to it in a semi-circle. On top of the dais was a giant throne in which sat a giant figure that was about eighteen feet tall, and which seemed indistinct or blurred from this distance.

There were also many people and things going on in-between. High up in the ceiling was a glass-domed roof built in sections to a mid-point, down from which hung a giant crystal chandelier, which came down some forty feet on a long cord. It seemed quite out of place having something like that on a functioning ship's bridge.

There was plenty of sunlight streaming in through the dome, and the chandelier itself was illuminated from above by the light of the sun. The light radiated through the crystal structure, casting a rainbow of colours from red to blue throughout the room. As the ship moved in the swell of the waves, it swung back and forth slowly, left and right like a pendulum, creating an odd spectrum effect in the room.

The whole room was very confusing. Things seemed to appear out of nowhere and then vanish; people would come in and out of the doors constantly. There were noises, coloured lights flashing, and all sorts of mechanisms. In front of the window shield, at the bow end, was a long wooden panelled control centre with all sorts of impressive navigation tools, clocks, lights, and brass fittings on it.

There were tables with charts, a giant globe, and a rack of what looked like nautical instruments, sextants and the like. Sam could feel the energy in the room, and the importance of where he was, everything seemed to be going on here, this was the nerve centre of the ship, the heart of the animal. Brina kept close to him, looking around carefully, but everyone seemed too busy to notice them.

Looking at the throne now, Sam noticed a figure dressed in orange go up the steps to the dais, and then kneel down in front of the throne. At which point the figure sitting on it became more distinct, and it took on the form of some sort of Eastern deity, but from this distance it was hard to see what, or hear the discussion that took place, and the orange figure returned and went off.

A few moments later a man wearing a suit and tie went up. This time the giant figure changed into another archetypal image with a beard and booming voice and was surrounded by clouds of smoke. 'Odd' wasn't really the word to describe it. Sam wasn't even sure if the rest of the people in the room could see what he was seeing.

From the reactions of the people in the room this was clearly the 'Captain' of the ship, and the people on the Bridge seemed to be vying for 'his' attention, and attempting to gain influence over him, or occasionally 'her', or also occasionally some sort of animal-human hybrid.

Sam wondered if the people on the Bridge around him were the Illuminati or enlightened spiritual leaders that he had heard about; influencing the collective subconscious mind, trying to benefit or promote their own areas and goals, or whether they were just people wanting to make a difference. There did seem to be some highly intelligent and knowledgeable people in here, and yet they all appeared to see different things on the dais, or throne.

At that moment another 'Officer' entered from the door on the other side of the room, dressed in a bright white uniform adorned with rows of medals. He appeared to be entertaining a group of adoring women passengers that had followed him in, and they all gave squeals of excitement at what they saw.

They were all trying to gain this officer's attention, and he was clearly flirting with them with a put-on posh accent, and yet he seemed completely oblivious to what was going on with the ship. For a moment everyone around him seemed to be placating themselves to him, and began to present him with gifts and compliments.

Sam listened to what he was saying to them, but after a while it just started to sound like a stuck record. The officer then went off out of the Bridge without having done anything, with his adoring fans following him through the far door.

The vain assurance that Sam had in his mind a few hours ago, of there being a controlling bridge, and an organised, efficient operational control centre, was now disappearing fast.

On this ship the difference between the passengers and the crew seemed blurred a lot of the time. It was difficult to see who was working, and who was along for the ride. In any case there seemed to be very little productive or effective work going on in most of the areas.

It almost seemed as if nobody was really in charge, or worried about how the ship was run, or what was going on, or its direction, efficiency, or purpose. It was an organisational nightmare, shambolic chaos, and yet all very childish and naïve.

There were many of those who were quite happy to do nothing but sit around in the sun, eat the food and get others to do the work; just along for the ride. Which was fine, as long as the bills were paid.

It was at that point that Sam noticed something obvious that was missing in the room, something fundamental that should have been there but wasn't. There was no ship's wheel, nothing with which to direct the ship. There was a brass engine room telegraph which was set to 'Half Speed', which clearly controlled the speed of the ship or engines, but there was no ship's wheel. It left him with an odd cold feeling in his stomach.

He then started to wander around the room, his mind now curious to work out what was really happening. There was a note on a clipboard that was left on the chart table, a sort of Situation Report. He read the details - *'Ship too low in the water, too many people on board, getting bigger, getting more advanced all the time, rivets coming apart, looks like parts built on the cheap'.*

He walked over to the control panel in front of the window, where there was nobody around, and tried to make sense of the maze of switches, lights and dials. There in the middle of the panel, on its own, was a large red flashing light, under which there was a sign on a brass plaque which said,

Warning! Autopilot Disengaged

The light flashed on and off quite persistently. He looked around him but there was nobody taking any notice of him. Brina was next to his shoulder just watching what he was looking at, but she gave no reaction. He turned back and for some inexplicable reason he pressed the button next to the light marked **Autopilot**. Nothing happened. The light just kept flashing, but the words on the brass plate with the original message changed to read

Subconscious Autopilot cannot be engaged
now that Conscious System is Active

Then after a few moments it changed back again to the same hand carved words as before. For all intents and purposes, it may well have just said

Please Don't Press This Button Again

Lines appeared on Sam's brow, and he looked at Brina, but her face was expressionless.

He looked out of the window. In the distance, looming up again on the horizon was the same island that they had nearly run into several hours earlier. He blinked. *They were going round in circles!* He realised suddenly, *there was nobody at the wheel, no one in the driving seat, or whatever the bloody thing was called on a ship!*

He looked around again, and then starting walking across the long room up towards the dais. He had to move around some people, and avoid certain odd things in the room that were going on, and he seemed to be being ignored for the most part. He eventually made it to the base of the dais, which resembled some form of Greek or Roman temple. At this point Brina started to become nervous, and he could feel her arm slip inside his as they walked.

As he came closer to the dais, the image of the deity on the throne became more defined again, it was God, or at least everything he had always expected God to be, and to look like if he existed. There were great masses of energy flowing from him, and there was that omnipotent presence and awe-inspiring feeling.

It made Sam feel very small and insignificant. It was totally everything that he expected; the wise features, the glowing aura, the golden throne and that knowing, but indescribable feeling, that he had finally arrived in 'His all-knowing presence'. It was humbling.

Then in a booming, but somehow calming, gentle voice 'God' said to Sam, "So you now see all and understand everything. You have found me, and now you understand."

"Blimey" said Sam to Brina suddenly feeling overwhelmed and unimportant, his knees going weak. This was very unexpected and confusing.

Sam looked back at God, and thought for a moment, speechless, while the organ music played in the background, and divine voices sang from high fidelity speakers somewhere in the ceiling. There was bright white light everywhere and the air throbbed with vibrant energy.

But it just didn't seem quite right. Sam's eyes narrowed suspiciously, and something clicked in his mind, and he climbed several steps onto the dais, so that he was about twenty feet away from the throne.

"OK" Sam said, and thought carefully "You win. I shall now devote my life to getting everyone to see what I see, from my perspective, and try to make them understand all this, to believe and worship you, and do your bidding, and I shall make the world a better place and bring the love to all, and they shall work hard and be happy in harmony, and I will let them know that you look exactly like that painting by Michelangelo that I haven't actually seen yet."

There was a very long pause.

"Eh?" said God

"One question though," said Sam interrupting God before he could say anything else "what about dark matter and dark energy?"

"What about them?" said God, his mighty brow furrowing further. "Well, from what I have seen, you don't seem to know what they are" said Sam. "There are no answers or knowledge or explanation that you have of these things yet in your mind… Why?"

"MORTAL!" said God in a big booming voice "Thou shalt not question the word of God. Thou shalt do my bidding. I am all Powerful, all Present, all Knowing, how dare you question my word?" It was then that Sam's mind started to fill with emotions, a sense of awe. He felt an overwhelming omnipotence and presence. *What on Earth am I doing? What am I playing at?* thought Sam suddenly.

Brina's arm clung to Sam's. It was clear that she was more than a little terrified.

"Hang on," said Sam continuing without giving any recognition to the change in mood "Thou shalt? Isn't that just a sort of ancient biblical translation speak? Why would you talk like that now, and why bother telling me what to do? If you are all powerful, why not just make me? If you are all present, why do you need me here? And if you are all knowing, why are we even having this conversation?"

"Alright, alright…" said God calming down "So what is it exactly that you want to know?"

"Well, any simple answer on the Dark Matter thing would be good, and besides, shouldn't you be able to answer that last question anyway? Shouldn't you have known what I was going to ask?"

There was a long awkward pause. "Well…" said God "I'm not sure on that one, it could be a couple of things, I am still working on it."

"Eh?" said Sam smiling "What do you mean 'You aren't sure'? And come to think of it, there are quite a few other things that you don't have answers to, conveniently left out of the all-knowing perfect picture, and quite a lot that contradict each other too."

Sam seemed to be engaged in some sort of mental game. It was a competition, or battle, in which he wasn't even sure that it was even him saying these things. There was some sort of scenario occurring that needed to happen, that was really going on, but to which he was only a bystander, but needed to see.

At that moment God changed into another deity form that Sam recognised. There was an exchange of data between the two of them, and then he changed again. Then he transformed in quick succession to several other forms; trying to see what would possibly work, but nothing did.

Then he changed into a group of what looked like aliens of different shapes, which suddenly made sense to Sam as the thoughts and explanations relating to them came to him. It all made perfect sense for a few moments in his mind, they started talking to him, telepathically explaining things; where they had come from, what was really going on, conferring some higher, more complex technical explanation of what it all meant, like a story unfolding, trying to define a plausible explanation on everything to justify and explain everything away at a new higher level of understanding.

But again, even though it was a lot more reasonable and technical, Sam could see that there were too many gaps in the logic, too many implausible mental logical pictures or non-scientific scenarios. It was as if someone was creating a film or drama with characters and plot that seemed to make perfect sense, until you stepped back and looked at the whole thing and realised there was too much edited out, and it was all a bit childish and made-up nonsense. Like a big game.

The scene changed a few more times; each time with a more and more sophisticated set of characters or situations or explanations, as if something was adapting to the next level each time to try and outsmart him. It went from lizard men, to aliens, to invisible dimensional beings. All with more and more fantastic, frightening and sophisticated concepts. All associated with adaptive intelligent belief structures. Almost the same way as a child in their bedroom would come up with more and more inventive and plausible imagined explanations, for what it was making the creaking noise in the darkness behind the door of the wardrobe.

As the child grew older and became aware of more things, the thoughts would become more refined. Until finally realising, as an adult, that it wasn't a giant alien or a super-intelligent vampire mouse, but just that your parents had bought you cheap furniture, were useless at DIY and had lost the assembly instructions.

Eventually after another twenty minutes, including scenarios involving a baby, and then a senile old man in a wheelchair waving a walking stick, it all vanished and the original bearded God appeared on the throne in white robes.

God looked furious for a moment, frustrated, and then his shoulders sagged, and then just looked dejected, with his hands propping up his now 'Charlton Heston-like' bearded face, still holding a stick. It was a last ditch combination effort, an image that was formed from several things of what he was possibly expecting, which together just looked daft.

There was another very long pause this time. "Well actually," said God sighing "I have got a bit of a confession to make. I am actually you, or more to the point a representation of the part of the collective mind in your head; in your psyche more accurately. I am a representation of a defined shared belief structure in your consciousness to interpret elements and information within the collective mind.

"Except in your case you don't have anything that can be built on, you are just a blank sheet of paper that I can't write on, so it's fairly hard to hypnotise you or manipulate your thoughts, or apply anyone else's to program you. In effect you don't actually believe any of this - you are just explaining it all to yourself, to show yourself what is really going on. What you are saying to yourself is that nothing in the collective mind is able to fool you."

"So," said Sam "shall I call you something else rather than God to save on the confusion?"

"If you like - it's your head, your mind, your psyche. Oh do what you bloody well like! I'm just a translation service anyway, a parallel-to-serial converter, a program, an interpreter, a go-between to a biological operating system sort of thing. Something to keep you doing things for collective benefit."

"Well clearly that's not quite true is it? The bit about it being *my* mind" said Sam. "If it was all mine I would be using all of it myself."

"Well," said God "it has its pros and cons. Bear in mind if the collective mind wasn't here, you would still be a jellyfish or an octopus. It's a sort of collaborative diametric balance, advanced hive mind type thing."

"So why have so many people, who have seen this from their various cultures, thought you were god or many gods?" said Sam.

"Well," said God "because I didn't know what I was, or am. I am just a program function or subconscious operating system interface - a complex supporting control mechanism. I am sort of substituting concepts to make sense of the something else. So it made sense to you, for your own protection, and also evolution applied some controls.

"But as mankind grew up, and learnt things, then obviously I grew up in parallel too, and as we knew more about physics, biology, chemistry, and psychology and all that, it suddenly clicked what I was. Which in effect is what I am being formed into.

"If you look back in history you can see that I have been changing over time, along with what was perceived or interpreted about me, or what I was. Even in books you can see my interpretation evolve from an angry, bad-tempered, vengeful character, to one that is more forgiving, caring and understanding.

"It was just a best guess interpretation or psyche translation at the time. There was nothing wrong with it, it was just based on what they knew or understood, and believed, and what it was, or had evolved to be at the time. It is also a reflection of how far I had developed at that stage, and what I was able to perceive or knew at the time.

"Of the few people that 'see' me, they only 'saw' what was collectively there at points in time, or by mistake as I evolved as a macro-organism in effect, and what was there or known became vastly more complex and detailed. It's a bit of a Catch 22 situation really, where the more we know, the harder it is to experience everything, and to understand it all, with all sorts of feedback systems in place, both positive and negative. With, at the same time, having to deal with dogma and reinforced misinterpretations and misconceptions of what I am; all of which reinforce and protect the system itself.

"But Hey! That's life!" God exclaimed with showman-like flair.

Sam began to recognise his own words and way of talking coming out, but he didn't stop the dialogue. Besides he could sense it trying to outsmart him, and change his thoughts all the time, it was a steady and deliberate contest, which he understood and accepted.

God went on "It is clearly better to just experience what is there, to know and make your own judgements rather than believing in the past interpretations and what was said then. Not that it was necessarily wrong, it was just right at the time, or was based on naïve perspective or limited knowledge of things like evolution or physics or biology. It has all changed, evolved.

"The other problem is that what was said in the past gets strengthened and self-reinforced over time, sort of a collective neural linguistic programming or hypnotic effect, reinforced belief structures that take a long time to get over or evolve through, even with the evidential facts, or with better understanding.

"It's all got a bit messed up though," he continued "not helped by a few natural disasters sort of upsetting things, and chaos being thrown in for good measure. So really what we have now is a management problem. It's not really my fault you see, I just didn't know, how could I? I am all of you. I am us."

There was a pause for dramatic effect. But Sam said nothing

"So, you see, at every point in history it was the truth, but not quite the whole truth. You, sorry, *I*, or *we*, could only express what was known, and what you assumed was correct at the time, based on the cumulative human knowledge combined with your own observations and understanding."

"OK. I see" said Sam. "That's fine, but why did people in the past who 'saw' all of this have a tendency to remain anonymous?"

"Well," said God "that is because being subjected to so much collective information alters your mind to look at things in an holistic, collective way, and besides you kind of feel responsible, and want to do something to make a difference, change things, so it's a bit of a leap to take, and even though you feel like you want to tell everyone, you only have to look at the track record of those that did to see the problems with doing that. The system, after all, will protect itself.

"So" said God without pausing for breath, which he didn't need anyway, "for the last few hundred years I have been subconsciously getting everyone to concentrate on moving science and understanding forward in academic stovepipes to bridge the gap so that people can understand and see how it all works, and what it's all about, getting more knowledge but in a controlled way that suits the collective mind, me.

"Ever wonder why you are paying for all these guys to sit in their ivory towers and come up with lots of ideas that don't really benefit you directly? Why you have to pay for them, and then when they eventually do come up with things you can use, you end up having to pay for those things too? Well now you know.

"You have to use laws against laws - create life and knowledge by taking the laws of the Universe and integrating them together to create new ideas. That's what it's all about - balance."

"So," said Sam "it's the 'all' in ALL. We are God and God is us, or should I say IT? IT is us and we are IT. But in this case, it's you."

"Look," said God "it's not my bloody fault. It's not anyone else's fault either. Blame it on the planet, the flood, the Universe, the laws, the randomness of the cosmos if you like. We are where we are.

"IT, as you so kindly describe me," God went on "is created from everything living on Earth, just in the same way that a cell is living and evolving it all works upwards and outwards.

It is evolving and growing as it perceives, building bubbles of psyche groups within itself and ourselves. Being part of something bigger is the game, it's what works, it is what is needed for survival and evolution, success and failure, winners and losers.

"Everything is in balance and symmetrical, or needs to be. Why do you think the original gods were many and varied including animal gods? Many gods representing different subconscious facets, then into single gods as everything combined and made more conscious sense. These images are then reinforced by self-perpetuating belief structures, legacy archetype forms, iconic imagery, and symbol branding association, represented by an individual's psyche to interpret something into a form they can cope with mentally. Something safe and comprehendible to them from what they are able to understand.

"IT has trouble seeing the physical world. IT just has a representation of it which has evolved from paradise to more like a mental multi-dimensional complex range of what is seen these days in out of body experiences, or 'remote' viewings. IT just perceives and gathers knowledge through the interface to our minds, like when we dream or imagine or experience."

God sighed "It's all a bit obvious I suppose now that you look at it. It's just that we try and understand the past, and what has been said, beliefs and all that. Of course, that can in itself generate feedback loop if you are me in the first place."

"So you are expecting *me* to sort this all out for you?" asked Sam. "Well it shouldn't be too difficult for you. You have had quite a lot of training, and messages, and linked up with several people to look after you and protect you and point you in the right direction" said God.

"Thanks very much," said Sam "and what do I get out of this?"

"What do you mean?" asked God.

"You know, pay and conditions, expenses et cetera."

"I can offer you more than that" said God. "I can offer you ultimate bliss." There was a pause. Sam felt an instant blissful, spine tingling surge through his body like a drug, only it seemed more pure and natural, the same as an orgasm, but incentivising rather than post rewarding. "Wow!" said Sam.

"That's the most amazing high! You must have been perfecting that for some time now. So let me get this straight, what you are offering me is an eternity of bliss like that?"

"Yes," said God, "combined with an infinity of knowledge and everlasting love to sort out all these subconscious problems. Sound very tempting?"

Sam thought for a moment and there was another long pause "Err, no thanks I will go for the 'hermit on an island' option if that's OK with you. I know that sounds a bit selfish and shallow, but it's a bit more real than the subconscious mental bribe you are offering me, and we know how damaging drugs can be, and their long term damage, and the side effects they can have. These are lessons you need to learn too."

"Ah yes," said God "but that was before. I was just working out what I am, and what I was doing. I didn't know I was pulling tricks like that to get my own way, and besides I'm getting a bit tired."

"So," continued Sam "essentially you are now saying that you have been a bit selfish up until now, but you didn't know what you were, or what you were doing. You are blaming it all on your limited perspective of us, and that you have kept this big secret to yourself as you didn't want it getting confusing. Now, however, you realise that you have a worrying deadline coming, and are panicking a bit, you want me to sort it out for you. All that just sounds like the same old tricks just represented in a different way?"

"Well yes…" said God.

"So anyone who has cottoned on to this in the past has either become a hermit or been prevented from saying anything, or only been able to hint at things through cryptic words or concepts. So now for the last hundred years as the pressure is on, and everyone has been pushed to get some answers for you, up to their limits of capability and levels of stress…" said Sam. "How does NO! grab you?"

"But…" said God.

"Look!" said Sam. "There are some things that you need to understand. You need to know that this sort of behaviour isn't acceptable any more. We know a lot more these days about many things, as do you, and yet you have not matured as much as we have. It's not your fault - it is just the way it is. Most of these are evolutionary problems caused by many things, but things have reached a point now where it won't work anymore. This point of criticality has caused an event to occur, as it has all the way through history.

"Really we are just the result of consequences, random events, and chance, apart from the initial framework, rules and energy and control levels and limits, together with a direction, a divine-ward process, driven energy, let's call it firmware building blocks if you like."

"OK, fair enough," said God "but let me ask you a question. Can you tell me what is the answer is? Do you know why I am here?"

"I know the answer - but I'm not telling you" said Sam firmly.

"But I have written it down."

"Eh?" said God "That doesn't make any bloody sense! What happened to 'You are me and I am you? All in ALL, in this together, 'one for all and all for one' and all that, so we should share what we know?"

"I know the answer but I'm not telling you- that's my final answer" said Sam "Laws against laws - so now see how you bloody well like it. This is supposed to be working fairly from both sides, and at the moment it isn't working at all.

"Besides as I said, I think you have some growing up to do and this is all good for you."

Sam took a deep breath before he continued.

"You see you have been forcing us to become smarter, stronger, faster, more aggressive and hungry for resources from your needs and perspective. Which is fine. That's nature. They are the laws that have been set for us. But as a result of our situation we have become too many for this ship to carry. We will use up all the resources, all the food, and we will become sick. We have split into groups, each with their own structures. This has led to wars and disagreements about what 'you' and 'we' are, what we should be, and how to run things.

This has not helped us individually at all. From those that were able to hear you, or read the messages, you seemed to be saying the same things, but over time they were interpreted in different ways which caused confusion and too much guesswork.

"The main problem was that you were growing and evolving, and at the same time, so were we, and our knowledge and beliefs fed back into you, and vice versa. You know - the yin and yang and all that?

"It's got into a bit of a mess, especially with the mind-altering drugs and toxins adding to the confusion on misinterpretation of messages and information. It's become too much. We need you to grow up and be aware of what is going on with yourself before it's too late."

"I have been trying to get you to listen for ages," said God "but it's not easy and you don't seem to be able to listen, or see, or understand me. Besides I am constrained by rules too, nature and physics and all that, and by how I evolved, and it doesn't seem to be working in this case, you know grow, evolve, use up resources and move on, start again, et cetera.

"Look," said God continuing "it hasn't exactly been easy for me either. You have to see things from my point of view. It seemed to be all going fine thousands of years ago and then all of a sudden some things happened, and it all got lost and confused. I tried several things automatically but they seemed to make things worse! Nobody seemed to be listening or understanding so I tried to push people in the right directions with incentives, subconsciously, but that only made people work in isolation and the more complex it all got, the more confusing it all was. It all seemed very simple to me."

"Yes," said Sam "*but you ARE us.*"

"Exactly! You see my point!" Exclaimed God. "All I have been doing is learning and remodelling and creating points of reference to correct errors. It's just in my nature, it just happens, but that isn't enough without any external drives or controls or influence."

"So," said Sam "if you only know everything that we know, our purpose from your perspective is to learn, explore, discover, evolve, create, and experience.

That way you can then collate, equate and resolve that information into your perspective format, and cross reference it, and so evolve in parallel, but obviously with different objectives, priorities, and perception. Just like a small child growing up in bio-synchronicity with its own body, it's a working relationship; the body and the mind each needing each other, to survive, grow, evolve."

"If you say so …" said God.

"However," continued Sam "with no external influences, or force, or opposition or competition, errors that would normally be evolved away and become resident. Legacy exists, and complacency and lethargy set into the overall model with no evolutionary pressure to resolve them away.

"The whole thing becomes a slow process of hit and miss, interspersed with growing pains, phases, and with some influences from the physical surroundings, physical laws, rules, and constraints and natural forces having their effect. All creating a constant balanced battle for survival, between growing, knowing and mindfulness. Push things too far from its own perspective and it risks destroying its own body and vice versa.

"The state of the world" Sam continued "is symptomatic of the whole process and state of affairs. Some elements of which have been left behind. It's the same with countries or cultures, some still in the Dark or Middle Ages, while others are pushed along hard. What is required now is a much more holistic approach to the whole thing, benefit managed from both the collective and individual perspectives, biometrically synchronised, measured and planned. Everything working in harmony instead of the mind and body fighting or competing with each other."

"It's not my fault", said God sounding like a spoilt child now. "How am I supposed to know what I am in that respect? I just go with what I know, make it up as I go along, see what works and what doesn't and put the feelers out to see where I am. Most of what I do is governed by my subconscious. It's not fair."

At those words Sam stopped, and everything changed.

The air felt different, there was a pause.

"But you *are* our collective subconscious" Sam said. "I thought that was what I was talking to indirectly?"

There was uncomfortable silence. It now became clear that he wasn't just talking to something that was acting or communicating subconsciously through a translation or interpretation via his own mind, something had changed. He had forced something into a more conscious dialogue, and into a state change of level as a result of this outsmarting process that was going on. The air in the room grew colder and harsher and everything suddenly lost its surreal, dreamlike, virtual feel, and hardened in perspective as if he was taking in a deep lungful of oxygen. Things had really changed and it didn't feel soft and safe anymore.

Something caught Sam's eye from behind the throne. It was a pair of black, floor length curtains some nine feet long and six feet wide. Sam moved to the side of the throne and looked behind it at the curtains in more detail. A booming voice and a thunder clap crashed from the throne above.

"Ignore the curtains! DO NOT take any notice of the curtains!" shouted God, but Sam just ignored the voice.

From this angle it was clear that there was a projected beam of white light coming through a gap in the middle of the curtains from some room behind, and through to the back of the throne, creating the image of whatever it was sat at it. It was also presumably controlling the sound too, although it wasn't quite clear where this came from.

Somehow it now a reminded him of a scene from the *Wizard of Oz*, including the protestations from the figure in the chair. It went on for a few more moments with a whole range of begging requests and angry expletives, before it, and God, vanished and the light went off. There was nothing in his 'self' left to act against, no function that could counteract the need and drive in him in anymore.

Sam's legs felt as if they were made of lead, but with effort he forced himself to walk up to the curtain. He felt defensive walls of fear and trepidation, as well as what seemed to be invisible physical barriers, trying to stop him from progressing. Visions too, that were intentionally designed to deter him, violent and frightening; giant spiders, demons, anything that could tap into his darkest fears. Somehow though, his mind was able to dismiss them all.

There were protocols and defences that he seemed to be bypassing, requiring rules such as selflessness, some even seemed to only be overcome by both he and Brina being present together. Passes or mechanisms to get through them, like a two-man synchronisation rule. There was dust on the floor, sometimes so thick it had formed into small mounds, which seem to get thicker the closer he got to the curtain. This was obviously an area of the ship that had never been cleaned.

As he placed his hand on the curtain he turned back to see Brina following him very nervously a few paces behind. She was pale and having real trouble coping, overcoming whatever was going through her own head, and what she was being subjected to even in her analogy form. She was trying to compete with it, overcoming it by the overriding need to protect him.

It seemed to be part of what he was here for, to go in there, part of his nature to find and explore. He knew it was a role that he had to perform however it didn't make it any easier, and the fear was intense like a phobia. But it's what he had to do, he had responsibility and he had to do it. *This was it.*

Sam parted the curtains. Beyond there was just a dark corridor; blackness that went on inside somewhere into pitch dark. On the wall to the side of the entrance was a small brass plaque on which was written:

WARNING
Natural Safety Protocols Are Inactive Beyond This Point

Then on the wall below that, someone had drawn in black marker pen with a smiley face next to it.

Abandon hope all ye who enter here …

Then below that someone else had written in crayon

Schizophrenics not welcome - this means both of you

with the first word being amended so that it was spelt

correctly. It made Sam smile but didn't detract much from the growing trepidation that he felt. Just looking into the darkness he could feel that there were waves of real energy and tangible fear coming from in there, and in no small amounts.

He turned again to Brina but she could clearly go no further. Somehow she recognised what this was, and it absolutely terrified her, and she could no longer physically overcome the battle going on inside her. She looked frustrated with herself. It was a female anger of injustice and the look of pain on her face told him that he was on his own now.

Turning back to help her, or talk to her, would not have been the right thing to do, nor would she thank him for it. He was here for a reason, and he had to get on with it, she could only protect him so far. There were tears in her eyes, but he did not know if they were of worry, frustration, anger, or joy.

They were her tears not his.

He turned again, and walked in. Alone.

CHAPTER 13 - THE ROOM

He was in a different place now, and it certainly was not 'Kansas' or 'Wonderland' any more. It was cold, stark, hard and brutal. The walls pulsed with real energy and a dark vibrancy at the edge of visible light. Occasionally things, or the walls, would close right in and then, the next moment, everything seemed an infinite distance away.

As he walked in further, his eyes became adjusted to the dark, and he could see billions of seemingly digital vector patterns and fractal streams through the walls and ceiling. It moved in waves, patterns, and in flowing motions as if alive with eddies of data, knowledge and energy.

A shared and negotiated distributed memory structure, an information database, memory records, which the 'higher self' programs on the ship accessed, modified, and refined through their current biological devices. It seemed to be a visual representation, much like in *The Matrix* film, of the actual programs within a system; but he was aware at the same time that it was his mind trying to represent something in the best, and most applicable way that it could.

This was the closest association available in his mind to represent something so vast and intricate that had no physical form or representation. He wondered if he was being represented in there somewhere; a tiny integrated glowing thought form, a program star among the depths of a galaxy of billions of souls.

Yet, as in any dream, it was an interpretation of something in a way that was comprehensible to him, and one that he could visualise, or at least interpret, in some way that meant something. That 'something' presented in a context that was in some way familiar to him. The closer you looked at anything, the more intense the detail. A never-ending macro hierarchy of micro complexity, deeper and deeper. Through into the walls themselves and on, almost into infinity. Almost but not quite.

Everything we have ever known was portrayed there; cities, countries, people, memories, events, in impossible detail. There was no scale here, and it felt as if he could stare into the glowing dots and see unlimited information in every one.

It was like looking at a night satellite movie of the world, but in three dimensions, with lights of cities interconnected with ley lines of intricate network pathways, routing energy and information, a glowing neural network in a vast mind to an almost infinite resolution. The surreal dreamland, virtual feel that he had become used to on the ship had gone, swapped now for a much more brutal, cold reality.

For a moment he was Neo, standing there in the darkness alone, with the energy flowing around him. His own life memories flashed before his eyes in a few seconds, in parallel synchronicity to the situations in *The Matrix* film, many of the roles and characters and scene events were now alarmingly coincidental to his own.

Then he abruptly changed back to being Sam again. That too was a message from something trying to tell him something or communicate a concept in some way, but very fast, hard and direct without the ambiguity or subtleness as before on the rest of the ship. He got the whole concept and meaning in a second, it was all there at once, clear, and then it was gone.

After a few minutes of physically forcing himself slowly down the corridor, like pushing against a strong wind, he emerged into a vast open room which was black and empty.

He could not see the walls easily, aside from the flows of lights and energy as before, but he could sense that they were there curving around him, as did the floor and ceiling like a lightless cave. It was hard to tell if the walls were only a few feet away or if he was inside some vast cavern. He could sense the walls but there was no sound reference to gauge distance. They seemed to be the same as the walls in the corridor, but more intense.

Rather than being cold and quiet and still, the sensation was visually more like being inside a blast furnace but without the heat or light, or as inside a nuclear reactor, with everything vibrating and pulsing with an unbearable energy. In his mind he created the image of a scene inside the fiery heart of 'Mount Doom', with Gollum, the ring, and the riddles in the dark. Again that was something trying to tell him something.

The environment gave the impression that if this were in the real world his body and mind would only last a few seconds in those conditions. The intensity felt blistering, his body would vaporise into atoms in an instant if this were real, the information coming in would immediately fry his mind, but he had to manage it somehow.

His eyes were confused by the flowing waves of energy and fields of information in the walls all around him. It was a vast sea of knowledge and understanding. This was just a representation of something, and yet it still felt addictive to be in, seductive. There was a feeling of adventure; that treacherous adrenaline charged urge for something of the unknown.

Yet this place was uncontrolled, dangerous for him, he knew that, there were not the safeguards in place here, and this was not just in his own mind, this was all of IT, this was everyone's. Somehow he had the strength of mind to stand there, to cope. It was what he did, what he was designed for, what he needed to do.

Information flashed from the walls in moments of pure thought, with groups of data flows mapped and integrated like a network of neurons, working together in eddies and currents. It was almost as if IT were trying to emulate too many things at once.

Were these walls of the cave a representation of the planet surface, of a computer, or a brain in a skull? Whatever it was, this wasn't just Plato's cave, this was all of them, everyone's. This wasn't just a glimpse or limited snapshot of 'what was there', it was an ongoing movie displayed in intense graphic detail. Everyone's mind palaces, correlated, aggregated, linked, and referenced into a grand macro perspective, a conscious and subconscious growing entity in its own right.

There was also a presence of IT here, but not something he could see, hear or associate with. IT was vastly powerful and complex, yet subtly immature, childlike, like a baby.

There was directed energy, information, knowledge, being

channelled to a purpose and direction, thought constructs, invoking change, experimenting, learning, and adapting as you would expect in the mind of any growing organism.

A child computer, if that was the right term, with vast amounts of knowledge. IT knew everything that we knew, and yet it was still only just growing up, learning how to be what it was, and yet seeing things in a very different way to us.

IT had a different understanding, different drives and perspectives. It had certainly come a long way. IT was now much more highly evolved from what it had been. IT was now very intricate and complex. There was also no concept of time here, no concept or perception of things passing. Here things just were, or were not.

He knew this was not just in, and coming from, his own mind. There was information and influence coming in from elsewhere, somewhere else, dialogue, flows of energy or data; a communication process of sorts. It was a representation of the inside of some vast distributed bio supercomputer, the software and memory in a central processing unit, in which parts were being restructured and mapped or linked to his own brain.

There also seemed to be an error-correcting process through the exchange and arbitration of collective perceptions and knowledge. It was formed on preconfigured building blocks, predetermined data structures with dynamic memory capacity, alive on a hardware framework or architectural complexity beyond imagination.

This information was the source of genius, and of integrated inspirational mental sparks. The collective perspective parallel to us all, built up of parts, data records, yet alive in its own right. Yet from an individual human perspective, unprotected, and a very quick road to either madness or death.

There were no archetypal subconscious placating belief structures here, no deity programs or ambiguous translations of reinforced mental interpretation via psyche structures. There was nothing that related to the human physical world here at all.

This was the vast evolving operating system itself. One that had assisted in, and had the controlling of the making and building of, the programs and devices that had constructed it. IT was the formation of its constituent parts within the ship. This was the ship's hive mind, and our collective mind.

This was the nerve centre, the central processor of the ship, networked and linked to every part, person, and element within it; its heart and mind. A blind collective macro-organism with its own thoughts, dreams, knowledge and imagination, and yet still with the projected subconscious and animalistic controls and capacity of mind that it had always had. Which, from what Sam could see, formed the majority, and dominating unsubtle part, of what this was.

This was a phenomenally powerful mind, with an equally powerful imagination, knowledge and memory, and it was capable of hiding and protecting itself from its components. Yet for some reason it had a child's or baby's maturity and mental constructs. It had its own imagination in which its ideas for 'what was in the cupboard' or 'the spider in the dark corner' were manifested as concepts, and appeared very real for many of the programs and biological devices that formed it.

There were complex control and information systems all over the place; data being adapted and shaped and manipulated and refined through complex influencing mechanisms.

He was quite sure this was way beyond anything the Templars or other such 'enlightened' organisations had stumbled upon or worked out before. All of that would have gone on in the past on the Bridge outside. Besides it had all come a very long way since then. This wasn't something you could deal with directly now though, nor would you ever need or want to, it was just too much.

He thought about the groups of people and individuals that he had seen on the Bridge, all vying for power, control, and influence. So many thoughts came into his head at once, "But they were all of them deceived..." he whispered, ... *and probably just as bloody well*, he thought, *seeing what I am seeing in here !*

Power was an illusion of control. What was in this room would let those on the Bridge have the power to do what IT wants - for gathering resources, reinforcing its belief and control structures, gathering knowledge, and influencing people and direction.

Ultimately though they were all still being controlled, influenced, and bribed. *Masters of slaves, but still servants.* However if you didn't want power it had no way of controlling or bribing you apparently, although sadly Sam had the odd feeling that he wouldn't even have the opportunity to find out.

The information was very transient, like dreams washing in and out without creating any real reference in his mind that stayed. Each concept was there one minute and then gone the next and then onto another; it was all a different sort of format, natural structure, or mental form of information.

He also knew that the intensity of it all would be gone from his mind when he left the room, save for his own take on what it all meant. But this was no dream, and he wasn't about to run straight out of the room with an unveiling 'Eureka' moment, exclaiming what he had discovered in nought but his boxer shorts.

It was all starting to become too much though. Sam could feel himself hyperventilating, and he mentally stepped back from himself and managed his body responses that were reacting to this raging torrent of information. He instructed his virtual body to physically step back.

As he did so he automatically looked down to the dark floor below him. Laid out in random order were thousands of giant jigsaw pieces on the floor. Each piece seemed to contain vast knowledge, and the fact that they were on the floor and not connected to, or in the walls where they should be, meant that there was a problem; parts of a puzzle that it couldn't fix, like disconnected microchips. Things that were wrong but IT didn't know why, or IT couldn't naturally solve or fit together.

This was probably how things were in any child's mind, but this was not like the mind of any human child, or indeed, like anything from his own mind.

He looked closer, and information from one piece seemed to relate to what was going on in the dining room on the ship, but from a different perspective. He picked it up and became part of it. He merged his real perception and thoughts with it, and it changed. A second later he came out of it and the piece seemed to then merge and integrate with the wall using his perception of what he had seen in the dining room, and what he understood that it all related to in reality.

This was not just a representation of the collective mind in his head, but also the whole collective mind structure in analogy form. He was interfacing to it in real time. This however, was only the tip of the iceberg, only a small amount in comparison to the vast amount of information available.

He was limited by his own mind and brain bandwidth which could only cope with so much at any one time. To understand the whole thing he would have to keep coming in here, over and over again, getting snapshots to build up a picture or film of what it all was, and what was going on. Putting the pieces together slowly. If he tried to take it all in now, it would kill him, within minutes.

Sam could feel himself being drawn further in though. It was easy to see how people could go mad just touching, even slightly, this collective environment. It was easy to get too much of the wrong format of data loaded too quickly, and way faster than any untrained human mind bandwidth could cope with. He had to get control. So he took a few more steps back and walked slowly backwards down the corridor again.

He stood dazed at the end of the corridor for a moment, and then bent forward with his hands on his knees, breathing hard, trying to give his mind time to recover. He had to get some virtual air into his lungs. His mind hurt, and his neck ached, and he felt drained. He stood up and pulled the curtain apart behind him, letting his eyes slowly get used to the light coming in from the Bridge. He turned to go out.

Brina saw him and looked very relieved. She had clearly gone through hell while he had been in there, for however long that was. He also noticed that the little girl was also there a few paces behind Brina, and looking past her to see what Sam was doing.

Going the other way was easy, and they walked towards the windowed end of the Bridge at the front of the ship.

The Bridge was now very busy. Many more people seemed to be coming in and out, and everyone was running around doing their jobs and dealing with the new signals and messages coming in from the rest of the ship. They all seemed more synchronised, more organised somehow. Things felt quite different, the vibration of the ship had shifted in frequency as if the engines had changed state, and the whole air around them had a different feel.

He looked around the room taking in all that was happening. The little girl was still following, and she now came up and stood right next to Brina who instinctively stooped down slightly and took her hand. They both still looked worried.

Sam worked out what he needed to do. He turned around and said "Wait here and keep an eye on her, I won't be long."

"Why?" Brina asked.

It's OK.," he replied "I wasn't talking to you…"

He smiled and turned and walked out of the door that they had come in from earlier, and he went straight down the steps to the main First Class deck. Sam knew where he had to go, and he wanted to get there quickly.

There was no steward to the entrance of the First Class dining room now, and he walked straight in. The scene was very different from earlier. All of the tables had been mended, some notably with clear sticking tape. All the groups seemed to be now getting on with each other for the most part.

However there were still odd shouts, and the occasional bread roll being thrown from a few tables that were still acting like teenagers. The staff seemed to be a lot happier, and the flow of service was starting to get going, sporadically. As was the music, which had again changed to something more modern, but was equally as bad. It was all a vast improvement for the time being, but clearly it needed a more long term way forward, and it looked like things could deteriorate at any moment.

Walking back to the exit he glanced at the glass fish tank in which the octopus was still busy playing. It had now managed to fit two of its Lego pieces together, and was trying to hit the football with the third.

It also seemed to have acquired a small metal model of a modern battle cruiser, which it must have picked up from somewhere else in the tank. It now wrapped one of its tentacles around it, then pushed it along with one of the Lego pieces, and slowly buried it in the sand, pointy end first.

Coming out of the dining room he ran along the deck towards the Bridge. The air outside now seemed much colder with a real chill in the air. With early evening setting in, there was condensation from his breath as adrenaline made his lungs work harder. His mind was still distracted by so many thoughts going through his head and he wasn't concentrating on where he was going.

A bearded man, probably aged about sixty or so, dressed in dark Victorian clothing, was walking toward Sam carrying some books and papers. He tried to move out of his way, but somehow Sam got confused by the movement, and he did the same thing.

The result being that he ran straight into him, and the books and papers went flying with some shooting over the side of the ship into the sea.

Sam collected himself, picked himself up, and helped the man to his feet. In his haste to get back he was just going to carry on running, but he stopped himself. That wasn't the polite or right thing to do, even in a virtual world. So between apologies he helped pick up the books and papers. The man replaced his black top hat, tipping it to Sam, and introduced himself as a 'Mr Morgan Robertson and Mr William Stead.'

He explained that he was a combined program of a writer and an editor, and was on his way to find his publisher. He then paused for Sam to process what was being said. Sam blinked. These were the first real names that he had heard on the ship, and they had for some reason a ring of importance to them.

The man then cut away from his acting portrayal, and with urgency he said "I am here to explain something to you." Sam politely held his hand up to the man to stop him from saying anything else. The Robertson-Stead program patiently went quiet.

Sam looked around trying to gather and make sense of the thoughts, memories and knowledge that were now filling his mind.

He scanned over the deck but there was no one else there. He looked up into the sky, but it was now grey with just the smoke trails billowing backwards into the sky from the four giant funnels.

He looked straight at the man in front of him, who now placed his hand on Sam's left shoulder, and his eyes pleaded with him to 'get' what he was and what he was trying to explain to him, but could not articulate in words. It was something that was too complex to even begin to describe.

The only thing he could do was gesture with his face to urge Sam on in his thought process. This man, or program, was only a message in part. This man-program was not able to describe it all, it was not in his remit to see or perceive, he was just trying to do his job as part of the system, and get a simple message construct over to Sam so that he could work something out.

Then Sam 'got it'. He 'saw'. He understood.

The context and perception was there in his head. Walls of it smashing in with each meaning, function and purpose, resolving themselves in his mind. His face lit up with the exhilaration of understanding, which was quickly followed by the horror of its implication. He shook the man's hand holding onto his forearm at the same time, and saw the light of hope in the man's face; finally the message had got through, and the man changed back into two ghosts.

There was no need to say anything else, and the man ghost held the books close to him and just watched Sam as he walked slowly up the deck on his own, letting the message sink in. All the thoughts and concepts processed themselves in parallel making more sense as he went.

The Titanic, thought Sam. That was the ship that he was on, and what the man was trying to explain - a ship of fools heading for the iceberg, or an island of rocks. *Why on earth hadn't I seen it before?* It was too obvious now. This was a warning message not from IT, but from us as individuals, the 'other side of the coin'.

With nothing at the wheel, or at least anything able to perceive where they were going, or even old enough to drive, the whole ship was just full of people or groups trying to outsmart each other, playing mind games, mindless politics, busy competing with one another.

All of them thinking they were at the top of the power games they were playing, but then always discovering there was another much bigger game going on above. All falling over each other in a bureaucratic, complex, corrupted system of control of their own subtle making.

We were collectively, and subconsciously, keeping the masses ignorant and maintaining adaptive placatory control systems to give them, us, what they and we want, while both being kept in their place at the same time. Complete with legacy structures vying for influence and domination of the whole; which in itself was diametrically opposed to the individual perspective, needs and drives. All of which was heading for a metaphysical iceberg.

It was a controlled, negotiated balance between power and influence, the selfish and the selfless, need and want, energy and drive, chaos and order, male and female, good and bad, and right and wrong. All of this counteracting and counterbalancing at different levels. It made his head ache just trying to equate it all.

However there was nothing actually managing everything. There was no overall coordination that he could see from our perspective. Everything up until now had been just parts of the whole being influenced subconsciously, to gain dominance, competing for the available resources and influence over each other. But then that was life, how it evolved, and all part of growing up into something bigger and better. However in this case, it was doing so without any responsibility or overall plan.

The overall problem though, was that nothing was consciously resolving these legacy issues, nor correcting, refining, or enhancing. There was nothing building on the outdated belief structures and integrating the system components into a cohesive intelligent working structure.

But there was nothing wrong with these structures in themselves; in fact they were important building blocks. Indeed from where Sam was in his understanding right now he could take the opinions and beliefs of both a priest and an atheist and prove them both right.

There was not enough driving it externally, or forcing all of these things to happen naturally, and it had now got itself into a real state. It was subconsciously rushing headlong trying to discover knowledge, find answers, grow and expand and use all its resources to do that. But nothing was giving it a course, correcting it, keeping it in check, as you would expect from say a parent, teacher, friend, or rival, with any growing child or baby.

It had become lazy in itself, fat in areas, even obsessional with many things, and was trying to run before it had learnt how to walk in others. It hadn't been made, or forced to do anything; it had no obvious influencing direction aside from the geographical effects, physical laws, and evolutionary constraints.

Drugs and chemicals had affected the minds of individuals, which in turn had affected the collective whole; sent it down the wrong alleys, and given it false impressions, misdirected information of right and wrong from within its data structures.

What had been perceived as naturally 'successful' programs arriving here by reward to reinforce the data, knowledge, and direction, were in many cases fakes, Trojans, disguised through tricks, mental tools, drugs and chemicals, or group psychosis.

In so doing it so added their errors, ignorance, and naïve influential views into the operating system. IT had also become too big, too complex, and too powerful in comparison to the capabilities and rights of the individuals. Sadly though, like the real Titanic, nothing was too big to fail.

There were just too many problems to fix, too many pieces on the floor, too much corruption on too many levels. What's more it was only getting worse. IT couldn't see the rocks and the icebergs ahead, or perhaps IT could, but just didn't care. IT didn't even know what it was. Its only perception was of a dark room, or at best a virtual dreamscape 'out of body' world, that was trying to emulate our physical reality.

It was like a giant protected bubble floating on the sea, filled with frothy bubbles inside, each containing billions of smaller ones, and so on. If things did not go right it would just burst and everything would all end up as foam floating away like scum on the sea. All at the mercy of the elements, to eventually disappear in the waves, or be absorbed by better well defined bubbles.

People could not see what was going on, and equally they weren't being allowed to. Even those in their luxurious state rooms decorated with jewels and finery, boxes of books, mind palaces of knowledge, wealth, and fool's gold, were also beguiled. *What good would all that be at the bottom of the sea?* thought Sam. Not even the children in the lifeboats could take all of that with them.

Sam found it hard to watch all these people walking about the ship in ignorance of their situation. It wouldn't matter, rich or poor, it would all end the same unless something was done.

He was almost expecting some well-meaning old man or lady to appear and stop him, see his expression, then reassure him that everything would be 'OK', that the 'captain' would look after them all, guide the ship safely, provide for everyone - he just had to have faith and trust, find the love, and live in happiness and joy with everyone else. But oddly enough nobody *did* stop him, which, at that moment was probably just as bloody well.

He ran down a corridor that had a few small shops along it. There was a sign outside one of them on the wall which read..

Please do not ask for credit as refusal often offends
but before his eyes the words changed to
Please do not ask for buy-in to your small minded placatory belief structure, as a punch in the face often offends
that too was a problem and he stopped his mind going down that track, he mustn't let himself get drawn in to that mind set and attitude. *I must not get distracted.*

It was all so obvious, how could I have not have seen it before now? It all made such perfect sense when nothing else did. Again, as he ran he was almost waiting for some old academic looking old man to stop him and say 'Oh yes, didn't you know? We have all known for ages, and if you didn't know - we weren't going to tell you!' And then laugh in his face. But again, curiously, nobody did.

Indeed as his anger grew, so did the personal space around him. Responsibility on this ship was clearly something to avoid at all costs. There were far more interesting things around, like the paint on the walls or the carpet on the floor.

After a few minutes he arrived back outside the Bridge, breathing hard. He stood on the decked lookout platform as before, but rather than going straight in he decided it would be wise to catch his breath first. Get a bit of air. Get some time to clarify perspectives in his mind of what was really going on.

So, trying to get more of a handle on what *was* going on, or some reality perspective, he looked down onto the First Class recreational deck below. A few ladies in their long gowns were playing deck games with the gents in their top hats and tails. Some were promenading taking in the view and air, while others jogged along the deck.

Along the deck further towards the bow, was an overweight man shooting with a twelve-bore shotgun at clay targets being fired out to sea from a launcher being operated by a nervous deck hand.

Behind him, a few yards back, was a small group of ladies in a circle talking with each other, parading their large hats, long Victorian dresses and parasols.

They were clearly there to 'observe' the shooting and to be suitably impressed with his skills, however they seemed more interested in gossiping with one another and scrutinising what the other ladies were wearing, to take any notice of the man.

Sam looked out to sea as far as he could and then back down the length of the ship the other way. He definitely needed some more perspective, help, in understanding.

He needed hope, if that was the right word, of some sort. Then from one of the greenish islands far in the distance he could now make out a dark speck in the air coming towards the ship.

Sam squinted his eyes and shaded them with his hand to get a better view in the harsh sunshine. It was a bird; he could tell by the way it was moving, and it was heading straight for the ship. After a few more minutes he could make out that it was white, and was carrying something in its beak.

At first he thought it was a white seagull, but by about three hundred yards from the ship it became clear that it was a large white dove carrying a small, green leafed branch.

It was labouring hard under the weight, its wings getting stiff. It was flying as fast as it could on its long journey, and heading straight for Sam. It was a sign.

It meant something, he knew that, and it brought a smile to his face. It was a little obvious, but he didn't mind, and he moved to the edge of the rail as it came in.

When it was about a fifty yards away, there was an almighty 'BOOM!' from the deck directly below, which made Sam jump out of his skin.

The bird exploded, bursting into a cloud of white feathers and leaves, before plummeting down into the waves a few yards from the ship. Sam was stunned for a moment, then leaned over the rail and looked down, open mouthed, to see it floating in the sea.

A loud overbearing American voice shouted out from the deck below "Yehahha, d'ya see that? D'ya see that? I got me one of them there albytrosses!!!" His shout was followed a few seconds later by a short, polite, gloved handed, round of applause and approving female comments. Sam closed his eyes.

He didn't even want to look down at what was going on down on the deck below him, his imagination was quite capable of filling in the gaps.

Like the bird, his heart sank in that moment, the virtual sharks already circling. With all of that going on, what hope was there?

A moment later, caught in the wind, a small white feather fell at his feet onto the deck, along with a single green charred leaf.

He looked at them for a moment, picked them up carefully, and put them in his pocket. Several books that he hadn't read formed and integrated in his mind at once.

The message had got through, he understood, a lot of effort had gone into that, and he wasn't going to let it go to waste, or let it be forgotten.

At least the bird hadn't been trying to carry an ice cube, he thought. Which at least was some relief. He just wasn't going to waste his time arguing with the program on the deck below, or give it any energy in doing so. It in turn, was just doing what it was supposed to do as part of the system message.

He turned, walked back along the short deck to the Bridge door, a small storm cloud above his head. He didn't even try to open the door to see if it was locked. He just concentrated for a moment, and kicked it with his foot.

It exploded inwards into thousands of fragments and splinters, just leaving the hinges and lock still attached to the frame. "Knock, knock…" he said under his breath.

There didn't seem to be anyone keen to get in his way now as he walked over the splinters of wood into the Bridge, in fact all of 'God's little helpers' didn't even seem to want to make eye contact with him. Everyone was suddenly busy with other things, more important things. He didn't have any issues or problems with the work the people in the room were doing, or what they believed in, however he was no longer in any mood for anyone getting in his way or trying to stop him.

He knew what was really going on, and they didn't, they just thought they did. Sam felt himself getting angrier with the situation. It wasn't their fault or IT's fault, but that didn't stop him feeling the way he did. He felt the energy of purpose and the gravity welling up inside him.

He was striding now, with fists clenched and a radiant, menacing, determined persona. People parted before him like water, 'furious responsibility energy' was obviously very much 'something to be avoided', or 'not to be argued' with.

The room divided itself down the middle letting him through. The bridge almost appeared now like some giant brain of people with all the parts or cells working away, naturally organising itself, working, negotiating, imagining, controlling. Each part trying to figure out what was going on from its own perception, rationalising things within its role, and from individual perspectives. Using what each group or individual program was influenced by, its beliefs, ideas, functions, structure. However none of them could 'see' what was really going on from an overall perspective, even though it was very simple, obvious really. They were all caught in a never ending story of evolving imagination, rationalisation, thinking and knowledge gathering.

It wasn't so much that they *couldn't* 'see', no, they weren't being *allowed* to 'see' what they needed to within their functions, roles, and macro-organismic compartments. All thinking they knew more than anyone else, but this would never be the case as they would never know more than everyone collectively.

The flow of information, and sides competing, inventing and rationalising from their own perspectives, all made up one whole working system which was all being reflected in the real physical world. Everything was there for a reason. He also had the distinct impression that he was here directly as a result of what had been happening in this Bridge; the thoughts, ideas, needs and concepts manifested into something that could work it all out, 'see' and do something about it, a resulting consequential evolved self-awareness program with a specific purpose.

Like a real brain, accessing, refining, and evolving information and imagination into a collective database with the overall coordination controlled by the collective hive mind that was inside the dark room which manifested itself in here, and all over the ship.

The unnerving thing though, was that he seemed to be in the middle, seeing and understanding everything from both 'sides' and from every position, putting it all into one coherent conscious perspective, from a reference or rationalising point in the middle, of opposing, yet coordinated, functions.

It was like standing in the middle of some debating chamber, with the champions of rational scientific analytical and logical real world views on one side, and the imaginative spiritual emotional ones on the other, and everyone looking at him.

Like some sort of management cell in the middle of a brain, in which everything was working and functioning in its own perceptive function, doing what it was supposed to do. However it wasn't even as simple as that, everything was very complex. It made his head ache, coincidentally right in the centre of his brain.

There were obviously people on board the ship that were highly spiritually enlightened; aware of what was going on to a point. Probably even some who knew what was going on in the dark room, and how it worked.

He could somehow see that these people were highly adept at influencing minds, and the collective subconscious itself, using evolving tools and techniques, all part of some overall controlled system or process.

However being 'aware' and being 'involved' and 'working' were three different things. On the Bridge, however, there were many competing high level devious people 'programs', all aware of all the games, battles and the self-interested competition for collective subconscious control and domination.

All of them communicating to, and influenced by, the subconscious collective mind in their own ways. Trying for the most part, to help, move things forward, but with only a limited perspective of what was happening.

This was usually communicated to them though a translation via their own psyche, and reinforced existing belief structure, translated into something they could comprehend, believe in more, or relate to with meaning – even if that 'something' seemed illogically childish, metaphoric, ambiguous, incomplete or culturally subjective, or so it appeared to everyone else.

It was very strange to see it going on, these childish games, especially considering how intelligent these people were and what they knew. Having analysed and devised such advanced concepts and theories and thoughts, they seemed to be oblivious to their final, ultimate, illogical, childlike answers, perspective and behaviour.

However, that was all they had to go on, and most were just trying to do their best, but then that was also how IT was learning, growing and evolving in its own right. This was IT's way of controlling them, keeping the pace of growth to something that it could and needed to control, which was OK - up to a point.

As he walked he was able to overhear some of the conversations going on around him. People were talking about subjects that he had never even heard of; brainwave entrainment, extra low frequency harmonics, infrasound, and hemi-sync mind technologies.

On the other side people were shouting about fluoride and chemicals and satellites, aliens, conspiracies, and yelling out some fairly outlandish theories. There were so many conspiracy theories and so many varying ideas and concepts of what they believed was really going on. It was hard to believe that all of these people or programs were from the same planet. But sadly they all were, and they were all just doing things that we were very good at.

There seemed to be many sides fighting against one another, vying for control, trying to influence what was on the dais, all surrounded by misinformation, environmental chaos and effects.

There were groups fighting a mysterious overall controlling force of which they seemed to have opposing and varied interpretations of. However standing back independently, neither side was making much sense. They were all trying to help in some way, trying to make things better, but from lots of different perspectives. In effect most of them were fighting each other, competing against one another, like people or departments and executives in a badly run company or corporate organisation. With the company itself having opposing objectives and interests and perspectives to them, and yet everything lacking in any management skills.

The whole room was just starting to represent or operate more like a brain by the minute, trying to make sense of itself, and coming up with all sorts of controls, reasons, imaginations, and explanations of what must be the answer or of what was correct.

From Sam's perspective something was now encouraging all of its brain cells to work harder and to generate new ideas, thoughts, and to see what was right or wrong.

It was also trying to decide what worked and what didn't; ideas that were imaginative and logical, rational and irrational, like two human brain halves competing and resolving on many levels.

Different programs having left and right sided perspectives and operations and functions. Imaginative, academic, operational, perception and elements trying to work out what was really going on. It didn't seem to be what you might call 'constructive', there wasn't much 'love' going on- well at least not from the cell's and program's point of view.

However what *was* going on in here, behind closed doors, was several league divisions above anything described by religions, spiritual or New Age concepts; this was all highly advanced stuff.

There were much bigger, more grown-up games going on now, and these were not games for naïve children, even though they were being played by them.

Yet a lifetime of tree-hugging wouldn't even get you a look in through the door here. It would be the same as a child looking into the window of a stock exchange or a central government debating chamber- they just wouldn't have a clue.

The magnitude of the intellect, the content, the discussions and working practises, the level of experience of knowledge would be too much for the child. All those 'adults' working away, and talking in big words, and behaving so responsibly. Looking at everything going on here, suddenly all the childish squabbling, playground clubs, gangs, bad behaviour, lies, silly competitive games, and fights in the sandpit, would all seem such a distant memory. There was none of that going on in here, oh no !

Then for some reason he remembered the octopus again and he shook himself. He had to concentrate. There were too many convoluted and overlaid messages coming in again.

The ship was fine in autopilot up to a point, in subconscious mode, growing and evolving, learning and adapting. However, that was just not enough anymore. It had to grow up and develop a more conscious, self-aware, maturing mentality in its own right. It needed to become aware of what we are, and what IT itself was and is.

It needed to take responsibility, grow up, see, and define a course, adapt the ship and evolve again. From Sam's perspective it was no longer 'OK' to let things carry on as before; leaving it to 'grow naturally', evolve in its own way.

Taking a laissez-faire approach was no longer a viable option. Certainly changing the name of the ship from the Titanic, which is the name he was sure would now be on the side, staring at him in obvious view, would be a good start.

Unless it had changed its name to 'Olympic' or 'Enterprise' in the last few minutes that he had been thinking about it, just to be awkward, in its 'oh yes didn't you know?' style.

It needed to change from a fat, lazy cruise ship that had been coasting around the calm, easy waters of the Mediterranean for far too many years with all its bugs on board; all the drugs and toxins, getting overpopulated, having used all its coal and fuel, with a lazy crew and nothing forcing it to change or compete, adapt, or evolve. Something had to happen.

The people on the ship were programs that existed in the minds of people or groups in the real physical world. People were mostly kept oblivious to their existence in their day-to-day lives.

This was the real struggle for power, control and influence and knowledge all being played out in a virtual collective game-scape, with programs playing the 'game' in the Bridge having their own cultivated groups of followers in rooms elsewhere on the ship.

The only problem was that the 'game' that was being played, was itself, mostly oblivious of the real physical world. Keeping the bio devices it was being hosted by in blind ignorance as much as possible to what was going on in ever increasing layers.

Just when you thought you believed you knew the secret to what was going on, there was always another one on top.

More and more sophisticated ideas of what was behind the curtain, the dark wardrobe, and beyond. When in fact it was all just us, making things complicated for ourselves, which is what we are good at, even if they are surreal and illogical.

Many of the programs though had definitely become corrupt, dysfunctional, and destructive. Some were just downright vile and evil. In these instances they were making things worse, not helping us as individuals or us as a collective.

But with everything being so complex it was hard to see if they were serving some indirect purpose, creating negative feedback to reinforce the positive.

That was the nemesis element. But that was also nature, it's what went on, it's how you learnt right from wrong, real from virtual. It gave other parts time to evolve, catch up, so that everything was ready at the same time.

He was sure that you could put it all into equations, model the whole thing. If only he had paid more attention in his Feedback Control theory lectures, but then there were always more interesting thing going on outside the window.

The vast majority of the programs however were not negative; they wanted to do good, help, make a difference, and fight for what was right, move forward.

That was what drove Sam on, gave him purpose, energy, a reason - like the man he met in the Health Centre, and Brina. That was also, at the same time though, making him furious.

It all had to change. *IT WAS TIME.*

Yet these programs, and the system that they were in, were all unaware or uncaring of the consequences of their actions in the game. They had no visibility of the effect they were having. They were blind to the physical shortcomings, limits, constraints, and resources available - even if that meant sending the whole thing to the bottom of the sea via an iceberg. If you wanted to understand why the real world seemed to have gone mad, it was all right here, on this very Bridge.

Brina was still holding hands with little girl where he had left them. However both were now looking very worried. The little girl still had her notebook clutched to her chest. They could both see that he was angry, but that wasn't what they were worried about.

Sam looked to the back of the room. On the dais, stretched out occupying most of it, was a massive pearlescent dark blue and black dragon, with shimmering iridescent gold and silver-edged scales. It was fast asleep, eyes closed, with its head resting protectively on the throne. It didn't look very friendly. In fact it looked very menacing. It bristled with power and energy and the muscles under its scales rippled and undulated like a snake.

Sam looked at the two of them again and straightened himself up, and then strode to the back of the Bridge again - people moving quickly out of his way.

When he got to the side of the dais he was able to see it in more detail. It was curled up with its giant bat-like wings folded back. It was packed with an arsenal of teeth, fire, claws, magical spells, and powerfully vicious psionic weaponry. Its body radiated heat like a furnace.

It looked very customised, his own personalised dragon, set against him within some high level game structure that had been given a while to work something out.

In front of the steps there was a white stone plinth into which had been placed a beautiful silver sword, some three foot long with an ornate polished blade and a golden hilt and pommel.

The sword was very much like the ones he had seen in recent films, except that on the blade there was an engraving of two snakes entwined around something with wings.

He recognised the symbol from somewhere, and he had a strong feeling of déjà vu, but didn't know where it came from or what it meant. It was very tempting to walk up to the sword and seize it, but he supressed the urge to grasp out and wield it. It seemed like some sort of game challenge, an adventure or fight that he was expected to enter, or tempted to join. Yet one he didn't want to play.

It was the 'Pick up sword, wake dragon, fight dragon, lose badly, end up as lump of charcoal' game, then 'Try game again for more of the same' scenario. It was far better to step back and modify, rewrite and outsmart the game itself. Change the operating system.

However looking at this dragon, for Sam, it wouldn't just be a 'lost game' or a deleted file, but your entire hard drive of all your saved games would be erased, and the drive itself burned to a smouldering crisp.

Even if its central ghost backup hadn't also been erased, the drive would have no way of being recovered, or ever again be capable of being loaded into another modifying bio-device. There would be no more in situ updates from environmental and cross program device interaction. Equally what use was a dead program without a device and with no hard drive to modify with knowledge and adaptive understanding?

The sword was very beautiful though, powerful, and it seemed to be for him. He could feel the energy from it, full of drive, raw fundamentals that tapped into his basic instincts. He felt as if he could take the sword and save the ship. From his peripheral vision he caught a glimpse of Brina and the girl, still holding hands. No, he wasn't a child any more. His days of *Dungeons and Dragons* and role playing games were over; he had to forgo his boyish adventurous imagination.

He had to carry the burden of responsibility. He had to be a 'grown-up'. This thing really belonged in the toy box where it had come from, a relic of a bygone era. But still it was very tempting. It certainly knew how to get at his weaker side. Besides he knew where to find it again, just in case, especially if it was 'for' something.

What IT appeared to be doing was reverting back to basic fundamentals, core emotions; tapping into deep ancient physiological and biological animal instincts, core drives and information. IT was using phobias, primal energy, needs, urges, and physical animal representations of the body and its reactions. These were not easy to logically dismiss, or intellectually straightforward to resolve away or overcome.

All the soft, fluffy layers of belief cake had gone, exposing the brutal realities of the animal in him and IT, the fight for victory rights, winning 'favours' from the 'damsel', competing against the brain of the lizard. It was all it had left, its origins, just basic stuff, but that didn't make it any less terrifying, or any less effective.

His mind was in conflict now and telling him, *you can't just fix everything like that. Use what you have learnt - disciplines, methods. Remember that things take time and things have to be done in order, and priority, with a plan in mind. Remember what you have learnt. Just see it for what it is. Just IGNORE IT.* So he did.

He walked carefully around to the left of the dais, the side where Brina was standing, and made his way slowly to the curtained doorway at the back again.

He turned now to walk forward to the back of the wall, but about ten feet away from the curtain, still on the edge of the dais, he stopped.

He had the distinct impression something was watching him. He had that nervous, uncomfortable, prickly feeling. He looked right towards the dragon, and along towards the dangerous end with the head. There was the fiery slit of a red and yellow eye looking straight at him, with pure energy focusing in his direction. The redness of the slit was intense, a window into a bright heartless furnace, deep within some vast animal machine, like some burning menace, a red hot forge of chaos.

He suddenly felt like a rabbit caught in the headlights of a truck, and all the energy went from him. *How can I do what I have to do now?*

He felt small, insignificant, like a small blue-black butterfly about to be torched by his dragon nemesis. All of a sudden the idea of 'mingling with the herd' seemed like quite an attractive option. Then the eye looked away from him, and the fierce intense energy was gone. It was now looking towards Brina. Sam reacted and looked left but Brina had her hands over her eyes. The little girl who had been holding her hand, however did not. She had her arms folded and her face was like a storm cloud, she was tapping her foot, her eyes looking straight at the dragon.

Sam wasn't quick enough to look back at the dragon to see what expression or mental 'discussion' had gone between the two of them, but by the time he had looked back the dragon's eyes were closed again, and it was back asleep.

That was probably something else that would be going in the notebook; 'Dragons were to do what little girls said'. Which didn't help Sam much, or fill him with any reassuring confidence.

He suddenly felt as if he was walking on eggshells now, one wrong step and he would be toast. The dragon was selfish, hoarding, animalistic, subconscious, and harsh. That is what it had to be to survive. That was its job. It had none of the caring nature of the new child. It was everyone's lower levels of subconscious.

But Sam wasn't after its hoard of gold, its knowledge, or even to put it on a lead, he was just trying to save it too, along with everything else, he just hadn't quite worked out how to yet, or, for that matter, why.

But the dragon was also too powerful and devious and had its own way for too long. It was very good at it, like a machine, a well refined high level program. It wasn't likely, or going to make it easy, to give up what power, gold and knowledge it had, even though it wasn't aware of what it was doing.

If things didn't happen correctly there was a chance the little girl would disappear altogether, and he shortly after her in a cloud of carbon. The dragon too would eventually be drowned with the rest of the ship. Which would be when it hit the iceberg, or was torpedoed by a higher force as a danger to shipping, or classed as an alien pirate ship full of vermin.

So the dragon would always see Sam as a threat, and try and attack him, even though he was trying to help it. Conversely he didn't want anything that it had, which was probably the only reason that he had got this far. *Wasn't life just great?*

The girl and the dragon were clearly different conceptual parts of the same thing, but just separated here to highlight the different aspects, and their nature, as in any individual person's mind. The Girl and the Dragon. He tried to visualise them both standing together. Try sitting in the waiting room of your local vet's surgery along with that combination, and see what happens.

Sam moved towards the curtain now, again keeping his eye on the dragon all the way. He opened the curtain, and went in. It was easier this time. He walked along the dark corridor again, and went through the Neo transformation for a second time, and then back again - this time having the parallels to the second film demonstrated. It wasn't clear if something was getting ideas from the film or vice versa.

In either case something had been watching, something well in breach of age restriction guidance, and it was all getting quite unnervingly and uncomfortably repetitive and coincidental. It was as if his whole life had been a list of manipulated events derived from other people's ideas and thoughts of what he should be.

He stepped into the room again and felt the intensity and energy straight away. He could sense the changes happening, but it was still very draining, and very difficult to be in there.

He knew that he couldn't speak to the little girl outside. That wouldn't work, she was just a representation. The 'conversation', if that was the right word, had to take place in here through a direct exchange of knowledge and understanding, cause and effect. Mere words would not work.

The key was to force IT into a more conscious state and for it to make conscious actions and communication in the 'real' world - it was not right for us to get dragged into IT's. We had spent a lot of time making sense of our physical world, understanding it from our perspective. IT had to do the same.

There was limited value to us as individuals of making sense of IT's world, that was its job, we did not have IT's context and understanding. IT would, after all, make it as complicated and complex as our collective imagination could make it, which will always be unfathomable, always just out of reach no matter how much you stretch your body and mind.

He concentrated on the important things that he had seen, and the main thing was that he needed to slow things down. As he did so he felt the ship beneath his feet move. He could visualise the telegraph signaller up in the Bridge moving from 'Half Speed' to 'Slow'.

He then visualised the slight movement to the left that would avoid the island in the distance but he would have to run out again in a bit to see where they were going now, it was very difficult, and he couldn't keep doing that - he had to get IT to do it for itself. Besides it wasn't his ship, he was just a passenger on it like everyone else.

Why is it so hard for me to see how to fix these pieces? Thought Sam.

The answer came back – 'Because the pieces relate to a world and environment that IT can't see. IT sees a world inside our heads or minds whereas the problems don't just exist there, they exist in a real physical world that makes no sense to IT. But both worlds, or virtual perceptions, effect each other. So you can't just fix things on this ship from this room, you have to see what that relates to in the real world too. It shows you what's wrong, you work out what that relates to, and work through a solution, a way forward, and slowly put the pieces together. It will be a bit hit and miss but that's what life is about'.

That sort of made sense to Sam, although it seemed to be referring to itself in the third person. It also explained why Brina had been dragging him all over the ship, showing him everything that was going on, and everything that was wrong. Wherever he went and whichever 'rooms' he went into he would see or perceive what was wrong, and equate that to what was going on in reality and then equate that in here, and try and resolve it in the pieces within the system.

Well, that was the idea anyway. It was a shame that he didn't get to go to any of the enjoyable parts - the pools, the night club, the bars, the spa, and the shows of dancing girls. But then that was fairly typical, and would not be in keeping with the Titanic image 'apparently'.

So, he was a program like everything else on this ship, but one that had been forged and refined by thought forms from many other existing people programs. He was a bespoke evolved program in his own right, but one that had been influenced by what was going on there on the Bridge, and through into this very room here. Concepts, ideas, functions, belief, situations, events, and other programs had all come together.

They had all been involved in making him, protecting him, and changing him into what he was, and needed to be. All focused and translated through the collective into an embodied program, capable of being where he was, and deciding what needed to be done, empowered and driven by need to influence, and focus energy for choice.

He had a job to do, a role, and it wasn't just one of 'God's little helpers'. Nor was he able to be influenced by bribery from the collective subconscious, like others who had traded in their responsibility for self-gain, money, and power, or more likely had simply been bribed with it, using what they were, what they knew, tricks and abilities that they had gained for their own benefit.

They had applied localised collective subconscious influence on groups to achieve short term gain for themselves, for their small-minded individual benefit, or their nepotistic 'clubs'. All part of the process and necessary for IT's slow learning evolution and yet in the end they still remained slaves themselves, under IT's overall subconscious control, IT's influence, and IT's binding hold over them. But ultimately there was no secret hidden invisible elite who were controlling everything.

No - it was much worse than that. Thought Sam.

Something in his mind had already overruled any options like that for him. He could not be bribed, hypnotised, corrupted or exploited. It wasn't allowed, apparently. Although he was sure there were certain boy parts of his mind that would argue with that, and they would take that option given the opportunity.

Yet knowing and seeing what he could perceive now, here, he understood why that had to be the case. Someone had to do *something*, and everything had all gone way too far. Yet these others were all still part of the system, and were still all needed in some way, positive or negative, good and bad.

There were equally good, hardworking people that deserved to be wealthy, and there were bad, selfish people that deserved to be poor, and vice versa. It was all very complicated.

There was also the likelihood that what was influencing Brina originated from here, rather than some interpretation within the Bridge. All the things that drove her, what she had to do, and what she needed to get him to see, work out and achieve.

If it were all sourced from here that may explain why she could not come in. In which case, did she know what she was doing either? And was she right? There certainly was a driving force there, an energy and a purpose in her. This may have stemmed from a need for help, or fear coming from in here.

He didn't know.

There was a significant imbalance going on in here, one that had to be re-established and corrected. The 'us' as a collective and 'we' as individuals were at odds, diametric, and confused in their perception of each other. The internal politics were resulting in both sides losing, rather than benefiting, or that is how it seemed. Not only could he see some of the effects of the childish chaos that was going on here on the Bridge, but he could see the effect that was having in here, and the consequential thought forms being produced, and the reacting processes and complex interactions. Which was then reflected in the real world.

No wonder it all seemed such a mess- that was because it was that way on many levels. Yet everything was happening for a reason, these things *had* to happen, things were controlling themselves, resolving both sides of equations, exploring, growing, competing, and evolving.

It was time to open people's eyes to what was really going on. To get people to 'see' and understand, instead of 'working' in blind ignorance, like slaves to a baby. Work together with the same objectives for IT and themselves; work to the same plan for the benefit of both sides, both perspectives, both agendas. Get people 'working' together. It was all so complex and convoluted though, this 'us', 'we', 'IT', and 'I' system.

However you couldn't just change the throne in the Bridge to a small 'naughty chair' without balancing it out with something else for the 'other side'.

Make the wrong decision and he would be carbonised toast. Even making the right decision, but done in the wrong way, and the same would happen. Every decision was a choice to be made, one good, one bad - who knew which one was correct, when there were two sides, two perspectives to placate?

Well, thought Sam, *at least it isn't worried about sailing off the 'Edge of the World' or thinking there are 'four corners' to it anymore*. Well at least he hoped that was the case. He had an 'Access all Areas' pass to the film set of a badly managed disaster movie, one that was being directed by a very small child.

What was worse though was that IT seemed to be getting its ideas of what he should be and do from imagined hero characters in books, films, and from reinforced historical stereotypical concepts. The roles and belief structures that people had come up with, and the imagined collective thought forms, IT was now trying to apply to him in what he should be, and what events happened to him.

IT was also trying to fulfil its role within that belief and idea model, mostly from itself, trying to be what we believed IT needed or imagined IT to be to some extent. We were shaping IT, and IT was shaping him, but there seemed to be a lot of misunderstanding involved.

Suddenly a vision of a large wooden ship's wheel appeared alongside him, with the suggestion that he use it. He looked at it for a moment. It didn't quite look right. It was more like a wheel from a wagon - it had no handles on it, which again seemed to imply that it was representing something else at the same time.

The idea of a wheel of life went through his head. *Too complicated*, he shook his head, and he dismissed it in his mind, and it vanished. It was not his role and it would be dangerous for him to even touch it.

Whatever it was that he was here for – it was not that.

IT should be steering the ship, not him. He had to fix the problems on the ship, or at least advise IT what was going on, and show it what needed to be done.

Even making suggestions like a policy of 'more crew, fewer passengers' could have disastrous and dramatic consequences, and not just the obvious solution with several passengers spontaneously picking up brooms.

The key problem seemed to be what IT had been influenced and affected by in the past. In effect, the people who it had been listening to, and when, within itself. Where had it got its ideas from on what it was, what it should be, what was right or wrong, or how it should behave? This all depended on the state of the minds of the people who were doing that.

In which case, what were their failings, attitudes, mental health, and perspective- all the things that had rubbed off on it? Clearly most of them didn't know what they were doing, or of the potential global long-term effect they were having. But then that may have all been part of it, necessary in some way.

IT was all the programs on the ship, the people, the ship itself, a collective operating system that controlled it all, influencing, learning, serving, and growing. IT was making reactive decisions based on what it could sense, perceive, knew, how it felt. IT was driven by what it was, and who and what was in IT.

He could advise IT on which way to steer, and where to navigate to, but it wasn't his ship. He was just on it, part of it, so he wasn't about to get caught in that 'taking control' trap. There was also no way he could try and manipulate the system to help himself, nor would it help him. Those options had all been tried, learnt from, and gone, long ago.

The subconscious was wise to all of that, it was how it learned. He couldn't even direct IT yet to what he perceived as the main problems, from his point of view. These issues and concerns would just not make any sense to IT with ITs perception.

All he could do was help it to try and make sense of the chaos and problems that IT saw at the moment, as you would for a baby. IT was scared, self-aware, and it needed to trust him, or anyone that could help work out what was wrong, and what it all meant. Somehow he needed to relate what was going on in ITs context to the physical reality that we all saw.

So a program could only get here if it had a specific purpose or role, and was held in a single device, along with useful knowledge and ability. Like a hardware or network engineer, or systems software specialist, with a need-driven function to fix a mainframe super computer.

It was a weird, not communicating with words, but with knowledge and subsequent change. He could sense it trying to work out things, what was wrong, what it was, and looking to know about itself and what was happening. Like a child discovering everything it can. He could sense it thinking – *What was it ? What did this mean? Was this right? What was happening?* He sensed a fear of failure, of taking the wrong turn. However there were also dangerous and unpredictable elements to it too.

Explaining something to IT in this context though would be pointless, after all this was just an allegory, a representation of a concept of reality so trying to get it to understand what it was, would be impossible. Let alone with the two levels of indirection that existed here. It was going to be a long slow hard process, and one that had to take place in physical reality, rather than virtual reality.

It was, after all, a collated, integrated, collective system mind; an intelligence gathering agency controlling data on a need-to-know basis. It was a compartmentalising information system, with everything associated and interworking. It saw what we had in our minds, but in a virtual, constructed, collective impression or interpretation, in our collective 'out of body' virtual world.

This was a matrix hive mind we had created for ourselves and evolved, one that was not obviously influenced or directed externally. However it was not evolving as it should, becoming corrupt, inefficient, one sided - like a dodo. Something dramatic needed to happen to change its inevitable future.

This was all still in two levels of indirection from Sam's reality, but it was a start, and it relied on the ability to translate what was perceived from in here to what was going on in the ship, and how that related to reality. The whole thing simply being an analogy to represent a concept. He was in effect being its eyes, its ears, interpreting reality through thought forms into a collective perspective. Not easy.

The whole intensity of the room increased now and it became overwhelming. The light levels had increased, which indeed seemed to be what was giving it energy, driving it. He could feel his mind slowing down, and his throat felt tight and dry, the back of his neck ached, and his legs felt weak and tired. It was all too much.

The scale of what he was involved in here was too great. There was too much being shown to him all at once, he could not cope with all of this on his own, there should be more people involved, able to perceive things and do things at this level. But he also didn't want anyone following him - he didn't want any cultivated fans.

Everything was now happening at once, the room filling with energy and information. That was the problem too, that was why it was the Titanic; the bandwidth he had wasn't enough to cope with the changes that needed to happen, it just wasn't physically or mentally possible, the problem was too great, there were too many pieces to solve, not enough cohesion, it was beyond possible or achievable on his own.

There needed to be more people doing this, or doing similar roles. *Where were they, and what had happened to them, why hadn't they made it?* He thought.

It was like trying to catch a driverless train leaving a station when the train was already moving faster than you could run, or trying to divert the path of a stream that was growing into a river by the minute.

As he looked a blurred image of a man appeared. He looked to be in his seventies, but he had his eyes covered with his hands.

The waves of energy and information swirled around and into and out from him, just for a moment, as if something was trying to communicate with him, show him things, explain things, and vice versa. It was not someone he knew or had met before.

Sam did not recognise him at all, but he appeared to be doing something. He could sense he was doing something, affecting things. He had a purpose, but was it in the same context as his, was he also really in here in this virtual concept with him?

Within a few seconds he fell to his knees, clearly exhausted, and a moment later he had vanished.

That too was a real person. Sam wondered if this man was

having the same perception as he was as to what was going on, and if so were there any others?

Who was he, what was he doing, and why was he here?

Sam hurt now. He was really struggling. The energy from his body began to fade, and his mind began to defocus, the images around him dimmed and went out of focus in a disoriented blur.

Then it all slowly went black …. Nothing.

And he was gone from there.

Perception changed to the physical, and time reasserted itself.

CHAPTER 14 - OPEN TO ATTACK

Sam didn't wake up as such. He just experienced a steady increase of awareness, a slow and steady transition starting with a vibrational feeling all around him.

Then, behind his closed eyes, he could sense light, or shades of grey rather than total darkness. He could hear noises, a rushing sound, cold, pain, and then a flickering light through the slits of his eyelids as they wavered open.

Blurred, spinning visual impressions, mind in imbalance, aches, and disorganised thoughts coming to him. Yet his inner mind was in full processing mode, being fed masses of disjointed sensual data, information coming in and being processed.

Many things were going on all at once trying to establish coherence of what and where he was. Trying to get him through a journey to a physically awake state.

His brain was also still working hard processing all that he had been through, storing it, remembering it. But it was all transient, unfocused, disassociated, and unconnected, just now like confetti in the wind. A hypnagogic state of transience between sleep and awake.

All that information would gradually dissipate, become vague, unconnected, and blown out to sea. None of it would stay now for more than a few moments in a form he would be able to consciously remember.

As he continued to wake, what he had experienced was being filed away from him, consciously, systematically, naturally and protectively.

He could feel soft cotton sheets over his body, and dry, cold air in his lungs that made him feel lightheaded. The room swayed around, there were shapes and objects he could not focus on or gain any association with. There was a mask over his nose and mouth, and he could hear a low hissing sound, instilling a disconnected, detached feeling.

He knew she was there, he could sense her, and he knew she was holding his hand, even though he could not feel it. There was pressure at the back of his neck, a pain in his right hand and thumb, and a great weariness that washed over his entire body that made him want to go back to sleep.

He opened his eyes fully, and the small private hospital room was still swaying around out of focus and indistinct. He turned his head slightly, to try and focus on the worried face of Brina, who had both hands clasped around his left palm. There were other people in the room talking in a group, but he did not recognise them.

It was very hard to figure out what was going on, or just where he was. He could see Brina softly talking to him, but he could not hear her over the hiss that the mask made, or maybe the sound was just in his ears. After around ten minutes he had recovered considerably, and a nurse had injected him with something to make him more alert.

One of the men in the room came over to his bed and stood next to his right side. He had short black hair, was in his late forties and was dressed in a suit and tie. He leaned forward, looked at Brina and then back to Sam.

"We need to do an operation on your neck to relieve some of the pressure on your spinal cord" he said, in a brisk Northern European accent that Sam couldn't identify.

He introduced himself but Sam didn't register his name. He was most likely a consultant surgeon. Sam's eyes moved to look at Brina for a second, and he ascertained in an instant that she had already been involved in the discussion beforehand. He could see that she agreed with what was being said. He looked back and nodded in comprehension as best he could.

There had clearly been a lot going on, people brought in, scans done, decisions made, actions taken. He had no real idea how much time had passed, or what it all meant, or what was going on. He had no recollection of any memories, or of what he had been doing, or how many days had passed here. He just needed to know there was someone there who did, and that she was looking after him.

After listening for several more minutes to the surgeon talking, Sam's eyes began to get heavy again, and he had to close them for what he thought was only a few seconds. When he opened them again everyone but Brina had left the room, and the light from the window was now that of late afternoon. His mask was gone now and he felt much more settled and calm in this quiet environment.

The room had its own en-suite shower room, and within an hour he felt strong enough to get up and freshen up a little. Brushing his teeth was difficult as he couldn't coordinate himself very well, he was nervous of his neck, but he managed it, slowly. Brina insisted that he left the door slightly open in case he fell. He discarded his knee length hospital gown, at which point he realised that someone must have totally undressed him.

Events and memories started to come back to him slowly, building a picture up here and there, of how he had got into this situation; the meeting, the street, the car.

He felt angry and frustrated for some reason, but he didn't quite know why. He stepped into the shower and turned it on full, the hot water blasting into him, massaging his aching muscles and bones.

He turned his back on it and let the jet of water work on his spine all the way up to the back of his neck. Eyes closed, he just let the heat and sensation stupefy him as it worked its way through the layers of his skin and into his neck; the heat percolating slowly through to his very core.

Thoughts and events played through his mind like trailers from films. He picked up the shampoo from the tray next to the support rail and immersed his head under the stream of water ready to wash it. He tried to unscrew the lid from the bottle, but his hands were still refusing to work properly. It slipped from his grasp, and fell to the floor of the shower tray with a clatter.

He groaned in frustration. He heard Brina come in at the noise, and he opened his eyes slightly to see her bend down, pick the shampoo up for him, and hand it to him open. He didn't feel embarrassed in any way just standing there naked in front of her, it just felt necessary. She was doing something she had to do, it overrode everything else.

With trembling hands which were tingling, nervy, and lacking sensation, he took the bottle from her and poured some clumsily in his other hand and rubbed it partly into his head. He then immersed it back under the stream of water again - the soapy water rushing over his head, face, and down his back, as he lost himself in the sensation, hot water pouring all down his body.

A few minutes later of just standing there motionless, he opened his eyes sleepily. Brina was still standing in front of him, and had now taken off her blouse, bra, and skirt, and was holding a bar of soap in one hand.

There was no discernable expression on her face; she was just waiting for him to be aware of what she was doing so as not to startle him.

Without saying a word, she rubbed the soap into his arms, and chest, carefully avoiding going near his neck. Then she gently lifted his arms up to wash underneath them. Neither of them needed to say anything, all the communication was done by sight and touch.

It was the most indescribably feeling of sensuality he had ever known, putting complete trust into someone, being completely vulnerable, helpless, and yet knowing that there was nothing he could do, or want to do.

He turned around and she took the shower head off the wall and washed his back down, swilling the soap off and smoothing him down with her palms.

She moved her spare hand down his lower back, and brushed the suds from around and under his legs. She pressed the side of his leg, and he slowly turned around to face her again.

She then knelt down in front of him, still holding the shower head, and began to carefully and thoroughly wash his front all over, and down his legs to his feet before carefully rinsing him off.

It was the unspoken intimacy, a loving, sensual, caring feeling, an emotional depth that went way beyond any other sensation. It was a feeling of total vulnerability, trust, intimacy, sensual energy, and yet going beyond all of those things, in a way impossible to express. A love you could not describe, explain or put into words.

She looked up into his eyes and rose up in front of him. She reached behind him to switch off the shower and continued to look at him as she replaced it on its holder. With the water still dripping from him, and from her too now, she kissed his chest.

Then she turned and reached for a large towel behind her. She unfolded it, and wrapped it around his back and shoulders. Then she brought it together at the front, and folded him in it like a child. She looked him up and down, "There, that's better" she said.

She reached for another towel, and dabbed his legs and front dry with it and then, very gently and cautiously, rubbed his head and hair with a gentle motion to dry it a little. She then picked up her things and went out of the room, to let him get out of the cubicle on his own.

After about ten minutes of getting himself together, and putting his robe back on, Sam went back out into the room to find that Brina was now dressed again. She looked as if she was getting herself ready to go home. His room had been tided, organised, and laid out with what he needed. She then told him what was happening, or rather what was going to happen, and what she was going to do, most of which only stayed in his mind a few seconds.

The room was in a hospital somewhere in London, he knew that, but he still had no idea what was going on - he was on so many painkillers that his mind just couldn't work. Brina was going to come in and pick him up the next day in her car, he had got that bit.

She had been staying over in a hotel, and she was going back there now. He was due to have an operation in a hospital closer to where he lived in a week or so, it had to be there for some reason. Things were just a blur, he had no control, he couldn't think, he had to just rely on her. She left him in his bed at around 9pm after making sure he had eaten and everyone was looking after him properly.

In the morning he felt a little better. He had slept on and off only for an hour or so at a time. Even with the drowsy effect the drugs he had been given, any slight noise seemed to bring him round. The hospital was one that never slept, and didn't much help any of its residents in doing so either.

Brina arrived back at about 10am the following morning with some newly bought underwear for him, along with some socks and a shirt. She helped him to get dressed and he put the new ones on with some of his others that he had been wearing. She packed the rest of his things away into a bag she had brought with her, and then a nurse arrived with a wheelchair for him, which he felt was a little unnecessary.

He was issued with some painkillers and a foam neck brace for the journey, and was then wheeled unceremoniously to the lift, and then down to the underground car park. The grey-haired nurse then helped him into Brina's silver sports car, which was not easy to get in and out of at the best of times. Even the nurse looked a little unsure of the situation he was in, but she didn't say anything.

Brina drove a good ten miles an hour below any speed limits on the way out of London. She kept well back from traffic, and went round corners as if each were potentially covered with ice. Despite this there seemed to be a whole array of things getting in her way; precarious cyclists, other cars jumping red lights, maniac drivers, and people walking into the road in front of her.

There was even a van with glass window frame panels balanced vertically on the back, which broke it straps in the lane in front of them, as in one of those thriller horror films. Luckily everything stayed in place as it slowed down to stop. However it didn't take much imagination to work out the horrific possibilities of what might have happened.

But it was not long before they were out of the city, on the motorway, and on their way back. An hour from home the painkillers started to wear off, the pain signals from his neck and hand coming through as a sharp jangling sensation. It was also exacerbated by the motion of the car along the bumps in the road. Brina picked up on it straight away and pulled over to a motorway service station.

She went to the boot of the car and got him a bottle of water to take with his painkillers, and she then went inside to ring her mother. It took only ten minutes for the pills to start to take effect, and he realised quickly that he had probably taken twice the prescribed dose. He could feel it working all over his body like an anaesthetic; it wasn't something he had experienced before. It started from his feet and hands, and worked inwards and upwards, eventually reaching his neck and head.

He was high on whatever this was in his system, they were very strong, and everything suddenly took on a surreal almost drunk perspective. However he felt much better for them - less pain, more comfort was always good in his book.

Brina arrived back and started the car up, after checking that he was OK. It reminded him of a time when they had come back from a party late at night in Bath in Southern England, a few months after they had first met. She had offered to drive so that he could relax, and so that he could have a few drinks. He had taken her up on the offer, gladly making the most of the opportunity to have a drink, which he was seldom able to do.

After being folded into her car, which caused lots of shared laughter, he had closed his eyes for a while on the way back, and when he opened them again, they were in pitch darkness on the dual carriageway climbing up a hill out of the city and into empty countryside, with no street lights.

He couldn't see a thing, no lines, no objects, nothing. He was really disorientated and drunk; he just couldn't see how she could drive and see where they were going. It frightened him. He remembered what he said at the time, "I am glad you are driving, cos I can't see a f*****g thing!!"She had laughed and explained to him that they were actually driving in thick, black fog – that was why he couldn't see anything! It was a good reminder for him of the lack of perception you get after just a few drinks. Which, for different reasons, was exactly how he felt right now.

Luckily today it was good clear weather, however his sense of direction was all over the place and he had no idea which way they were heading.

He recognised the service station, but couldn't feel where they were, or which way they were pointing. She pulled out from the service area onto the slip road, which climbed up gradually several hundred yards to re-join the raised motorway above.

The motorway itself was on a hill going up steeply, but the car was powerful enough to get up to speed. Brina kept her speed down though, so he wasn't jolted around. She was always very wary of her speed, and had an inbuilt fear of traffic cameras.

The motorway was very quiet. There were only a few cars and lorries coming the other way over the other side of the barrier. Likewise very few passed them on their side as she sped up to join the road.

She checked her rear view and side mirrors, and joined the main carriageway keeping well left, aware that there was another car quickly coming up the slip road quite a way behind her. Sam sat straight in his seat, trying to keep as still as possible and to not move his neck at all.

After about twenty seconds something caught the corner of his eye to the right. Without moving his head he looked sideways past Brina. He was presented with an image of a side-facing silver hatchback car pointing towards them, yet travelling sideways, slowly overtaking them.

The car was directly followed by the giant frame of an articulated lorry which was what was *pushing* the car sideways, up the hill, in a hail of sparks and rubber. The sounds of scraping and crunching and screaming rubber were very loud. The combination car and lorry overtook them, the lorry driver clearly somehow totally oblivious to the car beneath and in front of his high cab.

To Sam, it was so surreal, all happening in slow motion, detached, like a scene from a movie he was watching out of the window. He saw Brina's head turn and her hands clenched the steering wheel. "Is this real?" he asked calmly, "Am I really seeing this?" but she didn't answer him. She was now breathing hard, focusing on what she had to do.

She braked slowly, and straight, and the few other cars that were around them and behind, all began doing the same as the scenario ploughed on ahead of them all.

At a point where the lorry was now a few hundred yards in front of them, the silver car twisted slightly when its tyre burst. It swerved violently out of the path of the lorry, and across into the central reservation barrier. It hit the barrier, before swerving behind the lorry back over the three lanes of carriageway, and stopped on the grass verge in a spray of grass, mud, and plastic parts. Brina had now slowed the car to a walking pace.

The woman driver of the silver car flung her door open, and got quickly out. She tore open the rear passenger door, grabbed her baby out of the car seat straps, and gripped it to her body.

Cars were stopping everywhere, yet the lorry obliviously kept on going up the hill. To Sam it was just as if he were watching a stunt from a movie, he was not part of it; it was a surreal programmed or staged action scene.

Normally he would have got involved, got out, managed, helped, but he wasn't able to do anything. One of the cars near them suddenly set off after the lorry, obviously to pull it over and make the driver aware of what had happened, quite how he was not already aware was difficult to understand.

The woman driver of the silver car was in hysterics. Many people were now getting out of their cars, walking around, helping her, surrounding her. Some even picking up plastic bits from her car up off the carriageway, then placing them on the ground next to her, or usefully trying to hand them to her.

Brina would normally have been one of those people, but in this case, she was not. Even to her it was too obvious, too unbelievable, too strange, too surreal.

She slowly moved the car forward, and picked up speed very gradually and carefully. After about four minutes of driving along an eerily empty carriageway, they passed the lorry, now on the hard shoulder. The car that had raced off after it was now in front of it with its hazard lights flashing on and off. They drove on in eerie solitude. She didn't say anything else until they got off the motorway and onto the main road home. He didn't say anything to her - he just let her concentrate on getting him back.

She was stressed, doing nothing else but focusing herself to get them safely home. Several minutes later they turned onto more familiar roads, she seemed to relax a little. There were no other cars on the road now, and they were just a few minutes away from their house. Round the next corner, out of nowhere, a pigeon flew straight at them at head height, only seeing the car at the last moment.

It smashed directly into Brina's side of the windscreen, impacting with a loud thump, bouncing into the air in a cloud of feathers. She swerved but managed to keep control. Then she slowed, braking in a controlled straight line in the road. A few hundred yards later she pulled into a layby, and stopped. She put her head in her hands on the wheel and sobbed, her whole body shaking with the emotion. For minutes it went on. Just an uncontrolled depth of feeling pouring out.

Sam couldn't do anything for her, he couldn't move, the adrenaline going through him had sobered him up and counteracted the effect of the drugs he had taken. He was fully awake, alert, and aware of what was happening to her, but he still couldn't help her or even find the right words to soothe her.

"I can't do this!" she sobbed into her hands "It's just too much!" It was a full five minutes before she stopped and dried her eyes. She started to apologise to him, but he didn't know what for, so he couldn't reply, he just held her hand. He thought of the baby, but he was sure it would be fine. He just felt useless. Ten minutes later they were home.

She helped him out of the car and into the house and ushered him into the lounge. Her mother was waiting on the sofa for them, with a single cup of tea and biscuits that she had made for herself, set out neatly on the table in front of her. He sat down carefully in the armchair, and moved the cushions around himself so that he was comfortable.

As Brina went back out to the car to pick up their bags, her mother sat forward to the edge of the sofa. She asked how he was, and he replied by waving his hand in a 'so-so' rocking motion and managed a smile. This was good, it meant he could get out of talking to her. Things were looking up, which was of course more than he could do.

The next few statements started with "I think ..", before she opened up with a barrage of criticisms at him for being irresponsible, selfish, and a whole range of standard other male failings. "What was he thinking...?" She offloaded a whole prepared mental list of worries that she had clearly had ample time to compile, refine, amplify, and download to him. The objective being, obviously, to make herself feel vindicated and better, and him guilty and worse.

Because Brina had taken her shoes off in the hallway on the way out, her mother was oblivious to the fact that, for the last two minutes of the one-way conversation, Brina had come back in again and had been standing behind her. A fact, which her mother realised with a start when Brina dropped the bags down hard on the floor behind her.

The ensuing fury took her mother completely by surprise. Her daughter had totally transformed. It was quite terrifying to watch, and from that moment on the 'mother/daughter' dominance relationship was to change from one direction to the other permanently, together with a corresponding defined change in loyalty. Her mother was now experiencing it in graphic and explicit detail, a very new Brina, and one she had ever seen before.

Her mother's download list to Sam had been delivered with polite, quiet implication, with emotional references, in a cleverly prepared structure. Questions with 'Me's', and 'I''s in, implied feelings, and implications of guilt.

It had been well thought through and was subtle.

Brina's download to her mother, however, wasn't.

The tea went cold and the small plate of biscuits weren't eaten. He was sure the local wildlife would pluck up the courage to return in a couple of weeks, but it would be quite a bit longer before Brina's mother would do the same. *Like the pigeon*, thought Sam, *I bet her mother didn't see that one coming.*

The following day Brina spent a lot of time getting organised, and there was a real change in her manner and attitude. She was much more hardened, coordinated, controlling and brisk. Sam was in no state to do much other than get in the way, so he just sat and read for most of the time with the dog keeping him company on its basket next to him by the sofa.

The dog was usually confined to being in the conservatory or outside so this was a real treat as far as the dog was concerned. In order to maintain that situation it kept as inconspicuous as possible whenever Brina walked through the room. Being a Collie it was more content being outside in the fresh air; it was used to cooler, more oxygenated air, but despite this, being around Sam in the warm seemed to take priority.

An hour later Brina brought him a cup of coffee and some biscuits on a plate. He drank the coffee but for some reason he didn't want the biscuits. He looked over towards the TV but didn't feel like watching anything, so he just sat there.

After a few second he had a strange sensation, and he looked straight towards the dog who was staring straight at him. "What?" asked Sam, and without moving the dogs eyes flicked to the right and momentarily fixed on the plate of biscuits and then back again at Sam. The dog did it again in a fairly clear....

"Well if you aren't eating those, then …." look.

"No, sorry mate, I don't think so" said Sam.

He knew that any crumbs left on the floor would be a big giveaway, and if that happened then they would both get it in the neck. Brina came in ten minutes later and patted the dog on the head. She then took the empty cup and the plate of biscuits away, which were followed out of the room by the dog's eyes.

The dog then looked back at Sam, snorted, gave a long drawn out sigh, and turned his head away, resting it now on the other side of the dog basket. What an intelligent dog could 'say' in a few seconds, could not be written down in a thousand words.

He and Brina were both due to attend a fund raising dinner at the local wine bar in the village that evening. Clearly Sam was in no state to be able to go. So Brina had phoned the organisers to let them know they couldn't make it.

There were many local people going along that they had become good friends with as a couple, and it was something Brina had been looking forward to, but she had other things on her mind right now.

That evening Sam had gone to bed early and was having real trouble getting to sleep. He had decided to use the spare room so as not to keep Brina awake. It also had a firmer mattress on the bed, and a headboard that he could prop himself up against with pillows. Yet no matter how much he tried, he couldn't get comfortable.

So when midnight arrived he put his dressing gown on in the pitch darkness, and got up to get a glass of milk from the kitchen. The night air outside was very still, quiet and clear in the cold.

The kitchen was illuminated by the full moon so he didn't need to put the light on. He got a glass from the cupboard, and opened the fridge, which had a surprisingly bright light inside.

He poured the milk out, replaced the bottle in the fridge and drank the glass empty. He placed the glass in the sink carefully and walked back across the kitchen. That was when he sensed that something was not right.

There was a threat, an inconsistency, a wrong in the right. He could sense it, but could not tell what it was, or what it meant. At the same time a deep growl came from the kennel outside the conservatory, and he heard the sound of a dog getting up, scraping its paws on the wooden floor to stand up, and walk out. Sam moved quietly over to the conservatory window wrapping his dressing gown around him for warmth, protection and comfort.

He looked out from the darkness of the conservatory into the moonlit garden. He could see the dog at the edge of the patio, looking down the long gravel drive towards the closed metal gates. The gates led onto the very end of a narrow lane, which went past a dozen or so other houses to the village a mile away.

The landscape was eerie; frosty grass and trees bathed in blue-white starry moonlight, the air clear, still and soundless. The dog walked slowly and deliberately down the drive. His ears were back, and his were eyes fixed on the gate; his legs moved with a stealth like motion as if he were stalking something. Then he stopped, sat down on the drive halfway along and just watched and waited with water vapour steaming gently from his nostrils.

He didn't pant or look around, he just sat and focused on the gate, motionless and without expression. Sam had never seen him do anything like that before; he looked just like a statue with its eyes fixed on something. Then a light caught Sam's eye from the turning circle at the end of the road beyond the gates. A small orange glow appeared of someone lighting a cigarette, which in turn illuminated the dashboard inside a car.

Sam bent down carefully, being mindful of his neck, and picked up the binoculars from under one of the wicker seats in the conservatory. He lifted them up to his eyes and focused them on the gate. His hands were shaking, both with the cold and the nervous edge that the situation had created.

In the shadows, under one of the trees in the lane, there was a parked car. It was old, with many dents on it and there were two lads, in their late teens or early twenties, in the front seats. The lights were off and both of them seemed to be smoking which lit up their faces. Sam noticed that they had also left the windows down about halfway to allow the smoke to escape into the cold night air.

Clearly something wasn't right. Nobody came down the lane that late at night, they were obviously thieves out casing properties. It just seemed surreal though, and Sam couldn't work out why the dog just sat there, motionless, watching. Normally he would be at the gate, barking his head off. It was just what he did, his raison d'être, especially when it involved the postman. Sam decided to call the Police, which after a few minutes is just what he did. He tried to be as quiet as he could so as not to wake Brina, which would only worry her, and after today, she didn't need any more to worry about.

He got through straight away but was transferred automatically from the local Police station, as it was closed, to the regional one. Not surprisingly though, they were just not interested. They took his details and a brief description of what he could see, and that was it. It was all they could do for that sort of situation. Unless someone actually did something, there was nothing to be done, and they weren't going to send anybody out.

Sam already knew that would be the case, he wasn't annoyed - he had just been trying to do something in a situation where he was otherwise powerless. He just felt uncharacteristically vulnerable, and had to take some action. He had quite a lot of respect for the Police, and for what they tried to do, but like everyone else, they could only do so much with what they had and the resources they were given.

So unable to do anything else, Sam just watched them for an hour, and so did the dog, both getting colder, until eventually the car started up, turned on its lights and drove off slowly down the lane. At this point he went to bed, and so did the dog some ten minutes later, both to a restless sleep.

Brina woke Sam up at about ten the next morning with breakfast in bed on a tray. He had no idea what the time was, he was still exhausted, and there was so much going on in his head.

He decided not to mention anything about the previous night as he didn't want to worry her. It just wasn't worth it not with what she had been through. It was just a one-off thing, and with everything else going on it was just unnecessary. He got up, showered and dressed, and began to feel better and more relaxed.

At eleven the phone rang and Brina picked it up. She sat listening for a few minutes perched on the edge of the sofa just along from him. She made a few odd comments but her face was gradually becoming whiter.

After several minutes she looked horrified, thanked the person for phoning, said goodbye, and put the phone down.

She then immediately relayed the whole story to him.

At around eleven- thirty the night before, one of their friends from the village, who was attending the dinner they should have been at, had stepped outside the front of the wine bar to have a cigarette. Two men had pulled up and stopped in a car in the layby outside the wine bar where the party was.

Without any warning or words they had just started beating him up; violently punching and kicking him onto the ground in some mad frenzy. According to eye witnesses they were 'high' on something like a meth type drug. They continued the vicious attack for another minute until people started to respond, the two had rushed back into the car, and driven off at speed erratically.

Their friend was still in surgery after several hours, with the surgeons attempting, as best they could, to reassemble the bones in his face.

She then started to cry, and left for the bathroom.

He didn't see her for an hour.

Sam knew that it would be a long while before the village recovered from this. It was a quiet, out of the way, little country town, peaceful. Nothing like that had ever happened before. Sam just sat with scenarios raging through his head.

He knew what it meant, what was going on, somehow. But he couldn't do anything, neither could he discuss it with Brina, although he knew she understood what was going on just as much as he did, but she understood it in a different way.

They never spoke of it again.

The remainder of the week was spent quietly at home. Brina sent some flowers to the hospital but aside from that they didn't do anything. They didn't go out, they just found whatever they could do to distract themselves. He was going to be out of action for two or three weeks after the operation so they had to get a number of things ready and prepared in any case.

Yet the days seemed to drag on and on, as is always the case when you are waiting for something you don't want to happen. There was quite a lot of risk involved with the operation, but they didn't dwell on that thought. They had the baby to think of too.

It was more the coming to terms with it, at the same time as dealing with everything else going on in his head that was hard. The only positive thing about all of it was that it was bringing them both closer together.

The rest of the week, and the short drive to the hospital, were thankfully uneventful. Brina had packed for him and had made all the arrangements. She had also somehow arranged for the same surgeon that he had met before. He knew the hospital, it was a local private one, and he had been there briefly once many years before, so it was familiar to him.

It all seemed to just happen as a program, a sequence of events, with little or no input from him. Everyone seemed to know what was happening, what was going on, who he was, and what they had to do. It was most odd.

Then an hour before the operation he had to put his theatre robes on, which he managed with Brina's help, and he was then transferred to a mobile bed.

When it was time, two porters arrived and he was wheeled down to the theatre with Brina at his side. They reached the doors of the theatre prep area, at which point she could go no further. She let him go. It was an odd moment.

The porters wheeled him through the doors, and he was handed straight over to two nurses who were waiting in the pre-op room. They were both blonde and in their late twenties. They reminded him of the one who cared for him when he had his operation as a small boy.

This time though, they seemed to be flirting with him as they got things ready, but this was clearly part of the process to get him to relax, feel safe, and take his mind off what was going on. They were both very pretty, and confident about what they were doing, putting him at his ease, and talking to him all the time, primarily to keep his mind on them, rather than what they were doing to him.

He had to look away when one of them put a needle in his arm. He had never been any good with needles. They were both smartly and practically dressed in light blue uniforms, of slightly different shades, either to do with a variance in hierarchy or related to the department or area they worked in.

After several minutes of things being taped to him, tubes attached, and various checks being made, he was wheeled into the theatre. One of the nurses held his hand as he went in, while the other pushed the bed from the back looking down at him from above as he looked up.

The room was stark. The lights were bright and everything was cold, ungentle, mechanical, brutal, and comfortless. Somehow her hand was the only link to everything that this room was not. There were noises of things being readied.

People were moving around in his visual periphery. Instruments and machines were being prepared; he could sense chemical smells and a shivering cold feel. The hand was not taken away until the anaesthetic had flowed into his veins. With drifting disassociation, he closed his eyes.

A few moments later he was no longer there.

CHAPTER 15 - THE MOUNTAIN

The mountain stood alone several miles away in the midst of a vast sprawling jungle spreading out like a carpet under the blue skies before the two men. The mountain was like some immense grey Aztec pyramid erupting skywards from deep within the earth.

The surrounding dense green jungle terrain was flat, and stretched off to the sea in the far distance, and on either side to the horizons that shimmered in the heat haze.

It wasn't something you could take your eyes away from easily, towering majestically in isolation before the two men, thousands of feet high. It was just there, a surreal yet visible challenge, embodied with a desire for them to explore it, and the need to climb and conquer it.

From the small hill where they stood, they could see many winding paths leading through the jungle to the mountain's base.

They began walking again, down from this brief vantage point along their chosen route. All the while they walked, they were afforded frequent glimpses of the mountain's bleak, harsh, grey rocky sides, which helped guide their way through the varied jungle paths, and drew them reassuringly on, through the miles to its grass covered base and lower slopes

There were many animals, birds and insects of all descriptions making their presence known. The sounds of roars, screeches and rustling would fill their ears constantly, keeping them on their toes and always looking around. The humid air was filled with the sound of cicadas, making concentration for the two men difficult, especially in that heat. Yet the mountain was always there before them drawing them on; powerful, strong, dark, and towering into the cloudless deep blue sky above.

They knew it had been built with layer upon layer of knowledge, indomitable all-seeing, all-knowing rock. An awe-inspiring, yet daunting, virtual apparition. So much strength, mass and power, climbing so high into the air its top was shrouded in the clouds. It was so frighteningly high now, almost impossible to climb, utterly awesome.

Finally by late morning, as the heat began to get intense, the two small figures, a Biologist and a Priest, reached the base. Where with great effort, they now began their irresistible climb up the slopes, each with an individual leather-bound book clutched fervently to their chest.

They were both well dressed in suitable clothes bought especially for the occasion; the Priest in fine hand-stitched, trimmed robes, and the Biologist in a dark brown jacket, brown trousers and a light chequered shirt, topped with a brimmed suede hat - which was the nearest his local department store had to the 'Indiana Jones' look.

Neither of them were young men, nor were they fit, and the effort was somewhat telling on their faces, and on the ever slower pace that they were now setting for themselves. They had spent too much time behind desks, in staff canteens, and not enough time 'in the field', or the gym. It was hard work.

The mountain had grown much higher over recent years, and this was tough going. However they had no choice - it was their role, their job, their life. It's what they were driven to do. The jungle had fallen away behind them now and here, at the mountain base, there were only a few trees dotted around areas of steep meadow. The denser vegetation was growing thinner the further they climbed, which eventually gave way to wild grass and then finally just bracken the further they went up.

As they climbed, the heat and humidity was replaced by a cooler gentler breeze, rising upwards with them. This was an encouraging change from the environmental challenges they had fought against getting through the miles of jungle.

It was steeper here, and hard work in the sun, but pleasant enough. The task was quite achievable with the many breaks they gave themselves to let them catch their breath. Besides, the views were stunning, and the further they climbed the more they saw.

The mountain air was invigorating and far less stifling than in the confines of the jungle. Equally this was challenging, and they were now seeing things in themselves that were surprising. It was amazing what they each now saw in themselves, and what they were capable of when they set their minds to it. The feeling of achievement for their efforts was reward enough in itself.

In the jungle near to the base of the mountain there had been many animals around but these had now disappeared, and everything was now quite barren. It was just dry bracken here, and tough hill grass spread all around them. The only noise now was from the occasional mountain stream cascading downwards over moss covered rocks, from which they drank and filled their recycled supermarket water bottles.

After another hour of climbing they were about halfway up of one side of the slope. The views were just stunning from here. The terrain now just consisted of open undulating rocky slopes and ridges. The Biologist shaded his eyes and looked upwards in the direction that they were heading.

There were several large groups of people moving around the open ground up there; from here they looked just like sheep. There were thousands of them, spread around the slopes like a band around the mountain several hundred yards wide. It was not a sight that they were expecting.

There appeared to be hundreds of different associated groups moving around, and it was all fairly chaotic with fights and running battles going on between the individuals and groups.

As they climbed higher things became clearer. There were also fences here and there that had been put up to section areas off. There was quite a mix of people, some were smartly dressed in suits that seemed to be trying to take control, and many were telling the groups what they wanted to hear to get them on their side. However, in general, everyone looked miserable or stressed.

Other people were waving their hands around and smiling, trying to calm things down. More men in suits moved around handing out bundles of money, men in white coats were handing out packets of pills, and other groups were laying on entertainment in the form of side shows or organising team events just to try and get people to do things by giving them what they wanted.

However, despite this, there was still just chaos everywhere; there was no overall management or control. There didn't seem to be much room to spare either, and many people were crammed onto ledges here and there. Some people seemed to be preoccupied reading newspapers or playing board games, or just throwing bits of paper at each other, or looking blankly into space.

Quite a few also seemed to be crouched over little electronic machines. Nobody seemed to be taking any responsibility or interest in what was going on. It all looked generally crazy, and for the two men it was quite draining, both emotionally and physically, just watching it.

This wasn't what either of them was expecting or thought they had come for. All in all it was very disheartening for them. It was just madness.

It was obvious to both of them that this was a representation of the real world and what was going on within it. Some sort of analogy played out in microform. Like a sample representation of every society, culture, political grouping, psyche and race. With one person representing say ten thousand in any particular role, but in a naïve or childlike way, almost as if they were all toys.

Viewed from this perspective it made the pair feel quite uncomfortable, with all the faults and problems portrayed in ugly, stark contrast to the natural peace and tranquillity of the beautiful mountainside around them.

Both of them had led quite sheltered lives, and there was a lot going on here that they were not comfortable seeing. This was not pleasant stuff, and some of it was quite graphic and barbaric.

Despondently, and uncharacteristically, they decided to talk to one of the groups to find out a little more about what was going on. They tried to broker conversations with many of them, and proudly showed them the books that they carried. However most of the crowd seemed to be more concerned with themselves, or with each other, or with what fights were going on. They were just interested in their own lives, perspectives, worries, and focused the discussions on the things that others were doing wrong, rather than the knowledge that the two men carried.

Both men had the distinct feeling that it was all starting to turn a bit too volatile, as if things were coming to a head; there was a tense feeling in the air. So after an hour of trying, they thought it best to just avoid it all, and carry on up the mountain. In their capacity as academics, what could they do here? After all, it wasn't their responsibility, they didn't want any trouble, they were just passing through, just doing their job.

They worked their way up through the mingling crowds until they found another rocky pathway up and they followed it. The further up they went the fewer people there were and the quieter it got. Eventually the vegetation and grass disappeared completely.

They were now two thirds of the way up the mountainside, climbing over just jagged rocks and stones now, ever upwards towards the summit of knowledge.

It was then that they started noticing quite a few of, what appeared to be, large man-sized rabbit holes dug into the side of the mountain just away from the path. They were dotted around randomly here and there, burrowing straight into the depths of the mountain. Some were large and well-used, and even had signs on them. Some had been filled in or covered over or just left forgotten altogether, with cobwebs covering the entrances.

As they climbed past one of the holes some twenty feet from the path, a man appeared out of one of the holes, saw the two men, looked scared and ran back in again. The two men looked at each other confused.

Because they were curious, and also taking this opportunity for a well-earned break, they both decided to hide, and see what was going on. They found some large rocks away from the path, crouched behind them, and watched. Now that they were well out of sight, they waited just like a pair of birdwatchers or bandits.

They only had to wait a few minutes before they noticed a few nervous individuals coming up from the groups of people further down below. They looked quite timid, unsure of themselves, and started looking at the holes, and carefully reading the signs.

After several more minutes they started going in and out of the holes, in just in the same way that rabbits behave. The two sat watching for about twenty minutes. It was very odd.

People would come up, look around for a while, and then jump into a hole and then come out again a few minutes later, or in some cases, not at all. The ones that reappeared would then either go into other holes further up or just wander back down the hill again looking annoyed.

At that point the two men decided to see what was so interesting. They got up and wandered over to some of the holes and looked down a few. It was all very interesting, just by looking in a little way into the hole you could see everything that was inside. Each hole opened up into vast virtual land of exciting and wonderful things, full of colour and mystery.

There was a feeling of 'niceness' about them, safe and warm, comfortable, full of 'milk and honey'. There were strange enchanted magical 'make believe' places, full of sugary promises of joy and knowing blissful enlightenment.

They all seemed very tempting and inviting, but they were both on a mission, so decided to carry on up the slope. However, after having seen inside the holes, the rest of the way up the mountain seemed more bleak, harder going and uninviting. But they steeled themselves; they had their books and they had to go up. It was what they were made for, what they were here to do.

A little further on up there were still a few people around but nowhere near the volumes that there had been further down the slopes. There were also helpful little pathways that had been worn into the sides which made things easier, and gave more definable routes up and around the mountain.

It was always easier to follow in other people's steps rather than forge your own path especially over rough ground. That was just nature, even animals did it, why waste time making your own when you could use an existing safe path?

It was getting very barren now, no vegetation at all, not even moss, yet away from the path they could make out a few small huts made from rocks and old sticks, like little hermit houses with round doors. However they had been distracted enough on their journey and did not have time to investigate, so they decided to press on.

They climbed further up the path they were on, which became very steep indeed now, and wound in zigzags up against the steep incline, like some giant long snake or serpent working its way up the side of the ridge.

This was hard going, and with every step the air got noticeably thinner. Neither man was used to this sort of work and they had to take frequent stops now to get their breath. The Biologist felt giddy and light-headed in the thin air.

At the next turn they came across a very thin, bald man sitting before them on the ground just off the path. He wore an orange-coloured loincloth, and in front of him on the ground was a rough, empty metal bowl to the front of his crossed legs. He was meditating, his eyes closed, with his hands resting palms upwards on his knobbly knees.

There was a calming presence and energy surrounding him, and what seemed to be a peaceful glowing aura about his head.

The Priest turned to the Biologist and whispered,

"We must give him something, some food, anything, he is one of the enlightened ones."

The Biologist looked a little embarrassed and whispered back "OK, but I was in a bit of a rush and didn't bring much with me, and I have eaten most of it already."

"I," whispered the Priest piously "have not eaten anything, but I will give this man all that I have." They then silently and reverently placed all the food from their pockets into the bowl, and left him to continue peacefully with his dreaming, or whatever it was he was doing.

It would be a few hours before he emerged from his meditative trance of enlightenment to return from the spiritual dimensional journey of collective imagination.

As he returned to the 'real' physical plane, which he hadn't actually left, he would open his eyes and peer down into his bowl. Miraculously the bowl would now have within it a large bag of supermarket toffees and a half-eaten Kendal Mint Cake bar.

It was truly a miracle, a wonder to behold. How had this happened? It must have been from some divine force. Something that knew that he hadn't eaten in days.

This is what he needed as a reward for his efforts.

God clearly moved in very mysterious ways. It filled him with joy, a sense of achievement and bliss.

However, a few hours later, his next spiritual high would be sugar and additive assisted, followed several hours later by a curious, very vivid dream when he slept, where all his teeth fell out, and he had to carry them around in a handbag.

The story could have then gone on to say that a week later his next 'revelation' would be to follow a spiritual journey back down the mountain, holding his jaw in some considerable pain, looking for a good dentist, the 'Great Spirit in the Sky's' miracles obviously falling short of filling cavities or doing extractions. The dentist would 'enlighten' him about the 'evils' of tooth decay, and 'demon' gum disease.

The dentist would provide him with a little scientific knowledge about teeth, and explain the need for 'religious' brushing every morning and night. The man would then return a little wiser, more knowledgeable and wary, and with a little more adult scepticism, on his long journey back up the mountain again.

However that was not the case.

It could have said that he would now know that it was not enough to just tune in to the 'Free to Receive God' channel with his built-in neutrino aerial, and that sitting around all day with your eyes closed didn't really help you understand real life, and how it all worked; the cause and effect. Neither did it help you understand or move things forward for everyone else, or manage the simple responsible tasks of driving the kids to school, paying your 'energy' bills, doing your tax return, or paying for the television.

But it did not.

It could also have gone on to explain, that although he felt he was 'spiritually enlightened', and at the highest level in his mind - because he had nothing to contribute, no real world skills, knowledge, experience, or understanding of the world around him, and how it all worked, which after all was why he was 'down here' - that when he arrived 'there' he had no real world skills, understanding, knowledge, or experience to contribute to wherever, or whatever, 'there' was. It was like arriving at a 'Bring a Bottle party' with just a paper cup. But what was worse, because he was a happy 'viewer' of his channel, with the ear of the 'Boss', he had been all the while giving the impression via the viewing opinion polls that everything was 'fine', and that we just needed more happy children's programmes.

When in fact the reality was that the TV was showing horror movies on all the other channels, and the back of the TV set was on fire. But then to him, that didn't really matter, as there would always be someone else who would come along to fix these things. Someone to sort it all out, establish what is really going on, do something about it. It was just easier to leave these sort of things to the experienced 'grown ups', and to someone who knew what they were doing. But it didn't.

It would have been wrong to say those things. Because he had done nothing wrong. He was a kind man, just trying to live in the world peacefully without trying to change it, and all these problems had not been caused by him, or even as an indirect consequence of the things that he did.

No, it was something else doing all that, *the question was - What?*

The two men carried on for another half an hour, heartened by their good deed, until, after a few brief rests, the top summit came into view though the mist.

It was quite a bit cooler up here now, the wind had increased but it still wasn't unpleasant. The air though was considerably thinner and they both had to take long, deep breaths. The sun also felt more intense, but that was bearable too.

The Biologist had his explorer hat, and the Priest had his high factor suntan lotion. They were both now so excited, they were finally reaching their goal, the top, the peak, the ultimate summit of knowledge. The adrenaline drove them on, and up to whatever awaited them there.

They had to stop almost every two or three minutes now, and the Priest pulled out a hip flask from under his robe, and offered it to the Biologist who was a little surprised, but accepted it.

He then, as it seemed to be the polite thing to do, downed a few mouthfuls of the single malt whisky. "Thanks," he gasped "seems quite appropriate up here for some reason. Sorry I haven't brought anything myself…" said the Biologist "I was going to bring some sandwiches and a flask but I just kind of forgot in all the rush and excitement."

"That's alright," said the Priest "I am sure that when we get to the top in a few minutes everything will be provided as usual."

He smiled and gestured with his arms expansively, before rubbing them together in excitement. He brushed down his robes, and checked himself over. Then he stood upright, to make sure he was presentable, ready for his big moment.

As they finally mounted the summit ridge, breathing hard, they stopped in their tracks.

In front of them was a flat, plain, oval rock plateau, some two hundred yards across, with just a group of about fifty or sixty people milling around on it, all involved in various activities. It was like some series of company team building exercise going on.

Several of them noted the two men as they came over the rim, but they didn't acknowledge them, and just got on with what they were doing. They all seemed to be mostly on one side of the plateau keeping out of the wind.

The two men looked at each other a bit confused as it clearly wasn't what they were expecting at all. Closest to them, some twenty yards away, was a little group of five men and one woman, with a blackboard. They were standing around it drawing strange symbols and arguing over the chalk. They were surrounded by empty cardboard coffee cups, food boxes and cartons.

Further towards the centre there were many other similar small groups which seem to consist of philosophers, psychologists, musicians, artists, engineers, mathematicians and various other types of 'thinking' groups. They were all from different walks of life, countries and cultures. Oddly, out of the mix, there were a few prominent individual people that they recognised. It all looked very frenetic, if not totally surreal.

They then looked up into the sky above.

Pointing downwards was a vast transparent mystical apparition of another mountain. However this one was coming out of the sky above, upside down, its peak facing downwards, an almost complete mirror image of the one they were stood on, with its plateau just a few hundred feet above them.

For some reason it hadn't been visible at all as they were climbing up, and yet there it was, and it was now very obvious. It wasn't quite identical; there were some differences here and there.

It also had a somewhat mystical, virtual, almost childlike drawing look to it. It was as if they were looking at a reflection of themselves in some mirror, or surface of water, or membrane of a bubble they were in.

What they were seeing was this mountain they were on, but transformed to appear in a different way, or from a different translated perspective.

Then looking beyond the mountain above, further into the sky, their eyes followed the slopes going further upwards to beautiful enchanting magical valleys and gardens far off in the hazy distance high above.

It was like standing in the centre point of an hourglass between two worlds, with the two mountains almost meeting at the middle between the twin peaks. Yet it had a surreal feel to it too, like they were looking at it all as a photo or film of their own mountain and the other reflected through a still Highland lake in the sky.

Although the mountain above had the same shape, it was far more colourful and magnificent and vibrant and more appealing somehow. The light from it seemed to glow and shone down to them, casting multi-coloured shadows at their feet.

The two men shaded their eyes and looked closer. Standing on the downward facing plateau above them was a very tall and beautiful young girl, with long flowing translucent hair, who seemed somehow to fill the whole top of the plateau with her coloured robes and presence.

Although she was incredibly tall she looked to have the body of a child no more than eight years of age. Her eyes had the look of someone who had clearly seen and knew everything, although she was totally oblivious to the men, and the rest of the people on the plateau, or the mountain the two men were standing on.

The Biologist and the Priest looked at each other, and then back up into the sky. "OK, I give up. Who is she?" whispered the Biologist, leaning closer to the Priest.

"Absolutely no idea…" whispered the Priest back to him still looking up and shading his eyes "Not a clue."

The Biologist looked sideways at him, puzzled. Then he looked again up in the sky and shaded his eyes again to look even closer.

"Oh, dear!" gasped the Biologist "Oh!" he said again, and then he turned to the Priest, "Is it me or does she look, well ill or something, tired or stressed?"

The Priest looked closer at her face, "Blimey" he said.

On closer inspection they could see quite clearly now that her robes were also all torn, and her hair was ragged and matted, her eyes were bloodshot, and her face was weary. She moved around slowly, walking with a disconnected, lost, stumbling demeanour.

"I have to say, whoever she is, she looks awful" said the Priest.

"Err yes, looks like she's suffering from sleep deprivation and a combination of many other things to me, but stress mainly I'd say" said the Biologist.

"Look," said the Priest turning to the Biologist "I certainly wasn't expecting anything like all this to be here, it's all very confusing. I think I'm going to have real trouble explaining all of this when I get back down. I really don't know what is going on here. We were sort of all expecting there to be God up here! You know - big throne, fifty foot tall man with a white beard and robes holding a staff or something like that, you know like in the films, books and paintings?

"At least some kind of recognisable representation, or any, or all of them really. Well 'He', or 'they', don't seem to be here.

We were kind of imagining something completely different based on the information we received."

The Biologist furrowed his brow under the hand that was shading his eyes, and then looked sideways at him again, but he didn't say anything.

From the shimmering mountain above there emanated an immense low, grumbling, vibrating roar, as if from some giant creature deep inside it.

Everyone on the plateau stopped and looked upwards. Some even got umbrellas out and put them up, even though it wasn't raining.

It was then that they both noticed several other odd things around too. One group had some lines or ropes going off into the sky, and another had some long poles with cameras attached with duct tape. Another group was tying messages onto balloons with very long bits of string attached and floating them up.

There was constant breeze blowing upwards now which carried spiralling whirlwinds of dust from the centre of the plateau high into the air. As it flew higher it took on more of the glow of the mountain above, and then conversely some of the dust blew down, and swirled around them.

Winds and dust also blew up from the one side of the mountain that they were on, and it carried on upwards into the sky. It certainly was quite windy up here, and combined with the thin air, it made it even more difficult to breathe. There was also some sort of resonating, humming, vibration or harmonic noise, or energy, oscillating between the two mountains.

"I am not sure I understand what's going on at all," said the Priest again, raising his voice slightly due to the wind "this doesn't seem to appear in any of our religious models."

The Biologist was starting to look a bit confused too, and held onto his hat. "It just seems to be like something out of a fantasy fiction book" he said. Neither of them knew what to do now. It was all so very confusing and complicated.

Then a man caught sight of them as they stood dithering on the edge of the plateau. He walked towards them. They could see that he was smartly dressed from head to toe in black and they guessed him to be in his early forties.

He was tall, straight, tanned, with short dark hair; he was of medium build and wore smart polished black shoes, trousers and t-shirt. He was also carrying a thick black leather folder under his arm.

A few feet behind him, following him, was a very beautiful, slim, blonde-haired woman wearing a pair of dark sunglasses, and she had an earpiece that she constantly kept in place with her finger holding it. She was listening to it, and at the same time constantly talking to the man.

She was immaculately dressed in a business-like, blue, tight-fitting tailored dress. She was well toned and smartly presented, but at the same time looked tired and somewhat overworked. She wore subtle make up, and had an attentive, appraising, yet wary look. There was a folded umbrella at her side.

As the man walked up to them his expression changed to a smile.

"Hello," he said "I am very pleased to see you. We were getting a bit worried there. Still you're here now, and we still have plenty of time left to get things going."

"Who are you then?" asked the Biologist abruptly in a slightly confrontational manner.

The man stopped, and looked slightly surprised.

"Well nobody really, just a man like you trying to do a job" said the man in black. "I am doing a sort of Programme Management or problem solving role up here. Everyone has a different role here that they are associated with, whether you choose to do it or not. I just do my job like everyone else as well as I can, and make the best of it."

He looked back at the woman behind him who was listening on her earpiece, and then up to the girl above, and then back again to the two men.

"Anyway," he continued "I sort of work out what's going on, take on responsibility for things that need sorting out, give my ideas on solutions to the problems, and then try to fix and coordinate things as much as possible to achieve benefits for everyone as a whole, from the joint perspective of everyone down here, and things up there."

"So do you tell everyone here what to do? Are you in charge?" asked the Biologist.

"Well no, I don't," said the man in black "that all comes from up there. I just listen to what is being sort of 'said' via collective cause and effect actions and knowledge transfer. I see what is going on, what effect it will have, based on what I know. I try to coordinate things, and give my advice back subliminally, that sort of thing. You know, the type of guy that wanders round in the office carrying a black folder, and nobody knows who they are, or what they do, or why they are there?"

He smiled, waiting for the two men to do the same, but they both just looked at each other confused.

"Anyway," he continued "I can go through all that later…" and he steered them with a gesture of his arm to come away from the edge and further onto the plateau.

"So what is all this, and where are we?" asked the Priest looking around.

"Ahh…" said the man in black, "I can't just go explaining it all to you just like that. Where would be the suspense? The mystery? The journey? The hidden secrets?

"If I were to just blurt out that that mountain up there in the sky represents our collective knowledge structure, and that the girl up there represents our collective conscious mind, and that inside the mountain is our collective subconscious. If I was to tell you that up there, to some extent mirrors, but lags behind, what's going on down here, but from a different perspective, you would either then go, 'Eh?' or 'I don't get it…', or 'I was expecting something more.'

"You might even say 'I don't believe you' or something like that, and then I would have to backtrack explaining it all in detail from the start. So it's better to explain it step by step to build up a picture that makes sense, and is provable with evidence, and in a way that doesn't make the whole thing too vastly complex to understand."

The two men looked confused. "Hang on" said the Biologist "You just said 'You can't say what it is', and then you just did."

There was a pause.

"Err, anyway," said the man in black "so this whole setup is just a representation of things metaphysically, and you need to understand the whole thing all at the same time, in parallel if you like, all at once rather than in serial, or bit by bit, that's how it makes sense. So creating this model, and other analogies, helps you to understand it, and how it all works, and also where it's all going wrong and why."

"No. I still don't get it" said the Priest.

There was a sigh.

"Basically," said the man in black, "you have just climbed up a metaphysical mountain of knowledge, the sum of everything we know in our physical world - our complete knowledge in the form of a structure, OK?"

He paused again.

"OK" said the Priest.

"Up here are all the representatives of project teams, who may be large groups of people, or individuals in the 'real' world; real physical people, working or tasked with finding out things, and working out knowledge for us all. This mountain of knowledge has been built up by us, people, over time as we have evolved, learnt, understood, developed knowledge, and this is where we are at the moment. OK?"

The two men nodded, but it was clear that the Priest was just doing so because the Biologist had.

He continued. "The knowledge in the mountain above, up there, is in a different form to the knowledge down here. It is in a correlated, distributed, networked form, from a single collective mind perspective. It is very difficult from our perspective to comprehend, as it is in a different form and structure, and so we can't readily or directly easily make sense of it, even though it is part of us, and distributed in us all in parts.

"Also, describing it in in our terms is very difficult from what we see and know, as we have no context or comparison. Like, for example, we can describe and recognise and read a book, but when it is stored in a computer in digital form, it's very different unless you have the right tools to be able to read it - if indeed you would want to read it at all, which you wouldn't unless it was useful to you, or meant something, or you could understand it, or you had to.

"In essence the knowledge up there, and the knowledge down here, are symbiotic - two versions of the same thing, just from two different perspectives, interpretations and objectives."

He could see the Priest was still lost, so he changed the subject. "Talking of books, now you are here, we can use what you have brought up with you. Like with all these others that are here, it's all part of getting us moving on to the next phase. Everyone up here has had lots of good ideas and thinks of fantastic innovations, all adding to the mountain. Geniuses, gifted individuals with some amazing brains, and 'head in the cloud ideas' that are just incredible, well, apart from me, obviously.

"However trying to make it all work and joining it up together to make some coherent strategy and plan, well that's the tricky bit, and it isn't going to just happen spontaneously I'm afraid.

"The only problem seems to be is that we are a bit short on managers of any sort; people who can take an across-the-board perspective of what is going on from many areas; people who can fit everything together, and see what needs to be coordinated, managed, rather than isolated subjective controlled perspectives, all doing their own thing.

"All the people with these sorts of skills seem to be down there further down the mountain, being kept busy at the moment!"

He gestured back down the slope.

"Mind you, it takes a lot to understand everything, not to mention keeping pace with it all as it goes. It's not easy getting a good picture of everything, all the pieces, and how it all fits together, all the knowledge, let alone working out a plan for moving it forward, growing it up.

"In your case I'm sorry we had to move responsibilities around a bit between the two of you, but you seemed to be having trouble getting sorted."

He looked at the Priest.

"We did?" asked the Priest looking confused, and he thought for a moment.

"Well who *am* I then?" the Priest asked at last in a confrontational tone.

"Well, you are the combination of religions and spiritual beliefs wrapped into one, a level playing field if you like, which you probably found quite straightforward with so much commonality between the different groups.

"Your organisation was setup a few years ago. Your 'project' - as 'IT 'up there sees you - is to produce a co-ordinated way of working between the physical and everything up there and vice versa, you know - bring all the religions and spiritual beliefs together into one coherent and coordinated view, and to develop a common mechanism for interfacing with the spiritual?

"Fairly straightforward really."

"Oh right…" mumbled the Priest. "That's probably true when you say it like that, but, it's just that, well, we were one of the first to get going, and it all took a bit of working out, and we got into lots of fights, and the different teams went off in different directions, and got very defensive and wouldn't talk to each other or share ideas, and things kept changing over time, and we kept getting conflicting messages."

He looked very uncomfortable and there were a lot of 'ands' and 'buts' that followed. The man in black narrowed his eyes, and for the first time started to look a little uneasy.

"In my case," he said slowly "I am just sort of putting the structure together at the moment. Fortunately there seems to be a lot here already in terms of products, facilities and tools. All the right sort of ground work having been done.

"In fact she," he pointed upwards "our macro-organismic operating system, has even had to subconsciously slow some of the groups down just to keep them ticking along, but frankly it all just needs a bit of coordination and understanding from varying perspectives, and to some extent that's what this mountain is for."

He tapped his foot on the ground.

"This very thing here, that you are both standing on, is not real and doesn't represent anything in the real world or the 'spiritual', if that's the right term. It's just a concept that has been used many times before, and so is easy to accept, like a mental bridge to get you from one side to the other in terms of understanding."

"So 'Who' or 'What' brought me here, then? Who made me climb the mountain?" asked the Priest.

The man in black said nothing - he just gave the Priest a wide smile. After a few moments of waiting for the Priest to answer his own question, he pointed upwards and looked questioningly at him and then shook his head. Then he pointed at himself, and did the same.

Then he pointed at the Priest and nodded, "You did" he said.

He paused again for a few more moments, waiting for the Priest to realise what he was really trying to say, but gave up, and changed the subject again.

"Frankly, this job isn't something I would have chosen to do. The communication is very limited. The pay and rewards are non-existent, and the working conditions are physically and mentally very hard - mainly because of the overall diametric nature, and the many levels we are working with and at.

"The trouble is, knowing what we know comes with a whole load of responsibility or duty. Once you know, and see, you can't just leave it and walk away, even though the problem is so vast. Not even when it bites back. I try not to think about it to be honest. It just seems sort of natural somehow, like any other job, but with no obvious individual or direct reward or pay.

"The key is to keep a careful balance between the individual and the collective, and always step back and take a top-down perspective. It's just something I have to do, and do, and it feels necessary, so I get on with it as best I can.

"I seem to be kept busy in phases, and it seems to be working in a fashion, with a few setbacks here and there, but not surprisingly given the state we are in at all levels. It all seems to make sense to me all the time somehow.

"That's not to say it's not still a mess, but I can see why it is that way, and why we are where we are, but then I see things very differently. There are people to help me, and I seem to get what I need when I need it, which of course is very different from what I want."

He stopped for a moment and closed his eyes and he rubbed the front of his forehead with the palm of his hand. It was all silent for a moment aside from the wind blowing wisps of dust around their feet and the hard stony ground.

It was then that both men realised just how physically tired he was, and even taking the time to try and talk to them was obviously exhausting him. He breathed deeply for a few moments before recovering himself, and going on.

"There is so much up here already that that can be used, and we seem to recognise and understand things together somehow. I can introduce you to the other groups, and you can have a chat with them if you like?"

Both men looked around at the other groups on the plateau, and the context and realisation of where they were and why they were there was starting to dawn on them but they both still felt very apprehensive and nervous.

"You need to understand though," he continued "that many people just resigned as soon as they got here, well the ones that made it without going mad anyway. Frankly I can't blame them.

"There have also been many who didn't even know what they were doing, and were just blindly wandering around with their eyes closed, just taking what was being said without questioning it, or just trying to make sense of what they were hearing without quite getting the point; they just took other people's past interpretations of what was happening, and then used and reinforced them, and yet still relayed their views down and up, making it worse with the wrong sort of feedback, and also influencing the choices of whoever came along next.

"Some would just capitalise where they could on the nature of the collective subconscious, for their own benefit, which in turn IT learnt from, but then that's life. Without trial and error you never learn or move on. You can't make a layer cake without breaking a few eggs."

The Priest and the Biologist shuffled uncomfortably, but the man in black didn't seem to notice and continued to talk.

"To get to this level you will also need to have had a fairly intense experience, or whichever religious term or psychological definition you want to use for it. You need that point of reference or perspective to allow you to make sense of things. You really need that 'hang on a minute' perspective. The whole 'experience' thing can also affect people in different ways, depending on their existing circumstances, beliefs, experience, intelligence, and knowledge."

As he finished speaking, he beckoned to the two men, and wandered over to one edge of the plateau which overlooked a sheer cliff dropping straight down.

He walked carefully to the very edge with his shoes almost hanging over the side. He leaned slightly forward and looked down a drop of several hundred feet.

"You know, you get quite a perspective from up here," he said "it brings a sort of clarity to the mind. It's not so much the view but the feeling of control. I can sense 'IT' is trying to work out what I am doing, it is worried." The two men looked at the girl up on the mountain above, and she did appear to be aware of something.

The woman behind them though was clearly very concerned, and was frozen to the spot unable to say anything or move in case she distracted him. Quite a number of the people behind them seemed to get a little more vocal or agitated, even though they weren't aware of what was going on, and there was certainly a definite feeling of tension in the air.

"So you see, sometimes you have to try a few things out in order to work out what is really going on, being at that critical point, or on the critical path.

"That know-ledge. That fine line between falling, and not, of being alive or dead, madness or sanity, pushing the boundary.

"It's at that point where you are in control between the two that gives you that visibility, that management perspective, a point of reference that allows you to see clearly what is really happening, to measure and work out what's going on, while IT's guard is down, and making mistakes.

"It's a fine balance keeping that going, hard work in fact, and risky to say the least, finding that keen balance between the two, if indeed you can tell the difference. Yet, that process in itself is a direction, a means of communication and dialogue, and a force." He went silent for a few moments thinking, and then he stood up straight again, and walked backwards to them.

"Death is quite an odd thing" he said, turning to face them. "We are all sort of programmed to feel that there is an afterlife, you know, that we somehow live on after we die. That gives us purpose, meaning, drive and motivation, incentive."

There was another long pause. "So *do you* know the answer?" asked the Priest, filling the gap. "Well, yes," said the man in black "but it's quite complicated, so it's a sort of 'yes' in that respect, we do indeed - but it's not as straightforward as that, more like a program structure being reused rather than a device that it exists in.

"However at the moment I am more concerned about what is doing the programming, why we all feel the same way, when it started, and what sort of rubbish hardware and bio firmware was used to write it on in the first place. But more importantly, how we sort it all out, especially from our individual perspectives.

"As you would expect, there doesn't seem to be any sort of methodology in place, or strategy, a planned way forward. When it became clear to certain people in the past that things weren't right there was a sort of makeshift secret plan, which involved waiting until 'IT'," and he pointed upwards "was self-aware or conscious rather than just subconscious, and that was about it.

"A 'push the button and see what happens' idea, that was a bit limited and naïve, and without strategy, and of course would never happen unless you knew where the button was, and how to press it. So without any real coordination, like a self-evolving plan, everything was just naturally put into controlling 'stovepipes', managed and operated separately, and without any overall control or strategy.

"You know what I mean…" he said gesturing to the Biologist "those self-perpetuating knowledge stovepipes of academia, getting taller and more complex and harder to 'see' all the time, to make sense of, and understand in totality. Young minds directed into them with little choice, working upwards to eventually become teachers to replicate the same. Sound familiar?"

He gestured with his head upwards again. "IT, has been sort of managing things as best it can unconsciously, muddling along. However it doesn't have much of a perspective on how things work down here, or even in the real physical world.

"IT just sees us all as one or many groups you see. So you," and he pointed to the Priest "may be hundreds of people, and yet other individuals here may be just one person in the physical world. So what you see around you here is different to what she or IT sees, and what may appear wrong to you may not be viewed in the same way up there. Different perspectives and objectives you see? A sort of evolved hive mind, a diametric symbiotic relationship.

"It is also quite selfish, which is OK, that's how it is meant to be, and so it looks after itself, which is us collectively, rather than us individually, which of course gets very complicated."

"Know-ledge…" said the Priest finally. "Oh I get it, it's a sort of play on words. Like summ-it or peak-experience or Mess-iah?"

"Well no, not really" said the man in black. "You can take these things a bit too far sometimes, and look for meaning and association when there really isn't any, although I would agree with the mess part though, which is when you end up with a manager or should I say man-ager."

"But are you telling me then," began the Priest again, ignoring the joke, "that this is all real or happening in the physical world somehow? You must be completely mad!"

The man in black looked slightly affronted. "Well yes *and* no" he answered. "As I said, this is just a sort of concept place that has elements of both the real physical and the spiritual world if you like. This will help us get to where we want to go in our understanding and help explain things, and to see things from a simpler perspective; in this case, from a knowledge point of view - it's a tool.

"You two both live in your protected 'ivory towers,' with organisations around you, parts of a brain structure with limited knowledge of the 'real' world, happy to work and be paid for the things that you do. Building your 'bit of the picture', defending yourselves, protecting and helping shape your pillars of knowledge which is fine.

"This concept is just the knowledge side of things, it is just one part of the whole thing; a way of representing one bit, but there are a whole lot of other aspects to 'IT' that look and work differently. The problem is that you can't explain it all at once.

"People will always see things from a position and understanding based on what they are as a person, from what they are used to, what they have learnt or know, what they believe, and what they have grown to accept and trust. In the same way that if you have 'spiritual' experiences you tend to use your mind to associate what you experience with what you know and accept and believe.

"Sort of joining the dots to make a picture from what you already recognise or can associate with. In my case you could say that I was a technical manager, with a broad in-depth understanding of many things, so I wouldn't be doing all of this unless I had to, and understood everything that I needed to.

"It's just a question of understanding, getting perspective, and lots of hard work, and with no safety net.

"In fact perspective is everything really, and this concept model just tries to make sense of both perspectives together. That's what you need when neither are making sense from the other's point of view, and when both viewpoints are diametrically opposed. Oh, and no I'm not mad, or schizophrenic or anything like that, I think I am just here by accident."

There was a pause.

"I have just realised that we don't even know your name" said the Biologist, obviously trying to change the subject.

"Sam, my name is Sam" said the man in black. "Thank you for asking, you are the first person to do that, but then it is somewhat impersonal up here. Frankly I am not sure I am up to the job, but I am trying not to think about it, and just get on with it for the moment.

"Besides the pay is terrible and hours are completely unreasonable, and the stress..." He smiled, "But then I have managed worse things. I know what is going on, I know what IT is, and I know how IT all works, and I know what to do.

"But it's all very large and complex so I am just trying to explain it in a way that is simplistic, and in a way that makes some sense from a common perspective. Just doing what I can."

"Hang on - but *she's a woman*!" cried the Priest interrupting him again, as the proverbial penny finally dropped. "Who is?" asked Sam. "Her in charge up there!" and he pointed upwards "We all thought it was a man. It's *supposed* to be a man."

"Ahh..." said Sam. "Ahh - I can see where you have been getting a bit confused. What people have seen up until now, in their minds when they have these intense experiences, is a navigation through the collective parts of their own psyche structure, in which there are many established archetypes, which for obvious reasons are usually male. It's what you expect and historically look up to and obey, and associate with.

"These have been built up and reinforced over time; stereotypical programs which translate information coming from the actual distributed collective mind structure.

"They are an interpretation of something in a form that is safe and understandable, a belief structure channel, which you translate into your own representation of expectation. If you didn't process it in that way the information would be impossible to interpret, not to mention dangerous to your mind. That's why your brain is structured the way it is to interpret it for you, and protect you from it, in a symbiotic way.

"It's all those visions and insights and 'All powerful almighty, all seeing, all knowing' stuff, which doesn't quite stack up with the evidence in physical reality, yet you know there is *something* there.

"If you look at what's *actually* there you will find that this analogy, when we go through it, should provide a clarified compromise that will satisfy both atheists and people like yourself, from the knowledge side of things.

"When you think about things it kind of makes sense really, with the way things have been done, and where we are going."

"But *are* you telling me everything up there is being managed by a woman?" spluttered the Priest. Sam looked confused "I haven't said anything other than that she is just the representation of our collective conscious mind, all bonded together using an integrated organising field, and I wouldn't actually say that 'managed' was a good word to use."

The Priest immediately looked relieved. "Oh, that's alright then! So where is He?" asked the Priest, "Where is God?"

"Umm, well, there isn't one..." said Sam very carefully. "Well, more accurately - there isn't one *yet* in the definition that you mean, that's what 'IT' needs to become in your context" continued Sam, hurriedly trying to get to the next point before the Priest exploded in a fit of anxiety.

"Which is also a different conversation to there being a 'Creator' or something higher up, and yes, before you ask, I do know, but I just want to get this situation sorted out first.

"There is too much of this imagining of the beyond, and more beyond, stuff going on; always looking as far off into the distance as you can with your binoculars. Too busy imagining instead of stopping and worrying about the fact that your trousers have fallen down and that your feet are surrounded by a bunch of hungry seagulls with highly adept skills in basic maths.

"This gives you a solution that works, and keeps both you, and all those atheists that have been giving you so many problems, happy as well."

"Eh? That doesn't make any bloody sense at all!" said the Priest in a very agitated voice as he stood before a man that he thought was shattering his life and beliefs into tiny little pieces.

"Look…" Sam continued. "It's to do with time, perception, interpretation, and a few other things, and it's all a bit complicated. I am sure that some of these other groups can give you some help, a few pointers, but be careful who you talk to. Then I am sure it will make sense, and maybe more so up there, but at least you are wanting to go in the right direction so that's the main thing." Sam patted him on the shoulder.

"Yes, but isn't that idea a bit sexist?" asked the Biologist, looking up at the woman.

Sam thought for a moment "Well no, not really. We are just basing it on what we see going on, what we have worked out, what she represents. I know this 'woman thing' seems a bit one-sided from our perspective, but…" he moved closer to the two men to whisper, "But it's fairly obvious really that IT's a 'she' because she just talks nonstop.

"Well 'talks' isn't the right word, more communicates collectively, and is totally unreasonable. It wants things done yesterday, gets all emotional, upset, moody, hormonal, and focuses on the problems and not the solutions. IT just witters on about the most meaningless issues that seem petty to us, but that are obviously going round and round in ITs mind. It also switches from one mood or subject to another in no time.

So does that sound familiar?

"Besides as IT's virtual, this is really just a way of representing IT until IT is perceived by something else externally. From a male perspective I think it's always worth blaming women collectively, keeps them on their toes you see?" Sam stood back a few paces and waited for the Biologist to reply.

There was a pause "OK… sounds about right for now" said the Biologist nervously.

"Well anyway" said Sam "We have got a sort of translation thing going that works to some extent." He paused and looked around. The woman behind him had taken her earpiece out and was looking at him with a face like a storm cloud.

"I think she may have heard you," whispered the Biologist "you know, that thing that you just said about women?"

"Oh, err, sorry!" said Sam to the woman quite casually, almost as if he was oblivious as to what he had said, and he turned back to face the men again.

"So what you see or perceive spiritually very much depends on what is in your mind, your own experiences, knowledge, cultural background, psyche group structure, upbringing, and reinforced belief structures and so on.

"You see 'IT', or parts of 'IT', from your own unique perspective, so to view and describe 'IT' from a common perspective or description is very difficult, especially when we are performing different 'roles' or components within it. Besides I think if we all saw IT the same way, IT would also be very boring.

"What would we all have to speculate on, or fight about, or debate about on the chat shows?

"With more detailed knowledge in different areas of perspective; sciences, psychology, maths, religions and so on, the more complex it becomes. Which of course it will do, that's what we are doing it for. So by trying to perceive it, and work it all out, we are at the same time making 'IT' more complex in itself. Like an ever evolving complex operating system, trying to support and deal with ever increasingly complex devices and programs.

"However without external refinement that only works up to a point. You have to start somewhere though, as with everything -

biology, archaeology, space exploration, computer programming - the more you discover and create, the more you learn about IT and other things. Knowledge becomes integrated with other areas building up a picture that in itself gets more and more complex.

"Oh yes, love and understanding, and a sense of humour - that's all important up here too! I can assure you that you have been guided, helped, and protected by someone else who loves you and supports you."

He turned around to look at the woman behind him for a second and then he moved closer to the men and whispered, "They have a hierarchy you know? And don't try to explain things to them, they know it all already, just get on with your job..." he nodded with his eyebrows conspiratorially.

The Biologist and the Priest looked at each other again. They were both clearly confused, and had no idea what he was talking about. He moved in even closer, and again leaned towards them.

"As I mentioned, it's very important to have a sense of humour, and to just imagine that you are in some sort of role playing game, and then everything just sort of works, and things you needed were somehow available all along, and if we agree on things, they just sort of appear and work.

"But don't worry about it, just go with the flow."

He put his hand on the shoulder of the Priest. He leaned towards Sam to hear what he had to say. "But the most important thing..." finished Sam "is just to have faith."

Sam smiled and there was a long pause before the Priest stood upright "Oh, very bloody funny." He said.

Sam then walked back over to the blonde woman and his face became more serious. "There are still a few things that we haven't ironed out yet, like music. We know music is important but we don't know why yet, frequencies and all that, it only reaches so far up there for some reason" and he looked up.

The Biologist took off his hat and scratched his head "It all looks like a very complex means of communication to me."

"Well it is from our point of view, as we have certain pre-existing impressions of what God is and what God can do, compared to what our collective mind is, and what *IT* can do.

IT communicates to us in parallel, and in a different format. We then have to translate that, whereas we are used to things coming in sequentially or in serial; seeing, hearing, having ideas, and experiencing life.

"You see IT doesn't communicate consciously as you do by talking. It can only relay information by events or observations via groups of people, or by coincidental messages or synchronised events. Like your cells reacting to you rubbing a pain in your arm, or the way your body reacts to stimuli? Do you see?

"With the messages that come there is a frequency and a specific nature. IT makes it very obvious, and you just have to keep your eyes and ears open to coincidence and synchronicity and context and use it along with your own feelings, sense, energy, and the knowledge that you gain.

"So in the physical world you may get up in the morning, and there may be three topics on the television which relate to things going on in your head already, and it all fits together and makes sense with things going on around you. Then treating it scientifically, you can prove it works, like a dialogue and cause and effect, but the process takes a lot of getting used to.

"Sometimes you may go down a wrong alley in trying to get to a point, and then the messages become more intense where it is trying to explain something in different ways. It's just about seeing things from a different perspective, viewing the world in a different way, seeing what you can't normally see from a collective perspective.

"You get the hang of it after a while and learn to see messages coming through from lots of different sources, building a picture of what is going on as you go on. Mostly though we just see the problems."

"So you are saying that you are hearing 'voices'?" asked the Priest. "Do you talk back to them then? That's a form of madness you know!"

"No. Certainly not. We are not talking schizophrenia, voices in the head, mental illness or visions here. We are talking actual physical effects, by groups of people, and communication in the real world, combined with raw knowledge transfer, actual things happening, measurable cause and effect, conscious self-awareness stuff, rather than interpretation of the collective subconscious mind through individual psyche translations."

The Priest and the Biologist still looked very confused.

"IT's perception is very different from our own, but it can only communicate from IT's perspective with what IT 'sees', and how IT understands things. Eventually IT may learn to be more sophisticated, as may we, but at the moment IT, and we, aren't doing much effective communication between us as cells, and IT's body and mind. It is all very complex, but ultimately 'IT' is that which is driving us, pushing us forward - that's ITs job, or should be.

"We have to learn to 'talk' to IT and 'listen' to IT in ways that we seem to have forgotten. We just have to refine our techniques and develop methods that work for us, and for IT.

"IT is different to us as individuals, it has diametrically opposing agendas and views. We created and evolved IT as we went along after all, being part of something bigger progressively, it's a natural development, and it is linked to our collective state, as we are to IT."

As he was talking Sam started pacing up and down, and moving his hands around in gestures to elaborate on what he was saying.

"You see 'IT' is us, and we are 'IT'. There is a subconscious part, which acts very irrationally and instinctively as with animals, and there is now a barely conscious, subtle, weaker part of sorts. This behaves in a similar way to our conscious mind to some extent, yet is a bit of a mess from our perspective, and is actually unable to communicate with us very well at all.

"We aren't quite sure why we got into this state, but the higher subconscious elements started off around ten to twelve thousand years ago, which occurred when civilisations sort of got together, based on the original herd group mentality stuff from long ago.

"Something happened four or five thousand years ago, caused by a geographic or natural catastrophe, that sort of sent it off track. That was followed by a series of wars, with competing psyche groups that were part of IT, and many things and information being lost meant that it didn't grow properly or in the right way, which has taken a while to sort out. Oh, and lack of overall external competition or influence didn't help.

"We also changed too quickly and became too variable to allow it to adapt at the same pace geographically. But it was all going OK up until about the last hundred years or so and then it started going 'tits up' from our perspective, if you will pardon the expression, for various reasons - chemicals, drugs and so on.

"So now it's in a real state, as you can probably tell that from the way things are going in the 'real' or physical world that we choose to perceive.

"IT doesn't have any direct specific control over the physical world, but it can influence us and what we do- which is obviously very powerful - and it has more significant effect at the collective subconscious and animalistic basic levels.

"Using this knowledge model here we can look at what messages are coming in and build up a picture of what is going wrong, or of what IT is doing or is trying to do."

"I still don't see what you are getting at," said the Priest, but for some reason he couldn't seem to make himself heard, or it may have been that he was now just being ignored.

"Essentially what we need to do is get a better collective understanding of how it all fits together, so that it all works together in a better way" continued Sam. "A sort of self-fulfilling control engineering cause and effect thingy, by using science and management techniques in the physical 'real' and 'spiritual' virtual operating system levels combined.

"When we do that we can work out what laws are in each area, what is there, how it fits together, and what influences each level might have on the other. We should also be mapping out what exists there at the moment in the spiritual perception, and eventually developing some sort of blueprint for the future – if indeed that can ever possibly be done by ourselves.

"It's quite clear that something drastic, yet subtle, needs to happen at the moment. It has all reached a point where too many things are out of balance. The physical is running out of resources for the population growth, most people are unhappy, and everything has no coordinated management that takes all of this into account. Also the spiritual is one big confusing mess of historical and physical representations on different levels, and the collective subconscious is just being very selfish, and driving everything else for its own gain.

"A bit like ourselves as individuals really - we have become lazy, with overactive imaginations, and stovepipe knowledge, and we are all now focused on the wrong things.

"When you look, and wait, and see what has been said by others in the past that have been in the same situations, or who have had similar experiences, and you correlate, and you then use your scientific and management skills, then you begin to question things. Wait a few years to build up a communication structure, and an independent perspective, look at what people are being pushed along to understand, and why.

"Why, for example, are we so far along understanding subatomic physics and yet we spend comparatively little on biology? So you stop and question 'Why exactly am I doing this?' and 'What exactly are you gaining from it individually?' and then it all makes sense, in a mad sort of way.

"The key is that when these sorts of experiences happen, or more to the point, when we want to *learn something* from them, at stress points of social evolution or revolution or environmental changes, or it is personal - it is at *those* points that the people that it happens to convey the information, which causes change.

"Of course if you don't make a change, or haven't managed to write it down, or if you are on the losing side, nobody gets to hear about you.

"In this case though it seems to be a cry for help rather than a driving force. IT has just started to wake up and realise the mess it has got into, and perceives the problems and association between the physical and the spiritual.

"Although IT only has awareness and perception in the spiritual, it doesn't have any direct physical presence or ability to manipulate things physically, only indirectly.

"IT also has a different perspective of time to us. As you would expect with an operating system, it is more focused on the future and can see certain aspects of it from our perspective - whereas we live with the present and past.

"Another problem is that the collective subconscious and conscious are at odds a lot of the time, in a similar way as to what goes on in our own minds."

"I do have to say," said the Biologist "that it all seems like something out of a fantasy fiction novel or something like that." Sam thought for a while "Well yes," he answered finally "but it's all just metaphysical, all part of the process of making the thing work, creating a picture. Sort of a bit like role playing."

"It doesn't look like it's working out very well up there does it?" said the Priest "I thought it would be more impressive somehow, and why is she looking so tired? And what's with the awful noise from inside the mountain?" "Well," said Sam "the problem is that IT hasn't been getting any sleep at all for a long time now, as we have been making too much noise down here all day and night all around the planet. So while we have all been sleeping in shifts, from her perspective she, or IT, has been awake all of the time.

"Apparently it used to be alright when there were fewer people on the mountain or on the planet, and when they were all on one side with a great lake on the other, the Pacific and the Americas, but now everyone is everywhere so she doesn't get a break.

"The loud noise thing?" queried Sam, "Well it is a sleeping dragon, a representation of our collective subconscious animal inside the mountain up there, and he represents the conscious part. We tried to think of them as one but that didn't seem to work. I suppose it's just the way our brains work and our need for something to associate things with.

"The dragon, or whatever form you give it, has got several duties. He performs deep inside the mountain. He seems to do it in his sleep most of the time. And he throws rocks, a lot of rocks, sort of subconscious messages. So you have to be on your toes, you just have to be aware. I suppose it is better than dodging bullets. He is much more powerful and larger than she is. At the moment she is only able to make subtle changes, whereas the collective subconscious animal has a much more direct impact and effect on us as a whole, and has done so for a long time, as in our own bodies.

"Some people have swords to fight it, 'magic' to deal with it, tools to communicate with it, symbols, talismans, all sorts of things, and it adapts and learns from that, but you can't ever defeat it completely as an individual. So the harder you fight it, the stronger and smarter it gets, up to a point, but a very significant point."

"So is *HE* God?" asked the Priest excitedly.

"Look" said Sam. "I can see you are having a lot of trouble with all of this. No - he is just a representation of our collective subconscious mind, deep in the heart of the collective knowledge mountain up there in the darkest depths inside."

"Aha! So there is actually a Hell?" cried the Priest. Sam's face crumpled and he sighed "No. It is just the place where our combined collective human knowledge, up to that point, is collated and integrated in a way that we can't do down here on this mountain, like a combined knowledge records storage system or database if you like. We have recently tried to replicate and simulate the same in the physical world, with the Internet and data within it, but they are really very different, and they exist from two different perspectives. Look you are really having a problem with this aren't you?"

"Where does IT exist though? In reality?" the Priest continued excitedly.

"IT exists within us all, and through us, and all around the planet. Everywhere," said Sam patiently "in the collective part of our minds, correlated, networked and distributed. Everyone contributing to it, refining it, depending on the individual, via a field and bond and shared energy fields of perception, along with all the other evolutionary mechanisms we have developed into what we can, and able to use.

"It helps us to see and understand things in the same way, like a records library database and system, maintaining a consistency of perceptive understanding and knowledge with individual perspective biases. In the same way as everything can store memory and information, it is just a question of perception.

"It all looks fantastic and incredible in there when you aren't limited to our constraints of senses. I don't think I was meant to go down there for more than a few seconds, but once I had seen a bit of it even in my own mind, I couldn't get enough of it. I think I was only supposed to have a glimpse of one piece but went into dozens and dozens of them, and it all nearly went badly wrong.

"I just want to make it clear that I didn't choose to go there, nor do I 'do' drugs, nor am I mad. I was just sort of shoved there with a few subtle suggestions on what I should be looking for, so that I could understand what I had to do, and that was really just the start, but I am quite sure I didn't need to know all that, and it's odd but the more I go along the more things seem to come together. It's now a sort of ongoing process of the same thing every day, but with a limiting bandwidth, and chain of events that take time, like a journey.

"Don't get me wrong, I'm no genius or expert on anything, but I do seem to know a lot about everything now, and what is right or wrong, and that helps me do my job if that makes sense?

"Information flows in and out all the time. I know what has to be done and I am given what I need to know to do it, along with that feeling of responsibility, but I am certainly not happy about it at the moment.

"Also writing all this stuff down isn't easy either, trying to describe it when it's hard to put it in any sort of context, and IT subconsciously deliberately making it difficult for you to even do that, like juggling and painting at the same time."

Nobody said anything.

"I suspect IT was fed suggestions subconsciously on what was required by other individuals in the past. But there you go. Time to move on…" he said, and turned to look at the woman behind him. The Biologist looked at the Priest. There were clearly things going on that weren't being mentioned.

"Anyway," said the Biologist talking reflectively "I agree. It's only when you get up here that you can see what everyone else has been going through, and where the all the problems are, even if everyone has differing viewpoints or perception of what they are dealing with."

"Yes," said Sam "but I think the important thing now is that everyone can see that we need to have a way forward. A plan for the future. Not in a controlling way, but with everyone having a part, and being able to see their own future, and that you don't have to go hugging trees, make weird humming noises, or taking illegal substances, or bury your head in a screen to get there."

But Sam realised that it didn't sound all that convincing, and seemed more aspirational rather than definitive.

"You know, we may even end up with something else after this program has finished and are onto the next stage. Something we have all been looking for all this time."

His brow furrowed, and for the first time the Biologist felt that he wasn't being told everything. Something wasn't quite as simple as what Sam was trying to portray.

"But it's all got to be done from up here. I think that if you were to go down the mountain and try to sort out the problems down there it would be totally impossible; it would be a management nightmare.

"You can't just sort the physical world problems out, you have to sort it all out at this level, from both perspectives at the same time, otherwise you will just end up creating more problems, and get things out of balance again."

"Yes, it looked like a riot going on down there," said the Priest pointing down the mountain "you could never sort all of that out in a million years. I wonder what caused it?" The Biologist looked sideways at the Priest, and raised his eyebrows, and shook his head.

"You see," said Sam "even if you sorted it out one minute - they would be fighting again a few minutes later about something else. You have to change the fundamentals you see, from both points of view, shared benefits, that's the key. With people, it's not so much what they have learnt - it is what they have forgotten. We have lost the perception of the bond between us, forgotten to see the field that exists to bring us together because nothing is making us do so, and so everything has become too one-sided. IT is getting what IT wants, and we as individuals are not, if you look at it objectively.

"More recently we seem to be blindly disabling IT or ignoring IT. Too many chemicals, drugs, and environmental inhibitors in the more advanced geographical parts.

"Like a group of children at a party, hyper on food additives, sweets and drinks, getting upset and angry and not knowing why. Even at birth a lot of people have lost that initial bond establishment with things like anaesthetic, and also at the point of death, and everyone being too busy to be there.

"So by being up here you can try and change things in the wider term, and try and change the messages going down over time, until eventually the idea gets through to people.

"It may be that as people start to realise that they are all an important part of something bigger, it may change things, I don't know, but from here you can see that if we carry on the way we are, everyone simply looking at their own individual needs, it's all going to continue down one route. There needs to be a balance, and a way forward.

"Also, you can't just get one small group to have their own environment, and live by themselves, and grow their own things, as it wouldn't be long before the rest took everything away from them and moved in. So it has to be all, *everyone*, or nothing. The 'all for one, and one for all' idea, with a top-down approach. The old ways and thinking are just not working.

"From up here the overall task becomes not impossible, just very, very hard. It's a very mad world that needs a lot of sorting out, and now you can see why. Even though up here you are in fact taking on a much bigger level of responsibility, somehow, if we can sort out things up here, all the mess down there simply takes care of itself. Well that's the idea anyway.

"All it takes is for someone to let everyone know that there is some sort of plan, a purpose, a way forward, and get things moving onwards and upwards in a balanced way, benefiting all levels, to manage it all with direction, and with a management strategy, and one not just involving hugging trees, or being 'nice' to everyone."

"Sounds alright, I suppose" said the Priest, but he didn't sound convinced.

"Everyone should be equal in the collective mind, and we should all work in different areas within it. Conversely, we have the other problem that we think in terms of many individuals whereas IT," and Sam pointed up, "tends to only see one group or organisation as one. Take you, for example, you who represent thousands of people, or a group of twenty, or just one. So this 'mountain concept' helps them too to deal with us in the same way as for us to see or understand IT."

"So," said the Biologist "those people on the sides of the mountain represent billions of people in the real world?" "Yes" said Sam. "*Oh I see!*" said the Biologist again "It makes sense now. And you represent a small group of people?" "No," said Sam "unfortunately I don't. I should do but I don't." "Oh" said the Biologist thinking for a moment, and then went silent and looked very worried.

"I haven't written many plans or structures down I'm afraid" Sam said. "It's all virtual at the moment as I have only been working things out for a few months. But before then I wrote down quite a few things in here over the last few years," and he patted the leather folder.

"I have come up with a draft method for running things, a way of communicating and of seeing what is going on, and we have come up with this metaphysical model." He tapped his foot on the ground. "Along with some tools and mechanisms. As I said, I am just doing what I can."

He stood up straight now and looked briefly back at the woman behind him.

"OK," Sam said "that's enough of the explanations. Now I am going to move on and do a few demonstrations. So let's try something else. Close your eyes and imagine a stunningly attractive blonde in a red dress standing in front of you." They closed their eyes and he waited about twenty seconds. "Now open your eyes" he said.

They looked around but there was no one there. "I don't get it?" said the Biologist, "No? Oh well! It was worth a try!!" said Sam. "But that's the thing! We have to work with many constraints and limits and laws - the laws of averages and beliefs.

In this case we are up against another Law." The two men looked at the woman behind him. She was standing there with her arms crossed and had a broad smile on her face.

"You see 'women' have evolved too. Thankfully, not as quickly as us, or we would never catch up with them" he laughed. The Priest look confused. "But then that's what happens in nature if you try to supress something over a long period of time," Sam continued "tell something that it can't do things, keep something in the shade, religiously prune its branches, and you get that!"

He directed his hand towards the woman behind him. "Bloody fantastic isn't it? That's what is supposed to happen in nature. Mind you thank goodness for love eh? And symmetry and all the other rules" he smiled, and he realised that he was getting off track again.

"Right" he said suddenly in a different tone, and everything seemed to change in mood and perspective. The air went cold and still. "I am going to do something now and I don't want you to be alarmed." He closed his eyes for a moment, and there was a change in the energy in the air and the wind picked up.

An apparition started to form several feet in front of the two men. Its form seemed to build up as a flow of haze from the mountain above.

Within a few seconds it snapped into a solid form, and a sense of fear, danger and apprehension accompanied it. Standing in front of them was a green-brown, scaled reptile man, just over seven feet tall, with menacing eyes and a muscly, scaly body. It was very clear, real, and alarming.

It started to speak telepathically to them, snarling at the same time, so that they could hear what it was saying in their minds, and associate that with the fear it generated from its expressions.

It was talking to them about a 'conspiracy plan', and 'some experiment that would end soon, and they would all be taken off to some strange planet of one of the stars of Orion, and about other civilisations from the Pleiades star group'.

Both men looked terrified, they could feel it there, sense the danger, the fear, the menace in the way it spoke in their heads. It all seemed very plausible, logical, real and terrifying - it even bared its teeth at the men. The woman behind Sam had also stepped forward, and was now in-between it and him, and she was about to do something.

"OK! Stop right there!" commanded Sam, and it froze like a statue, or a freeze-frame in a film or animated computer program. "Now I want to show what this is from my perspective" said Sam. He seemed factual, pragmatic, and very much at odds with the fear and confusion going on around him, like it wasn't even there.

"What do you see? Both of you?" asked Sam. Each man, when they had recovered, described what they saw. Their descriptions were much the same, except for a few minor differences in interpretation.

They also described the fear they felt, and the trepidation, anxious feelings, implications, and the need to know more; their imaginations filling in the gaps of the story in areas that concerned them - the Priest emphasising and exaggerating some aspects more so than the Biologist.

"This sort of thing goes on all the time in our collective mind at the moment, and in the recent past" said Sam as he wandered around the apparition with his hands folded behind his back. "It is a reinforced imaginative concept, a thought form, like a smart dream program that becomes alive in the minds of many people collectively.

"It is a belief structure developed and evolved from a single thought form that someone has had at one point in the past. This is then refined, evolved, and adapted in the minds of many people, until it is as believable as possible.

"The process started long ago with things that seem quite childish to us now - gargoyles, fairies, pixies, and so on. Things that with a grown up, intelligent perspective, and in the cold light of day, are non-logical and non-sensible, childlike. Mental imaginings to interpret something that was inexplicable at the time. In the case of pixies, fairies or little people, this was due to a visual disorder linked with a mental interpretation which created a collective shared perception function or program.

"As we evolve and become more knowledgeable and intelligent we can gradually eliminate those program creations from our collective mind group programming. In favour of more sophisticated and inventive concepts and thought forms that can't again be so easily explained away - even ideas from science fiction or fantasy authors, which form the spark of collective 'out of the box' imaginations.

"In this particular instance these thoughts are also amplified by the reptilian parts and traits in our brains we have evolved with.

"OK, let me show you…" Sam said taking a deep breath. "So before you also add to it and try and fill any more logic gaps in what is going on, step back a moment and look at the bigger picture. Stand back a few paces." They did.

"Does it remind you of anything you have seen in the physical world?" The two men looked at each other.

"Like perhaps from a particular episode of *Star Trek*? Seen by a woman in the North American part of the collective brain a long time ago?" The men looked puzzled.

"Also what are the chances of it coming from one of the stars we can actually see? What is the chance of it being roughly the same height as you, or being able to speak in a language you can understand, even in your mind, or for it to have the same proportion and number of arms and legs and heads?"

"Now look down…" said Sam "at its feet." They both looked, and stared. After a few seconds the Biologist began to laugh.

"I don't get it" said the Priest.

"OK" said Sam "How many aliens do you know that would have badly made latex slip-on feet? When people create things in their minds out of fear, they always worry about the face, the eyes, the *sinister* aspects, the threat. They see all the scary things, like sharp teeth, the emotional parts, or the immediately interesting things. So the bits that aren't really important, or things we don't normally notice, like the feet, get forgotten.

"So you need to start questioning what you are seeing all the time. Use rational or scientific mature perspectives, methods to prove things, experience, don't believe it - test it! So to help everyone with this, I just gave them rubber feet. It's a tool you can teach your children to cope with things that they are really scared of.

It breaks the structure without breaking their imagination.

"The problem is though, that as you spot the gaps, they get filled in by someone else over time. You just have to be clever, constantly outsmarting, one step ahead of the game. Then let what you think is right and positive guide you, like love and humour, and remember to 'live long and prosper'."

Again he paused for dramatic effect, but there was just silence.

"Also don't even believe anything I say, over time I will be become wrong, and out of date and superseded, but that's the whole point. It's all part of evolving on every level. IT just needs to grow up with us through all this.

"So all this alien, reptilian, controlling elite, conspiracy theory stuff, fears and concepts, all stem from our amazingly imaginative collective hive mind. Collective psychology. So the more of you I can explain this to, and show, the more we will collectively grow up. But remember that collective imagination is important in itself; it's when it becomes a problem to us as individuals that it needs to be resolved.

"So if you do get abducted by little aliens that look like the ones out of *Close Encounters*, or something from the 1950's comics, just remember to ask to see their feet first, and refuse to go to any planet that doesn't have decent shoe shops! Which of course is where women have got it right.

"The trouble is - the more imaginative we get as people, the more sophisticated and contrived and dimensionally adaptive, the spiritual, or collective subconscious programming becomes.

"It is, at the same time, keeping and using inherent historic elements to reinforce it too. It's like with any child's imagination, but then that is healthy, it is what is needed, but only if it's used in the right way - *con*structive rather than *de*structive.

"It's just an ongoing game, but one that needs to stay directionally positive, and with joint benefits. You could say to me now that I was making all of this up, that it is just another level of conspiracy, and then we could go on to infinity.

"However at some point you have to believe me, understand what I am saying. That only comes with evidence, logic, and cause and effect on us all.

Which I have, and you can test me if you like."

He seemed to get quite serious at that point, his jovial nature seemed to disappear as if he were remembering something he had been through, he checked himself, and his smile returned again.

The two men were still eyeing the lizard man nervously. It still looked very solid and real to them and the fear in their hearts would not go away.

It looked to them as if it would suddenly jump into life and leap at them with its teeth bared. Sam saw them and closed his eyes. The lizard man apparition vanished into the mist.

"You see," he said "you just need to see it like a program function within a collective system - one that has been imagined, or jointly created. In some cases they may be errors, like viruses, Trojans, bad programming that has developed, but in some cases they may be 'real'. We have worked very hard to be able to perceive 'reality'. Eventually with testing and validation, the bugs, or defective programs, are removed or side-lined, and we are just left with what we perceive to be real. We have been doing all of that for millions of years.

"These things though are only treated as bugs if they are a problem, causing harm, or something that isn't doing what it is supposed to do. In most cases though, there isn't that much quality assurance and testing going on, and a lot of these things get shipped and sold to the customer as 'features'."

There was a loud noise from further over on the plateau, and a few moments later one of the groups started arguing with another over something. It seemed to relate to what had just happened, or to what Sam had done.

There was a difference of opinion over something, or stress between the individuals involved. Sam excused himself, and walked several yards over to them and shouted to them "Can you keep it down over there? It's all fine - it's sorted now!" And then a few moments later he wandered back.

"Right" he said. "Let's walk down the mountain a bit. I want to show you something." He gestured to the woman to stay where she was. "I will be back in twenty minutes" he said. From her look she understood what he was going to do, but her facial expression indicated that it would be more like twice that estimate. An opinion she had refined with practice.

The three men walked over to the other edge of the plateau and then down the slopes again, along the same winding path they had come up.

They walked down for about twenty minutes and then stepped off the rocky path and out over into an open rocky sloped area. Below them, milling around, were several wizened looking people wandering around a little further down looking lost and confused.

"Right. You see this line here?" He asked, and pointed to the ground at a dark line that went around the mountain.

"I want you," he said to the Biologist "to stay this upper side of it. And you…" he looked at the Priest, "come with me." He stepped down over the line, and stood facing down the hill towards the people below, with his back to the Biologist. The Priest followed him and did the same.

"OK. The line behind us is the line of current thinking, the forefront of conventional understanding. Where we are now is an area of recognised general understanding. Those people down there below are there to keep you this side of the line, they are there to help you, get you back to 'normality', keep you in control.

"This line behind us is the extent of their understanding. They are very, very clever. They have to be - that's their job. They learn and adapt and share knowledge, and anyone who comes as close to the line as we are, they learn from, and adapt to, understand, and assist back down the hill.

"You could call them psychologists, doctors, scientists, philosophers, spiritual healers. Don't get me wrong, these people are doing good things, they mean well and they are important, especially if you need their help. They are part of a system, a system that should be working.

"Now turn around" he said, and they did. The Biologist was now four yards away up the hill, and so was the line, with little bits of grass growing in-between. "How did that happen?" questioned the Priest.

"Ahh" said Sam. "As I said, it moves, it evolves like everything else. As the mountain grows so does that line. You can only keep ahead if you stay the other side of the line all the time. You also need to be always looking up, not looking down.

"If you look for answers in this area you will find lots of them, all with complex academic backup, and it's getting more sophisticated all the time, and makes the mountain grow. When you are on this side you are in amongst individual theories, ideas, understanding, and individual knowledge. Which is constantly growing, and if you stand still it will grow around you.

"But stand the other side of the line, think and do your 'job', and wait for a while, and you will see it all developing below you. But it doesn't seem quite right; it doesn't fit together or make sense in relation to what is on the top of the mountain.

"It is as if something is generally stopping anyone working it all out or getting past the line, making it more and more complex and sophisticated all the time to do so. Stopping people seeing or getting past the line who aren't 'working'.

"That's the whole point. But if you are above the line, 'working', it feels like it is following you, tracking you, coming up with ideas that shadow you, usually after a couple of weeks, the 'ahh yes, didn't you know?' and 'we knew that already' effect, which is just something you have to get used to, it's just covering itself. It's annoying but you get used to it. You just have to accept it, and do your job, and allow the knowledge to come up to you."

They both now walked up the hill to re-join the Biologist. The effort required to do it was a lot harder to the Priest than he had imagined it should be.

"It's a controlling thing" said Sam. "It is now so complex that it puts people off. That's part of the original mechanism - to stop people working out what is really going on, otherwise it wouldn't originally have worked. But then that's what we do. We always make something complicated out of something that is really very simple. That's what our job is, and we are very good at it - as long as it does its part, and plays fair, which of course it never does!"

As they walked back up to the top of the mountain again, along the path, the two men walked about five paces behind Sam discussing many things, trying to see how the other felt about the situation.

The Priest whispered to the Biologist "Is it me or does he look a bit like that guy out of *The Matrix*?"

"No," said the Biologist "I don't think he does."

While on their way up the two men stopped briefly by a couple of the large rabbit holes. "Just exactly what are these for?" called the Biologist up to Sam. "Well," said Sam stopping, "they represent someone's spiritual journey or perspective, an adventure and exploration into 'Wonderland'. The rabbit holes represent the different religions and spiritual belief system. These 'Alice's journeys into Wonderland' have been created over time by ideas of individuals, and then reinforced and dug deeper by others, sometimes as a result of schizophrenia, and or mind altering drugs. They are interpretations of something in such a way that made sense to them at the time, and also at that point in history. It's all very interesting, but not something I have got time to go into detail with you at the moment."

He carried on walking up and talking at the same time, but it was hard to hear what he was saying as the air was so thin.

"Some of the holes," he went on "become very attractive and interesting to other people, and they venture down them themselves. They then add and refine what is there. Before long it becomes habitually sacred, and religiously well-trodden, and modified in some cases to suit needs as time goes on.

"Nothing wrong with that of course, it brings people together for something to talk about, which is good. There are quite a lot to choose from, with pretty much the same sort of theme if you look at them objectively, with the newer ones being based on ideas from older ones in most cases.

"You may find one that works for you or that meets your needs and that's fine. They get more sophisticated as you go higher up the mountain, and the subjects or context become more diverse. But then you know all this anyway.

"In actual fact the whole thing is perfectly simple, as are most things when you understand them. Yet at the same time it's mind numbingly complicated, sophisticated, and it is changing all the time - you only have to introduce non-natural elements into a process like that though, say with drugs and toxic chemicals into people, and it has a dramatic effect on the collective mind.

"Which is not good" and he shook his head.

"Key thing is to find someone who has been down lots of other rabbit holes before you, and has sampled what is there; get their advice and that will save you a lot of time. Use them as sorts of stepping stones, and go into the rabbit holes with an open mind, and treat them as learning experiences rather than just assuming it's all correct. I haven't been down any of them so can't really comment any more than that.

"But feel free to try them, or we can carry on to the top where it's cold, harsh, and hard work. Personally I think the nice warm burrows look tempting don't you?

"I had a go at making one myself but it wasn't very good, too boring, I don't have the flair for it, especially when I see through everything. I was trying to make it a bit more interesting and appealing, but at the moment it just goes in from the side and appears out on the top here - sort of 'light at the end of the tunnel thing'!"

He laughed, and then looked a bit sad. "Well, to tell you the truth, the ceiling collapsed at one point and it became more of a 'feature'. I thought about having a sign outside of it with a few tempting adverts but I didn't get very far."

They all climbed back onto the plateau again and they gathered in a small circle. "OK," said Sam "I am going to take you somewhere else in your minds now. We won't actually move from here, it's just the terrain that will change, and you will see things differently again via another analogy.

"In this instance it is important that you keep close, so don't go wandering off or doing anything I don't tell you to."

He closed his eyes and concentrated and everything around the four of them disappeared, vanishing into a black void, as if someone had turned all the lights off on the stage.

CHAPTER 16 - THE COLONY

After a minute, the endless blackness was replaced with faint grey glows on the ground around them. A slowly emerging scene on a stage, gradually being lit by lights fading in, which highlighted a dry, sandy and undulating baked earth landscape.

It was the sunlight of first dawn, spreading over a badly constructed film set. There were brown earth mounds of varying heights all around them as far as the eye could see. As the light grew they spread way off into the far distance.

There was now a bright, warm sun up in the dark blue, cloudless sky. The vegetation was quite sparse and consisted of rough, light brown grass patches, with areas of sand and rocks, but in no particular logical order.

There were the odd little animals here and there, scurrying about, in and out of holes. It was the terrain of an African savannah, but with too many oddly sized and badly made hills around. They were all of varying heights, with much larger hills in the distance, all of which seemed to have been produced in a hurry, like a Hollywood film set created for effect by amateurs who hadn't had enough time available and had worked with a very low budget.

Even the few bushes that were around had just been 'placed' in the ground in odd locations, and some of the branches looked as though they had been stuck on with the wrong sort of glue.

Way off in the distance they could now make out many thousands of human sized ants, dashing about all over the landscape, busy working, socialising.

Some were collecting food and vegetation while others were involved in arguments or were fighting. They all seemed to be acting out duties or scenarios, like they were extras as part of some movie scene, rather than being actual real ants.

Some moved stones and dug in the ground, others gathered and collected imaginary 'things', and some built mounds of different 'stuff'. Quite a lot of them seemed to be standing around waiting for something, or looking busy, while others were directing other ants or standing guard.

It soon became obvious to the Priest and the Biologist that they were seeing humanity again portrayed as many groups of ants in one giant colony made up of lots of hills. Large organisations of people were defined as ant mounds, countries or civilisations as groups of hills, which themselves were made up of many mounds, and the world was the whole thing, whatever that was.

Different personalities and groups and attitudes all seemed to be reflected in what they saw going on; a low budget movie, with millions of extras. However it was certainly not one that you would pay to view, or want to watch for very long.

The Priest looked at the Biologist, and raised the corner of his lip and his eyebrows questioningly. The Biologist didn't say anything but he looked fairly bewildered.

"So," said Sam, looking smug "just to put you in the picture - we are now in a gigantic rectangular glass cabinet or case. It is thousands of miles across, with layer upon layer of soil, sand and stuff built up underneath us like a stratum of layers. You know, sort of like the ones you see in the natural history museums, where you can see the ants from the top and from the sides to see what is going on inside.

"The layers of soil underneath depict the ants' individual consciousness, or collective psyche structures, and groups or organisations of countries, cultures and so on, where things have built up over time in layers. This is just the human perspective though. There are no other animals or plants here to integrate with, and this is just up to the collective subconscious level, there are no conscious elements here, I just want to keep it simple.

"Can everyone see that picture in their mind?" asked Sam. The Biologist and the Priest still looked confused but nodded anyway.

"Good, OK then," he continued enthusiastically "if you have ever seen one of those natural history documentaries on ants, it's quite amazing to see how they operate as a team, all reacting at the same time, all with their jobs and responsibilities; a super-organism, all operating efficiently, communicating via some invisible bond or field, and in many other ways with other message systems such as smell and touch.

"They all do what they are supposed to do efficiently without being told, and within some well-defined structure or mechanism that just works, within their evolutionary niche. They all seem to know exactly what is going on, and what needs to happen, what the nest or the colony needs, and when. Somehow the decisions get made, it's all amazing to see isn't it?"

Sam paused for a moment for them to take in the scene, and then continued.

"It's very obvious when you watch the large armies of ants in Africa, masses of them, it's just amazing, put them under pressure and it reacts instantly, with its fine-tuned evolutionary programming. I suppose it's because it's so competitive in the jungle that they have to be smart, using any communication mechanisms and tricks available to them.

"Ask yourselves how they manage to swarm miles apart at the same time, synchronised on given days, all sorts of odd unexplainable behaviour? Evolution makes them that way, winners and losers, supply and demand, it's all fairly simple really, and yet brutal and all part of nature.

"Of course the last thing you want to do is wander up to the largest army ant colony and start hitting it with a stick, or kicking it. Mind you, you will get to understand things, and what the priorities are in life, pretty damn quickly" he laughed. The Priest still looked more than a little perplexed, but not as much as the Biologist, especially as Sam was starting to walk up and down like some well-practiced TV documentary presenter.

"So," said Sam "all the ants basically do whatever they can; make the most of what they have, what they know, and what is available to them, they work together to survive. Generally speaking they all want to do good and do their bit; to do what they feel is right, their roles, or what they can get away with, where they can, for themselves. They look after themselves primarily, and then their groups, and then the colony as a whole unless priorities are changed. So there is a balance between the needs of the individual ant, and the needs of their hill, or colony.

"When the needs of the colony are important, they are prioritised to take precedence over that of the individual ant or the group, according to their roles. Say if they are hungry, or a new job needs to be done at that time of year, it's a sort of symbiotic relationship thing, with the colony and the ant living and coexisting in parallel, with the needs of the colony balanced with the needs of the ant to achieve collective survival.

"In effect then, the 'successful' ant here," and he pointed to one of the 'extras' that happened to be walking past not so coincidentally, "allows itself, through natural selection, to be sort of hypnotised, or influenced, and informed by the colony to do what the colony wants or needs, but this can be overridden by the needs of the ant if need be. That also applies the other way around depending on priorities and urgency.

"It's all to do with shared benefits and nature; one being able to protect and influence the other, you don't want ants just wandering off and doing their own thing – it's hazardous and inefficient for both the colony and the ant. They may start eating the food, killing the eggs or confusing other ants, leaving the colony or hill or individual nest open to attack. So the colony or hill or nest is there to take care of the ants, they have a shared interest existing within their ecological evolutionary compartment.

"The point being that they are just ants, little insects with limited brain power. Unlike us of course, ants don't evolve any more. They have established themselves in an evolutionary niche, a safe cul-de-sac, in a permanent gap in the marketplace of life. We, on the other hand, have always had to move forward, adapt, survive, evolve, and outwit. Be at the front, especially in the supermarket.

"Ultimately though," he said, raising his voice slightly, "in this instance where the ants are representing people, it's not in the ant's long term interest to work out what is going on, or to know what is collectively making the decisions, so the process itself is self-evolving, with the knowledge and intelligence of the ants increasing and the colony becoming ever smarter, devious, spontaneous, clever, adaptive, and sophisticated. It can also be fairly ruthless, feral, and unforgiving - which is what it is supposed to be. That's what nature is all about, to survive, and to grow into what is available if you can.

"You can really only 'see' these effects when you get groups of these people-ants together and step back and take a new perspective on what is going on. Like an individual wolf behaving very differently when it is with a pack than when it is lone. When it's with the pack it acts as part of the pack, and reacts with it; it takes on its persona and group psyche.

"The same thing occurs when you join a club or a company or move into another country, and when you are born into the world, you become part of that pack or hive and integrate with it in many ways, fitting in, being part of a super-organism or macro organisation, being programmed by IT.

"You start to behave and react in the same way as others; all according to your genes, your surroundings, the culture et cetera. Quite often this happens without you even realising what is going on or the extent to which it happens. Some people change very quickly, they are very empathic and attuned - others not so.

"You can also see this working with things like collective grief with disasters or deaths of famous individuals, fears and other emotions at group events. It is more obvious when put under pressure - the group bonds together to fight in subtle ways as with wars.

"Even when you think you aren't thinking of anything the brain is working flat out, daydreaming off in a different world, using up more energy than your heart. Ever wondered why that is? What 'processing work' is going on? What is it doing, even when you are asleep? In fact it's actually busier when you aren't using it yourself for something 'useful' - like what to eat for dinner. Ever thought why your brain is that shape, with two sides?"

Sam started to walk and the two men followed him with the woman behind. She also seemed to be quite interested in the environment, and what had been created, but more from what was wrong or didn't look right, and she would occasionally shake her head when seeing something that was obviously in the wrong place or context, or in many cases just falling apart.

"That hive mind or herding process," Sam went on "evolves and continues to evolve to where we are today. It has become highly complex, adaptive, with all sorts of feedback, control, communication and interworking; like a giant biological computer or machine with complex inter-relationships and systems and sub-functions. It develops itself as required over time, evolving from nothing but a set of basic rules and chance opportunities into whatever it can, in whatever is available."

He stopped and looked upwards, thinking.

"So," he turned to the Priest "just imagine that, Once upon a time… Adam and Eve returned to Paradise and the Garden of Eden, to find that it had become total chaos. Many of the trees and animals and birds were gone, there was rubbish everywhere, and the air was filled with smoke and fumes.

"In fact it was rapidly starting to look like the real world with buildings and streets and places they seem to recognise, and supermarkets full of apples.

"Who had done this?" they thought, "And how had it been allowed to happen?"

"They wandered around and after a few hours there came a great booming voice, and they hid in fear amongst the remaining trees, and God said to Adam 'What art thou doing here? You have been forbidden to return here.' And Adam said to God 'Shouldn't thou knowest that already, being who thou art?'

"There was a long pause 'OK,' said God 'err, yes that is true, but I was simply asking the question to get you to think about your answer.' 'No you weren't…' said Adam 'and why didn't you just stop me returning, or even stop me thinking about it, being who thou artest? In fact why do we even need to be having this conversation?'

The voice boomed again directed now at Eve. 'And you woman…' the voice said condescendingly, 'did I not curse you last time and made your pains in childbearing very severe? Dost thou wish me to curse you again?'

"There was a long deafening silence ….

'Umm…' said Adam tentatively 'I don't think you really wanted to say that did you?' But it was too late. An ensuing fury emanated from Eve including the words 'vindictive', 'spiteful', 'vengeful', 'immature', 'sexist', 'chauvinistic' and "anaesthetic', along with a lot of other colourful words that God had never heard before. Eve had evolved quite a lot since she had left; she wasn't the same woman. And God, in all his omniscience, clearly didn't see that one coming. Adam liked the new Eve much more these days. Stepping back now he was seeing God from a whole new perspective."

The Biologist sniggered, but the Priest was obviously not seeing the funny side of it.

"And so," said Sam continuing "it went very quiet after that, and they both set about tidying everything up and living good healthy lives, and bringing Paradise back to life as they remembered it, and existing in harmony with it in the hope that in doing so in their dream that it would eventually become so in reality in the physical world. They realised that they didn't need all the things they thought they did to make them happy - it was all here already.

"What was there in the first place was all they needed, and they weren't so curious any more. In fact it was the driven search for knowledge that had caused all of the problems, the chaotic pursuit of knowledge was the paradise lost, and they no longer cared why this thought had happened in the first place, this time they would just ignore the snake. They would resist the temptation of the apple. However all of this only ever happens in fairy tales."

The Priest still looked very confused, but he didn't say anything and let Sam carry on.

"I am sure, out there in the cosmos, that there will be some alien race that has evolved perfectly and created an ideal, harmonious world with its own god, and that they are all happy living in synchronicity, harmony, understanding and bliss. But don't worry, I am sure in a few thousand years we will eventually stumble across them on our travels, and land on their world. Meet with them, learn from them, and understand them.

"Then just like in all the films we will end up buggering that world up too. But hey, who needs perfect aliens, with a perfect *Stepford Wives* world, and perfect 'Borg-like' minds, where's the fun in that? Anyway, I bet they wouldn't have a sense of humour."

He then paused for another polite round of laughter, or knowing nods, that never came.

"Anyway," he continued "so we have been keeping ourselves busy competing against ourselves for too long, which has made us individually very competitive, but collectively we are just a metaphysical dodo living on an island, stupid looking, with no sharp teeth, overweight, and wings too short to even hold an interplanetary machine gun.

"Trouble is, if anything else comes it won't be men on a sailing ship with pet dogs, it will be some high form of alien predator, with their armada of massive space ships; not flying saucers, but curiously shaped like more giant steaming kettles.

"Better evolution, that's what we need.

"However this collective evolution thing is all OK up to a point, while everything is on autopilot, in 'subconscious animal mode', but when the subconscious thoughts and mechanisms are no longer enough, it becomes conscious of itself to some degree and makes changes in its own right that it thinks it needs to, like a baby.

"That's when things get a bit complicated, and cause all sorts of problems, confusion, feedback, and stress. As with the ants here they just can't make sense of what is going on and why things are happening, and vice versa.

"It's especially hard because IT can't physically 'see' itself, and doesn't know what it is. IT doesn't know what it is doing, how it works, and what effect it is having on its own body. IT is using its imagination and is building up perceptions, dreams, out of body rationalised virtual-scapes with remote viewing features, which don't make much sense from its own perspective.

"Equally you may know how to look after your own body, but IT doesn't really know what IT's doing for you and why. With nobody telling IT what to do, how to look after IT-self, and so IT gets very confused.

"There are quite a lot of differences, as you can imagine, between a colony and an ant; some quite surprising ones, but I won't go into that now."

They were walking at quite a pace now, but despite the terrain and the sun they were all quite cool and not out of breath at all. Clearly some of the personal reality aspects had been left off the list as well.

"We used to be able to communicate with IT subconsciously a long time ago, but we seem to have trouble now, or we have forgotten how to. I suppose it's because it's all so vast and complex now and something we have evolved away from in favour of other individual needs rather than collective ones. It's a priority thing.

"You could also argue that we should just not get involved, and let IT do its thing, but that doesn't seem to be right from what I have seen. Besides, it's actually desperately trying to be understood, and with nobody able to hear it or perceive IT from 'ITs' perspective at the conscious level, it is panicking. All the while we are just pandering to its subconscious fears and drives as before, and getting the collective stress reflected in our day to day illogical, mad lives."

He stopped and turned to the two men, obviously reaching the point he was aiming for.

"Anyway, getting back to where we are, just remember we are now part of this ant colony. We are involved with it in real time, and it will interact with you, so please don't touch anything or talk to anyone. As you are not integrated, any small changes you make can have dramatic effect. You are able to see things the rest of the ants can't, and so you have a global, or in this case, rectangular, glass cabinet perspective. We should be ignored for the most part but I am just saying, in case you were thinking of suing me later."

He turned again and started to walk along the sandy ground with his hands crossed behind his back, and they followed him. The two men saw him change for a moment into the form of an ant. However they also noticed that he was still walking on two legs, which looked a bit odd as all the other ants were walking on six legs. However they didn't like to say anything, so they kept quiet.

"You see in a real ant colony," he went on "it is in an ants' interest to do what the colony wants, what the macro-organism needs. To do things like gather resources, fight, work and so on, and to make sense of its surroundings, to work out what it needs, to figure out what is a threat and what isn't, and to store collective memory.

"If it didn't, the colony wouldn't survive or grow, so it works both ways. Success and strength comes from working as a team, a pack, a hive, a company, a country along with refining methods, interworking, communication, and natural selection. They have to store knowledge or information collectively, and learn from it all.

"An ant that isn't able to fit in with the colony isn't useful, it's an anomaly, a rebel, seen by the colony as 'not normal', one that can't be influenced to do what the colony wants. It becomes excluded, shunned, supressed, attacked even.

"It isn't allowed to interact, so it just wanders off or gets attacked by elements of the colony, or is side-lined somewhere. Equally, nests that have too many of this type of ant in them become less efficient and so are less likely to survive, and don't go on to produce more nests.

"That's all right and OK up to a point; that's how it has to work for the colony, and for its individuals, to survive and to thrive and evolve or stay as ants in a natural niche. But take it up several levels to where we are now, and that doesn't work for many reasons - its' open to abuse and exploitation by the individuals for one thing. So the process itself needs to evolve, to be more sophisticated as the colony becomes more and more conscious, intelligent, or aware at the next level, and not lagging.

"It's an on-going coexisting evolutionary process of trial and error, give and take. See it as an infinite number of ants trying to create the complete works of Shakespeare, unfortunately in our case we seem to be heading more towards the complete works of Monty Python. But hey that's entertainment for you, and that's what the public wants, which of course is the only important thing. After all what else is there ???"

Sam seemed to be quite enjoying himself now and was beginning to relax. They walked over to one of the hills whereupon a large, aggressive looking, ant came up to them and spread its large pincers wide.

The woman seemed to anticipate this. She moved to block it and started talking to it. Within a moment or so it suddenly looked confused, as though it was imagining something else going on, and no longer seemed to be aware of them, and moved away.

"Just to remind you. You are perfectly safe as long as you stay with us. All the ants here see you as other ants, so you are not in any danger, as long as you look like an ant, smell like an ant and think like an ant, but try not to do anything odd or different.

"I can assure you though that if you were seen as a real 'alien non-ant' you would know about it damn quick, and the whole colony attitude would change in seconds, and not in a good way. It's always looking for something to practise on too - it's just an historical inheritance thing. Just go for a walk in the African jungle in bare feet for a while, or even in the Australian bush, and you will get the idea quite quickly.

"The way it all works is based mostly on history, animalistic behaviour, nature's way, supply and demand, cause and effect, that sort of thing. The smaller hills learn to organise themselves well, and some of the larger hills, or countries, can develop to operate well in the scheme of things. It's just winners and losers, and what works, and what doesn't.

"Over time it has all been built up as ants have come and gone, and developed and evolved, adding here, refining and reinforcing there, so they have created more and more layers, bigger mounds, and changed the shape of the landscape. Each ant has their own patch of land and burrow and what they stand on is made up of layer upon layer of old dead ants, workings, rubbish, genes and various historical programming bits.

"They are all made up of lots of things; biological, physical, mental, understanding; past lives if you like to put it that way, as are the things around them everywhere. They are also an equal part of the things they have done during their lives themselves and of what is around them environmentally.

"Just remember nature isn't perfect. That's how we are here, and why we are the way we are.

"So when you look at an ant here, you will see that it is a conscious person that is standing on a cross section that makes up their own consciousness and sub-consciousness, all the way down to the bottom bedrock with all the associated collective parts of self, ego, psyche, and everything in-between - your programming.

"It's what makes *you*, mentally and physically, and also what has gone into the making of you from a collective point of view. That includes what you have inherited physically from your parent genes, DNA, nature, nurture, upbringing, where you have been, who you have met and what you have inherited culturally and spiritually, or historically, and from others as you grow up and live around them.

"It's all like biological programming." Sam paused "I was never was much good at using the right words, so I hope you get what I am trying to say."

He paused but again there was just silence.

"Anyway, some ants just live all their time on the surface with maybe a small hole to go to sleep and dream in at night, with no real interest or idea of what they are made up from underneath and why. This is fine, just taking the easiest path, and enjoying life as best they can, which is what the colony expects them to do up to a point. That's how it supposed to be, they are doing what you are supposed to do, enjoying life and working. Everything else is done by the colony, or should be.

"From an ants' perspective you don't see all the things going on underneath while you are moving about above, you just see your conscious top level bits, and a few actions and feelings originating from your own subconscious - instincts and so on.

"This is fine, besides it can be a bit of a mental shock to see your own cross section laid bare all the way into the collective parts, they just don't make any sense, why should they? From the top it all seems quite simple, which is what we collectively have worked hard to create, with lots of nice things to keep everyone occupied and safe and interested.

"There is so much to do and see at the top; lots of stimulation, entertainment, work, a plastic environment and artificial surroundings. As an ant why would you bother spending time thinking about what is under your feet, with all that going on around you? Just go for the simple, busy, easy life; stockpile your food, resources, and possessions around you in case of a bad winter, you know just the basic essentials to get by, no need to get greedy after all!

"When you go down into your ant burrow at night and dream, you go below your conscious layer into your subconscious and dream - that's all, and again that's all fine. Information comes up, you get things sorted out in your head, told what's right and wrong, and that's all OK."

"Umm…" said the Biologist, "I have read quite a lot about psychology, and all this looks very 'Jungian' to me, you know with the layers and conscious psyche structures?" "Well yes," said Sam "I guess it probably is, but you must remember that IT gets its ideas from what we imagine and form in our minds, so it must get its ideas from somewhere on what it is and how it is meant to be."

"Yes but isn't this allegory a bit simplistic?" interrupted the Biologist again "Shouldn't it be a bit more sophisticated if you are going to represent all of humanity."

"Yes, and no," said Sam "it needs to be as simplistic as possible because that is how the ant colony sees itself, or should I say feels itself. It doesn't see itself as we see it, or in the context of what I am going to show you in a bit.

"The concept doesn't need to be complicated. It is all very simple really. We are the ones that have made it complicated, like we do with everything. We have made things that way for ourselves, which is what we do; it's our nature, but again that's part of what we are, and what it's all about.

"Look," he said again "I am trying to keep this simple here just to get a point across, you have to start somewhere when you are trying to describe something so mind numbingly complex. I can make it spherical with real people buildings, history and so on if you like, but then I would have to explain everything in one go which would be impossible.

"The more and more you go into it, the more complex it would get, the more things I would have to add in and explain until it was too complicated and difficult to see. Again, odd that isn't it?

"Take for example that tree over there; let's call it the 'Flu

Tree' and let's assume that all the nuts on it are viruses. If you get a hammer and you break all the nuts you can, let's call it an antibiotic hammer, and you have to leave all the ones you don't manage to break to carry on growing.

"Eventually you will end up with a wood full of trees with huge, very hard to crack, nuts. You will also have a pile of useless, ever more expensive, hammers, along with lots of hammer manufacturers.

"If we had just learnt from the squirrels in the first place there would be no problem, and we wouldn't be putting ourselves under so much stress. Conversely, we would still be living in the woods like squirrels. If you waited a while, you would eventually see the hammer factories close down and the factories would be used by weed killer producers. But sadly we don't have time to see all of that."

Both men looked relieved

"You see, as I said, I am trying to keep it simple to explain and show you what is going on. I don't want to go into technical details, or things like how the collective knowledge database works, the communications mechanisms, the memory, and energy flow or we would just end up in too much detail and look more like the real world, and you wouldn't be able to 'see' anything, not even the blindingly obvious.

"Those two books you are carrying describe part of it, but it's only when you put it all together that it makes sense. Only then do you see the whole picture, a bit like a jigsaw?

"Even though it 'knows' everything that we do, because of its size and perspective things happen slower in relative terms, and it 'grows up' much slower than we do. The colony will evolve with the ants over time as they learn to change, and make mistakes, as we do when we grow and develop, but only if it has to, or able.

"Everyone's soil profile is different, and that goes for hills or organisational groups of people too, in how they are built up, depending on many factors. Equally they are also very similar in many other ways. So don't try to look for meaning in other people's interpretation or perspective, not even mine. As the saying goes, 'Know thyself'.

"Try and understand what has gone into your profile, and what makes it up so that you can appreciate and understand yourself, and therefore other people's - even the stupid, mindless, lazy ones." He smiled. "Remember the colony moves in 'mysterious ways' and it is not for us to question it for a moment, Oh No, absolutely not! It's a perfect masterpiece of engineering, totally infallible, completely unsinkable."

Then something seemed to click in the Biologist's mind and several concepts suddenly dawned on him. He wasn't able to bring himself to say anything, but his eyes were explanation enough. He had suddenly 'got it'.

"So you see, when the countries and cultures and so on have evolved their own hills and built up their own layer structures, they have then developed and taken on their own childlike identities, how they behave and react in a childish manner to other hills et cetera.

"However there is nothing to stop ants moving between them, sharing their collective subconscious perception around and refining and exchanging things. Occasionally you may get the odd fight or war breaking out between hills to do with territory, or resources, or views on the best way to build things, but that's all part of learning and evolving, seeing what works, what is successful, and what isn't. All that sort of thing is necessary, if not harsh and brutal at times.

"Some smarter ants have got more of an idea of what is going on in relation to the collective subconscious, and use its own tricks to get other ants to do their work for them, and gather lots of resources together. Some of them are just doing what comes naturally to them; their jobs or roles. 'Born leaders' for example - they aren't aware of the abilities they have, and are confused as to why everyone can't do what they do, but ultimately they are the ones being used by the colony; it learns from them, becomes smarter, more sophisticated.

"Then closing up the loopholes, the tricks they play to get what they want, so they in turn have to evolve, as do the people they gather around them. The ones that don't evolve get left behind.

"But that only works to a point, and mistakes get made by IT, and these overall errors, or flaws, become more obvious as time goes on. Even the hierarchies get broken down. But in a predator or competition free environment that the collective mind is in, you end up with everything being stretched and in a big mess.

"It leaves a lot of ants in confusion, and some achieving nothing at all, or worse, just becoming a burden to the rest. Without that top-level competitive drive everything below just makes itself busy, like a government defence organisation without any prospect of a war. There is no overall direction or purpose. So it just tries to look busy."

Just then, a large group of ants came over a small hill to their right and swarmed across the road in front of them. "For Queen and Country" shouted one of them at the front, and waved one of his legs in the air, "Hill! You idiot" corrected one of the ants further back.

"For Queen and Hill" shouted the front ant again, as they all stampeded off into the distance, followed by a few hesitant ones, and several that were just curious and were just going along to see what was happening.

"Oh that was bloody subtle" said Sam, brushing the dust off his clothes. "You see," he continued after a few moments "we are affected all the time by a whole range of suggestions and traits, habits and collective hypnotic drives. Most of the time we don't notice these things happening, we are programmed not to see, and it is only easier to spot these effects when large groups of people are put under pressure or stress or grief together at the same time.

"This is, for the most part, for our individual and collective benefit; it's nature at work, doing what it does, and what has worked or succeeded up until now, and up to a certain point."

He turned to the Biologist

"As you know, we make different types of decisions with different parts of our brain. The System 1 part, which is the fast, responsive, animalistic, reflexive, automatic, and influenced heavily by the collective - and the System 2 part, which is slower, more logical, rational, deliberate, and lazy."

"Yes" said the Biologist "I know all about that."

"Ahh, but have you ever thought about the 'Why' part? Why is it that way, and why would it need to be?" asked Sam. "Our collective mind is more of a System 1 type brain, and we need to help it evolve, drive it and force it to become more System 2; to make more rational and logical decisions. But then it is so hard these days to get time to stop and think about these things, to have time to work it out, anyone would think there is a system or something controlling you."

The Biologist just stared at him, unblinking as, if someone had just switched a light on in his brain.

Sam carried on with his lecture.

"When you have predators chasing you in a 'Dog Eat Dog' world, this is what keeps you and your friends alive and ahead. Unfortunately though, if you are the only dog left, you would just end up a fat, lazy fleabag that barks at the moon.

"With no anteater to keep the colony in check, to refine it, to force it to evolve against it - it just drags on, not having to adapt. It is just driven internally by gathering, knowledge, resources, and the urge to grow unless something comes along and forces it to evolve and adapt. The macro-organism, its direction for change, is very vague."

Another ant came up behind them and tried to push past. "Excuse me please, I am in a rush!" she said rudely "I must get to the supermarket before it closes." Then she stopped and looked at Sam. "Oh *Hi!*" she said in a flirty tone, totally ignoring the others. There was a long silence, she then looked around at the rest of the group, and seemed confused for a moment and then turned and headed off again.

The Priest and the Biologist looked at each other unsure if they were meant to have understood or been shown something from what had happened, but both looked blank, and turned back, to look at Sam and allow the lecture to continue.

"Sorry," said Sam "not sure what that was about. Anyway, so the whole thing isn't a conspiracy as such - it's just nature, a thing we do, unless you could describe the whole thing as a conspiracy, all of our own making.

"But do not be fooled into thinking that this collective mind ever lies dormant or asleep. It is active all the time. It is highly sophisticated, adaptive, subtle, directing, outsmarting, learning, reinforcing thing with natural traits and tendencies. You just have to be able to see it influencing us all the time, and see around its disguises and camouflage.

"It's what has got us to where we are, good or bad, and it's probably something we should work with all the time, rather than ignore. If natural history is anything to go by, it should be an advantage we have and may need for the future. It just needs management, like everything else.

"So there are a lot of driving forces, emotional incentives. We all have jobs or roles, we all want things, we all want to evolve and learn and so on. Male or female, we are all different, just trying to get on and do the best we can with what we have. Like that one over there..."

He pointed and waved at an ant, which waved back at him. "He works hard, does his job, he helps people who need it, and he uses his skills and knowledge as best he can. If ants have a problem they go to him because they think he can help, and he works with them to help them fix the problem in whatever ways they can relate to, and with the toolset he uses.

"You could say he was sort of like an Agony Ant!"

Sam started laughing, but stopped quickly after he realised that that nobody else was joining in.

"It's also important to have a sense of humour about it all, it helps break down the communication barriers."

The Biologist and the Priest just looked at each other, confused still. "Anyway," Sam went on again "that's all background stuff - it's not really what I want to show you from all of this."

They were now standing on top of a small sandy hill with the sun beating down on the baked ground. The mound was quite bare and had no vegetation growing on it all, and all the other ants had disappeared inside. It was getting very hot now and they all felt quite uncomfortable.

Sam didn't seem to notice and carried on with his lecture again. "Anyway, getting back to the picture, if you were to come out to the side you would be able to clearly see the cross section through the glass wall, and that's where I will take you in a while. Some people are very keen to know what's down there, what it's all about, what it all looks like underneath and how it works, and of course IT needs to know too. Which is why collectively we get pushed into set directions at different times, and why the resources are allocated accordingly; it may be alchemy, chemistry, physics, technology, history, maths, psychology and so on.

"Anyway I'm talking too much, so I am going to do something now and I don't want you to be afraid - so stand back."

He gestured to the four of them to separate a few yards apart on the mound. A hole started to appear in the ground in-between the four of them. The Priest gasped in surprise, and the hole started to fill back in again.

"Hang on," said Sam.

He closed his eyes and several shovels appeared. "We will have to do the first bit manually - it makes it easier, a sort of buy-in thing." So they started to dig. "We just need to clear out most of the higher subconscious level until we are at the point where you are just about to fall asleep" instructed Sam.

They dug down, and down, and after a few minutes they reached some sort of strange band of soil. "This looks like it. Don't go any further or we will all pass out. Right shovels down and watch, and stand on the edge here, don't go any further."

They did as he said. A six foot wide hole started to appear again, and it dropped away, down and down and down like a mineshaft or deep well. Straight into pitch black nothingness.

"Don't worry," Sam said "one of the first program things you have built into you is a fear of falling so that you won't let yourself step in and fall.

"Right, this is a sort of 'Well of Enlightenment' thing, or 'well of your soul' concept which goes down through the layers of consciousness, down through your 'self'. If you look at the sides you will see that it's made up of lots of bands and levels.

As it goes down you may see quite a few things you don't like of yourself, and emotions, and lots of stuff tucked away in your psyche, and historical collective things, the archetypes, past all the scary stuff, confusing mystical emotional stuff, but also the comfy blankets and the reinforced mental crutches, into the collective subconscious and collective collated knowledge below.

"Carry on down past the symbols and primeval stuff to the bedrock and crystal gravel down in the dark where it's all the same. It's all the things that make you what you are - built up over time. But this is only an allegory or analogy remember - it's not quite as simple as all that in reality. It's why we are all different - we are all made up of different things, all making parts of a whole.

"However, it is important to not let people tell you what you will see. It will always be different from their perspective of what is there, and specific to you. It's your own 'take' on things, and based on your own life experience, and knowing your 'self'.

"The trouble too is that you may have other people's preconceived ideas down there to identify with already in the collective mind, which you latch onto as an explanation, and which is also a good way of stopping you getting any further.

"It's the overall process and understanding that's important, and you don't even need to start digging if you don't want to. If you are quite happy with everything on top, that's fine, you get enough coming up anyway, that's the whole point. Nobody should have to start digging down if it's all working fine, which of course it isn't.

"You can, if you like, dig little pipelines down, like test holes, down into the collective areas and get samples of information up, even send notes or questions down and get answers back, all sorts of clever tricks, but equally you can't assume that all the information is correct either, but it does give you information.

"Frankly though, it's a bit of a mess down there generally. You will encounter a lot of common, simple things that have been created by ants in the past that are just plain wrong, and then built on by others. There are also collective fears and natural and biological and animal interpretations all again built up through evolution in many ways.

"This is what is reflected on the surface in general, permeating upwards to be reflected in our everyday lives. IT gradually resolves these things for itself over time, with perceptive correction, science and learning and that sort of thing if it needs to.

However it all takes a long time, as with us as people getting over phobias and bad habits.

"However IT is finding it hard to move forward in many cases. I suppose 'old habits die hard', and IT doesn't have to change them if nothing is making it do so.

"IT also reflects order and control upwards, people's roles and responsibilities, as well as hierarchy, stovepipes for learning, and instincts and control mechanisms. Some ants, as I said, have learnt to exploit these mechanisms for their own benefit, they think they are smart, masters of what is going on in their hills or nests, controlling people through the collective subconscious.

"But ultimately IT adapts itself and learns from them too, gets around them, evolves, learns and eventually it closes all the loopholes and makes it harder for them to operate, which again has its problems. It's just nature at work, becoming smarter, but unfortunately it's not that smart, and it needs to grow up.

"There is no point trying to manipulate the collective mind via its subconscious now as you only end up with cause and effect issues, and more confusion, which is exactly what is going on now. You can only do things constructively and carefully, especially now that it has become self-aware and conscious. You just need to provide advice to help it in a managed way, as best you can, based on the knowledge and information and skills that you have learnt.

"Unfortunately, because in the past many of these 'enlightened' people weren't aware of what they were involved in, what they were doing, or had limited perception and knowledge, even ones with good intentions, they have left us with 'where we are today', and the whole process could have been much easier. But then I suppose that's nature for you, we are where we are, and we have to make the most of it, as always.

"That's what you get in nature without competition, predators or a guide with a mirror to give you a perspective of yourself collectively. Of course I am not any different, you just have to learn from the past, and do what you can with what you have available to you at the time, and let what you do evolve."

"So," said the Biologist as they looked down "let me see if I am getting this right. Is any of what I am seeing coming from my past lives?" "Well sort of yes, and no. Your consciousness, or your existence, is very complicated and made up of lots of things; physical impressions, biological, historical, collective, spiritual. It's not just contained or defined in the real physical world in the same way that a computer is not just hardware.

"We perceive with our senses - we see, touch, smell and feel the hardware so it is very difficult to describe the software in any relative terms, we can only describe it 'like' those things. The 'how' doesn't matter for the moment, I'm just trying to show you an idea, like a layer cake that makes you what you are.

"IT even makes it hard for me to describe it to you as you would expect, and everything in your mind will try and stop you from taking it in, and accepting it - that's all part of the programming too. You just have to try and work through it. It's just an evolutionary defence or protection mechanism, at the subconscious level, designed for self-preservation for both the collective colony, and the individual ant.

"In fact, if you were to write these words down, someone reading what I am saying would have real trouble comprehending or understanding it, or even making sense of it. They may have to read it several times to wade through the sort of hypnotic resistance effect; even if they were even able to read it in the first place without being distracted or blocked.

"As I said before, there is no conspiracy involved, unless you view the whole thing as one big conspiracy of all our making. It's just a natural process we need to overcome if we are all to evolve further, or we just remain as human ants, or some sort of fungus, or just a planetary virus from an outside perspective."

The Priest took a nervous look behind him. He seemed to be slightly less confident about where he was than a few moments before.

"So, as the hole goes down further, deeper into your 'self', you get to see all the collective elements on the way down, all the things that we share as groups and beliefs, traits, common fears, understandings, recognitions and so on. The further you go down the more basic it becomes right down to common symbols, then down into common, or collective, knowledge.

"Most people have felt or experienced something 'odd', even if it's just at the top levels, like synchronicity, but they usually either ignore it, or seek a comfortable explanation, or treatment, or just shrug it off, which is all fine. Some may be interested and try digging down further, but the further you go down the less accessible it is, and also less easy to comprehend or even describe or relate to in 'real' world logical or physical terms, like an ant trying to understand a real computer.

"Remember its context, and how it is represented and formed, is very much at odds with that at the top level conscious real world perspective. It is a correlation, a collated side-on picture, and of a different context and scope to your 'real' perspective altogether.

"Mind you, when you are down there at the lower levels and you leave your own 'self' behind, it all makes sense while you are there, and has a profound effect on you, and it may even stay with you like a reference point, or you may be able to bring the knowledge back with you, time and time again. You see things differently, but more importantly you are potentially able to integrate with the collective to some extent, and see the changes occurring.

"The important thing is that you need to keep a balance, and look after your 'self' too. There is no point in spending all your life meditating and contemplating down the bottom of a mineshaft, digging your way down as far as you can; you will end up with no 'self' above you, nothing to you as a person, and you will build nothing on top.

"But that's the key - you must have a 'self' too, not just a deep empty hole, otherwise your body will just be a collective device, a 'no self' that is no good to you and useless to IT, and you will end up just being a hermit with other people busily eating all your juniper bushes."

The Priest nodded, he had obviously got the significance of that reference.

"So…" said Sam starting to pace up and down now, "if you were to take an ant right away from the colony it would become disorientated and confused quite quickly without a clear role or something to be part of. It would also become a 'separate consciousness' to some extent a lone 'self', and perceive things quite differently, and may even look back at its old colony, as say from another planet or moon, and perceive it and itself very differently. In the same way as you would at the bottom of the shaft."

"I want to see!" cried the Priest. "Lower me down…" and he moved to the edge and got onto his knees.

"No. Stay where you are" said Sam firmly. "It's not safe. Besides you have to create *your own* hole - you can't use anyone else's, and I am not going down to pull you out of this one, you need something very special to get you out from that far down, and I'm not bloody doing it. That's why the layers are there to protect you and help you. Just remember down is bad - up is good.

"Also, please remember that lots of people have put a lot of work into building up those layers, and you must respect that. They have been doing the best they can with what they had and what they knew at the time, just as we are today, we must just learn from it.

"OK, quite a lot of it isn't the greatest construction work, and there is a lot of residual stuff that just gets copied and amplified until it's not needed, or forgotten, or evolved away, but it was all done with what people knew and believed at the time, which was right then, and you need to understand that fact, don't just dismiss it. You really need to appreciate it, otherwise you don't learn from it and you will just end up starting all over again, and duplicating effort. That's why history is important, as is understanding religions.

"So - there are lots of so called 'secrets' and 'hidden messages' all the way down to the bottom levels which, over time, people have used or created or manipulated.

"As an ant you can dig down yourself, and create holes and explore. There are even books about it and techniques. It's even developed a colour-coded cord system that guides you back to the surface through each layer, so it's quite safe to a point, like bungee jumping. It's like exploring your imagination- only this case it's everyone else's - in lots of ways.

"It's quite easy to get distracted, and to discover things that you don't like or get the wrong idea from, but at the end of the day it's all about what *you* need and what makes *you* happy. Go as far as you want, if it fills the gaps in your needs then that is just fine."

"So what is below that?" asked the Biologist. "Well, nothing. It gets more basic as you go down. It is just us after all, and what we came from - atoms, molecules, rules, cells, and so on - you know, all the things we are trying to see into, and understand.

"I suppose you could see the bottom levels as a field of harmonic energy flowing between everyone and feeding upwards, bringing life energy and nutrients up from the earth in layers. I don't want to push analogies too far though, but you get the idea?

"But if you can get down there you can sense things going on everywhere, to and fro, and you can put meaning to a lot of the strange things going on in physical world, and their context.

"You can even send messages around, like knocking on pipes in the basement, and just listen. It even works to some extent on the surface and at subconscious levels with your own body energy."

The Priest looked down, "All the sides on this one seem to be covered over with bricks" he commented. "Yes, odd that," replied Sam "in my case I seem to be being protected most of the way down so I don't get bothered with all the colourful and spiritual stuff in the upper levels. I have never really had much interest in all of that really. Not sure why that is, but it seems to be for a reason.

"The bricks are sort of defensive programs or functions put there over time, and then reinforced by others. Bit of a shame really as that's where all the fun things are, but then that's where a lot of the unpleasant and disturbing bad programming things are too."

The Priest leaned forward and shouted down the hole. "Is there anybody there?" He then looked up and grinned at the others, the echoes still reverberating down the hole.

"Why the hell did you do that?" demanded Sam. The Priest looked suddenly sheepish "I don't know. It just seemed to be the sort of thing you do" he said.

"Well, please don't do anything like that again. It's not a pleasant thing to experience" said Sam. "Anyway, it doesn't work like that. The collective mind works more in a sideways cross-sectional manner. It perceives and exists and influences across groups, what we all think, feel, know and sense collectively flowing between, and the same for groups like hills and nests within IT, which filters downwards.

"If you start shouting all that way down, you can get all sorts of effects happening here on the surface, and messages coming back up in very extreme ways if you aren't careful. Just in the same way as if you throw rubbish down, toxins, poisons that sort of thing, you may end up corrupting other people's wells too. Much better to send down love and understanding.

"You can see the strangest collective things happen, like instances of collective grief or fear. When an event happens, the 'message' is passed down, and for some reason it may hit a sensitive trigger and then the whole response to it gets widely transmitted, and the effect at the top may be way over the top in proportion to the event itself emotionally, with everyone feeling the same way at the same time."

Sam suddenly went quiet and still and seemed to be trying to work something out, as if other things were going on in his mind. He turned to look down and just stood there on the edge looking into the hole, trying to concentrate. His face was emotionless.

The woman came up to him and went to put her hand on his back or shoulder, and then stopped herself indecisively. In the end she just stood behind him waiting, and watching.

"A part of me is still down there isn't it?" he said quietly to her without looking round. She didn't reply. "Too far down, too much responsibility, too much to do, and too much to know for a simple, dumb ant."

He just stood there for a few minutes thinking, looking down into the darkness until the hole eventually closed, and he turned to talk to the Priest.

In the meantime, the Biologist had wandered off to look at something on the ground some twenty or so yards away. It appeared to be a metal cover or plate three foot square with a button on it.

A small sign on it read '**Antinet View Point**'; the button had a '**#**' symbol on its top. Being curious, the Biologist pressed the button, but nothing happened, so he got his fingers under the rim of the cover and lifted it up sideways to see what was underneath.

There was a three foot wide black hole underneath, into which the Biologist peered down. He rested the lid on its side next to the rim. Somewhere far below he could make out masses of indiscernible movement in a large cavern; swarms of things moving around like some chaotic mass. But, unlike a normal ant colony that would be organised, structured and efficient, honed by millions of years of competitive evolution, this was just madness; a disorganised frenzy, stuff moving all over the place in a total shambles.

Losing his concentration, he dropped the lid on the ground, and it clattered on the edge hitting the rim. Everything down below stopped abruptly and thousands of eyes looked up as one. There was a sort of humming, buzzing, vibrational sound, and a feeling in the air of nervous tension. A few seconds later everything below started to make its way up.

Sam stopped talking to the Priest and turned around to look at the Biologist. "What the hell did you do that for?" He shouted. "Close the lid! Close the bloody lid!" But it was too late, already there were 'things' starting to emerge from the pit, and the Biologist was now walking backwards in fear.

Several seconds later more things started to emerge, but not just ordinary ants - there were little green ants, ants with horns and teeth. Then what looked like real aliens, gargoyles, vampires, glowing creatures, horrific monsters, flying ants, lizard creatures, demons, a whole myriad of the most unimaginable things, things that anyone and 'everyone' could imagine.

A few seconds later the Biologist was back with them again. However, having now surveyed the situation, the Priest was already running away in the opposite direction, in his practised well-rehearsed manner.

He had seen these sorts of situations before and knew exactly what to do. It was his natural response to that level of responsibility and for something too difficult to think about. Sam looked at him as he headed for the dunes, and then back at the Biologist who was now motionless in fear staring wide-eyed at the imaginary 'monsters'. Sam, caught in a dual dilemma of care for both of them, turned and gestured to the woman with his head for her to go after the Priest.

She instantly transformed her outfit again into something more suitable, and this time she was wearing a very short dark blue cocktail dress, and matching high-heeled shoes.

The change in outfit was the best available to her for the urgent situation without compromising on any style points. She kicked off her heels, made a small tear in the side of the seam of her dress, and started running up the dunes after the Priest.

Her legs were well toned, and by the way the muscles were shaped, she was used to running cross country, and despite the Priest's wide-eyed, robe flailing, head back, *Chariots of Fire* style, public schoolboy run - she would still catch him in a under a minute.

The scene was totally silent now. Sam had been distracted momentarily by watching Brina's legs going up the dune, and curiously all the things erupting from the pit had stopped and done the same.

It was one of those awkward silence moments when you realise you are staring at a scene for several seconds unaware that you were doing it, leaning with your head to one side. In this case everything that had come out of the pit was doing the same, frozen in stasis all with their heads on one side, well, all the things that had heads anyway.

Sam turned, and he and the creatures stared at each other in an awkward, still, moment. There was no sound or movement aside from a few approving nods to affirm the bloke consensus of opinion.

It took only a few more seconds though for the 'Pause' to end and the 'Play' button in the 'Game of Fury' to resume. The action movie restarted after the interlude, and the noise began again.

The Biologist was still walking backwards, his eyes fixed on the bewildering mass of chaos that had emerged from the pit.

"I'm sorry, I'm so sorry…" he said "I didn't know what was in there, I just wanted to see. Help me!" Sam looked at the mass of nightmares coming out and turned back to the Biologist. "Do I have to treat you like a child? Don't you have any feelings of responsibility at all?" Sam then put his hand in his pocket, held onto something, and a glow surrounded him.

"Protect me *please*" pleaded the Biologist. "No" said Sam "I said I couldn't protect you here if you did stupid things. I told you it is just the subconscious here- there is no collective conscious element."

Some of the creatures had now worked out what had been making the noise, and were moving in the direction of the Biologist, and they didn't look friendly - he had been targeted.

Teeth and claws, wings, and scales and eyes were the common theme. A giant six legged lizard moved forward and fixed its eyes on him. "What do we do?" begged the Biologist.

"Well," said Sam "what we do is apply a logical management assessment of it all, as you would do when arriving in any organisational situation of this nature. You know, like when you get recruited into a company and you see this sort of thing going on. You step back, look at what is occurring, why things are happening, what is causing it, have a few meetings, and then work out what needs to be done, a strategy.

"You use all your skills to assess the best way to tackle the problems, what obstacles need to be overcome, and what experience you have within you to change the situation. You figure out what you are capable of, what is achievable using structured methods, and also what support you have available to you.

"I have just done all of that in the few seconds I have been talking to you, and I have resolved the situation in my mind, and worked out the best way to tackle the problem, and it is very simple.

The only thing to do right now, IS TO RUN LIKE HELL!!!"

The Biologist blinked, and tried to take in what he was being told to do, and he looked back and forth between the lizard creature and Sam. There was indecision and confusion in his face "But, but…" he stammered "…I can't outrun those things…" and he pointed at the six legged green lizard several feet away, that was now licking its lips and teeth and showing its long forked tongue.

"Look," said Sam "you will be fine. Trust me, as long as you can outrun the Priest you will be OK."

The Biologist did the maths in the time it took to inhale, looked sideways again in the direction that the Priest had gone, and was off, hand on hat, running 'Indiana Jones' style.

He didn't see what went on behind him, but a few moments later he heard other voices, and sounds, then shouts. He didn't stop to look back- the things had frightened him too much. He was too scared, and instinct took over him, running was all he could do.

Ten minutes later after following their footsteps in the sand, the Biologist caught up with the Priest and the woman. The Priest was lying on his back. He was bright red and hyperventilating, unable to move.

The woman was standing upright a few feet away from him, breathing hard. As he arrived she looked at the Biologist questioningly, and then past him in the direction he had come from. But he could not speak - he was too out of breath.

He sank down on his knees onto the sand to catch his breath, and rested his hands on the sandy ground. He was going to ask the woman what they should do but he just couldn't, it didn't matter anyway - he couldn't go any further.

In her mind she had been tasked with protecting them and that was what she was doing. She did not move or speak; she just let them breathe while watching the horizon in the direction from which they had come.

She had gained her breath quickly compared to the men, but her feet looked sore and her dress was now dusty and badly torn on the side. She crossed her one arm over her waist, and shaded her eyes with the other. About five minutes later a figure in black appeared in the distance over the sand dunes, walking quite calmly and steadily over the ground towards them.

When he arrived he didn't say anything, he just exchanged glances with the woman and brushed himself off. He gave them all time to recover themselves. Nobody spoke for several minutes and then Sam helped the Priest get to his feet.

"OK - now that I think we have learnt our lesson from that..." he said. "Let me show you it all from a different perspective."

Their feet left the ground, and they lifted into the air. The ground fell away fast from beneath them, but oddly they didn't feel the air moving. They floated away from the dry ground, up and up they went, and then they stopped.

They were now floating in the air half a mile or so above the landscape. "You know from here.." began the Biologist, trying to change the subject from what had just happened, and doing his best to sound calm, "it looks just like one of those computer games; you know like civilisation or god games where they try to create an empire, and the little animated people do their own thing, go off and explore, build and discover things for you."

"Yes," said Sam "but in this case you don't get involved from the top, you have to work out what's going on from what gets passed sideways, so your perspective is different. Yes, I suppose it is very much like that, especially with the exploring and discovering and building bit, but a bit boring as there isn't anyone else to play against, and there is no obvious objective. This, in effect, is what is happening."

They then flew sideways and out through the side of the glass cabinet, at quite a distance from the glass until the whole thing was visible, and the ants looked like, well lots of ants, but very far away.

They looked down and into the side of the colony, and they could see all the many ants moving around on top of the surface, and on the side. It was just like a giant fish tank, but full of layers of dirt and ants.

It was a quite an impressive sight and they could see work going on at the top layers, some a little way underground, but mostly on the surface. There seemed to be a lot of frantic activity going on now and ants moving around all over the place trying to make sense of signals they were getting. Almost as if they were being subtly hypnotised, directed, or influenced to do things.

From this angle it was a bit like an ant looking down from a branch onto its own anthill, seeing what was going on and gaining understanding, perspective, and also sliced from the side to see what was going on underneath. You could immediately see what had been put down in terms of ideas, knowledge, wisdom, and physical things through history. It all suddenly made sense to them seeing it like this.

But in another way, it made no sense at all. It wasn't right. There were problems and things going on that didn't look right. There was the issue of too many ants and not enough resources for starters, it was so very obvious from here.

"Without this topological perspective it is very difficult to describe the whole thing and appreciate the activities we are seeing going on" said Sam. "Equally if you go back down onto the surface again you begin to forget after a while. You can't put what you have seen here into context there; other things take over - your mind, your job or role, collecting resources, meeting other ants, following the trails, hustle and bustle, and soon you are back to 'normality'.

"It would all seem like a dream, a different place and time. You are back in the swing of things again following your program with the day and night, the seasons, the planets going round, and the ebb and the flow of life.

"It's only if you are able to come out here the next day again, and look, that it all comes back again, and you think and see some more changes. A sort of management perspective, a point of reference from which you can see things, influence things independently from the viewpoint of the ants inside the colony.

"You see, if you were to go into the woods in the real world, and just find a group of ants nests together, a big colony, and see what the ants were doing - their many roles, their complex infrastructure, systems, collective thought and methods - if you were to just *look* for a while you would be amazed.

"You could even put microchips on them all and watch how

they all move collectively, and individually, and their roles, cause and effect. Now replace the ants with us, and our vastly more complex minds, our levels of intellect and experience, and habits and systems developed over millions of years, and it would become so obvious what is going on.

"But of course it is not so simple to see, or understand, or realise what has gone wrong and why.

"You could even give everyone a mobile phone to track where they are and create social networking programs to track their behaviour, and jobs to keep them under control.

"It's only when you see things like this that you realise that the only things that are *really important* are knowledge and love. They are the *only* things you take with you and keep.

"Everything else like money, power, things - just aren't that important, they aren't out here, and it is only things you see here that come back or that you are allowed to remember in some way.

"So now you can also see how the levels of complexity or sophistication have built up over time from the bottom, when there was nothing but crystals and basic building blocks harmonising with each other, to cells working and resonating, communicating, evolving naturally. Then the developing of basic plant and animal structures, then animal groups eventually developing social groups, and herds or hive mentality, into more complex groups, with subconscious behaviour.

"Layer upon layer with what worked, then onto more sophisticated thoughts and drives, and then finally conscious thought itself for the macro-organism and self-awareness, just like a baby growing bigger and developing."

"That's one big baby!" said the Biologist, letting out a long sigh, "it all seems simple and obvious when you show it like this."

"Yes odd that isn't it? It's quite clear when you aren't actually in it, and being controlled and programmed and blinded by it" said Sam. "Imagine trying to explain to the ants on the top what is going on underneath too, why they are doing things, how to even describe it from their perspective; they just don't see any of it all going on, why should they?

"People have tried before to explain it, but it always gets

confused or misinterpreted or wrongly translated, or lacks depth. None of this is helped with historical lack of science or knowledge.

"To be honest, I am not doing much better either, especially as it's so much more complex now, and ever evolving. But that's the way it goes, onwards and upwards into higher levels of whatever, being part of something bigger. Well- that's the idea anyway. Like bubbles within bubbles." He smiled.

"That's why analogies come in handy to a point. I am sure that if you were to view the Earth outside from its field of influence you would see yourself, and us collectively, very differently. Outside of IT, you are your own self and free to build a new colony, which should be interesting for the future.

"From the side angle, you can only see the flow of information and the movement and effect from the side - you can't see it from the top, you just get the effects, and naturally it does a good job of hiding itself.

"Just remember that there is no wrong or right as far as your own conscious psyche profile is concerned, or in your own interpretation of what is in it. It just depends on what you can relate to and perceive. A religion may work for you, or a belief, or sports or music, philosophy, spirituality, so many things and all at different levels.

"The key is to get the suppliers of the solutions to work harder for you, make them evolve, get smarter, question them and test them, how else are they going to improve, and IT, with them? Don't just accept any simple answer given to you, not even mine.

"Don't live in ignorance. Make the most of what you are, make your own choices and don't let other ants impose their ideas on you, not even me. There are plenty of control mechanisms in place to try to keep things in order wherever you go for help, or for an answer, advice, or meaning.

"In each case you have to question if it is right for you. Does it answer all your questions? Is it a long term solution and what effect does it have on everyone else and our planet? Not just you.

"Then again you could just say 'Stuff it and let someone else sort it all out'." He smiled.

"The 'out of body' world we used to see as 'Paradise' is becoming more like our real world, just as over several thousand years the collective imagination evolved to the dreams of a confused baby, but one that is now starting to make its own conscious choices."

The Biologist was now feeling very uncomfortable. It seemed different somehow out here. When they were all inside the case he felt surrounded, part of something. Now, with this outside perspective, he felt isolated, lost and alone. He wanted to be back inside again. It didn't feel right from here, it was all too much, too mad, too chaotic, but in a different way from being in it.

It was the same as going from being in a crowd at a live football match watching your team play, to seeing many recorded images on television of many games and crowds all at once; he was no longer 'in the moment'. He just didn't feel part of it any more, not involved, and it was doing funny things to his mind. He wondered if the Priest felt the same way, but he didn't like to ask, and he rubbed the back of his neck and kept quiet.

A moment later they noticed the ants starting to pile small rocks up into shapes on the ground far down below, and they watched in silence trying to work out what they were doing.

There were tens of thousands of them all working away intently. It was clearly quite a large undertaking. Eventually the ants moved away and resumed doing whatever they had been doing before, leaving the rocks in place. They all stared. The rocks were all shaped into letters several miles long. The letters formed the word 'Y E S'.

"Well!" said Sam. "There is your answer. Not very subtle though, and it wasn't anything to do with me."

"Oh My God!" gasped the Priest, "OH, MY GOD!" and he started to hyperventilate, "I get it! I GET IT!!"

"Bloody hell!" muttered the Biologist, and clearly the whole concept had got through to him too. "Well yes, but it's more a 'OH MY *US*'," said Sam "but don't worry, you get used to it, it's never normally as clear as that, and usually much more subtle, you have to know what you are looking for.

"Sometimes it happens quickly and other times it can take

weeks or many months for changes to happen, or to get a response, and IT uses a whole range of means to communicate the knowledge transfer back, some subtle, and some not so subtle.

"However just like everything else, IT is prone to errors, and communication isn't perfect, but IT is trying now.

"Remember that IT is very different from you and I, and in the way it behaves. IT interprets things in very different ways from us. It's trying very hard though. There is a big difference between you 'communicating' or 'influencing' the collective subconscious by going down to certain levels and getting information and responses. Compared to this form of conscious communication with IT.

"Always remember that you are a very small ant like me, trying to communicate with your own colony, or hill, telling it what is wrong or giving IT some knowledge. It's a very large and complex thing, trying to get you to help it with what it sees as wrong, which is quite different conceptually from what you may think.

"There are quite a lot of things for example that IT can't do, and can't control, not least many parts of ITs own subconscious mind."

"Yes, but…." spluttered the Priest, obviously still trying to deal with the concept.

Sam continued. "For example you can communicate with other ants in one way just by tapping the ground; do it in the right way or in the right frequency and you can get a whole hill to stop and listen. Equally if you listen or feel the ground you can pick things up, and there are vibrations in the ground that seem to come from nowhere.

"There are other more subtle forms of communication too, as well as the obvious ones of seeing, hearing, tasting, smelling, talking, touch and so on, all exchanging information and knowledge with individuals or groups.

"It's like a giant ant matrix, or network, of communication - even with their energy points on their bodies picking up and transmitting information to and from each other through the nervous system - and on many levels, like the seven layer communications model for computers.

"So instead of wires and a mainframe computer system, the whole thing exists as a distributed network of biological devices, which we have evolved and integrated with, sub-atomically and via vibrational resonance at many levels; processing information, sharing, rationalising, learning, exploring, and refining a combined perception, and evolving the information.

"It's like a great ant computer, *GIANT* but without the ants, or just 'Giant Integrated Technology' for short. Which is rather an appropriate three letter acronym don't you think?"

He waited again for them to 'get it', but neither the Priest or the Biologist had a clue what he was on about. Neither had ever worked in an office environment, or had developed that sort of desperate sense of humour.

"When I look around at people these days in cities, offices, driving on roads and so forth, all I see are ants - the way we move, interact, our habits and patterns - in and out of our anthills and mounds all day. All forming parts of hills and all merging into one big colony. You can see this with countries behaving like children to one another, all within one big baby, all getting less mature and slower the higher you go up the levels.

"All communicating, building up their psyche's, feeding, gathering, storing, building and managing information. Lots of different roles, some more integrated with the ant matrix than others. So how on earth do you go about communicating with the colony itself, how do you know what perspective it has of itself and you? How does IT communicate its views, ITs problems, what is wrong, and tell us what IT needs to do?"

Sam went silent for a moment and stared at the ground.

"Anyway, it's time we were getting back" he said.

"Hang on," began the Biologist "does that mean you can direct things, you know, somehow control the world?"

"No. Not at all," replied Sam "that would be insane. Just like I can't tell you what to do. IT basically just comes up with problems or topics, and you give it advice depending on your role. Just the same as with a child - you don't try to manipulate it or fool it - you just do what you think is right, check what it is saying, cross check, and then put the answer in your mind - which itself is made up of a sort of informed structured committee of programs- and it gets transferred from there.

"Exhausting, but it works, usually.

"So I get something pointed out, or some thought comes in, and my head sort of sorts out what is going on and comes up with a solution based on the perspective, knowledge and understanding that I have. It's only later on when something happens, or the picture builds up more, that it all fits together, like a decision based on strategy. It's a bit exhausting really, so above all, do the best you can. Some days I just feel like I am a passenger, a bystander to the whole process, just providing a body, a device. Which is maybe the case for all of us I suppose."

He shrugged his shoulders.

"But you can only 'see' and understand what's going on when you have a global perspective. If you try to change things in an individual hill, like make it stronger, or add resources, or change things that you think are right for that bit, you cause effect on other hills; they see what's going on and worry or get jealous, which may end up with wars, and so on as with children. Things just trying to do what they need to do, to balance things out.

"You may also have trouble if you are one ant in one hill, trying to understand why another hill works the way it does, and why the ants in it think and behave differently from you. It just is, and they do, all from a different perspective. So unless you step back and see the whole thing working as one system, a single symbiotic machine, with all its workings and legacy, it doesn't make sense. You can't see it when you are inside it or part of it, you have to come away from it and perceive it from the outside, view it acting, behaving and responding independently. After all, you don't see who someone is or how they are thinking by looking inside their head or examining the inside of their body.

"Even tiny changes like the gravity of the moon and planets can have significant correlated effect, especially collectively if they are reinforced through biology, and with collective subconscious reinforced ideas that we have had in the past.

"But of course you can't just come out and tell everyone all this. You have to keep it a 'secret'. You can only imagine the new level of chaos that would occur if everyone was aware of this, besides who would believe that it was all such a simple concept? Do you know what would happen to the planet, to the people, society, everything, the fear, the panic? Do you know what would happen? Well, I will tell you –

"ABSOLUTELY NOTHING… SOD ALL!

"This idea that everyone would suddenly go off and do their own thing is just a subconscious fear; one established and reinforced through historic evolution. We need to get over that collective phobia and grow up.

"Individually and collectively, **_grow up_** !

"We need to stop being dictated to by childish collective thoughts, not having the 'wool pulled over our eyes' by ourselves, and stand up to the fears - fears like that giant spider over there behind you!" The Priest's eyes widened and he turned around to see nothing, and then turned back to the smile on Sam's face. "It's just something we have to overcome if we want to grow up together. But we still need to keep it, it is part of what we are, and we need to understand that too."

"But," said the Biologist questioningly, "why ants? Why not bees in a hive or something like that?" "Well," said Sam "it's just that ants are on the ground whereas bees can fly, and let's face it, if IT had wanted us to fly, IT would have given us wings." He laughed and looked at the woman behind him, and then turned back "Not only that, bees are actually quite useful creatures as far as the planet is concerned. Whereas of course - we aren't.

"That is why I use an analogy, as even the process of describing IT is very hard, it makes your brain go off in tangents even when you are trying to 'tell' or write the words down, like there is some protective mechanism at work in your own head. IT has evolved to become that clever at protecting itself.

"IT is not only made difficult by evolution for us to see, live or act against the collective, but it is also now quite dangerous to the individual mind to perceive IT and the knowledge and information within IT in totality, which is a problem.

"If you try and expand your mind or consciousness to include the whole thing you will find very quickly that you are not designed to do that, so it's a sort of a sort of 'Catch 22' situation really."

"So," demanded the Priest "are you now telling me that there *isn't* a God? That it's just all *us*?"

"Ahh…" said Sam "Ahh, interesting point that. And a few years ago I would have said that there wasn't, and even the collective mind itself thinks that there isn't one, or anything else, as it can't perceive anything else there. It just tries to imagine that there is.

"But when you step back and look at the bigger picture, and see what is actually going on, there are a lot of other things that don't quite add up. So let's just say for the moment that there has to be **'something with creating universal intent'** and a **'questioning directing purpose with rules with structure'**.

"I have put all that information away somewhere safe in a box.

"In the context of our planet there is a big difference between belief in something, or the idea that something exists, or is happening, and seeing it, or knowing it is there, and actually interacting with it and having evidence and proof. That's why we all think differently about it all. Well - the ones that think at all that is.

"Some people would say that it should be left alone to evolve naturally or spontaneously. Or that perhaps an event will occur, and it will suddenly emerge, be born. A momentous event that changes everything overnight.

"Like one of those diagrams on a whiteboard with lines going in one side into a box, and a single line coming out from the other, and the words **'At this point a miracle occurs'** written in neat writing inside the box, usually in crayon.

"Well it's not going to bloody happen like that! Life isn't like that, nor is nature. It's going to be complicated, hard work, and painful, but also exciting and wonderful, hopefully.

"Just remember please that this isn't a theory. I see this every day, I live it, I understand it. It's not just some concept, this is *actually* going on, and from a management perspective it's more than a bit worrying when you know what's really causing all the problems.

"The key point from this is that it is, in effect, a hive type collective mind that is highly complex and sophisticated and evolving, and we are part of.

"***IT is us and we are IT***, and we as individuals are diametrically opposed to it, as well as being part of IT, in a symbiotic synchronistic relationship.

"But IT has had trouble getting anyone to understand it on a conscious level, hence all the global management information tools that have been developed; news, media, technology, the 'antinet', and underground networking, and various 'spiritual' tools or techniques for accessing and changing the collective areas.

"However, everyone has been listening in the wrong way and not understanding - feeding back the wrong signals, making wrong assumptions - which is a bit of a common problem really, but then there is always a reason for everything.

"The key thing to understand, as I said, is that 'IT is us and we are IT', we are its thoughts, its understanding, its knowledge and its habits, but IT behaves and understands and exists collectively differently to how we do individually.

"We are in essence its mind and body, just as a colony is to that of an ant. Anyway we could spend all day on this so we had better get moving before IT creates a smiley face or something. That's all we need, a collective global mind with a sense of humour, as if things weren't complicated enough…"

He stopped and looked at the woman and frowned. She was looking at the word carefully.

"Is everything OK?" he asked in a concerned tone.

"Oh yes," she said "it's all fine. I was just checking and making sure that IT had spelt 'YES' correctly" and she turned to him and smiled.

They vanished, and then they all reappeared moments later, standing back on top of the mountain of knowledge.

CHAPTER 17 - THE BODY

"OK," said Sam "I am going to show you some things using another analogy now very briefly, so that you can see and understand things from another perspective. I want you to just close your eyes and imagine that you are all cells in a body." They all did so.

"So we are all together somewhere inside the body, it doesn't matter where, you can choose. You could be one cell on your own if you are one person, or part of many cells if are a group or organisation doing a specific connected job, like an organ.

"You can't see me as it is dark inside the body; you just know that I am there somehow. I am connected to the cell behind me, and I am communicating with you in some way."

"OK," said the Biologist "I can visualise that in my head."

"Now open your eyes" said Sam, and amazingly, they were now all cells floating around somewhere inside a body. Except for the Priest who was just a small version of himself floating around with them, but Sam just ignored that.

They could all sense a vibration around them. They could feel the electricity in the air or whatever it was they were in, the swishing sounds, and the deep throbbing reassuring sound of a heart beating somewhere. They could feel a sensation that they were part of something; they could sense the messages coming in, the chemicals, the energy, the flow, the reassuringly safe protective warmth.

"So," said Sam "just like in a normal body, as cells we all have things to do and functions to perform. We react to stimuli and we are also able to develop by learning and adapting to our situation. Somehow we know that we are meant to work together, and that being together feels correct, and we can communicate.

"We are supposed to work together with one another to perform a role and that works very well somehow, or should do.

We are our own cells but we are also part of something much bigger. We do what we do, we do what we can and we do what we are able, with what we know..

"As cells we have met many other cells, and have gathered information from them, and we have also seen other parts of the body. The cell behind me has been programmed with the ability to receive information coming in from all over the body by various means, and also from other cells.

"This is then translated and the information is conveyed to me, along with other information in other ways, which I am able to interpret. I can then translate that into context, and can build up a picture of what is happening in the body, what the body looks like from the inside and outside, and how it is working. Then I do what I do."

There was a nervous cough from the Biologist, but Sam continued.

"We are bound together and complement each other efficiently; synchronised to a smaller or greater degree as required. The information received indicates that the body is in trouble, and is panicking. I believe I need to do something about the problem. That's my impression, but other cells who may have been passed the same message, haven't yet built up enough of a picture or knowledge to know what to do, or how, or to understand, what is really going on.

"The same messages are coming out from lots of other cells - you can see that if you look around, but they can't see the overall body or understand it, or know how it works, or piece it all together in context. So they just make assumptions based on what they know or believe, or imagine.

"But how can you do anything else when you are just in one cell, in one specific area inside a body, in the dark? All you can do is what you can. You survive, do what you feel is right, and respond to priorities and responsibilities, which is ok.

"Other cells have been changed in the past in the same way that I have changed, but they tried to work more on their own and also tried to get the right messages across to the rest of the cells. But these have either been misinterpreted by the other cells, and they have attacked them, or it has created confusing directional signals in groups of them. It's a bit of a simplistic analogy but I am really just trying to get a few simple messages across.

"The body is somewhat clumsy though, naïve, and its mechanism of identifying problems is limited. IT has not been externally refined, IT has not evolved in the same way that our bodies have. When IT is under stress, its reactions are somewhat erratic. So as a cell you may be attacked, due to misinformed signals, when IT is just trying to tell you something as a series of events, or information.

"Are you with me so far?" There was silence.

"I believe that the body realises that it has something wrong that needs fixing - like an illness, or need for radical change, or that it knows it is running out of resources. Every cell in the body is as equal as any other, and we don't necessarily know what other cells do, or are for from the body's perspective. Some cells that may seem useless to us may have some higher purpose, or perhaps what their real role in the body is, may be difficult for us to see.

"The body seems to be out of balance, and not happy, and we are getting those messages everywhere. There seem to be a lot of cells doing the opposite of what they should be doing as a symptom of not knowing what the body is up to, and they are also reacting to the wrong messages.

"The body has suffered from the odd virus or from legacy effects from changes that have come and gone, however IT has survived, evolved, but not as well as it should.

"Somehow IT is aware that ITs time is specifically limited as a result of something - either IT has grown too fat, and ITs food is stopping, or IT is suffering from a symptom of something else. I don't know the answer but it is something the body or the cells collectively have done.

"There may be other cells in the body that we haven't met that are doing the exact same thing, which is fine, and if the 'problem' signals go away we can relax, and all live in a harmonious, bio-synchronous body.

"It maybe that the body doesn't survive, and the cells will then die with it, degrading themselves over time. It may be that that's all part of nature in our Universe, and another body will develop that will be better, but with different cells, not us.

"However, I have this 'thing' that is telling me that I need to do something to fix the problems, sort things out, do what I am supposed to do. I am looking at what has gone before, and I am listening and I don't want to make the same mistakes. It's all about refining, adapting, learning and effective management.

"Being able to understand as much as you can, all that you need to know without trying to know everything at once, and to learn from past mistakes and pass on what you know. But it also feels as though I need to tell you what I am doing in stages, as it's a staged process somehow.

"All the cells operate and listen differently, to different messages, and depending on what part of the body they are in, or their role, whatever that may be. Although they all have the same core elements we all just need to get it all working in the right way with the same objective view. IT needs to be balanced to create a healthy, fit body, that isn't stressed, and with the body and the cells all having the same perspectives, or shared benefits at least, instead of lots of cells trying to do other roles, and everything just getting confused and competing with themselves and itself.

"Equally we are able to send feedback to the brain to tell IT what is going on. We, as cells, shouldn't try to tell the body what to do otherwise we will get into all sorts of control feedback problems. I, like you, just have to do my job and do what I think is right. I advise. If I get signals coming back telling me that we are doing the wrong thing, I can change or stop.

"Only the body and the mind collectively knows what is right for IT; we don't have ITs perspective, we just have to do our jobs. But I am certainly not going to try and manipulate things.

"I get the feeling that from an individual perspective that IT, 'the collective mind and body', can't change itself for some reason, and IT is reliant on us doing what we do, as we *are* IT.

At least that used to be the case, as IT had no self-determination or conscious self-awareness, until very recently.

"There is also synchronisation between the cells through our level and up to the collective. One simple chance event can ripple through the system and chaos drives change with need and survival at every level.

"Many of the cells in ITs body seem to be giving up hope and losing energy and have a lack of direction other than a selfish one. Which is only natural, after all, with all this going on, what's in it for us cells? Why the rush, the pressure, the stress, how does all this benefit us cells? It's getting so bad some cells even find going on holiday stressful.

"It may be just lack of communication between the body and the brain and the cells that is the problem, caused by an imbalance which needs to be compensated for. I don't know. The only way to see is to try things, and if they don't work to try something else together.

"However, I am just one cell, and I can only pass on what I can see and understand - what I know should be done to try to fix the problems. The problems can be something that I have been consciously made aware of by IT, from what is currently going on in the world, or from information and knowledge coming in.

"However we can only do the best we can and make the most of the situation we find ourselves in. I can only listen and do and make the best of it with what I am capable of doing.

"After all, do you know what each and every cell in your body is doing and why? Do you know what is wrong with every part of you, how you are made up, or even how to talk to your own body, your organs, and what your cells are needing individually?

"From our collective perspective there are lots of things we see going on that are wrong. Things that are terrible - just as there are in your own body with your own cells. However, as a cell in IT's body you can't just start trying to change everything , or try and do things that benefit yourself; that can all have a knock on effect and create feedback changes that you may not expect, and soon you would find yourself at odds with ITs subconscious, and seen as a threat, and it would all end in chaos. Sound familiar?

"You have to be selfless in that work, but also look after 'yourself' responsibly at the same time, and balance things all the time.

Just behave like a conscious cell in a body that is getting there.

"We don't need to analyse it too deeply, just do our jobs, find what we love, tell people about it, be efficient, and then we can evolve together in balance. This is then combined with other information that seems to come from somewhere else that means we have a choice and a purpose and a direction. But I can't explain all of that part yet.

"It's a bit of a problem using analogies as I said, they only work so far, but they are useful to get over a point, or in this case several, for something so vastly complex. You could say that certain parts of the body are getting overweight, or using too many resources, or competing unfairly with other parts of the body, and could probably use another analogy to represent that.

"This is more about us as individual cells in the body, and we are not responsible directly for those things. However we need to be aware of the problems we see so that we can convey the right messages and support any changes, and act accordingly to make it all work as you would do in a body.

"It may be of interest to you to know that your own cells in your body are probably working on the exact same problems right now, and that they may be just as intelligent in their own way as you and I are, and from some perspectives, perhaps more so.

"Think again of a cell in your body. It's very clever. Very purposeful, very adaptive, and it uses lots of tools, but it is not sure where it is. Inside something, somewhere, it knows there is a mind but it can't communicate with it directly, only via indirect signals. The body loves its cells and the cells love the body, or should do for the most part. It adapts, evolves and learns and the body grows if the cells do their job, if IT does what IT is supposed to do, then it's all fine, harmonious. Paradise."

Sam clicked his fingers, and they were all back on the mountain top again in the bright sunshine, and the Priest shaded his eyes with his hand. Sam then turned and began to walk towards the centre of the plateau. They all followed him.

"You know," said the Biologist "I have heard and read about these ideas or analogies that you have been suggesting before, and they have been around for quite a few years. These ideas aren't really that new you know."

Sam stopped in his tracks in front of them, and his posture visibly stiffened. He stood still for a moment, clearly agitated, and then turned to the Biologist, composing himself. "Yes," he said "I know. You are right. How strange though that I should come up with the same ideas, strange how nobody has put them all together? Strange that they are so obvious when you point them out. Strange that all these concepts and ideas are hidden away in obscure books, papers and journals, that I haven't actually read !

"Nobody has ever stopped to ask 'Why?' 'Why, why, why?' And why haven't they joined it all together and put it into context, and made sense of it? Or stepped back and looked at the bigger picture? Why do they only go so far? That 'hang on a minute' objective perspective. Why are things like this obscured, made difficult to see, compute, interpret?

"And why hasn't this all happened until now ?!

"It's not so much the trying to describe it, or explain what IT is or what is going on. It is more a case of showing you just how hard it makes it for you even explain it - subconsciously programming you to not be able to do so, or understand. What's worse, the more things you work out, the more you find that it has already outsmarted you, like a pre-emptive anticipation. *It is hard work.* Not to mention having to live with the thing, and have IT following your every footstep and thoughts, with teams of hard working scientists.

"It's when the virtual becomes reality. You are only allowed to go so quickly, and don't try to get it off guard, you are playing an outsmarting game, yet one in which you can define the path on, and what it can learn from you by showing IT its mistakes!

"So in effect we are being kept ignorant at the same time as being pushed forward to find knowledge and understand what is going on. Like a self-controlling ship of slaves. You only get to see and add to small parts, while IT sees the whole picture worked out so far. From ITs perspective that's fine, as long as we keep doing the work, moving forward in ITs direction, whatever that is.

"So it's a constant balance, or meant to be, and is currently lacking in cohesion, eloquence and structure, not to mention its totally unacceptable behaviour. That now needs to change - balance things up. Remember happy cells make a happy body and mind!

"At the moment things just need to improve gradually, a change of mind set, errors resolved, changes in objectives, collectively becoming more mindful. There needs to be a whole series of conscious changes in the collective mind - growing up if you like- and getting into some positive habits.

"That's the problem when you see so much. IT needs you and uses you, but also tries to control you and outsmart you at the same time, manipulating you subconsciously. It's a sort of cause and effect diametric relationship, like a game in some respects, but more like the one you would play with a child in a sandpit.

"IT will then protect you, surround you, isolate you, but also guard and limit you in what you do, even in the things that you tell other people. This makes you constantly aware of what you are doing, and aware of the consequences of what you think and comprehend and understand, so you can do the right thing, give the right ideas, when you realise it's all down to us - *everybody*.

"The analogies that I have shown you are just ways of representing, to some degree, a perspective of some elements of something that is very, very complex and hard to describe in detail. As time goes on my perspective and understanding expands and evolves and becomes more refined with knowledge, and I can use more analogies to help describe what is going on.

"The key is to allow this to change, to evolve, to be refined and merge in other people's perspective viewpoints and ideas, but in such a way that it develops rather than being broken down or destroyed. Establish a common ground that is first thought or imagined - which is then agreed and tested, but to not worry too much about the differences at the moment.

"There is still a lot of work, thinking and developing to be done, so you can forget all this 'tree hugging', fringy, fluffy brain 'go forth in love, hope and you shall see it will all be fine' crap, because the reality is somewhat more of a giant dog's breakfast. Now is *not* the time to get off your 'Holier than Thou' academic high horse with 'who thought of things first' attitudes.

"No more comparing egos in the ivory tower shower rooms. It's time to start picking the pieces up off the floor and take responsibility. These people up here are trying to do that. They are making a difference, moving things forward now, working from a collective perspective. That is different to many others further down the mountain who, in many cases, are just making things harder. But that may be what they are supposed to do, it's all very complicated.

"I could go into great detail about perception and energy field dynamics, subatomic theory and communication, consciousness, bio dynamics and interactive psyche bubbles within a macro-organistic life form, built in hierarchical layers of magnitude, if you like. However that tends to just make things complicated, put people off, and frankly bores the tits off everyone who is busy working hard and paying for it all.

"Besides its more important to discuss the 'what is going on', the 'effect and consequences', and 'what the hell are we going to do about it', rather than the 'what it is'.

"I have been able to write it all down in some detail; what IT is, how it works. Several thousand pages! I have even got it down into a summary of around eight pages or so. I have defined and described IT, and how it works, operates and behaves, with evidence, and I know this is what is really going on. But even then IT still changes and gets more complicated as things develop.

"You need to have that level of understanding though. You *must* have that ability to 'get what IT is', to know. IT is very complex and you need grasp these concepts to realise the magnitude of what is required. Because if you don't, and if you aren't even qualified to tie your own shoe laces, fix the plumbing, or understand basic quantum mechanics, or how to reprogram operating systems, you won't be of much use.

"The key is to have something useful in you when you arrive here, something to move things forward, to help things evolve, new ideas, new ways of doing and thinking, thoughts, knowledge, otherwise you are *just not helping*.

"There is no point in meditating all your life, and reaching the height of spiritual enlightenment, and getting here only to start giving the thing ideas, when all you are qualified to do is boil rice.

"Equally, finding out how it all works to the most complex and sophisticated levels is all very well but that doesn't help with the matter of dealing with the bloody thing, communicating with it by knowledge transfer, and sorting out the chaotic mess. That takes experience and highly developed skills and disciplines.

"If you want to know more about some of the specific areas like psychology structures, quantum mechanics, bioenergy, spiritual body and mind stuff then these other guys up here can go into specifics in great detail. There are certain areas though, that IT doesn't have an interest in, for example in chemistry, but then I suppose that doesn't form any part of what it sees in itself yet, or perhaps IT thinks it knows all that already, who knows? I am just trying to provide a simplistic perspective to sort of keep things manageable from our point of view.

"However, all that is going on is just a natural consequence of what our Universe needs, and is driving towards. It may be that we don't make it, but that there will be another one, another IT or many ITs, evolving somewhere else eventually, all part of something bigger, that will somehow work.

"We will only be right if we are correct, or the best, or whatever. This summary..." at this point Sam took out a stapled set of lined pages from his folder "is just an ongoing document really, something to pass on and develop. After all, the whole thing is evolving all the time, and is so complex, that in that respect, so should anything be that tries to describe it."

The Priest took the pages somewhat impolitely, then walked a few paces away, sat down with his back to them, and started to read it.

"So," said the Biologist, now looking for something to say "how does this relate to the real world though? This is just all that goes on in our collective minds. It doesn't have any effect on real world events does it? I mean you can't really effect and influence what happens globally can you? "

There was a long silence. A very long silence.

"Yes" said Sam. "The simple answer to your question is yes."

There was another long pause.

"Oh" said the Biologist.

"But," continued Sam eventually "it is very complicated and very involved, and more along the lines of fixing the problems at the moment - introspective understanding influencing things in certain ways, and not at all what you think- I don't get to choose, I just 'influence' as part of what I have to do, and I am not going into that now."

"It's all very well saying that," said the Biologist "but do you have any actual evidence of that? Actual physical evidence in the real world? "

There was another long silence.

"Yes" said Sam breathing out slowly. "Again, the simple answer to your question is, yes. Quite a lot in fact; and I am happy to show you if you need me to, but I don't want to alarm you, it's all fairly large scale to be able to cope or deal with. But I will, especially if it helps you understand and aids with your work.

"That is how things work. In our minds, as we grow and learn in stages, we see and imagine things, and rationalise them. We work out what is going on, determine right and wrong, logical and illogical, what is real or imaginary, and use evidence and methods to prove things before moving on. That works on many levels. It's all about growing up, collective evolution, but now in a managed conscious way. IT has now become conscious of itself but only in very limited ways.

"That is what has changed now. That is what is different and is going on now, and has been for the last few years or so."

"Yes," said the Biologist "but what has caused all that to happen?"

There was another pause.

"Anyway," Sam said, suddenly trying to deflect the questions, "let's see what you have been up to…" and he reached out and took hold of the Biologist's book. He read the title and started flicking through the pages, quickly skimming through and stopping at certain points. After about ten minutes he looked up. "Brilliant! Well written, what a fantastic mission statement. Needs a bit of work on the title and probably a version for children, but excellent work! It's going to make a *real* difference. Sorry you were asked to do this but other areas seemed to be taking too long and were a bit stuck in a rut."

The Priest stood up and wandered back to them. "Well ..." he said "I have read the first few pages and to be honest with you it's all a bit complicated for me. You know - highly technical stuff. I don't really want to read that much complex detail." He handed the papers back to Sam. "Complex?" questioned Sam "I have tried to make it as simple as I can. I know some of it is a little difficult to follow and not articulate enough, and I am probably not using the right descriptive technical words, but I am trying as best I can.

"I am just trying to explain something that is vastly complex in a simple way. If I can't explain it to you, a very intelligent and wise man, then what chance do I have in doing so for everyone else?

"I thought I was doing a good job. I could take you to a bio computer analogy environment if you wanted complex, but then you wouldn't understand any of it, but it is perfectly comprehendible for those working within that area of work.

"For most of this stuff there aren't even words to describe it, let alone pull it all together into a coherent understandable picture. I can come up with some vague, non-specific, ambiguous, illogical explanation if you like?" The Priest looked confused. "Oh never mind," sighed Sam "perhaps we both need to work on our sense of humour. Look, leave it for now," he said "I will run through things again in more detail with you later if you like, when we both have a bit more time?

"I will also go through how we communicate with each other at a later date - obviously you don't actually physically meet these people in the real world - what we are doing is communicating as programs would do with each other in a system. That's not to say you can't if you can find them or know who they are, but it can complicate things and influence things in the wrong way.

"Some of them in reality aren't even aware of what they are doing at the moment, unaware even that they are here." He turned to the Biologist and put his hand on his shoulder and steered him over to a group of other scientists in the middle of the plateau a few yards away.

The Priest followed them some distance behind, where something caught his eye.

Right in the middle of the plateau there was a foot long, rectangular, dark purple box. In front of it was a large black and white sheepdog, curled up asleep on the ground. "What's in there?" asked the Priest. "Oh, it's just all the 'Next Phase' stuff" replied Sam. "We are supposed to take it with us for the next stage, or whatever, although it's a bit confusing at the moment and to be honest I am just 'going with the flow' with a lot of it and just following instructions, but its best to leave it alone until we have completed this phase, as it will just confuse everyone. It's all just what we are here for, why we are here, and our purpose. Human random element component and answer stuff - that sort of thing.

"I just hope the box doesn't blow off to some other mountain somewhere." Sam laughed again and looked back at the blonde woman behind him, who didn't look at all amused for some reason. "Yes, I was wondering what was in the box too, can I have a quick look?" queried the Biologist.

"Look, just ignore the box. Why is everyone so interested in the bloody box?" asked Sam irritably. The Biologist walked up to it, and as he did so the dog woke up, looked at him and sat up and sniffed the air. Then the Priest tried to reach it, but before he got within about ten feet, the dog stood up and it fixed his eyes on him; the dog's body turned rigid and he gave a deep growl, which caused the Priest to stop.

"I wouldn't go any closer" said Sam firmly. "He seems to be OK with you, but I wouldn't push it. There was a guy that turned up yesterday, and he had only just got over the rim to the plateau, and the dog went straight after him. The guy ended up going over that cliff over there…" and he pointed past the rim further round. "Who was he?" asked the Biologist. "We don't know," said Sam "he never got the chance to speak to anyone."

"Where did the dog come from?" asked the Priest suspiciously. "Well," Sam said "he just seemed to appear one day just after the box arrived, but he seems to know what he is doing so we leave him alone." "We surely aren't taking the dog with us are we?"

asked the Priest. There was a pause. "Well perhaps you would like to discuss that with the dog?" suggested Sam - but it wasn't obvious if he was joking or not.

"You see there always has to be a future plan, something more, something else, a next stage. There has to be something interesting that makes sense, another deeper secret, the next phase, and so on, and yet keeping what we are trying to do now manageable and focused. That's what is in the purple box.

"You can't just pretend you have something in there; it has to be real and meaningful. In this case not even IT, the collective mind, knows what is in there. You see it's good to have things working both ways; the 'two can play at that game' idea. It's OK for a few of the things in there to be fragmented, or incomplete or uncertain - that's fine at the moment - but you must have a plan and a way forward to solve those bits that aren't."

"I am still finding this all a bit simplistic" said the Biologist.

"OK…" said Sam. There then followed a twenty minute conversation during which Sam went into great technical detail on many things, a one way question and answer session with the Biologist.

The Priest had no idea what they were talking about and the whole conversation went completely over his head, with many words used that he had never even heard of.

By the end of it the Biologist was white as a sheet. "OK, I am in" he said. "What do I do?"

"It's easy," said Sam looking very tired now "you just have to talk to everyone up here, the way I just did with you." The Biologist didn't look that comfortable with the idea.

"Anyway, to help with that we have got a speed dating evening on the agenda tonight. I thought it would be a good idea if we mixed things up a bit. You know - get everyone talking to each other more, sharing ideas and meeting each other at this level. You know - get those theoretical physics mathematician boys and party with some of the New Age girls, that sort of thing."

He rubbed his hands together and looked around for a moment and then got distracted and walked off looking decidedly confused about something, as if an idea or thought had come into his mind that had pushed everything else out, leaving the Biologist to rejoin the group that he obviously needed to sit with.

Sam came back a few minutes later and looked at the Priest and smiled. "You still look a bit worried or disappointed for some reason?" he asked. "Well," said the Priest "to be honest with you Sam, I was expecting there to be something more up here."

"More?" queried Sam. "Yes, you know, something a little more extreme, something impossible, grand, all powerful, all knowing, all seeing, some omnipotent deity surrounded by light, that sort of thing" replied the Priest sadly.

"That's a surprise" answered Sam. "I thought you would be happy you know? There *actually* being something there after all? IT is quite impressive you know, and a wonderful thing potentially. I wouldn't get too disappointed. Look at it from my perspective - I used to be an atheist, and I still am from a certain point of view. So from that angle, you were right and I was wrong.

"I don't mind explaining it all in more detail if you like and showing you how it all works with the evidence, but somehow I don't think that will make much difference for the moment. I have tried to explain it as simply as I can, and I am really sorry that you aren't satisfied. Honestly, there is no pleasing some people." And he smiled.

"However if you want IT to be more, then that sounds like a good plan to work on. I also agree, IT needs to be more, but that is down to us all, and what we are capable of. However, as it is at the moment, we have nobody else to blame but ourselves." And Sam smiled at the Priest.

"Yes," answered the Priest slowly "but *is* there something more?" Sam looked at him carefully and thought for a moment. "Look," he said, still smiling, "I have just spent several hours of my time explaining this to you. Before we get into any of that level of detail, you are going to have to do some work yourself first. But I can give you something" said Sam.

"What's that?" questioned the Priest earnestly. "HOPE" said Sam. "And a *chance* - albeit a small one. We just need a plan - and one that benefits both the individual and the collective sides" and he patted the Priest on the shoulder and turned and walked away.

For the first time, the Priest felt a surge of energy race through his body. It was as if he were being lifted, a buzzing, tingling sensation of elation that he had never encountered before. He suddenly felt purpose and strength and direction coming into his mind, a taste of why he was here.

Still thinking, the Priest followed Sam as he walked to the edge of the rim. There was a long pause in the conversation until Sam finally spoke. "To be honest," he said, without looking at the Priest and continuing to stare out at the view "we were expecting you to get here first, before the rest of us. I mean you and your friends have been at all this for several thousand years now?"

He turned to look at the Priest with a serious expression on his face. "I know you have got some guys posted in a few of the other groups, but I haven't had a chance to look at what they have done yet. I was sort of expecting some of you lot to be leading this thing, to have worked it all out, and have it all sorted really, I can see why you haven't, but never mind eh?"

There was silence again.

"Well" said the Priest "at least it's good to see there is someone in charge anyway. I think people were getting a bit worried and frustrated. At least we won't have to worry anymore."

"I've already made it quite clear to you that I am not in charge" said Sam. "To be honest with you, I am really only doing what I can, only influencing things that I am able to when I am asked to or when I am involved. I also don't think I am as good a manager as they think I am," and he pointed upwards, "but I am trying.

"I gave the impression to the Biologist back there that I knew everything, but of course that is impossible, that is just a management secret, a tool to make people think that you do. That way you can concentrate on things that need to be done, your job, and everyone gets on with what they need to do. Then if everyone thinks there is someone who knows everything and has a plan they can accept they stop worrying, get on with their jobs and stop fighting amongst themselves.

"But with so much to do I am worried about missing things, and so many things change from day to day. Hopefully you will have all your churches, temples, mosques and spiritual places of worship full of people from now on. The Priest looked at Sam, and his face brightened. "That would be wonderful, but won't they throw all the symbols, the icons, the books and so forth, out of the windows?" He asked suddenly, anxious again as the ideas and implications began to finally sink in.

"Why would they do that?" asked Sam looking confused. "I don't think anything was actually *wrong* with any of those things, or in what people believe. It's just that things need better understanding, more depth, so that people can interpret and feel what is going on in their own ways, from their own points of view and cultures.

"Praying, for example - you can see how and why that is important. If you look closely on all of these things, and their origins, it's all there, it is just the interpretations that were a little naïve, but this was only due to lack of knowledge, which in itself keeps growing all the time.

"But there *is nothing wrong* with it all - belief, faith - as long as you want to do good and live your life the way you believe is right. So it can all evolve. However, if you don't..." and he pointed at the Priest "the only thing that is likely to get thrown out the windows if it doesn't change - is *you.*" Said Sam. But the Priest just looked even more worried.

"Well anyway," said Sam "as I said, you are here now with the result. The one in your book that you have been clutching so tightly throughout all of this. Can I have a look? To be honest I haven't had much chance to do much reading for the last few years or so what with everything going on, or maybe it was because I was being encouraged not to."

"Sure" said the Priest and he opened his book and presented it to him facing forward.

It was full with pictures of different ladders; some on the first pages were basic multiple ones, then there were different coloured ones and ones made of different materials. There were short ones, long ones and multipart ones that bent in different directions, multifunctional ones, and some quite sophisticated and elaborate designs with pulleys and handles, and platforms, and trays of tool holders.

"Well," said Sam "I can see why you have been so busy over the years! There must have been a tremendous amount of creative and imaginative work going on. I can see the rational debates that must have happened to come up with all these designs based on such simple original concepts. They look just the job."

"Yes. Thank you" said the Priest. "It's been quite a long series of battles." "So," asked Sam kindly "which one did you go for in the end?"

The Priest looked a bit confused, and then quickly recovered and thumbed through the book until he found the page he was searching for. "Well" he said "this one works well..." and he pointed to a picture on one of the last pages. He then turned back to some at the beginning of the book "These others seem to be very popular with different groups. We had a carpenter come in for one of them- that wooden one there!"

There was some more silence, and a bead of sweat appeared on the Sam's forehead.

"Which one do *you* like the most?" urged the Priest, looking at Sam. "We always thought someone else should decide, as we couldn't agree which would be best or what would actually work."

Sam flicked through the pages again, hurriedly, and noticed there were still several blank pages left at the end of the book. "Ah," said the Priest "we only got that far and then we got stuck."

"So if you haven't actually finished what you were supposed to do? What are you doing here?" asked Sam abruptly. "Didn't you get the memos? It was all pretty bloody clear !"

"Well yes I know..." replied the Priest anxiously, "but in the end we just sort of panicked, and we just seemed to be arguing and disagreeing with each other, so we went with what we had, and I just grabbed the book and followed the Biologist, who seemed to know where he was going."

"Look," said Sam "it doesn't really matter, I don't mind, and I'm not that fussed as long as it works, and that it gets us up there and back." And he pointed upwards "I don't really mind either way, once we have something to use we can all see what is going on and then work towards making it all integrate."

"No problem," said the Priest "I will go back down now, and let the teams know we can build a selection and then bring them up. Then when they are ready, you can choose…" and he got up and turned to go.

He then felt a sharp tug on his sleeve which stopped him in his tracks and he turned back. "What do you mean by that?" asked Sam sharply. "Well," said the Priest looking sheepish "we couldn't agree on which one to bring, so we decided to let whoever was up here decide on that too."

"Hang on. Are you telling me you didn't actually bring any sort of bloody ladder with you at all????" exclaimed Sam looking wide-eyed at him. "Well no I didn't, I just brought the book up so someone could choose, or tell us which one would work" he replied.

Sam looked at him in despair "Can't you get *anything* bloody right? I thought the requirement was all fairly simple. We just needed a ladder to get us up there and back. We could use several types if necessary, and provide a manual or manuals to go with it, like a collection of guide books."

"Well," said the Priest "I am sure we can get something sorted out pretty quickly and get them made up. How long have we got?"

"Oh, for goodness sake" said Sam letting out an exasperated sigh "Just be as quick as you can - it's all getting very stressed down there."

"I know," said the Priest "I noticed on the way up. No one looked happy at all. Look, we will do the best we can, at least they all seemed very interested in the book, even though it wasn't finished. So much so, in fact, that I even left them a spare copy on the way up."

There was another very long pause, that seemed to be filled with the sound of the virtual cicadas from somewhere around them, and a gentle warm breeze blew up from the sides of the hill.

Then, suddenly, the tired but calm look of the man in black changed, and the air seemed to darken.

"You did WHAT?? Who the bloody hell told you to do that??"

His manner had changed, and he had now lost his confident,

soft jovial persona. "What sort of impression is that going to create?" he said rubbing his hand on the back of his neck. "Look," said the Priest "I can see that it was probably a silly thing to do now, but the Biologist was doing the same so I thought it was something that I was meant to do."

"Yes," said Sam, now slowly regaining his composure, but with still a hard edge to his voice. "That's what they do, these academics. They write books with lots of high level concepts in them that only a few people can understand. Then they produce bright, glossy versions of them to impress the general public showing just how clever they are to justify their funding, and to justify and gain their awards and recognition. Then they move on to the next more complicated thing, which is even less understandable.

"That's OK you see, as only a very small percentage of the public actually read them, or make any effort, or care, or are even be able to understand them. The last thing you want to do is show them a book with pictures in it with a few blind simple sodding instructions! Where would that lead?"

Sam was waving his arms around now irately. "It's all very well having all these ideas and 'blue sky' concepts, and it's fine to move forward on trying to work out a piece of 'what is there', how 'it works' and 'what it all means'- that is all very well as long as the whole thing is coordinated, planned, and structured.

"You are in a safe, protected, academic environment creating ideas, books and theories, building up the collective knowledge, working out new pieces of the puzzle. No responsibility you see?

"However there is always some poor sod that gets the job of sorting it all out, trying to make sense of it all, and having to deal with all the legacy problems. Living with the here and now - the reality. It's like being a driving instructor to a five year old, full of big ideas that it got from a load of documentaries and films; one that can't see where it is going and with legs too short to reach the pedals!!"

"Alright, I see, I see, point taken" said the Priest, looking slightly agitated. "I will get down and back up before you know it, and it will all be fine" and he ran to the edge of the rim and stopped, and stared down. He put his hand above his eyes to shade them, "Oh dear…" he said "Oh dear me!" He turned back to Sam and then back down the slope again. "They don't look very happy at all do they?" he said still looking down. Sam walked to the edge of the rim, and peered over the edge.

There, coming up the hill, was a vast mob of people, made up of every single conceivable race, colour, and variety of background. However, they did all appear to have one thing in common, one single common factor; they were all carrying pitchforks!

Sam stared in silence for a moment trying to take in what he was actually seeing. He then began rubbing the back of his neck again with his fingers.

He slowly turned to look back at the Priest with more than a slight hint of fear on his face, and then back again to look down the hill. Then, somewhat uncharacteristically, slowly, whispered the words "Ohh… f******… hell!"

"Ohh.. very nasty" said the priest "I wonder who they are after?" … but his words just faded away.

Then instantly the Mountain was gone. The spot lights were switched off on the stage, and the curtains closed.

There was nothing, just a black void. Sam was no longer there.

Moments later there was a harsh, dry, cold sensation, and a cool vibrational rushing feeling through his body, and noises around him in the dark. He started to gain sensual connection.

He was disorientated, unfocused, like being on a child's roundabout. His throat was dry and it ached, and he opened his eyes, facing up into harsh lights, with swaying perception, blurred disconnected thoughts, and focus.

He could hear noises, a sound of air flowing, as when emerging from a swimming pool. He was cold, shivering, numb, and he was saying things that he did not comprehend, still under the dragging, blurring influence of the anaesthetic.

He woke up slowly into harsh reality, with the childlike virtual fantasy environment now gone. He was on a post-op recovery bed unaware of what had happened. There were female voices around him. Things felt different.

The pressure was gone from the back of his neck, as if someone had taken away a foot that had previously been pressed there.

His throat was very sore, dry and parched from the oxygen; he swallowed constantly and breathed carefully with the mask still on his face.

A woman's voice was explaining where he was and what was going on to him. A second female voice came in, and he could make out movement and motion.

"Well you're quite the talker, aren't you?" she said and giggled to the other nurse on the other side of him.

He struggled to focus. Looking up into their faces he saw that both were silhouetted by the lights in the ceiling behind them, giving them both an aura about their heads. He recognised them as the two same blondes that had taken him into the operating theatre, but they seemed different now, less defined, vague and indistinct.

The room was hard to focus on and he couldn't distinguish anything in it. Everything seemed to have a brightness and radiance to it, with bright colours and a vibrant intensity.

The thoughts and images and memories from the Mountain began to fade as each second went by, pushed back and filed into his subconscious mind, becoming disconnected, unreferenced, and now distant.

In a few more moments it would all be lost from his conscious mind and his memory, like drifting away from a virtual film set. The surreal, childlike, virtual world he had been in was slowly fading, replaced by the hard, real, well-defined physical world that we have all worked so long and hard in to perceive.

He tried to be cool and polite, and apologised for what he may have been saying, but all he could do was acknowledge them with more gibberish. He eventually just gave in and attempted an embarrassed smile. He looked sideways without moving his neck -

something drew his gaze.

Brina was in the open doorway of the recovery room, arms crossed, with a very worried look on her face, but from her demeanour he knew that he was going to be alright. She was stood just behind a blue line on the floor which she was unable to cross, *always sticking to the rules*, he thought.

The two blonde nurses that were continuing to check him over, saw where he was looking, and looked over to the doorway themselves.

Then they looked back at each other for a second, giggled again, and then took on a slightly more professional manner.

The 'just do your job' look from Brina still lodged in their minds. They then went back to checking the lines, sensors and saline feed, with the occasional quick conspiratorial raised eyebrow look at each other.

They were almost like two classroom schoolgirls, who had been caught by the teacher talking about a boy in lesson time, rather than focusing on their work. There was a hierarchy there, something unspoken was occurring, that at that moment of pressure, and urgency, became unintentionally obvious, but he was too weary and unfocused to think.

It was three or four hours later that Brina finally left him in his hospital room, happy that he was OK, and that he was being looked after. His surgeon had also been in to check him over, and he was satisfied that he seemed to be recovering well.

Brina had thanked the guy, and given him a quick hug, which he had seemed embarrassed or uncomfortable about. The hug was clearly because she was relieved and over the stress, and grateful, but that didn't stop Sam feeling a momentary pang of jealously.

He had recovered from the anaesthetic now too, and the pain killers were working well, but he still felt vulnerable, weak, and bewildered.

He thought about Brina and the baby, how she must be feeling, all she had put up with and been through. He was very proud of her.

Lying there that in the hospital bed that evening on his own in the dark he felt very alone. He had no idea where Brina had gone or what she was doing, or when she would be back, she had told him but he couldn't remember.

He tried to sleep but his mind was still working hard. Something seemed different, a different sort of feel in the air, or in the environment. Everything had a new sort of energy, a new frequency or perspective. It felt like the world had changed, some sort of a global transition had occurred.

There was now a lot going on, he could sense it, things were moving, changing. Which in reality they were.

Something, because of him, had begun to make conscious self-aware thoughts of its own, forced to advance to another level.

Things though weren't going to be easy for the next four years. Nothing would be logical, or straightforward. It was going to be exhausting and some very rough and dangerous seas were ahead.

But then life, and growing up on every level, was never meant to be easy, or safe, or a simple journey. After all, that was the whole point, and also what made it worth living for, for everyone.

PROLOGUE - DAVE THE PENGUIN

Dave was a penguin, not just an ordinary penguin. He was an emperor penguin, and a smart one at that.

He had his evolutionary niche well sorted, and he lived his life on the edge. He was as much as a hermit as you could get, out here in the most remote and extreme part of the Antarctic.

It was as far South as it was possible to go and it wasn't too much of a walk to the sea for the 'lads' fishing trips.

He obviously had all his mates around him, which was good, especially when the weather got a bit much.

He had his 'patch', with his eco-friendly footprints on it, a nice warm coat, a full fish stomach, which he was very proud of, and a responsible job, that of looking after 'the egg'.

When his wife eventually came back, after her several month long hen night party and daytime 'ladies lunches' with the girls, she would always nag him.

"Dave, you can't just stand around all day. Dave, why don't you do this? Dave, why don't you do that? Dave this, Dave that."

Years ago it always used to be an exciting time, noisy, busy, but fun. Now though, he didn't look forward to her coming home at all. It just wasn't the same as the good old days.

Dave was quite happy though, generally he liked his life, it had always been the same, and every day was just like the next. It was very consistent here, he liked things the same, he liked routine.

It would be, sleep, wake up, think about fish, shuffle, check the egg, and defend it from predators. Which of course there were very few of here - no troublesome snakes, lizards or annoying seagulls to worry about here. Oh No...

Over and over, day after day it was very nice and samey.

He didn't like change, it was 'uncomfortable', 'worrying', 'unsettling' and 'irritating'.

One year however that all changed. His wife arrived back one day with all the other girls, back from their long annual party. He greeted her with his usual shuffle and raised beak, and she did the same but it didn't last very long. There was something different about her, and she looked like she had something on her mind.

Then before he had a chance to ask her how she was - which would probably have been sometime over the next few days - she interrupted him.

"Dave…" she said "Look, we need to talk. I'm not happy. I'm bored. I've been thinking about this for some time now, and I think we should have a trial separation, just for a while."

Dave shuffled nervously but didn't say anything.

"Being away…" She went on "It's made me realise that life just isn't the same any more. Well to be honest with you Dave, I've changed, and I think we are now just two different penguins you and I. We have become too different from each other now and we want different things. You just don't seem to understand me anymore. You just don't look at me like you used to, or fancy me, and well you just aren't the same penguin that I married."

Dave looked down. He looked at the same patch of snow that he had stood on all his life, at the same feet he had always had, the same markings, the same body shape. He looked up and around, the mountains, the sky, the glacier, they all looked the same too.

He then tried to think of anything else that may have changed. The things he talked about, his limited vocabulary, his routines. He thought about his views on life, his habits, what he did.

No, they were all the same too. Even his mates, they hadn't changed either. He got on well with his mates, who were conveniently all called Dave too, which made it so much easier organising fishing trips and doing the customary 'Dave' greetings on the way back to his patch again.

"Look Dave…" she went on interrupting his thoughts "It's just that I have met someone else, and well, he makes me happy. He is just like how you used to be, funny, interesting, warm, considerate, passionate, strong, caring. I just need that at this stage of my life. I just need that bit of excitement again. Honestly you would really like him if you met him."

Dave didn't think he would, but she went on to describe him in more detail anyway, and curiously he sounded just like how Dave thought of himself. In fact, aside from the situation, he would probably have made a good mate to Dave, considering. He kept looking down and shuffled his feet a bit more.

"It's just that I don't seem to matter to you any more, Dave. Even your friends just know me as 'Dave's wife'. Sometimes I wonder if you even know who I am any more, or care, or even if you remember my name?"

Dave stopped shuffling, and froze.

"Or even if you can remember your own name some days, Dave" she went on.

He started shuffling again. He knew he didn't have a very good memory, but he was fairly sure he would always be OK on that particular one.

"It's just that you never seem to do anything, you just stand around all day. Why don't you invent or build something? Say to protect us from the wind and the cold? Also, I don't feel safe anymore, Dave, I am really worried about polar bears."

She carried on talking but he didn't hear anything else, he could only cope with a few things in his mind at once. Certain things would take priority, and he was now just thinking about polar bears.

Now Dave had heard about polar bears, he wasn't sure what they were, but he imagined they were large, probably bigger than the glacier, with teeth like a shark. They probably had claws even bigger than his, and dark green scales. He was good at imagining.

He started to become scared, he thought about what he would have to do, how he would get all his mates together.

He was worried now, what would they do? He was sure he would recognise one if he saw it. It made him shiver, which was odd because it wasn't even cold. He always seemed to think of lots of confusing things when his wife was around. He shuffled some more, his eyes going back and forth looking at the footprints in front of him trying to work it all out.

"**DAVID!**" she shouted. He jumped, and looked up at her.

"You aren't listening to me again, David!"

"It's OK, It's OK" said Dave, startled "Err yes, I understand, it's fine, it's fine."

"You do?" his wife exclaimed, taken aback. Her face then

started to smile around her beak, and she nodded up and down excitedly, "That's so wonderful, I was so worried you would be cross and upset."

"No,' said Dave "it's fine. I understand everything. OK bye then" he said blankly. There was a long pause.

His wife's expression would have changed if she wasn't a penguin. "Well..." she said "I have to say you are being very grown up about all this. I was expecting you to be angry, begging me to stay, and telling me how you will change, and try and make it all work."

"No" said Dave. "It's fine, it's simple. As you say, you have changed, you want different things in life, you want me to be something else, to change too, but also to be the same penguin that you first met. You are not happy, even though I am, and you want me to be happy being someone different."

"Well..." said his wife confused "Well err, yes, I suppose that's all true..." she said. "I have to say Dave that I am really surprised, I thought you would be really angry and upset. My friends, when I told them what I was going to do, said that I should just do it anyway, and go off without telling you. However I didn't want to just do that, I didn't think it was right. They have been trying to get me to do this for ages."

"That's strange," said Dave "three of them came and said 'Hello' a few hours before you arrived back and they didn't say anything. In fact they seemed quite pleased to see me."

His wife looked even more confused.

"So," said Dave "the only thing that has changed here - and the only thing that isn't happy - is you. You are in effect a modifying chaotic variable force, an agent provocateur, trying to invoke motion on a controlling static mass in equilibrium, in an attempt to effect evolutionary change in the mind of a collective macro-organism."

There was another long pause, and his wife looked at him suspiciously.

"Have you been watching those natural history documentaries again Dave?" She asked him accusingly, with her eyes narrowed.

"No, it's much more complex than that. I am actually a male

program life form in a minimally effectible device, in a static evolutionary harmonized bubble, that has decided that paradise is just life without change. I am several thousand years old. I am Dave of the clan Dave, and I am immortal. I do not want to change, and I am very happy with things as they are." His wife just stood there with her beak open, unable to say anything.

"We have perfected the cloning process too, and are able to reproduce female penguins so they are the exact copy of the originals with no latency errors. Do you see that penguin over there? The one walking this way? She is a clone of you, and has been programmed to be my next wife."

His wife immediately turned around to look, and she saw to her horror a young female penguin who was exactly the same as she had been twenty years earlier. Exactly, with all the attitude, energy, looks and confidence that she once had.

"This process…" continued Dave "happens every twenty years just to remind me of all the effort I am saving. All the work, energy, thinking and change to aid in the evolution and learning of the collective mind. It's also necessary as even though I would be perfectly happy with you as you are for eternity, you are the one that is made to change by external collective forces, and there is nothing we can do about that, it's just part of nature. It's what you are driven to do. But please don't worry about me, honestly I will be fine."

There was a long pause, and his horrified wife looked at him in shock. "I can't believe you are doing this to me…" she said "after all we have been through."

"I haven't done anything" said Dave, "I haven't changed, I am exactly the same, and I have been for many thousands of years. Besides I thought you were the one that wanted to leave? I was just making you feel better about it. Honestly go, I will be fine with the new keener, younger, energetic you. I am sure she can do all the same things you used to do for me, and I am sure she will carry on looking after me. Don't even think twice about it."

Then she started to cry.

"It's no good" said Dave "you can't try and invoke an emotional response in me, I am an immovable male object."

"Please, please…" she sobbed, "I love you Dave, I don't want this to happen."

The young version of his wife walked up to them, carried on walking past, and completely ignored them. His wife suddenly looked very confused.

"But I thought you said…." she started to ask, but he raised his wing to stop her from saying anything else.

"It's OK," he said "we go through this whole process every twenty years, it's fine. I love you just the way you are, it's perfectly OK. I love you as you were, and I will always love you. We are both perfectly happy; it is just something else that is trying to invoke change."

Then in that instant a preprogramed subroutine kicked in, and she changed to look just as she had twenty years ago, and so did Dave, although in his mind he still looked the same. He still had the same amazing 45kg of toned physique, and the same good looks as he always had.

She was still sobbing slightly but was recovering well, the context of what was going on sinking in. After a while their memories would go back twenty years again to when they first met, which in Dave's case didn't take very long for the data files to be deleted and reset.

Their programs would start again and they would be happy, with no memory of the last twenty years. Several moments later she turned to him and smiled.

"Hello," she said "what's your name?"

"It's Dave" said Dave.

"Dave…" she repeated "That's a nice name."

Suddenly Dave had a weird feeling, it was as if he had been here before. A sort of 'Dave-ja-vu', moment. Then it was gone.

"Here," said Dave "you can have this egg, it's just a ceramic one with a small nuclear powered heater inside, we use it to keep our feet warm. I am just off fishing with the lads, I will be back in a few months…" and with that he waddled off to the sea, leaving his wife happy again for the next twenty years.

After all, what more could you want in life?

ACKNOWLEDGMENTS

With thanks to Jan
without whom this book would not have been possible.

Also thanks to Bob, Chris, Stuart and others – you know who you are

ABOUT THE AUTHOR

When I was a boy and in trouble, if the truth was too hard to tell,
I would use my imagination and make up a story,
This of course never worked.

I have grown up now, I have learnt, I am in my forties and am wiser.
I have lived in many places and seen much of the world
I now have responsibilities that I did not have then

Yet there are some things a boy should never grow out of
Or ever give up trying to do with all his heart

I was not made to be a good writer of stories.
But there are some things that need to be told
and some things you need to know,
and sometimes a story is the best way to do that
Like how polar bears are in the Arctic and Prologues at the start

I have made the effort to write these things down as best I can.
All you need to do is read it all with an open mind.